Zowie! It's Yaoi!

Zowie! It's Yaoi!

Western Girls Write Hot Stories of Boys' Love

EDITED BY MARILYN JAYE LEWIS

THUNDER'S MOUTH PRESS
NEW YORK

ZOWIE! IT'S YAOI!
Western Girls Write Hot Stories of Boys' Love

Published by
Thunder's Mouth Press
An imprint of Avalon Publishing Group, Inc.
245 West 17th Street, 11th floor
New York, NY 10011

www.thundersmouth.com

AVALON

Compilation copyright © 2006 by Marilyn Jaye Lewis

First printing, October 2006

Library of Congress Cataloging-in-Publication Data is available.

ISBN-10: 1-56025-910-8
ISBN-13: 978-1-56025-910-7

9 8 7 6 5 4 3 2 1

Book design by Maria Fernandez

Printed in the United States of America
Distributed by Publishers Group West

CONTENTS

KAI STUBBORN

NIX WINTER

To London, always London

There were two of them, standing by the ocean, a lone bed and breakfast in the distance. One was tall, wearing a black trench coat, jeans, bare feet. His blond hair lifted, dancing tangled as the breeze danced lightly down the beach. Cigarette smoke curled back and around him, lazy and yet also tangled on that breeze that promised the world had not really stopped for them. He drew his hand slowly to thin lips, the white filter of his cigarette tucked between two bent and stiff fingers, to pull a slow drag of smoke in. Green eyes, half-closed, watched the weak wave as it broke down to nothing. "You shouldn't have come."

The man next to him was younger, perhaps, but not by much. In a suit and tie, polished shoes that left their own imprint in the sand, he stood with both hands in his trouser pockets, short dark hair untouched by the breeze. He could have been a samurai or a yakuza, a ghost of some of the things a man does for his country that are never spoken of, but when he leaned forward a smile lightened him and he was just a man. "I had to come, as soon as I knew where you were. Kai, I have missed you so much."

Surf came closer to them, leaving little bubbles unsaid of the ocean's soul. Kai touched the back of his wrist to his forehead, pushing suicide blond back, smoke trailing over the dark roots. "And now you've found me," he said, in English, voice mellow, a playboy's voice that could never quite give up on lazy sensual being. "You're going to miss the ghost I was."

"I missed the man much more," Dorian said. It wasn't a Japanese name, but it had been his name for as long as he could remember.

Kai pulled another moment from his cigarette, then tossed what was left into the encroaching ocean. "You should go away and pretend like you didn't find me. I can't work with the team anymore. Even Spades acknowledges that. I could never do intelligence only. I'm just not that smart." He held out his hand, the mangled remains of an assassin's skilled weapon, three fingers broken so badly in an interrogation, left to the ravages of infection and damage. The other two fingers were better only because they'd been broken for less time when the rest of his team had found him. The problem with being an undercover terrorist hunter was that it was sometimes hard to tell the good guys from the bad. "I'm finished, Dorian. Done. Ruined. You have always been smarter, kinder to the world and yourself. You can make a place for yourself in the organization, do something more than hunt and strike."

One hand came from the warmth of Dorian's pocket and reached for the twisted hand, but Kai turned away from the guilt in his friend's face, the reaching touch. "I didn't find you to invite you back to the team, Kai. I know that's done. If we'd rescued you sooner . . . if you'd just told her who you were."

"If I'd started talking, I wouldn't have ever shut up, and how was I to know if she was really a cop like she said? Terrorists lie, too, you know." Kai pushed his foot in the sand, plowing up a small trough that water slipped into. "I couldn't give her anything that might have been used to hurt you."

There were so many things that might never rise to the surface, like a soul dragged down to the bottom of the ocean. Usually, things that one hadn't meant to think or do. It didn't stop a person from wanting someone to love them, wanting to believe that someone could, not a ruined hand or a ruined soul.

Kai dropped then, to a squat, then down on his ass in the sand. Salt water and sand weren't going to ruin his faded-out jeans and he'd had about all he could stand of pretending he didn't care about Dorian being there. "Just get out of here. Or are you planning on breaking my fingers to make me talk?"

"Don't be a goddamn ass, Kai," Dorian snarled, dropping to one knee, a hand reaching cautiously for Kai's T-shirt, to grab hold.

Cautious or not, he had him, a fistful of black T-shirt and Kai looked up, not so cocky, more vulnerable and afraid. "Dori, you want to kick my ass, fine. But I can't go back to being who I was. I learned things about myself, too. It's not just my fucking hand."

"I understand," Dorian said, holding Kai's green eyes locked with his gaze. "I learned, too. I learned that I love you. I love you, Kai. You're the only person I've ever really let get into me that deep. You know me and I know you, maybe better than you think anyone can. It's more than just knowing you, it's something so primal. You're the only person I'm attracted to, and don't make it out like it's some kind of fucking joke. 'Dorian's a fag.' Whatever. I . . ." he paused, his eyes finally letting go of their hold as his power rolled back out like the tide, leaving little bubbles of feeling that he couldn't quite put words to. "I love you," he whispered. "I love you so much."

Kai's other hand had healed better and with it, he reached to touch Dorian's cheek, caressing smoothly shaved skin, his thumb moving over soft lips. It had always been that way between them, words of foam, but deep, moving emotion that pushed the current of their lives. Kai's other hand, his mangled one, rose, the side of his little finger smearing away a tear and he leaned close, shifting to one knee, smashing sand against Dorian's expensive trousers.

Their kiss was a tentative brush, a passing of spirits where there should be none, Kai's chilled lips against Dorian's blush-warmed lips that opened back with a willingness of Christmas just one day delayed, hunger, need roaring back from the oblivion of a soul which knows it's banished. Deeper into each other, tongues dancing nervous, afraid to touch, needing to touch, until Dorian took the kiss, his fingers combed into Kai's hair, holding to him as if he were the only breath. Cigarette smoke, salty ocean air, heat of needing the touch of someone you love and respect and redemption.

Kai moaned into the kiss, his heart and body both waking. Panting, Dorian pulled back, dark eyes dancing with hope and happiness. "And you love me, too. I know you do."

"I do," Kai said, lips full of color now, a crooked smile forcing its way into being. "I'm not any good for you."

"I'm a grown-up. I'll make up my own mind on that. Make love to me?" Dorian asked, the breeze now moving his hair, tousling it forward against his cheeks.

"If that's what you want," Kai said, swallowing. "Dorian, don't call yourself a fag anymore, ever, or I won't do this with you. Understand? I'm not going to do anything that would hurt you, not even you hurting you." He stood then, good hand on one knee as he pushed himself upright. It had been more than his hand that had been hurt and he would not have been fine even if he'd healed faster. There weren't any more bruises or open wounds. Those had been gone a long time. Now it was as if he'd aged twenty years, as if his soul didn't quite believe he'd survived and was waiting for him to just fall over.

"I want," Dorian said eyebrows drawing down. He'd found Kai standing on the beach and he hadn't been briefed on the stiffness Kai was moving with. "I want to make love to you. Why are you stiff? What happened?"

"You don't want to know, Dorian. Just let it go. I can't go back to the company for many reasons and maybe they wanted to make sure I didn't go to work for anyone else, either." Kai said. Where he'd come from, before the company, had been a permanent group, not the kind you walk away from, but the company had taken care of that for him. The company had taken care of everything, until he couldn't take care of problems for them anymore. "Dorian, are you sure this is what you want?"

"Do you know how hard you were to find? Do you know what kind of favors I pulled in to find you, and once I had, to make sure that the company left you and me alone? Kai, I don't want you to do anything you aren't interested in, but I'm not just going to go away. We have been friends. I want to be more, but if you don't, even after that kiss . . . come on, that was a good kiss, wasn't it?"

"It was the best kiss I've ever had," Kai said, wishing he had another cigarette. "That kiss, it just happened, Dorian. I can't say I haven't had my hand wrapped around my cock thinking about you plenty of times, because I have. God, you're so beautiful and watching you work is like watching one of the gods. You're just perfect. You're kind and you're human and I'd give anything to kiss you again, and if you want that, I want that, too, but listen to me," Kai said, watching as the sunset settled over the distance with the most striking of violets, storm clouds and sun, as if the two had anything to do with each other. His thoughts were a run on sentence and his soul a train wreck. "Dorian, I'll come back if you want, run the shop, be there when you come home. You don't have to suck my cock to make me come home."

"Kai, what if I want to? And I've wanted to for a long time, but you're such a stubborn fucking bastard that you wouldn't take a hint."

"You were young and innocent," Kai objected, his broken hand moving to push hair out of his face, then stopping, just leaving the pale brown tangle for the wind to pick up.

It was a habit as old as either of them could remember, and Dorian reached out to brush the lazy hair back, his fingers gentle against Kai's face. "I was with the company before I was ten and you were the more innocent one, if I remember. Kai, you're only two years older than I am, in the human world. Why do you always want to make that into a decade? I was nineteen when we met and that was six years ago. Why do you want to make me into a baby in your head? So you wouldn't want me?"

"I want to protect you, that's all. I just want to make everything good for you," Kai said, emotional confusion in his voice. Sex had not always been a good thing for him. There were reasons he'd become a yakuza before he'd been picked up by the company. "I don't know what's right."

"Kiss me again, Kai, please?" Dorian asked.

There was a vulnerability that cut all the way through to Kai's heart, that would have made him walk over broken glass to do anything for Dorian.

It set aside his fears from the past, his angst and guilt; everything that wasn't passion or Dorian's pleasure burned up in that vulnerable plea. Kai moved closer, this time watching his shorter lover, because Dorian had become his lover with that request. Those dark eyes watched him with hope and such innocence. Kai had always seen innocence in Dorian, and behind that, an openness that could have left the man unprotected. As nice as Kai wanted to be, the invitation woke a hunger in him. "What if I want more than a kiss, damn it, Dorian? What if I really want to take you back to my room and touch you?"

"Touch me? I was rather hoping you might fuck me, and let me fuck you," Dorian said, "Come on, have you never thought about it? About what it would feel like to have my cock in your ass?"

"Oh my god," Kai growled, jerking Dorian close, one hand going down to cup the hard curve of his ass through the fine wool of his slacks, to call the shorter man's bluff, "Where did you learn to talk so goddamn dirty? Your cock in my ass? What about your tongue stuck up my ass?"

Dorian rocked his hips against Kai's leg, rolling his hard excitement against him. "Sounds good to me, Kai."

"Shhh, don't say anything else," Kai said, backing Dorian up the beach, toward the little path which led back toward the bed-and-breakfast where he'd been living. It was new, so new, this invitation to touch someone he'd loved so deeply for so long. "I don't know what I'm doing with this, Dori—with us. Shhh, just listen to me for a minute, okay? Sex is like money, I trade it for things I want. People fuck me, they don't love me, but you're different. You're Dorian and I need you. Just the thought of touching you makes me so hard I think, maybe I've never really been hard before. You get that? That I've never done this before, touching someone I love. I can't just fuck you, Dori."

Dorian bit his lip, hand again fisted in Kai's black T-shirt as he backed up the path toward the big gray house. "So make love to me," he said. "Tell me how you want to touch me."

"Aren't you even a little afraid of me?" Kai growled, catching up, reaching around Dorian to rub his back with a not ruined hand. "I'm a scary bastard."

The wind stirred Kai's hair as excitement woke power he'd hidden away. Sex had never had that effect on him before, touched his more dangerous nature at all.

"Who do you think you're talking to, dragon boy?" Dorian asked, his body pressed closely to the slender tall body of the man he loved. "You've been out of town a while and I've learned some new tricks." The air began to glow as his fingers traced symbols into the air. "Some of them are really good."

There wasn't any smoke or light, no darkness, just the blink of an eye and they were back in Kai's room. Dorian grabbed hold of Kai, an arm easily reaching around him as he steadied himself. The power of the teleport pulled energy from the spell that hid his ears, so now the delicate pointy tips were clearly visible, three gold rings in one and a jewel for the mastery of water on the other.

"Holy shit, you gained a rank and mastered water? I've only been gone six months," Kai said, fingers reaching wonderingly toward the teardrop-shaped gem hanging from Dorian's ear tip. "You were afraid of water."

"I thought it would be good to face my fears, and you should know time is not the same in Underhill as it is here. Many things have changed."

A shiver went through Kai, rippling down his belly, over his manhood. "You are so hot with your ears showing!"

Dorian's fingers slipped under the edge of Kai's T-shirt, over hard abdominals, over the silky hair near Kai's belly button, following the hair back to the worn elastic of his boxers' waistband. "Your ears are pretty hot, too," Dorian said, eyes full of innocence and heat.

Kai laughed and kissed, sloppy and tender, over Dorian's jaw, down to his throat, pausing to breathe softly on his pulse, then back up to Dorian's ear, breathing whispers and kisses over the sensitive length, up to the very pointy tip. "Is it just my ears you like?"

"No," Dorian whispered, "I like your hair and your eyes, and the way you're more thoughtful and kind than you want people to think. I like how precise you are, while letting people think you're haphazard. I like the way your soul shows in your voice. Kai, I have loved you for so long."

Kai moved back toward his bed, pulling Dorian with him. There weren't words for what he wanted to say. Men didn't talk about how lonely they'd been, how they'd thought they weren't worth anything at all and how another man's hands sliding over their belly made them feel as if they'd been all wrong. They didn't talk about how it felt the first time anyone really valuable had ever touched them, how the tip of their cock ached. "Dori, what do you want, really? Don't play any games. I'll give you anything you want. You want me to come back, I'll come. You just say what you want and I'll do it."

"I want to fuck you," Dorian said, "I want to wrap you up in all that's warm and sweet and make you happy. I want to lick your nipples and I want to suck your cock. I want to have you play video games by me as I type until two in the morning. I want to make you pancakes and I want to help you bleach your hair."

"Shit, you do love me, don't you?" Kai asked, almost asking why—but Dorian's mouth caught the word in a kiss.

Dorian pressed him back, stretching out on top of him. "I do. Tell me why you ran from me, all those years we knew each other, and don't tell me you thought I was too young. I have been of age by human guides for twenty times your age."

"I didn't always know that, did I?" Kai hedged, trying to tickle Dorian off of him and making no progress. The elf was smaller, but much stronger, and in this moment very determined. "Dorian, what do you want to hear? Why are you looking at me that way?"

Dark eyes seemed to bore into him, to unravel the very

edges of his soul. "I want there to be no mistake, Kai. I am not here simply to have sex or fuck you, though I want that with sweaty passion. I also want to touch you, your soul. The part of you that will last forever. I want to love that part as well."

Kai's hands stilled against Dorian's waist, his good thumb moving in small circles. "Baby, my soul ain't really anything anyone wants, but I'm happy to be your lover. Just don't try to make me something I can't be, Dori."

"You don't know what you are," Dorian said, fingers caressing softly over Kai's lips. "I know about the Paris clubs."

Kai went stiff. There were clubs and then there were clubs. Just how much stronger Dorian was now mattered a lot. How much he didn't want those clubs right then shocked him deeply. It was finding out that a fetish no longer worked and not knowing what was on the other side of that. "Are you into that?"

"I thought about it before I came," Dorian admitted. "But then I thought a lot about it, and I needed to look into your eyes to see if I was into it or not. I'd follow you into anything, Kai, but I think you don't need that."

"You make me feel like I'm crippled and stupid," Kai hissed.

"And you make me feel like everything I might say could be wrong and I'll have the most precious person in my life slip away before I even know I've screwed up. That's why I studied you."

"I'm precious to you, really?"

"Really, so much more than anything else," Dorian said, promise thick in his voice. "I'm going to undress you now, will that be okay?"

"I can undress myself," Kai shot back, but his hand was working on Dorian's tie, at the button underneath. "I don't need your help."

"You are a stubborn bastard," Dorian growled between kisses to Kai's throat, as both his hands worked Kai's shirt up, inch by inch. "How long did you think you could hide from me?"

"Wasn't hiding from you . . ." Their hardness, veiled by jeans and slacks, rubbed against each other and Kai thrust his hips up against the man pressing against him. ". . . didn't ask you to come, either."

Dorian pressed down, rocking his hips. "Prick," he snarled, holding the tension between their bodies for another moment before he pulled back, straddling Kai's hips, the ends of his T-shirt held in his hands. "Take it off."

Tongue tip touching the center of his upper lip, Kai rolled up a little, enough to peel his T-shirt off over his head, revealing a red dragon tattoo that covered most of his chest, tendrils of smoke curling lazily around one nipple. The lines of his stomach no longer perfectly matched the shadows and lines over the dragon, but he had had the dragon of heart for many years. While he was up, he caught Dorian in his arms, fingers combing into dark hair, lips catching lips to pass secret words that the man in Kai couldn't say out loud, a plea for love, a plea for understanding and passion.

Dorian met him just as fast and hard, like two ocean waves that crashed one into another, trying to become one and overcome at the same time. As Kai held him, stiff wrist at the back of his neck, strong hand in his hair, Dorian slipped out of his jacket, rushed to undo his buttons, throw away the tie. The stiff and ruined fingers at the back of his neck made his heart ache, made him wish for magic he didn't fully understand, made him long to celebrate the courage and power in the man he loved, and he had no way of really saying those things to Kai, so he concentrated on the kisses, down his chest, to one nipple.

Kai dropped back against the bed with a groan, both hands working to push Dorian's shirt off. "So, ever put your finger in another man's ass?" Kai asked, watching

Dorian's face closely, and breaking into a grin as bright color flashed over Dorian's cheeks.

"Well, no," Dorian said sitting on Kai, his shirt down around his shoulders. "Have you?"

"Of course I have, and it's a good thing one of us knows what he's doing," Kai teased. "Go to the drawer and get the lube and pick yourself a condom."

"We don't need a condom," Dorian pointed out, "I am an elf. You can't catch anything from me, nor me from you, but if you find it attractive, you can wear a condom." Dorian moved off the bed with a grace that he was too distracted to hide. He peeled away his slacks and boxers with that same fluid grace, as if such clothes weren't really meant for the likes of him, all without really seeming to know that how he moved wasn't the most natural way for a human.

Unearthly, it would have been disconcerting if Kai hadn't spent enough time around a relaxed Dorian to have become used to it. "I'm not wearing a condom, but you can. You wanted to fuck me, remember? God, you're pretty when you blush!" Kai kept pace, shoving his jeans down and throwing them across the room toward a chair.

"My cheeks will burn up if you keep making me feel this way. Do you like being 'fucked'?"

"Yeah," Kai said, rolling slowly onto his side, one knee bent a little. "I like being fucked. Dori, you're really beautiful. Dressed, you're something, but naked, you're really—like the most beautiful anything I've ever seen."

Dorian grinned over his shoulder. "Is this the lube?" He asked, holding up a plastic bottle with a blue cap.

Nodding, Kai moved to the center of the bed, rolled onto his belly. Both arms folded under his head, he smirked. "You don't use lube? What do you put on yourself when you jerk off? Just when I thought you couldn't get any pinker."

"Do you think about me when you . . ." Dorian paused climbing back onto the bed, one knee pressing down as he reached out to touch Kai's bare back, trace along the line of red dragon there, "when you touch yourself? Don't look away, please, I want to see your eyes."

Kai turned back to face Dorian, blush on his own cheeks. "You? Maybe. Maybe stuff I'll tell you about when you're dark and jaded like me."

"You are not dark and jaded, Kai," Dorian said, reaching across him to set the lube down before he leaned over and kissed the round curve of Kai's bottom. "You are beautiful, my lover."

"Damn, Dori," Kai groaned, lifting his hips up, inching up onto his knees. It was a vulnerable position, offering himself. He moved his knees apart a bit, his cock swaying slightly. "Touch me, slide your hand down between my cheeks and look for my hole."

"Does everything have to be so rough? Hole? I think it must be better than a hole," Dorian murmured, moving between Kai's spread legs, fingertips lightly caressing down between the valley between Kai's cheeks. "I think it must be a lock, and I have the key, and together we will be joined."

"That's very pretty," Kai said, hips moving, passion dripping from the tip of his cock. "And I love you, Dori, I do, but mostly I just want you to touch me right now. Put a finger inside me. Put some lube on your finger first, okay?"

One finger found the tender pucker and circled it. Nothing but skin to skin, Dorian whispered, "Oh wow, wow. You're really soft."

"Okay, virgin boy," Kai smirked, arching his back. "Just put the lube on your cock, then, please? I want you."

"The book I read said to slip one finger, then two, to make 'scissoring' motions with them, to help you relax."

Kai laughed. "Oh baby, maybe if it was my first time. I'll do that to you."

"Have you been in love before?" Dorian asked, hand shaking as he reached for the bottle, which he flipped open with his thumb.

"Does it matter?" Kai asked, a veil of caution over his voice.

"No," Dorian said, "I'd love you even if you didn't love me back, even if you loved someone else, even if anything. I love you and I trust you."

"Good," Kai said, his customary smirk back, "Put the head of your, uh, wand, at my, um, cauldron, and push forward slowly. It's a good spell. You'll like it."

"You are such an ass," Dorian snapped affectionately, but he was doing as he was told.

"But you love me anyway," Kai asked, watching over his shoulder. "Don't you?"

"I love you anyway," Dorian said, eyes closing as he slipped into the heat of Kai's body.

Suddenly sweaty hands caught at Kai's hips, pulling him back, as Dorian lost his virginity, sliding deep into a silky heat, passing through a ring of tight muscle that hugged him just tight enough. Their balls touched when he was in deeply enough, and he held himself there, his toes curling, the sack of his balls tight, and his eyes closed.

He didn't see the tears in Kai's eyes, which was good because he would have mistaken them for pain, and they weren't that at all. Perhaps to really love, one has to be really known first and while Kai had felt devotion, infatuation, passion, he'd never felt as if a touch could open his very soul. "Baby?"

"I'm not hurting you?"

"No, pull back a little, then in again," Kai urged. "I want you to cum in me."

"In you," Dorian moaned, like he hadn't thought of that, but now could think of nothing else at all.

There is a spot in a man—not all men experience it the

same as Kai. For Kai it was like each stroke caressed him higher into the land of light and passion. The sound of Dorian's breathing, Dorian's touch . . . it had been months, years, if ever he'd felt anything this strong at all, and yet the orgasm strengthened until release peaked.

They cried each other's names and rolled to their sides, and it lasted forever, and moments, limbs tangled with each other and as Dorian came, he cried, too, tears wet against Kai's shoulder. It was redemption in a way, for both of them. Water in a desert, life where it had been dying, and they held to each other long after pearls had been spilled into Kai and onto his bed.

Kai didn't believe anything could ever be wrong again, ever. Even if he could never fly, even if he could never be anything except a crippled man who watched the sea, everything would always be all right. He rolled a little, pulled Dorian's head onto his chest. "I love you, baby."

"Kai," Dorian said, one hand in Kai's hair, curling soft blond around a finger. "I need to tell you something and I know you're going to be angry."

They lay together, still naked, covered only by the fading light of the sunset through Kai's window. Legs entwined; the glow between them was bright, tender. Kai scratched Dorian's back softly, "You can't apologize until you've actually done something, Dori. I promise, I'll still love you after I'm done being pissed off."

"I hope so," Dorian whispered.

"Shit, what did you do," Kai asked, lifting up onto one elbow.

"I came to warn you about something, but then we started talking and there was that kiss and I was afraid if I told you right then, I'd—" Dorian stopped, pulling away enough to roll out of Kai's arms and leave the bed. Contrite is not the same as vulnerable, in fact it's the opposite, guarded, pulled back from intimacy.

Kai swung his legs over the edge of the bed and reached for his cigarettes. "What the fuck, Dori?"

"Adrian is dead," Dorian began as he reached for his pants.

Adrian was the king of the fey, Kai's patron and the one who had called Kai to become a dragon, a protector and servant of the king.

"That's not all," Dorian went on. "Evian is king now and he's declared war on those loyal to Adrian. You're in danger. If I can find you, his people can."

Kai dropped his cigarette then struggled to pick it up with his ruined hand before grabbing it with his left. Both hands shook as he tapped the end against his bare leg. "Did you come to kill me and then got distracted by fucking me?"

Contrite turned cold to anger. "No. I was wrong. I should have told you first, but I wanted . . . I wanted this."

"Damn selfish way to start, Dorian. What else haven't you told me?" Unlit cigarette in his mouth, he reached for the bag under his bed and threw it at the dresser. "This was one of the dumbest things you've ever done! You know I'm on a hit list—that's what it is—and Evian doesn't play games, Dori! And you come where I am. You miss me so badly you want to die with me?"

"Yes, no, I mean, you're not going to die. Evian is using wraiths. You're a dragon." Dorian said this like it was the most logical thing in the world, no concerns.

Kai touched a stiff finger to the red dragon tattooed on his chest, the wing unfurled, a wing that could batter back the strongest storm. "It's not so easy. I miss it, being so fast. I miss the wind. That's why this room. If you look out the window, you can't even see the cliff the house is built on. It's almost like I can fly again." His moment of longing quickly turned to packing, the kind where a person throws all they own into a black backpack and sorts it out later. "I miss the sky so much, Dorian."

"You can't fly," Dorian said, soaking it in, understanding the ramifications. "We'll be gone before they find us. I have a car."

Kai yanked the zipper shut. "Elf, you never were good at understanding mortal technology. A car will only drive along and leave a nice, easy Kai and Dorian trail for them to follow—and they will have followed you right out of Underhill. You've got to teleport us farther than my room. Somewhere warm this time."

"Are you angry at me?"

"Hell, yes," Kai complained, throwing his bag on the bed and grabbing his pants. "Get your shirt on, baby."

Dorian grabbed his shirt with one hand and a sock with the other. "I'll make it up to you."

Kai's grin was crooked, slightly vicious, and the sweetest thing Dorian could imagine. "I'm sure you will, Dori. I got plans for you."

Shirt buttons misaligned, Dorian nodded. "We'll be okay. We have time and we'll be gone. Wraiths are only dangerous if they sneak up on you!"

"Right," Kai said, almost mockingly. "Next time you tell me the important news before I blow you, got it?"

"I promise!"

And then black mist started to rise from the carpet, so subtle it would have been missed if one wasn't on guard. Half transparent ghostly lace consolidated, misted away. It was too hard to really look at, but Kai was sure there were four of them. He grabbed for Dorian, catching him by the shirt before the elf could collapse.

Elves were very susceptible to the evil aura of wraiths. This was one reason the king chose humans as his guard, humans with special gifts that only he could give them.

"Transform, Kai. It's okay. You can't break your word to Adrian now. You're free."

Kai held his lover close, caressing his hair with this good hand. "I can't transform. My wing is deformed. I can't."

"Oh," Dorian said, slumped against Kai, as if he'd just found out that yes, he was mortal and the universe was about to prove it. "Shit."

"You ought to talk more, pronounce less, baby," Kai said, fury underpinning his words.

"You can, Kai," Dorian countered, his voice slurring as the toxic aura of the wraiths surrounded them. "You are still a dragon."

Kai wrapped both arms around Dorian, holding him with a great tenderness. "Stupid elf," Kai complained, distracted by the dark forms consolidating around them. "Just because time doesn't go the same in Underhill, and you've had time to get ready for this, it's only been six months for me. I can't make the shift," he said, the aura of the forming wraiths affecting him as well, making his words bleed from him, his worst fears dark and putrid. "It's agony, Dorian, to change without Adrian's blessing and I'll die from it. You wanted that, didn't you?"

"That's right," one of the wraiths hissed, but a melodic beautiful hiss, like a nightmare violin, "The elf can't stand that he loves you."

"It's a disgrace," another whispered, picking up the death song as if they were all of one mind. "Disfigured human, worthless. Disgraceful for the prince of the fey to suck the cock of a worthless . . ."

"Piece of trash. Did you think the elf prince loved you? Did you think anyone could love you?"

Kai planted his feet, his head spinning. Wraiths don't lie . . . because wraiths don't state anything, just ask the ugly questions from within one's own soul. "Dori," Kai asked, "Are you a prince?"

"It doesn't matter," Dorian said, words slow, slurred. "I researched it. I know you can transform, Kai."

"Didn't you have a nice little home before the nasty elf came looking for you?" One of them sneered.

The wraiths walked a slow circle around them, clothed in lacy mist robes of the souls they'd stolen, pale gray dead faces, black eyes with liquid red highlights flowing over them. Objectively, wraiths were Gothic beauty, death incarnate, delicate features, the perfect mirror of all that was dark in their prey. Once elves themselves, they evoked the greatest influence on other elves and Dorian already shivered in Kai's arms. Dorian would be near death before they even started consuming him. There had to be a way to protect him.

Dorian was so full of life, so just and noble and hopeful, and images of Dorian from all the years that Kai had known him splashed back, bright and cheerful and Kai clung to them, these memories that had sustained him in the months apart from his best friend and now lover. "I don't care if he's a prince. He's still Dorian. Leave us alone, or I'll transform! If I do, you'll die!"

"Can you kill those that are already dead?"

"Can you be a dragon anymore? Maybe you are just a worthless street thug with a pretty tattoo?"

"Are you going to cry as he screams? I think he'll scream as we eat him, don't you?"

"Shut up!" Kai growled. "I wouldn't let you hurt him!"

"Maybe you should break his neck? Maybe you should save him from all that suffering? Maybe you should try to help him a little, after all, you didn't even try to find him after you were hurt."

"I would have only brought him down!"

"Like you're doing now? Everyone you've ever loved, you've destroyed, haven't you?"

"Shut up!"

"Let us eat you and maybe we'll leave him alone. Isn't that what you want?"

Dorian had been so sure, so very sure that the transformation could happen still. Dorian could be an arrogant highbrow elf, but he wasn't stupid.

Out Kai's window, there was the ocean, vast and beautiful. The house had been built right up to the edge of the cliff and he'd taken this room because when he looked out the window, he could remember when he'd flown. The skies in the world of the fey are the same as the skies in the world of humans. They take up the same space, but are offset from each other just enough that a great ruby dragon could spread his wings and soar over vast planes and forests and there were none to complain. He had been someone. He had been a servant of the king, a friend of the king, and he'd lost that gift while protecting human life and the life of Dorian. He had bought good things with his life, and if he could do one more, he would count it as great worth.

The draining of the wraiths was making him shake now, too, and Dorian had completely lost consciousness. Kai held his elf to him, pressing with one hand, his good hand tilting Dorian's face up so he could run his thumb over soft lips, feel the breath there proving life. He kissed him then, lightly, a promise of love and respect that would always outlast anger and even life itself.

"It's so sad to love someone whose station in life is sooo far above you," one wraith said, sounding as if he really cared and how he shared in Kai's sorrow from the weight of that impossibility.

"Fuck you," Kai growled, and then he was moving.

Wraiths most often killed their prey by letting the prey do the work, then stealing their soul at the moment of separation.

Kai's favorite window shattered, sending glass outward over the ocean. The wood of the frame drove slivers into his shoulder, and there was the briefest moment of regret, of fury at not being able to think of a better plan. Dorian's weight dragged at him, caught on the debris from the broken window, and Kai held him, tugged, as dark mist from the wraiths clawed for them.

The moment they had broken free, the deepness of the despair evaporated, leaving them falling toward the ocean and rocks below.

Holding Dorian's hand with his good hand, Kai willed the transformation. If Dorian believed, so did he. He did!

He wasn't just some skinny suicide blond ex–drug addict gangbanger street thug! He was Kai! Both arms out, wind ripping at his back, hair tangling and whipping, he willed himself to fly. Like a paper cut that slid along his spine, stinging and long, then it peeled, pulling back the form of himself as a man. It burned, like a rug burn that tore away what he had been and bubbled out into what he could be. Arms stretched, bones elongated, and a blast of light and hope flashed from him, echoing out like a blast ring.

The effect woke Dorian, fed the wizard energy like plugging in a lamp. The wraiths fled or died, and Kai didn't care which. His left wing spread out wide, twenty feet of ruby red flight, catching as much air as it could. The left was twisted, bent, screaming in agony at his foolish stupidity. He was a crippled dragon, nothing more.

Dorian, being the wizard that he was, slowed his own fall. Kai watched the growing distance between himself and his lover. If he could have rolled, he might have glided better, but he didn't have the strength or the will to turn from Dorian on this, his last flight. Dorian was a prince. He could see it now, the power and nobility in the spell-wielding prince, the slacks whipping around his legs, hands drawing lines of magic in the air around him. Dorian would live. Now that he had his magic protections up, he would live.

Exhaustion softened Kai and he could accept. His life had started in Shanghai, a child his mother had wanted until she realized that his French father would not be coming back for her, a child that no one else could stand to look at. He'd grown into an angry man, running with a gang that was violent against the government, people, anyone in their way. He'd died the first time in an alley behind a butcher shop, bleeding out his meager little life from fifteen abdominal stab wounds. So he'd had nearly ten years of life after, living in the fey kingdom, knowing Dorian and serving Adrian, redeeming his life by saving the lives of others, stopping violent people, even the gang that he'd grown up in and died from. He'd had years of Dorian laughing and sitting by the dark-haired man as he'd typed out mission reports. They'd been so very . . . human in their lives. He'd loved. If the fey hadn't taken him, he'd never have loved.

Dorian had been right to have those moments together, before this. There could have been no other outcome. The wraiths would have found them on the run and he would have transformed to defeat them, and then . . . he was finished.

Really, it was best to leave the world in this form, as he'd left it once before in his human form and he didn't want to do that again. The last trails of his life left his mind as he hit the water. Sea surged around him and he sank, eyes closed, his imagination feeling Dorian's lips on his again, warm and full of life. It was worth it, this one afternoon.

Water fell back on him pushing him under. His crippled wing was agony under the weight of the water and light turned to darkness. His huge dragon form, before his hand had been ruined, had mastered the sky, diving, gliding, and he'd loved the freedom of it, missed it deeply, but it had never been designed to swim. The water currents shredded wing membrane, but he forced his mind to go back to when Dorian's head rested on his chest, soft dark hair tickling his arm.

He could almost feel the fingers caressing his cheek, warm and untouched by the water currents. Dragon scale was such odd stuff, insanely sensitive to the slightest touch of air or fingers, impervious to sword and bullet. Light flickered like crescent moons beyond his closed eyes, and he snapped them open, huge green emerald eyes. Surprise does amazing things to dragon expression.

Dorian, surrounded by golden light, one hand touching his face, so close to teeth longer than his fingers, was pushing the water back away from both of them, creating a bubble around them. The little blue gem attached to his pointy right ear glowed as if it were about to become a new sun. As the energy of water magery pushed away the water, it left Kai tingling, shivering, excitement going down his spine, over his tail. A mage's power came from deep within its soul and it was usually loathe to let that power touch anyone so completely.

Eyes closed, Dorian gave all his concentration to the spell he worked, leaving himself completely vulnerable to anything should it not go as he planned. Men are men, but men who are dragons are sometimes more dragon than man, and not always the gentlest of creatures.

Kai loved Dorian's bravery, was humbled by the offering of trust and love from the mage. Carefully he wrapped his tail around the fragile human, holding him with all that had ever been human inside Kai. And then the next part of the spell hit. Just as when they'd moved from the beach to the room, there was not even a blink of an eye, just an is/is not/is, and they were elsewhere. And it was hot!

"Africa," Evian sneered. He was just what one might expect of an elf king. Elegant in black velvet and tailored slacks, he did not hate humanity. Far from it, they were the most profitable sheep he could imagine. In fact, when they had fought each other to death, then he'd like the remaining pets of them even so much more. "What a splendid place for him."

The throne room had been redone, in the days since his

father's unfortunate death, and now it looked like a very fine boardroom; smoky glass table, Leonardo Da Vinci paintings never seen in the realm of humanity on the wall. He sat in a black leather executive chair, one hand absently petting the red hair of his father's other dragon.

"He has not the energy to teleport again, not for a long time. It was quite magnificent. He retrieved the dragon of heart from the sea and teleported them both. It was a splendid feat for one of his age," Birus said, pride showing her smile. She had been a servant of the royal family for five centuries, most of them spent serving Adrian.

Evian tightened his hold on the red hair between his fingers, pulling with increasing pressure. "Good. He shall stay in Africa. I hear humans starve there. Let him rot with the creatures he would call brothers. The dragon of heart is worthless, created from filth even the humans had no use for. Let them have each other. When he comes to me, begging to be allowed back into Underhill, then—and only after he has begged for the life of his pet—then I shall kill him."

"Majesty," Birus said, eyes narrowing. "There are no laws in our people which allow you to murder your brother, king or not. Dorian will not be so easy to kill, in any case."

The man on his hands and knees beside Evian snarled, eyes watering from Evian's hand in his hair. The air snapped between the three of them, and Kryie broke first. "Dorian and Kai will come back and kill your sorry ass! Dorian has right of duel for the man who killed his father, and a good king!"

"Oh, Kryie," Evian said, leaning forward even as he jerked the red head back onto his knees. "I hope so. Let my pretty little brother come and try. I still wouldn't kill him until he's begged enough. I'm going to make you and that crippled idiot dragon mate in the courtyard. So you have nothing to worry for, you see? You shall be serving the right king for years to come."

Kryie, like Kai, had not had a pleasant early life and had been saved by Adrian. He was the dragon of soul though, golden with blue eyes, even though his human form was that of a slender red-haired man with violet eyes and a small curved nose. He spat and it made it as far as Evian's polished Italian shoes. "You disgrace your kind!"

Evian sighed, not at all disturbed by the defiance, more pleased by it. "Birus, you served my father so well, but I think you've grown too old and set in your ways to be of further use to the royal house. I command you to return to your rooms and I forbid you to eat while I am king. You've grown fat on the kindness of the royal house."

Her eyes were hard, dark pools of rage, but she bowed. Her traditional elfish gowns flowed around her, long golden hair. Court politics had risen and fallen around her in the time she'd served Adrian and before him, his mother. Such a new king might not last the month, but as king, she would obey him. He had not commanded her to withhold aide to his opponents, however. "As it please My Majesty," she said, and she took pleasure in his smirk.

Of course, he meant for her to give aide to his challengers, and she knew it.

As she left, he pulled his captive dragon close. "Now, now, Kryie, you must keep your temper in check. You know I will make your Stephen pay for your bad behavior, don't you? You had best hope that I find pleasure in the day before we return to our rooms. Maybe our stodgy old Birus will cry for help to heroic Dorian right away. What do you think?"

"Peace," she said, arms crossed over her chest, face half-hidden in the shade under her hat brim. "Did you really think they were going to come to vaccinate our village? You really did think so, didn't you?

Hands on the wheel, Peace narrowed his eyes and stared at the road. His hat was cloth, pulled down on his head. A leftover from the Korean War, like the jeep they had, it was a little soft, but did its job. He was a lot the same. Light hair, straw colored, light green eyes, and a close-trimmed beard. The set line of his lips let her know he really had thought they could just ask the visiting doctor to come out to the village where they were working.

Muscles flexed under his worn cotton shirt. Once it had been army green, but now it was bleached and tie-dyed with local dyes. "They should! It's not even a full day out of their way! No matter," he said, some of the tension softening in his shoulders as he turned to look at her.

She looked away, up at the endless sky when he gave her "that" smile. She was pretty sure he didn't even know he was doing it, that soft smile, the light coming into his face like he was looking at an angel. For an American he was more peaceful than she'd imagined possible, and that's why she'd started calling him Peace. He sang all the time, helped people look for lost goats, fought snakes, milked found goats, ate no meat, and he was falling in love with her.

"You are a stupid idealist," she said, fingers still tucked under arms. She had gone with him to the next town over, a larger town, because she had to post her report on the status of the school she was building. Mitsui Setsuki had actually never known an American before Peace.

Peace turned his eyes back to the road, lips tight again.

He was quite handsome, for a gaijin. His eyes always had some plot or hope in them and without his shirt he was firm and hard, lines on his stomach. He was kind and gentle, and she wanted very much to reach out and touch him, tell him she hadn't meant her words so harsh as they might have sounded. She, too, was a stupid idealist. Her family told her this every time she asked for money, which she did frequently.

Even still, she spent less money in building up this village than she had when she lived in Tokyo. "The doctor will come."

"I wanted him to come because it was the right thing to do," Peace said, his voice a little deep, anger at the world coloring it.

"What difference does it make if he comes because my family tells him to, or because he wishes to be a good man, like you?" She said, leaning a little forward, a tentative smile on her face.

Setsuki was a Japanese lady and if she'd stayed home, she would have married well, had a splendid house, fine silks, a distinguished husband, and been yelled at much less frequently. She was her father's only daughter and she knew he was simply waiting for her to come home. Her father would never ever, not under any stretch of fatherly love, understand a tenderness for a sun-blond American who owned nothing and thought getting down to business meant doing work that caused one to sweat.

"You think I'm a good man?" Peace asked, that crooked, almost cocky smile lifting him beyond the dust and heat of the road they bounced on.

"Maybe," she said, then started laughing. "Peace! You're so cute when you are indignant."

Color flashed up his cheeks. "I am not! Men are not cute! You! Now you're cute! A cherry blossom!"

"Peace—oh my god!" Her eyes had gone wide and she was pointing ahead of them.

"Dear God!" Peace yelled, but it was more prayer than curse. He stamped on the breaks. The jeep skidded on the dusty road and Setsuki caught herself on the dashboard.

Her curses weren't prayers. "Turn around! Go! Fast!"

Peace leaned forward, looking over the top of wired-back-together metal-framed sunglasses. The beast was red, and big, like a huge painted elephant with wings, and a long neck like a giraffe. The wings were tattered and one was propped up, casting shade over a half-naked Asian man. "I'm not going to run! This man needs help!"

Setsuki cursed more, hitting him with her cloth hat. "It's a dragon! Don't they teach you anything in that rabble of a country you come from! An *oni*! If it wants to eat this one man, let it."

She chilled at his glare, and for once in her life, for maybe the first time ever, someone's disapproval mattered. She opened her mouth to speak, closed it, glared at him. "It's a dragon!"

Peace rolled his eyes. "What kind of rubbish do they teach you in your university? There's no such thing as dragons! It's just some great big red beast with wings, and steam coming out of its snout. I don't know everything that's in the world, let alone Africa! Even if it were a dragon, which it's not! But if it were, we couldn't leave it out here! This heat would kill anything and the man already looks poorly."

"Poorly? That's what he gets for sleeping with dragons," she shouted over the windshield. "Peace, please, I'm sorry, but let's go back to town and get help."

"Hush," he said, pulling the keys from the jeep's ignition as he stepped out of the battered old vehicle. "Hello!" he called to the beast laying across the road, and maybe to the unconscious man laying under the shade of the wing. "Can I be of any help?"

The beast, whatever it was, opened one great eye. The eye was the size of a baseball and it followed him as he walked nearer. It pulled the man next to it closer, protectively.

"I just want to help," Peace said, hands up. "Setsuki, bring some water. Water? Want some water?"

And right then is when Peace's solid little world shattered into a million pieces. The red beast, the lip of its snout lifting a little, spoke. "Yes, water, please."

Setsuki ground her teeth, the canvas covered canteen in her hands. "I told you! Oni! Demons, *baka!*"

The dragon's eye shifted toward her, his great head

lifting to look at her more clearly, and then he started in Japanese: "Please, Dorian's chi is spent. He needs food and water, please? The heat is too much for him. He is a water master. I will serve you if you help him."

She walked past her American, where he stood, hand on his cheek, eyes wide, and only his God-knew-what thoughts going on in that head of his. "We have water, food. We can take you to our village, but you must swear you will not harm anyone."

"I swear, lady," Kai said, "I am Kai."

"His name is Kai," she said back to Peace. "Don't just stand there! Get the extra shirt from the jeep. This guy's burned like a cricket on a stick. And he isn't human, either."

"He's not human," Peace said, moving to get the spare shirt. It was often cold when they went out in the morning, and having some extra clothes was always good idea. "What is he?"

"Don't ask me," Setsuki complained, "I'm a teacher of small children, not mythology. Kai, can you fly?"

"No," the dragon said sullenly, a strong breath from his snout sending up clouds of dust. "Where are we?"

"You're in Africa," she said, "Do you speak English?"

"I speak Japanese," Peace said, defensively, "Here, let me get him."

The wing withdrew and Peace squatted down, lifting Dorian easily. "Okay, so what are oni?"

"Spirit beings, not human, not bad, not good, just beings, like us," Setsuki said, worrying that Peace's religion would somehow kick in and make him take back the offer of help they'd already given. She glared at him, elf held in his arms and a deep confusion showing in his eyes. She'd seen that breakdown happen in her father when she'd told him no, she wasn't marrying the nice businessman that he'd found for her and that she was going to Africa to teach poor children. "Peace, your god is bigger than any one place, bigger than anything one person can know. What are a couple little oni to a god that big?"

"I am not little," Kai protested, not quite pulling off sounding offended, though anything that could speak with teeth as long as a man's hand, shouldn't have too much trouble sounding offended. "I am the dragon of heart, servant to the king of the fey."

Peace, recovering himself a bit, tilted his head, "Funny, you looked like a great red elephant with wings to me. I don't care who you serve, as long as you don't hurt anyone, but you're not going to fit in the jeep that way."

"Peace is a very practical man," Setsuki said, pointing to him, and when she smiled, he smiled back and Kai rolled the eye that watched them. If the attraction between this man and woman were magical energy, he could have pulled off the transformation back to human without so much as a twitch.

"Right. Good thing. Then he won't mind a naked man standing in front of his girlfriend," Kai said, the smirk making his teeth show. "Or maybe he will . . ."

He'd been told that watching the transformation was a beautiful thing. In the king's court it had been painless, pleasurable even, he could well believe that the transformation was a fireworks display of all the many magics that changed him. Here, as it had been on the fall from his lost house, it was agony. Like the sun falling in on itself or maybe being caught in a trash compactor. Even his scream fell back in on him as his mass as a dragon boiled away. Becoming the dragon was an exercise in hope and life, and falling back to what he was left him feeling the despair he'd known when encircled by the wraiths.

Collapsed stars become black holes after all, and maybe that's what being a man was, just a creature that sucked from the world around it and never gave anything back. Like all things fey, there was a timelessness to the processes, and he only knew it was over when he woke, head in Dorian's lap, a hand fanning him.

Groaning he tried to sit up, only to have Dorian press a hand to his shoulder. "We are near the village of Peace and Setsuki; rest a bit more, Kai."

"I hope they have a beer and some cigarettes," Kai groaned, fingers tenderly touching his forearm, trying to see if the shredding of his wings by the rough sea had carried over into his human form. "Holy shit, are we really in Africa?"

"You think that's hard to believe," Peace teased, looking at them in his rearview mirror, "I about ran a dragon over today."

"As if this shitty little car could have done anything," Kai snarled, finding his arms bandaged, all the way up past his elbows.

"Kai is often unpleasant of mood after he has transformed back," Dorian said, but smiling down at Kai.

"Well, if I could be a dragon, I'd stay one a lot. Fly around eating cows," Setsuki said.

"Eating meat when people are starving is not right," Peace preached.

Setsuki rolled her eyes. "It must be great!"

Peace was watching her, the delighted smile she had as she stuck one arm out into the wind. "Well, maybe dragons can eat cows."

"Flying was great," Kai said, finding it unreal to be talking about such things with two strangers, especially strangers so very odd from anything he'd ever known. "It was really great."

It was the real world though and his hand was still ruined. His wings were still ruined. And Evian had many more wraiths he could send to attack them.

"You mustn't tell anyone about Kai being a dragon," Dorian said. "There will be those seeking us. Rumors of a dragon would only bring them sooner."

"Oh don't worry," Setsuki said, "We won't tell anyone. No one would believe us anyway. We're not the most presentable of people ourselves."

"Speak for yourself," Peace said, wrinkling his nose. "I'm presentable! Washed in the blood of the lamb! And I suppose it wouldn't be very good to tell people. Some things people have to take on faith!"

Kai turned his head, rubbing his cheek against Dorian's leg. He needed the contact, and felt weak and worthless for it, but he needed to know that Dorian would still love him even if he were just a crippled man and a ruined dragon. His tears welled on the side of his nose, then rolled down to soak into Dorian's pants.

"Ril vey orisei," Dorian said whispered, voice as high and elegant as any elf could ever have done, a formal declaration of love that could never be taken back or removed. Saying it was a bond given from one of the noble house to the one spoken to and as immortal as the elf that spoke it. *"Ril vey orisei."*

Dorian wiped at the tears pooling by Kai's nose. Kai wrapped an arm around Dorian's leg and sobbed. King Adrian had been a friend as well, so there was much to grieve.

Kai had cried himself to sleep in that jeep, cried for failing in Australia and losing his hand, losing his wings, not being there when Adrian was attacked, cried for loving Dorian when he could never go back to Underhill with the elf. He cried for the pain his body was in and the sheer frustration of not being more than he was. He woke in a stifling little mud hut, lying on an old wool blanket. A light cotton cloth covered him and he took a deep breath of the warm, clean African air.

With his crippled hand he reached out to touch the hard packed mud floor he lay on. The answer was there, in the dirt. Life gave you what it gave you and you had to make do with what you had. Adrian hadn't been his father, but he had been more than just someone wanting to use him. Adrian had had such big dreams of peace and safety for people, of a bright future where elves didn't hide anymore, but walked as brothers to humans.

Kai had never really believed it. Humans didn't seem to like those that were different, even a little, but he had liked helping, saving those he could. He wasn't going to live forever like Dorian, but he wasn't powerless. Sitting up, he found a colorful caftanlike shirt and a pair of loose pants, a pair of sandals that surely counted as some kind of ethnic craft.

It felt private in the little hut and he found water and a cloth on a small table, so he washed, though he left the bandages on his arms. He had no idea how rare gauze was around here and he had never been wasteful.

A few minutes later, he was dressed and stepping through the cloth-covered doorway of the hut. It was Rudyard-Kipling-meets-a-video-about-saving-children outside, and he figured his chances of getting a cigarette had gone to hell in a handbasket and had not made it real far. As hot as it was, they'd probably burn up before evening started to fall. Hands shoved into the pockets of his rough-woven linen pants, he started down what passed for a street toward what smelled like roasting pig.

Closer into what turned out to be a town square, of sorts, he found people. A couple dozen children ran and played on the far side. A few more, maybe half a dozen sat around Dorian. Kai paused there, leaning his shoulder against another mud-brick house.

Just watching Dorian tell whatever story he was practically reliving for the children, Kai felt like the world was at peace, felt the exhaustion of their becoming lovers, fleeing, of finding out about Adrian's death, of everything. The elf's ears were hidden again, but those didn't matter, what mattered was the soul that lived in the body.

"Hello, dragon," the woman who'd helped them earlier said, having successfully sneaked up behind him.

"Hello, woman," he replied, fingers itching for what he didn't have. He didn't look at her. It was still a little embarrassing to have sobbed himself to sleep in the backseat of her car, not to mention the whole "being naked as a cream puff in an oven" before her.

"You love him very much, don't you?" She stood behind him, close enough to talk to him, so close he could have reached out and touched her. But she was hesitant, like she wasn't quite sure of him yet.

"Yeah," Kai said. There was little point in lies. "See him though? He's a dumbass. He's a royal prince and he hides it, because he doesn't want his friends to know. So here he is, sitting on the ground telling stories to children. Dorian," he paused, "is a very good person."

She took a step closer. "He is a prince?"

Dorian made the motion of a big explosion fingers spread wide, his cheeks filled with air until he went, "BANG!"

"It's hard to believe sometimes. I guess we're all things that are hard to believe sometimes. What about your lover?" Kai looked over his shoulder, tried to give the woman a smile. "He seems very nice."

Nervous, she crossed her arms over her chest again. "He's not my lover. He's an American."

"Oh?" Kai rounded on her, picking up on some hesitation in her. He hadn't survived the streets of Shanghai by being stupid or slow, and he'd only gotten better since then. "By that you mean he's not Japanese, don't you?"

"Well, he's not," she said, "Aren't you ashamed to love another man? It's so obvious. Do you, are you . . ." she paused, blushing, unable to bring herself to say the word *homosexual*.

Kai wasn't sure if he was pissed or amused, but amused won out. "Yes, when I can. You want to hear what we do?"

Blushing went bright red. "No!"

She held up both hands and in her eyes, Kai could see the echoes of a teenage girl secretly reading spicy manga, and he was again more amused than pissed off. "Fine," he said, a lazy smirk. "I'm sure it's not any different than what any two people do anyway. You were a little sheltered as a kid?"

"I didn't mean that it was different, but well, you're not married, are you?"

"Actually," Kai said, feeling a great warm glow in his heart, "We kind of are. Something he said to me, when we were in the car. He said it in Elfish, which is only spoken in his the, uh, the capital of his people or on very serious occasions. We are married."

"I don't think my father would let me marry Peace," Setsuki whispered.

"Listen, Setsuki, it is Setsuki, right?"

She nodded, and while she'd seemed so grown-up before, and he still would have put her age at least twenty-three or twenty-four, the innocence now in her made her look younger.

"So listen, Setsuki," Kai said, leaning forward a little, "People get in their minds what they think is right and wrong, but all that really matters is having enough to eat, being able to laugh and play with the ones you love, having someone around who wants to hold your hand sometimes, and loving how your heart really loves. I almost spent my life alone because I was too stubborn to admit I loved someone I thought I shouldn't have. I'm not talking about loving someone who would get hurt if you loved them, but how is Peace going to get hurt if you love him?"

"I will get hurt if I love him," she whispered. "My family will never talk to me again, but seeing him hold you today, I realized I would hold Peace like that, if he were crying, because I love him."

"Then your family will have to get over it. I wouldn't have planned on loving that idiot elf, but I do," Kai said. "You're some person, you know that? You didn't even flinch at me in my dragon form."

"Yes, I did! I told Peace to leave you both!" She looked down, chin touching her shoulder. "I would have been wrong if we'd left you. I came to Africa to help, to make my life matter, and to run away from a marriage I didn't want. I didn't mean to fall in love here."

Kai gave her a heart-stealing grin, a flirtatious smile that had made everyone think he was straight for years. "You think love waits for your convenience? Where would we get all our tragic romance stories then?"

Peace coughed as he came up behind Setsuki, and Kai threw him a steal-your-heart-grin, too, then blinked at him. "Setsuki was just telling me how nice you look without your shirt on," Kai said, dead straight, not a hint that he was lying.

Those pale green eyes went wide like a deer in the headlights and Kai wasn't sure if he'd run or fight. The missionary wrinkled his nose, then said, "She looks beautiful no matter what she's wearing."

"What about me?" Kai asked, touching his fingers to his chest, then making a small tsking sound. "So you have seen her naked then?"

"I have not! I wouldn't! I haven't even asked if I could hold her hand yet! She's too valuable for that! She's amazing and if you lay one hand on her, I'll, I'll sock you a good one! She's very precious! A great teacher and a she's smart and kind and brave!"

"Make a great wife," Kai said, again leaning against the

mud hut. "Two like-minded do-gooders out in the middle of hell's waiting room . . ."

"It's not that bad here!" Peace said.

Kai snorted, then looked at Setsuki. "If you don't kiss him, I will. He's just so cute."

Her mouth dropped open, snapped shut, then she grabbed the front of Peace's shirt, jerked him close and kissed him, full on the lips. Kai arched an eyebrow, then grinned crookedly. It was a chaste kiss, from what he could tell, just lips to lips, and Peace couldn't have been more surprised if, say, he'd almost run over a dragon, but Kai had the deepest feeling that they were perfect for each other. He had to do what he could for humanity, and "He's an American" was the worst excuse for rejecting someone that Kai had ever heard. Perhaps it was something to do with his own life, being rejected because his father had been Western. Either way, he'd meddled all he was going to.

When he turned back around Dorian was still telling stories, and he stood there for a moment more, loving the life in his lover. In a bright blue shirt, he looked about as far away from Asia as a person could get—well, and still be in the human world. Maybe it was all right here. There really wasn't any place else they had to be.

Dorian saw him then and his smile was so big. He didn't look like an elf, or anything unusual, other than a Japanese man lost in Africa, and for a moment Kai could believe that that's all there was, just two men wandering the world, nothing else. The thought was sudden: that's all there was now. They were free to just . . . go.

Kai's lip cracked as he grinned in response and held open his arms for his lover. Even in the heat, sweat running down his back he felt the chill of having Dorian wrapped in his arms. "Damn, baby, you make me shiver."

"After we eat," Dorian said, hard body pressed to Kai's,

"I'm going to show you what goes with the meaning of those words I said in the jeep."

Kai squirmed as Dorian's hand slid down to cup his ass through the thin linen pants. In Chinese, so they were the only ones to understand, Kai whispered, "I want you to touch me, like I've never wanted anything more. I've never slept with anyone else a second time."

Dorian gave his ass a squeeze. "Don't kiss anyone else, except me," Dorian said, voice low, words in lyrical Elfish. "We are Evraida and I will know. Your heart beats in time with mine."

"I don't know what to say," Kai whispered. "You could have warned me," he teased softly, his good hand caressing Dorian's hair.

"It wouldn't have mattered. We were Evraida before I said those words to you. How do you think I found you?"

Kai pulled back, remembering that he was angry. "So you're saying you lead the wraiths right to me? And what was with not telling me until we'd wasted the hours doing each other? Didn't you think I might want to know that Adrian was dead before I got my head wrapped around some thing as important as becoming your lover?"

Dorian reached for him. "Are you really angry at me? Kai, please, I was afraid if I told you first, I'd never be touched by you. I was grieving for my father, too, you know! He was the guiding force in my life long before you were even born! I needed you to steady my life."

"You needed. So you took, and it's okay." Kai growled. "I'll get over it. I need you to, but I'm tired of being manipulated. You only tell me what you think I need to know to do what you want me to do. What if you'd told me the truth, and I'd still wanted to be your lover? What if I'd been able to turn to you and hide my grief in you? But you didn't give me that chance, did you? You think you know everything, but sometimes, Dori, you don't."

"Kai," he said, hands made into fists. "You're right. I'm sorry. Forgive me?"

"In a little while," Kai growled over his shoulder. "Just leave me alone for a little while!"

Falling in love wasn't as easy as Kai had thought it would be. Happily ever after for his story started when Dorian had found him, had confessed his love. That's where the story should have ended. When he'd fallen into the ocean, when his life had passed before his eyes . . . that could have been the not-so-happily ever after. It could have been, but it hadn't been. Dorian had saved him.

A mile or so away from the little village, Kai had found a hill and the sunset gave him no answers. He'd been born a man and that was still all he really was. Too near death so many times and now, he just wanted to live quietly, but he didn't know how. How did a person go from crisis to crisis and then just stop . . . find a little mud hut and become what?

Could Dorian ever be happy without the excitement of court politics? There were questions Kai didn't have the answers to. When he'd woken up all the answers had seemed so easy. He scraped up a fist full of dirt and wondered what he could make of it, what he could make of what he had.

"Hey," Dorian said quietly.

"Hey," Kai replied, suddenly very interested in the red line along the horizon.

"You don't have to stop being angry at me, but I brought you some food."

Kai motioned to a patch of dirt right next to him. "So, Dorian, what do we do from here? Why didn't happily ever after simply start with me suddenly knowing what to do?"

"I don't know," Dorian admitted, kneeling down next to Kai. "I guess things are more intense when they really matter."

He opened a basket and pulled out a carafe of water, then a wooden bowl of food with a neatly fitting wooden lid.

Kai took it and set it on his folded legs. The scent of it made him immediately hungry, like he hadn't eaten in weeks. "I had an awful dream. I dreamed I was in my dragon form and I couldn't fly, so all I could do was chase this cow around."

"Did you catch it?" Dorian asked, taking a drink of water.

"No. It was a milk cow, too. I just kept running after it on my stubby little dragon legs. I got dissed by a milk cow."

"Bad dream," Dorian agreed. "I guess we'll get an apartment. Go somewhere where they don't kill gay men, and make a little garden, get a cat. I've always wanted a cat."

"I'm never going to fly again," Kai said, chasing a bit of hummus with a piece of soft folded bread.

"We'll get a plane," Dorian offered.

"Not the same. Aren't you going to miss Underhill?"

"Probably, but I chose you over it and I'm glad. I don't think I like eating goat, though."

"It's not pork?" Kai asked, looking sideways at his bowl now, then eyeing the shared water bottle. "Let's live somewhere that's not here."

"I was thinking France."

"I don't speak French. Do you?"

"No, but that will make it all new, wouldn't it? It'll really be starting over."

"We can't go back to my place by the ocean, can we?"

"No. I'm sorry, Kai."

"It's all right. We'll start all over." Kai smiled then. "I'll learn to eat left-handed. I'll become a therapist."

"A therapist? Like a massage therapist?"

"No, no, like a shrink," Kai said, still smiling. "And you, you can be my housewife!"

"Bastard!" Dorian snapped, pushing Kai over with both

hands. "I'm no one's housewife! You will be the housewife! Except you can't cook!"

"Oh yeah?" Kai teased back, hooking a leg around one
of Dorian's. "Let's see if I can cook or not," he purred as his
fingers worked their way under Dorian's pants, to caress
the smooth hardness of his ass. "I bet I can get things hot
as well as you can!"

With a moan, Dorian pressed against Kai's thigh, the
hard roundness of his passion pushing against Kai's leg.
Words deeper, slower, breathy. "Maybe you can cook.
Maybe we should see how good your spoon stirs."

"Oh, baby," Kai preened, pushing the front of his pants
down a little to let the hard, proud member stand straight
up. "I can sure stir something up for you, uh-huh!"

Sex under the African sunset can still get pale skin a bit
red, but they hardly noticed, with Dorian straddled over
Kai's hips. Passionate creatures, humans and elfs, and the
sounds of passion are not unknown on the African
savanna, but they were precious to Kai. Each moan that
Dorian lost to the coming night as Kai thrust into the hot
sheath between Dorian's legs—it wasn't so different from
any of the women that Kai had fucked. The pleasure had
been there, hot around him, stroking as he moved,
building, but being with Dorian was different.

As his own climax tightened in him, making him press
at the hard ground with an only half-sandaled foot, his
thrusts hard and deep, caressing the sweet spot within
Dorian, it was Dorian's expression that brought Kai's soul
into the act.

Head back, lips parted, eyes only half-open, moaning in
pleasure each time Kai so much as moved, it was that
addictive glow that he could bring such pleasure to a
person he loved. Intimate beyond what Kai had thought
sex was, he found himself crying as his hands held
Dorian's hips. In the touch he forgot about his ruined

hand, forgot about not being able to fly, forgot everything he'd remembered of his life when he thought he was dying. Riding passion together with Dorian was better than flying, and then it was his own voice, panting, groaning as he neared the tightest point of the ride.

"Kai!" Dorian cried out, his knees so tight against Kai's waist, body curled over around his releasing member. Pearls shot up, milking over Kai's chest and Kai returned them, completing the cycle, releasing deep into Dorian, as he cried out his lover's name in return!

The come-down was slow, sweet, and as the sun slipped away over the horizon, Kai held his Dorian and they lay half undressed and entwined with each other. It was the freest and best feeling Kai was sure he'd ever had. Love had been a myth, harder to believe in than when Adrian had offered him the chance to be a dragon, to have his life back. Yet, here it was, love.

So he was lying there, holding a sleeping Dorian, content with the world, when the end of the world happened.

Something in him had known peace wouldn't last, that they'd find them. You don't just put a hit on someone and then decide to forget about it. It started as an itch at the back of his neck, the opening of the portal. He let it come. There was no knowing what could be coming through and it hadn't awakened Dorian yet. It was possible that it was something that didn't mean to kill them.

Even before the manifest, Kai already knew what he had to do. It was this deep understanding of what he had to do to make Dorian safe, to avenge Adrian, that ended Kai's world.

Evian was Adrian's older son, born when Elizabeth still ruled the world, or at least her part of it. He was all elf, barely touched by the modern world and the sprawling expanse of human inventiveness. He was the kind of elf who could challenge his father and make the greatest man

Kai had ever known into so much spare spirit energy. While Kai didn't know all there was to know about elfish royalty, and he now felt a residual spark of anger that Dorian hadn't bothered to let him know that he was sodding elfish royalty, Kai did know gangs. Evian was nothing more than a fancy gangbanger in midnight velvet and gold. From a gang mind-set, as one of Adrian's lieutenants, Kai had the right of payback.

The manifest, whatever it was, was taking forever to come through. Impatient, Kai slipped carefully from under Dorian's head. He pulled up his pants, slipped his sandal back on, and it hurt, seeing a sleepy, dark-haired Dorian as he woke, eyes wide with gentle curiosity.

It was like standing with one foot in the grave and one back in life. The world hadn't ended for Dorian yet. Kai squatted back down, touched his lover's face, ran a thumb over his lips. "Hey, baby," Kai said. Looking at Dorian, touching him, Kai decided, was better than a cigarette after sex. "You're the best-looking thing on this whole rock."

"What's wrong?"

He wanted to say "nothing," wanted it with so much of his being. They could just run. He'd make up failing Adrian by protecting his favorite son. Yeah. "Manifest seeking us. Can't you feel it?"

Dorian yawned, sitting up and adjusting his pants as he moved. "I thought we'd have more time."

"I guess your brother loves you," Kai said sarcastically, and then there it was, just a flicker of light like a pastel firefly, and Kai's good hand snapped it out of the air. The information hidden in the little ball of light soaked into Kai's mind like knowledge he'd already had. "Birus is condemned to starvation. Kyrie and Stephen are being tortured by Evian."

"That was meant for me!" Dorian growled, on his feet

now. "Birus would have sent that to me, not you! It's got a reverse manifest, doesn't it!"

"Yeah," Kai said, taking a step back. "I want to live a quiet life with you, Dori. I want that so very much. I want to get a cat, and I'll be the housewife. Meet you at the door with a kiss."

"Oh shut the fuck up! I forbid you to go fight Evian! Don't do this, Kai! Don't be so stubborn! You've got that look in your eye like you know what you're doing, but you don't! Evian will kill you!"

"Have some faith! Will you? Have some respect! He killed Adrian. One of the reasons you didn't tell me about Adrian first was this reaction. This was why you were afraid we'd never get our apartment together!"

"Damn straight! You stubborn prick. Kai, please."

"I love you, Dori. At least I told you what I was doing before I did it." And then Kai was gone, blinked out of the human realm and into the fey with the same ease that Dorian could teleport, only it was a one-way trip on his own.

"Kai!" Dorian screamed to the empty air! "Kai!"

The trip ended in darkness. Kai froze, a different kind of fear grabbing him. It was the scent of blood and bile in the air, the slow steady breath behind him and then, fear turned to relief. Relief that Dorian wasn't standing in this very spot right then.

"You're not my little brother," Evian snarled, wet fingers caressing down Kai's cheek. "But you smell like him. You do get above your station, don't you, Kai?"

"Fuck you! I'm going to kill you for what you did to Adrian!"

"Adrian . . ."

The punch hit Kai in the small of the back and his legs went boneless.

"Adrian is dead and henceforth you will refer to my

father as His Late Majesty. My father was never on a first-
name basis with dirt like you. You have nothing which he
didn't give you. You should have licked his boots, vermin."

Kai's wits clicked back to him slowly. Evian was nothing
except a very powerful gangster, just a bully. "Oh, is that
what you would have wanted?"

"I want so much more than that, but the first thing I
want is to see my little brother die, painfully. Dorian, you
see, is a twisted creature, lulled into believing your kind
has some value beyond that of a pretty cow. My father was
so proud of him and all things that my father wanted elevated will be destroyed. Do you know how hard your kind
will work for bombs that blow up big? What do they call
them, nuclear?"

"You son of a bitch," Kai growled, getting one foot flat
on the floor.

"Tsk, tsk, Kai. Is that any way to talk to the man who
owns you? This is going to be so much fun, maybe I
shouldn't have killed Birus so soon. After all, if you'd been
my stupid little brother, everything would be over already.
Don't you wish that you'd let him come visit me instead?"

"He's going to kill you," Kai said, and it was out of his
mouth before he could think it through. It was true
though, all his hopes were pinned on Dorian.

"Well, you could walk, but it's about fifty miles," Peace said,
pulling his hat lower over his eyes. "It's a little hot out."

"I can't take you with me!" Dorian protested. "I just want
a ride to where I can get a flight! You don't want to go."

Peace sat on the hood of his jeep, watching Dorian from
under the shade of his hat brim. "If it's someplace a person
can go, I want to see where dragons come from."

"Now's not the time," Dorian growled. "I'll come back
later and take you for a visit. Don't you get it? Kai has gone
to fight the king of the fey. He's in trouble."

"Can't you just magic yourself to him? Poof. Isn't that how you got here?"

"Yes, that is how we got here, but I only have so much energy to do 'poof' with, Peace. And when I use things that make me go 'poof' it leaves a signature. I don't want anyone to see me coming."

"Are you a criminal?" Peace asked.

Dorian's left eye twitched, "If I were, I'd kill you and take your keys."

"I want to see where you're going. I can take care of myself."

"No you can't! Kai's lived in Underhill for years and he's been endowed with great gifts and he's still not even a moment's fight for Evian. Why? Why do you want to come?"

"I was praying this morning and the Holy Spirit told me to," Peace said, straight-faced.

Dorian swore and kicked at the dirt. "All my life, I have worked to protect and help! I have had a team of people at my command for as long as I can remember. When human means fail, I use magic and I have always solved every problem, except when I couldn't find Kai in Australia and now, when I can't follow him home! I have never killed an innocent person in my whole life, but if you refuse to help me and Kai dies, I'll start with you. This is not a game!"

"I'm not afraid of you or of dying. I know where I'll go when I die." Peace propped his arms on his knees and grinned.

Dorian rubbed his temples. "By human standards, you're insane."

"Naw, I just have lots of faith. I didn't say I wouldn't help you, I said I want to come with you. You have very little room to call me insane. You're having sex with a dragon who turns into another man and you're desperate to go to the land of the fairies. I've always wanted to see Titania."

"That's Shakespeare, dumbass," Dorian complained. "This is not a play. Just because it's something you don't know much about does not make it not real!"

"Exactly," Peace said, "I want to see what's really there. I need to know. I need to."

"Great. You see a dragon and a man with pointy ears and now it's a crisis of faith?"

"I don't have to understand why you need to go. You don't need to understand why I need to go. I own the jeep and if you don't promise to take me with you, you can walk."

"I want to go, too," Setsuki said, gliding up behind them. Her quiet request somehow had more steel and unbendable will to it than all of Peace's argument.

Dorian covered his face with both hands. "You're going to get killed! Who will make your school then? Who will help these people?"

"I will always do what is right over what is easy," Setsuki said.

"And what makes seeing Underhill right or wrong? That's not something noble, that's just something you want."

"It is noble to seek to understand the world, to know truth, and to embrace it no matter how frightening it might be," she said, her hand finding its way to the hood of the jeep, where Peace just happened to find his hand.

"Dragons are scary," Peace agreed, slipping his fingers through Setsuki's. "We want to go with you, and we want—"

"We want to help Kai, too," Setsuki said, "He helped us."

"How? By threatening to kiss Peace?"

"It was an odd way to help, but it did help."

"He never would have kissed me," Peace added.

"Yes, he would have," Dorian said, a growing smile on his face.

Peace's lips puckered and he scraped his tongue on his

teeth, as if he were trying to get a bad taste out of his mouth, which made Setsuki laugh.

"Shall we go then? How long will it take, once we get to the airport?" she asked, giving Peace a small, flirty smile.

"If you're homesick already," Dorian grumbled, "Stay home."

"It won't take too long! Not with the three of us doing it."

Time in the mortal world was different than time in Underhill. Dorian had not been expecting the backlash of emotion and physical pain when it caught him. He had spent most of his life in the human world and it was possible he hadn't understood the full effects of an *orisei*. It had been only hours since he'd committed orisei with Kai, only a few hours since he'd bound his soul to a human man, but he could feel the weight of Kai's experience. Distant aching despair; he had to save him. It was Peace who caught Dorian though, an arm around his waist, holding him upright when Dorian hadn't even realized he'd been screaming, or that his legs had gone weak.

"Don't have a fit over it," Peace half-teased.

Dorian muttered, in elfish, not even understanding it himself, but then he gathered his wits and pushed away. In English, he explained, "Evian is torturing Kai. I'm not going to need your help, after all."

Setsuki made a disapproving sound. Dorian didn't want the lecture he could feel coming from her. "Peace, let go of me," he said, calmly, for all the empty lonely ache within him. One hand on his knee, his stomach feeling hollow and twisted, he opened his eyes, and there it was. The little glowing firefly key that was the gateway to his home world. He'd been robbed, all that was most precious stolen from him and he hadn't even seen the con which set up the theft.

Grief and a feeling of being too small to fight, just some throw away chaff, smothered Dorian, but then tears wet through the dryness of his soul, like the last bit of his soul leaking down his face. Always he had been a strategist, planning, moving the dragons into the best position, but now, all the dragons were likely in his brother's possession and he was nothing. His planning had lead to this failure. His decisions. It felt like slow motion, his hand reaching out, closing around the small ball of subtle light the way Kai had taken the earlier one. Kai had given him love, acceptance. Finding love in the first place was very hard, protecting it often harder. Dorian would fight to protect that love.

The blink that took him home to Underhill was colder than his own teleports; longer, timeless. Memories of Kai filtered through his thoughts as he pushed to the other side. Kai with drying hair, a smirking smile, Kai after he'd just joined their team, looking lost, and there was always backstory, story within story, and all Dorian cared about was this story, saving his Kai.

"Your Kai," Evian asked, insult discoloring his voice. "Your Kai? You cannot have orisei with a human. Didn't you know that? Besides, I am king. He is my dragon. I can do with him as I will."

Dorian had teleported right into the throne room, a room of marble and gold. It had a Roman feel to it, arches, a garden beyond, but where the throne had once sat, there now sat a long glass table with black office chairs around it. Kai lay in the center, just wearing jeans, one knee bent, bare feet against the glass, dark pooling and slowly dripping from his outstretched hand.

"He was no threat to you! Why did you have to hurt him?" Dorian demanded, a terrible rage rising tingling over his shoulders, scalp. "What have you done, Evian?"

Evian smirked. "Anything I wished. That is the privilege of the strong, Dorian. Idealism is for the weak. Father would have made us weak, exposed us to the humans, but he was right. They are strong, aggressive, violent. Father was right. We do have much to learn from them."

A calm core solidified in Dorian. It was more than the orisei with Kai, deeper, the root of that bond, the validation of his own being, of the world. He held out his hands to either side and summoned the blades of his mother's house. "Prepare yourself."

"What? You're really going to fight me for the human?" Evian sneered. "He's not worth it. You can have him. Take him and go. Live in the human world and let us see no more of you, little brother. You are not worth your ears and title."

Slipping out of the thin sandals, Dorian got a feel for holding his mother's short swords. Elfish metal, older than history, bright as moonlight made solid, the hilts curved up around his forearms in a kind of protective armor, but the blades reflected the fluorescent-like office light around them. The gold leaves, etched into the cold silver, were said to be gifts of the elfish gods, each one a reward for valor and courage, for justice and balance. "My mother's people were healers, Evian. One thing I have learned in my life though is that one cannot heal if one cannot stop that which destroys. You were warned."

Dorian had spent years with those blades, learning the art of a violent dance of truth. He lunged, giving no quarter, no mercy, and only Evian's dodge saved him from having twin livers.

"Shitty brat!" Evian snapped, calling his sword, the Blood and Sorrow. It was red, ruby glass, two-handed, and he easily deflected the double blows that Dorian sent at him next.

They circled each other, so archaic, so out of place in the throne room done over into a boardroom. "I demand you step down and enter contemplation for the death of our father."

"Oh? Mercy is lost on you, isn't it? I demand you slit the throat of the dragon of heart and kneel at my feet as my servant." Evian swung his blood red blade with all his strength, but Dorian caught it in the crossed X of his own and kicked his brother in the gut.

As Evian staggered back, Dorian lunged, trying to scissor his blades over anything softer than Elfish blade. The stronger and larger of them, Evian pulled back quickly, drawing back for another blow, and Dorian struck his left blade against Blood and Sorrow. His other blade, Balance, sliced through Evian's fancy business jacket to leave wet on the silver and on the cloth.

Evian came back with a heavy overhead swing that knocked Truth down and would have had Dorian's shoulder if the smaller elf had not dropped and rolled.

"Do you really think those little blades can stand up to me?" Evian snarled, his blade hitting the marble with sparks as Dorian scrambled back. Another blow followed and then a swipe at Dorian's belly. "I am going to gut you, Dorian, and while you lay dying, I am going to do bad things to your human lover. Orisei with a human? Are you insane?"

Dorian swished his blades, dual figure eights, buying seconds to think. Sweat trickled over his temple and he searched for an opening. There were no thoughts of Kai, no time for his life to pass before his eyes, just the cold calculating predatory planning that a killer was capable of.

"So serious, Dori? You love humans so much, maybe you'd like to see the new spirit weapon of my house? My house! Not our father's house. I have made it my own!" Evian declared, holding his family's sword in one hand as a pistol appeared in his other. He aimed at Dorian's head, the red light moving from there slowly down his body.

Sparing no words that could break his concentration, panting from being on the defensive, Dorian struck, lunging in close and there he had his blades to Evian's throat, laid cross each other. "And now Truth and Balance have you in their grip. Renounce the throne!"

The bullet hit Dorian's ribs at point-blank range with a crack. It tore through him as only elfin-magicked technology could and he held there for a moment, eyes wide, fists slowly losing their hold on his mother's swords. Evian gave him a shove and he staggered back, one step, two, before Balance dropped to the ground and he followed. Truth skidded when she hit, dragging a trail through Dorian's sprayed blood.

Evian returned his spirit weapons to where they'd come from and delivered a stinging backhand to Dorian's cheek. "So noble! So fallen! You are not worthy of the royal blood in you!"

Dorian hit the floor, hands and knees, then down to one shoulder, blood coughing out of his mouth, and his brother kicked him hard in the shoulder. He rolled and Evian gloated.

The families of the fey appeared then, walking through the walls of Evian's boardroom as if they were no more than illusion. Delicately beautiful creatures, ornate and archaic, displaying fashion as old as the Greeks, as elaborate as anything a Paris runway had ever seen, and they watched, silently, as their royal house culled from its ranks. Faces impassive, pale ivory to the deepest ebony and all shades in between, they were only witnesses to the struggle.

Evian held his arms out to them, chin lifted, palms up to accept their adoration and acknowledgment of his assumption of the throne. "I am your king! It is a new age! Give your homage to me! We will dominate the humans as we have not for millennia!"

The faces around him remained impassive, unconvinced. A sharp burning cut through him and his eyes dropped to the blade point that now extended from his belly. He hissed sharply and spun, only to run into Kai's left hook, which caught him unprepared and sent him sprawling.

Pale, shaking, Kai grabbed the remaining blade and rushed to press it to Evian's throat. "Don't push me, fuckhead! Is this who you want for your king? Is this what you want? This loudmouth with crappy taste?"

A woman emerged from the silent witnesses. She was a snow queen, skin iridescent, eyes snow blue, hair more elaborate than Kai had time to think about. "Is this how things are done in your world? Kings are chosen?"

"Yes, well, presidents," Kai said, dropping to his own knees, Dorian's sword falling from his hand. "Save Dorian, please?"

"You are a true dragon of a king worthy of our race," she said, reaching out to touch his face with a graceful hand. "If I can save only one of you, would you have me save him or you?"

Kai found himself leaning into the warmth and comfort of her hand against his cheek. The pain fled with her touch, the darkness fled, too, and he knew that he would find all that he'd ever longed for in her touch. He pulled back though, tears of loss already chilling their way down his cheeks. "Save Dorian."

"The power of your heart pleases us," she said and reached down to touch the blade, which had fallen from his hand. A new golden leaf, really two, twined around each other, appeared. She turned and with a sweep of her hand Evian was swept away into whatever lay beyond the illusion of their throne room. The same hand motioned toward Dorian and his back lifted as he drew a deep breath. Then she turned again to Kai and took his face in both hands. "You are so noble, and you are welcome to our family. Your spirit will reside with the spirits of all in our family when you die. Do not be afraid."

"We were going to get an apartment together, and a cat," Kai said.

"Such a place must be quite lovely," she said. "You must bring me a cat in time. If you long for one so, it must be a fine creature. You will not die today, dragon of heart. Return to us when time has stolen youth from you and you may yet find peace and joy among our kind. For today, take our king and love him. Share an apartment with him. We have no need to move as quickly as your world seems to be so pleased with."

Kai swallowed tears, drew a deep breath and struggled to get his mind around that idea that he wasn't dying today. "What kind of cat do you want?"

She laughed, a completely out-of-place laugh. "What kind of cat do you want?"

The question echoed through the nonquiet of passive faces watching them. "What kind of cat do you want?"

The oddness of it sent a shiver over Kai's shoulders and he scrambled away from the beautiful woman toward Dorian. "Kyrie and Stephen?" he asked as he pulled Dorian into his arms, and only then did he realize his hand was whole. The fingers flexed and had strength again. He flexed a couple times then pulled Dorian close.

"What kind of cat do you want?" She asked him and then before he could blink, he was back in the heat. It pressed him down, clogged his lungs.

"Good Lord!" Peace exclaimed. "He's reappeared."

Setsuki swore in Japanese and Peace followed her eyes. "Wow, man, and now there are two of them."

"Welcome back, Kai," Setsuki said.

Dorian groaned.

Without sound, the other two of their team appeared, the dark and feral Stephan and the elegant, emotionally wounded Kyrie.

It was over that fast, like a car wreck. Blink and all that's left is wreckage.

Dorian's eyes opened to a smiling Kai. "Welcome to Africa, baby," Kai said. "Thanks for coming to find me."

Months later, in the spiritual plane over Paris, a red dragon spread his wings wide; a dark-haired man holding tight to his shoulders as they took the sky together. Wind whipping dark hair, the king was with his dragon and that was how life was meant to be.

THE HUNGRY GHOST

BIANCA JAMES

My parents sent me to live with my grandmother in Silver City in the fall of my seventeenth year, under the premise of curing my homosexuality. Despite my metropolitan upbringing in New York, my parents were old-money conservatives and it meant a great deal to them that I get married and settle down with a nice girl, give them grandchildren. I had managed to pass off my lack of interest in girls as a side effect of my solitary, bookish personality for the better part of my high school career. Then one day my father came home early from work and overheard my boyfriend Johnny and me having sex in my room. It was easier for them to send me away to the snowy one-horse town where my mother had been raised, than face the awful truth that their son was queer.

I didn't particularly want to leave my life in New York, but I suppose what happened to me wasn't so bad compared to what poor Johnny went through. His parents were Italian Catholics, and they'd sent him to a religious group home where they would supposedly "cure" him. I was cut off from Johnny with no way to contact to him. I even employed a female friend to call Johnny's parents' house under the pretense of being a girlfriend to get his contact information, but they hung up on her.

I began writing letters to Johnny everyday, even though I didn't know where to send them. I saved them in the drawer of my desk at my grandmother's house. Someday Johnny and I would be together again, and I could give them to him. We'd laugh about all of it, our parents foolishness, feeling smug and triumphant because we'd have survived it and made a life together. That's what I told myself, clinging to any scrap of hope to keep myself sane in the middle of my grief.

My life was easy compared to Johnny's because I still had my privacy, even more privacy than when I lived with my parents. Just me and my widowed grandmother Mabel in that big old house on the hill. My parents didn't even bother telling her the truth about why I needed to live in Silver City, they just made up some excuse about the schools in the city being dangerous. She was grateful for the company and didn't ask questions, preferring to spend her time alone studying scriptures. My time was my own.

My grandmother's house was located on the outskirts of what had once been a Nevada boomtown, now a minor tourist draw, a sleepy hamlet that was almost completely buried in snow in the wintertime. Silver City didn't have much: the supposedly haunted mansions of long-dead silver barons, an old Episcopalian church and cemetery, a tavern that served heavy food, domestic beer, and Irish coffee, with football or horse racing on the television; an ice-cream parlor, a pathetic excuse for a little casino. You had to drive to Angleston thirty minutes away if you wanted to go shopping at Wal-Mart or see a movie. There wasn't much to do in Silver City. The town's few teenagers would hang out in front of the ice-cream parlor in summer, get drunk in the woods, or go to parties elsewhere.

Silver City had an elementary school going up to eighth

grade, but older kids were bused out to the high school in Angleston. My grandmother let me use her car to get to and from school and anywhere else I needed to go, as long as I took her to church on Sundays and grocery shopping. I went to church with her even though I hadn't been raised religious by my parents. It made grandmother happy, and the gory drama of Jesus's brutal crucifixion held an exotic, detached appeal to me.

My great-grandfather had been the mayor of the town when it was prosperous, and the ghost of the Andersen family wealth lived on in that big mansion on the hill, full of empty rooms. My parents might have thought twice about sending me there if they had known what kind of disrepair the house had fallen into over the years. My grandmother refused to hire cleaners though God knows she could have afforded it, preferring to live in squalor with her three cats for company. In the beginning I made overtures toward helping around the house, dusting and washing dishes. But it seemed it made no difference to her whether I did or not, so after a while I stopped bothering.

Grandmother let me have my run of the dusty rooms on the second story of the big house. Grandmother's knees were bad, so her movement was restricted to shuffling around the first floor using her walker. I spent my first weeks wandering those decrepit rooms, fingering crumbling books, old clothes, and forgotten photographs, sleeping in a different bed every night. It was like being a princess in a fairytale. And though I missed Johnny terribly, I soon realized that I vastly preferred staying with my grandmother to living with my parents. Silver City had very little of interest compared to New York, but it was the first time in my life that I had complete freedom to live as I pleased.

I grew to cherish the weird hours I spent lost in the strange house, or wandering the decrepit cemetery down the road, with its spindly gates and forgotten tombstones.

I would help myself to a bottle of wine from the cellar, and would slip out at night, plant a candle in the dirt of the graveyard for its paltry light, and talk to the dead for want of real company.

So really, I suppose I have no one but myself to blame for what happened.

It was around the time that I stopped writing the letters to Johnny. Every day got colder as winter approached, and it seemed pointless after a while to pledge my undying love over and over again when my pleading fell on deaf ears. For all I knew, the Catholics might have cured Johnny already. My family was still holding out hope that I would come around. All I had to do was say that I was ready to make some changes, and they would have sent a ticket for me to come home. My mother told me she had met an admissions officer from my dad's alma mater, and it still wasn't too late to apply for the coming year. I could study economics like Dad, and he would hire me to take over the family business one day. They had my whole life all planned out for me. It would have been a guaranteed life of misery masquerading as comfort, so I held out, said I wasn't ready, said I needed more time. I wasn't ready to go back to my parents, but the truth was I was perishing of loneliness, and sometimes I wondered if I wasn't going a little crazy.

I had taken to sleeping in the attic room at the top of the house. It was the darkest of all the rooms, with no natural light except for a few small, gabled windows that looked out on the expanse of town below. I would sometimes entertain fantasies that I was a reclusive king surveying his kingdom from those tiny windows. There was a burnt-out bare bulb hanging from the ceiling. I ignored it and burned dozens of candles in glass pillars instead, which cast the room in eerie shadow. There was a big, tarnished brass four-poster bed in that room, with ancient bloodstains on the mattress. I pretended it was the scene of some gruesome murder in a Victorian whorehouse. I moved a clean mattress and new sheets onto the brass bed, and I began spending most of my time in that bed, reading books scavenged from the library in Angleston and writing stories in my journal.

Having been raised in a Manhattan apartment with one small room to myself, it was luxurious to have my own suite of rooms to do whatever I pleased with, complete with antique furniture, and my own bathroom with a claw-foot tub. There was an odor of oldness that had settled over everything, but I burned incense until it smelled like a church. The second floor and attic became a magical place where I dwelled in my dreams.

I had been sleeping in that weird attic room for over a month when Max appeared to me for the first time. I was laying awake in the big brass bed, when I noticed a light in the tarnished silver mirror on the wall opposite the bed. I had already extinguished the candles, but this was different from candlelight, soft and diffused like a flashlight shining through mist. The smoky orb of light seemed to float out of the mirror and gather at the foot of the bed, mysterious and indistinct. I sat up in bed, and squinted the way one does when a pile of clothes or a chair can mimic something sinister in the dark. The light shivered and I could make out an outline of a person, transparent and glowing like a moth. He was faint as a line drawing, a pale suggestion of cheekbones and glittering eyes and mouth in the shadows of the dark room. Yes, there was definitely someone there, perched on the bars at the foot of the bed. It didn't occur to me at the time to be scared, I was too much in awe.

"Who are you?" I asked. "And what are you doing in my room?"

"I could ask you the same thing. This has been my room since long before you were born." I wasn't hearing the voice with my ears, the words just appeared in my mind, but I could hear the person's voice loud and clear regardless.

"That's strange," I replied. "Grandmother didn't say anything about another person living here." It was a stupid thing to say, it was obvious that the man wasn't a living person.

"Your grandmother pretends she doesn't see me." He sighed, and I saw him strike a tragic pose with his wispy ethereal arms. "Her own brother. She didn't even attend my funeral. Drowned in a swimming pool, me, drunk on liquor. She thought I brought it upon myself. She thought it was fair punishment for my . . . unnatural tendencies," he finished with an amused smirk.

His outline was growing clearer, shaded smoky dark in places. He climbed down from his perch, crawled onto the bed and came to lay beside me. "Do you mind if I rest a while?" He asked. "It is my bed, after all. And I'm so tired." He yawned, and moved closer to me. The air around him felt cold.

I didn't argue, but studied him instead. He reminded me of an image from an old movie, flickering black and white, skin pale against indigo-dark eyes and black hair. His face reminded me of my own, except my hair was auburn and my eyes were green. He was good looking and young, like a 1930s movie star. I remembered that my mother had an uncle who had died before she was born, when he was only nineteen. Suddenly I knew this must be his ghost. I tried to remember the name. Mark or something.

"Max," he replied, as if he could read my thoughts. I could hear his voice clearly as he was speaking out loud now. "And you must be Mabel's grandchild."

"My name is Anthony," I replied solemnly. "I remember you," I said suddenly, as the memory came back, a memory I did not realize I had. "You played checkers with me when nobody else would."

I was only six years old then. The only other time I'd visited this house, a family reunion full of guilt and sighs. Bored, with no one to play with, I'd carried my box of checkers from relative to relative, until they all tired of me and told me to go play with the old toys in the attic. My grandma's dolls were there, packed in tissue and smelling so old. He had been up there, too, just sitting on the bed and smoking a cigarette. He'd talked and played with me, though he never let me win at checkers. I had thought he was just another family member, but nobody knew who I was talking about when I mentioned the "man in the attic," they had assumed it was a childish folly, an imaginary friend I had made up.

"I've been sleeping all these years," he said. "Nobody to disturb me. And then you came, and fed me with your dreams night after night, and I found my will to live again."

"But you're dead! What do you mean?" I asked, incredulously.

"Touch me now," he said. His face was inches from my own. I reached out to feel his cheek, expecting my hand to pass through air, but there was something there, soft and warm. As my palm met his skin, it glowed with color, as if it were real flesh.

"How?" I asked, baffled.

"You," he said. "Your energy, your belief, makes me strong. It's like an electrical current. As long as you touch me I can absorb your energy and manifest as real. But I cannot keep a form like this for long, it is very taxing." His color faded a bit, to near transparent.

"Close your eyes," he said. "Picture me, picture me as being real." And so I did, and so I saw him come to life on the backs of my eyelids, young and strong and beautiful, my great-uncle, not much older than I was.

He kissed me, and I felt lips on my own, and I felt hands—real hands touching my chest through the fabric of my T-shirt. It had been so long, and it felt so good. Just that little bit of physical contact was enough to make my mind race and my cock hard.

No, I thought abruptly, this is my own great-uncle, this is family, this is someone who would be old and decrepit if he were still alive. This is not Johnny. And the presence disappeared without a trace. I felt a pang of regret. I realized I was so lonely that I didn't really care about all those other things. *Come back,* I wished, *come back. I don't mind that you are family. You are just a spirit, a memory. Come back and touch me.* And gradually the figure regained color and touched me again. It was a feeling like being half-asleep, my mind drowning in sensual fantasies, but my body awake to the mysterious pleasures that were being played upon my flesh. He brought me to orgasm in a way that was not so much the result of being physically touched, but a physical response to the thoughts and feelings that accompany arousal. Max stimulated my sexual responses at their deepest core level, as if I were having a waking wet dream. He made me come, and then I fell into deep dreamless sleep moments later, my thighs stained with phantom semen.

I had forgotten all about it when I awoke the next day, preoccupied by the ritual of getting ready for school, driving through the snow to make it barely in time for homeroom. I drifted through my day, ate lunch alone in my car with the heater turned up, listening to my favorite CDs like I always did. I had been assigned a project in my history class to research my family tree and create a report. When I got home I asked grandmother if she had any old photo albums I could use for my presentation. She procured a dusty stack, which I flipped through listlessly until I saw a picture of adolescent Max in the prime of his beauty. My fingers froze as the events of the previous night came flooding back. I flipped through the remainder of the album, hungry for more, but found only gaps, faded white squares against the browned paper where pictures of the debauched young Max must have been. I stole the photo of Max when my grandmother had her back turned and took it back up to the attic with me.

I sat on my bed and stared at the photo, praying for him to return, talking to the empty air in the hopes that he would appear before me again. Disappointed, I drifted off into a restless sleep. I was awakened in the middle of the night by a chilly presence under the sheets. I twitched awake, still feverish from dreams, and stared into the ghostly face of Max.

"Hi," I said, in a sleep-thick voice. "I was waiting for you. Where were you?"

"I was looking for something. Your grandmother keeps things well hidden."

"Touch me," I said taking his cold hand in my own, "get warm." My skin felt too hot, I craved the coolness of his presence.

Max rubbed his phantom fingers on my arms and held me. His body felt refreshing as a cool mist against my skin. I sensed life flowing into his form as he touched me, and soon it felt as if there were a real body lying next to me.

"I missed you," I said. If Max was a figment of my lonely imagination, there was no point in being coy with him. "I forgot all about what happened last night until I found a picture of you and since then it's been as if there's a piece of me missing. Is that strange?"

"No, not at all." He smiled and looked pleased. "Come, I have something I want to show you." Max gestured to a paper bag on the bedside table that hadn't been there when I'd gone to sleep.

"What is it?"

"Open it."

I unfolded the weathered brown paper and pulled out a stack of old photos printed on yellowed paper. I gasped. "The missing photos!"

"Your grandmother hid them well, but I know where to look."

I gasped when I saw a picture of Max, looking just as he did lying next to me, wearing a silk suit and drinking a cocktail. I flipped through, and saw a picture of him standing with his hand on the arm of a blond man who was looking at the ground.

"That first photo was taken the night I died," Max said.

"If you're dead, why don't you just go to heaven or hell or just disappear?"

Max pouted. "Unfinished business. I'm trapped here. I don't have the freedom to move about like you do. Unless . . ."

"Unless what?"

"Unless you take me with you."

"What do you mean?" I asked suspiciously.

"Think of it sort of like possession," he began.

"No way!" I said.

"It would be a passive possession, as if you were carrying me around in your pocket. I will be with you, and I can talk to you, but I promise to behave myself."

"How do I know you won't try and take control of my body?"

"Lie still," He whispered, ghostly lips pressed against my ear, making me shiver. There was a sense of sinking in my body, not invasive, he went in easy and smooth and filled my body completely. It felt the way I always believed sex should feel. It felt like the first time I saw the inside of a church after a lifetime of being raised by atheists, or the feeling I got when I got wrapped up in an art project and forgot about everything else. It was a bit frightening, and for a moment I wanted to shake him loose but he held on tenaciously, like a snake sinking its fangs into my throat. I swooned, and there was a feeling of coolness all over my body. My heart was beating faster, and my skin stood up in goosebumps. My soul felt very full all of a sudden, as if my body wasn't big enough to contain my spirit and I would split open.

"You'll get used to it," he said, a voice in my head that was not mine. "Soon you won't feel me at all."

"I feel as though I've gone crazy," I said.

"Is this better?" he asked, suddenly appearing before me on the bed, in full color this time. I was struck by his beauty all over again. His hair was blue-black, his eyes were deepest blue. He was wearing the silvery-gray silk suit he had been wearing in the photograph.

"But—you're inside of me?" I asked, confused.

"Yes, I am. This is an optical illusion," he said. "A diversion. If it makes you more comfortable I can turn it off or on."

"How did you learn to do all this?" I asked, baffled.

"Fifty years alone in an attic, poking around the ether, talking to other ghosts. I've never had anyone to test my theories on until now."

I reached out to touch him. My hand passed through the air.

"This is just a visual projection," he said. "You cannot touch it because I'm still inside of you. But it can touch you." The ghost-image reached out its hand and touched my cheek. Goosebumps rose again on my arms.

"Ah, you like that, don't you?" he asked with a cheeky grin.

"How do you know?" I asked defensively.

"I'm inside of you now. I feel everything you feel, I know your thoughts."

"I don't know how I feel about that," I said.

"Trust me, there are benefits," He replied with a smirk. Take off your clothes and I'll show you."

I don't know how he did it, but he made it feel as though I were being made love to by someone who knew exactly what I wanted at any given moment, which caress I craved most. The fact that I couldn't touch him forced me to be passive and receive pleasure, and I was ashamed to admit that it was better than anything I'd ever done with Johnny. He even controlled my exact moment of orgasm, holding me back until he wanted me to come, as if I didn't have a choice in the matter.

It was strange having Max inside of me. Sometimes I could forget about him completely, drifting away in daydreams in math class, and Max would make his presence known again, tormenting me with invisible caresses so that it took all my willpower to stay quiet.

If I dared to get angry with him, he'd just smile and say, "You liked it. I know you did." He was usually right. And for the most part, Max kept his promise to behave himself. After months of isolation, his presence was tremendously comforting to me. I was never lonely because he was always there to talk to me. I had to be careful not to talk out loud to myself in public, so I trained myself to converse with him inside my head. When there was no one else around, he would create the visual so it didn't seem so strange that my best friend was the ghost of my great-uncle, who was also my spirit-lover.

Max liked to visit the decrepit old cemetery with me, where I once went alone to think. He showed me where he was buried, and we'd sit on his tombstone, me drinking wine from the cellar while he sipped imaginary martinis and smoked ghostly cigarettes.

"Do you ever find it strange that that box of bones beneath the soil was once your body?" I asked.

"One gets used to not having a body after a while," he replied nonchalantly.

One of the more interesting aspects of having Max

inside of me was that I could see and talk to other ghosts. There were quite a few that haunted the cemetery. There was an old woman with long gray hair and rags for clothing who crawled about on hands and knees searching for something. She didn't like to talk and hissed if we came near here, preferring to keep to herself.

"She was a spinster who ran a boarding house in town until she hanged herself," Max remarked knowingly, smoking a phantom cigarette. "She was very beautiful when she was young, believe it or not. She was engaged to my father once, but he jilted her for a society woman when he went into politics. After my father broke the engagement, she threw away the ring in the cemetery, and now she will never give up trying to find it."

There were friendlier ghosts as well—the cheerful red-haired Irishman named Tristan whom I had mistaken for living when I first met him. He whistled with a jaunt in his step and always had a friendly word for me.

"I don't understand why he's a ghost," I confessed to Max. "I mean, a spirit only lingers on if there was some lack of closure, something that went wrong," I said. "He seems so happy."

"Him?" Max asked "He killed his wife and son driving drunk. They went on to heaven but he decided to stay on to atone for his guilt. Now he spends his days pushing children out of the way of speeding traffic and other such good deeds."

"And you?" I asked. "What really happened with you, other than drowning in a swimming pool? If it was really an accident, why weren't you allowed to go on to heaven or whatever?"

"Your grandfather killed me," he said coldly.

"What?"

"He turned his back when he saw me drowning."

"Grandpa did this?" I asked, astonished.

"He would have never admitted it. Perhaps he never

admitted it to himself. But I never forgot. He was next in line for the inheritance and he didn't approve of my lifestyle. He wanted the fortune that was rightfully mine, so he let me drown."

"But Grandpa is dead now, too. His ghost must be around here somewhere. Why don't you confront him about it?"

"Because he's gone, died a peaceful death and disappeared without a trace. Maybe he never admitted his guilt to himself, maybe his love for your grandmother saved him. Me, I've been stuck here for years, for God knows why. But then I met you, and understood."

"Understood what?"

"I have been given a second chance to undo the wrongs of my life. You. It took fifty years, but you returned to me."

"What?" I asked, a little startled.

"You are the reincarnated soul of Clarence, the boy I once loved. He died the same year you were born. It's ironic, isn't it? My family shamed him and forced him to leave town after my death. He made a life of his own as an artist in Los Angeles, lived to old age, and his spirit was reborn in the body of Mabel's grandchild. It couldn't have been an accident."

It was weird being told that I was the reincarnation of my great-uncle's lover, and I felt a bit suspicious. "How do you know it's me?" I asked. "What proof do you have?"

"Oh, little things . . ." he said. "The way you look it me, the way you talk, the way you touch your hair. Habits the two of you share. The more time I spend with you, the more I am certain that you are him and he is you."

"Are you sure it's not just your imagination?" I asked him. "Maybe you want to believe I am his reincarnation because you miss him?"

"Doesn't really matter either way, does it?" Max replied. "I love you, whoever you are."

Over the course of weeks, I got used to Max's constant presence and even found it comforting. But he was growing restless. He wanted a host, a human body that he could borrow to go about his life. "I miss the taste of wine, of good food," he groused bitterly as I ate my evening meal. "I want you to be able to touch me the way I touch you. I want to feel whole again."

I had my doubts about how ethical it was to "borrow" someone's body, but Max assured me it would be fine, that he would cause the host no pain. It was just the question of finding a host in a town as small as Silver City. A disappearance would not go unnoticed. I didn't really understand how Max planned to go about his mission, and I did not encourage him. I hoped that a suitable host would fail to appear, and Max would be content to stay inside of me, where I was happy to keep him. But Max never stopped looking, and after a while, he appeared. The name badge on his uniform said Jayce.

We found him at a gas station fifteen miles outside of town, the kind of gas station that doesn't exist in big cities anymore. Full service, with a young man who wipes your windows and fills your tank. He had the sort of beauty that belongs to those who don't realize they are beautiful, those for whom beauty has no meaning at all. Tall and slim, with long rangy muscles under his white undershirt and blue service-station coveralls. Tanned arms and face, unkempt dirty-blond hair swept under a baseball cap, slightly crooked teeth that added to the charm of his smile. He was working class, smelling of gasoline and cigarettes. He spent his long empty days at the gas station sitting up at the counter reading comic books and drinking slushies spiked with moonshine, smoking up in the bathroom and jerking off to pornography to break the monotony. Max knew all this just by looking at him, and the images flooded my brain in one heady rush. I felt myself salivating and I didn't know why. He wasn't my type. I preferred dark-haired men, but Max had a thing for blonds.

Max and I debated this in my head, sitting on the worn orange vinyl seat of the waiting room while Jayce changed the oil and washed the car. I was sucking on a sticky-hard Sugar Daddy and flipping through a battered tabloid to pass the time, but Max's phantom image was watching Jayce intently as he buffed Grandmother's car with his lanky, scarred, brown arms.

Max devoured him with his eyes as he lanked back into the shop. "He's perfect," he declared with an air of finality.

"What are you talking about?" I accidentally said out loud, and Jayce's eyes wandered over me warily. "Sorry," I said, embarrassed. "I was surprised by something I read in this magazine," I said, feeling ridiculous. Jayce nodded disinterestedly.

He's nothing like you at all, I thought to Max. *Look at him—he's straight. He'd kill me if I made a move on him.*

"He's young, and he's beautiful. He'd clean up nicely. And his will is weak. He wouldn't be missed." Max replied in a voice only I could hear.

He's white trash!

"I'm not going to argue with you about this, Anthony."

I felt myself being lifted off of the seat against my will.

Max, stop it! You promised you'd behave!

"And now it's your turn to behave. Be a good boy, Anthony. I want him, and I'm not going to let your prejudice stand in the way of getting what I want."

My head spun. I felt my very free will being pushed into the background, like those poor victims of neurotoxin poisoning who watch in horror as they are buried alive, unable to move their muscles to speak in protest.

"Hey there, Jayce," I heard my voice say as I sauntered over to the counter.

"Hello, Mr. Smith," Jayce replied with uncomfortable politeness. "Is there anything else I can do for you today, or will that be all?

"That'll do it," I said reaching for my wallet, and peeling off a few bills, more than what was required. "Why don't you give me a package of Lucky Strikes, too."

Jayce fetched the cigarettes and rang them up without asking for I.D. "Anything else?"

"Actually Jayce . . ." *Oh God,* I thought to myself. *Here it comes.* "Do you know where to buy reefer around here?" I felt myself grinning maniacally. Did I actually say "reefer"?! I was amused by the outdated terminology, but the tactic wasn't too bad for a man who'd spent the past fifty years asleep in an attic.

I panicked when Jayce narrowed his eyes for a few seconds, but then his expression relaxed and his gaze darted around the shop. "Come back at nine," he said. "Wait out back and I'll pick you up."

"Thank you for your trouble," I heard myself say, peeling a twenty-dollar bill out of the wallet and handing it to Jayce.

What the fuck was that all about, I screamed in my head. *I've had enough, get out of me!*

"Soon enough, I will be," Max replied. "Be patient, Anthony, it will all be worth it."

Max was at least kind enough to appear as a projection again, even though it really made no difference. He could seize control of my will anytime he wanted, and I was powerless to stop him.

"Oh, stop throwing tantrums," Max said, and as he spoke, I felt myself opening the package of cigarettes and lighting up. "You should know I'm doing you a favor. You should be a little more thankful!"

"What the fuck, I don't even smoke!" I said, throwing down the cigarette.

"But I do," the phantom image of Max replied, bending over to pick up the cigarette and smoke it, which was weird because every time I'd touched the phantom it hadn't had any kind of substance with which to pick up a cigarette. It meant he was feeding on me to create a solid body. No wonder I felt so tired. Before I could protest any further, I felt something like a cool hand creep into my mind, relaxing my doubts, and I found myself stumbling toward the car, lying down and enjoying the best nap of my life on the fake leather upholstery. Maybe Max had taken mercy on me, knowing the idea of preying on the boy's body made me physically ill.

When I awoke, it was dark and I was alone. Max was utterly silent, maybe he'd gone somewhere. I got out of the car, stretched and pissed by the side of the parking lot. I looked up and saw Jayce watching me with his creepy yellow wolf eyes that seemed to glow even in the dark of the parking lot.

"Are you ready to go?" he asked, and I gulped and nodded.

I rode in the passenger seat of Jayce's pickup truck, perspiring in the hot hay smell of the cab. We rode in silence, except for country music buzzing low on the car's tape deck. He pulled up in front of a crumbling old farmhouse and turned to me with his vulpine face. "How much money you got?" he asked me. I took all of the money out of my wallet and handed it to him. He was gone a long time, and I began to panic, afraid that some small-town cops would roll by and bust us.

"Max, if you're here, say something. This is creepy," I pleaded out loud to the silence in the cab. "Max, quit fucking with me! It was you who wanted this, remember?" I tried the handle of the rickety pickup but it was stuck. I slid over to the passenger seat and opened the door, and was met by Jayce coming out of the house.

"Good shit," he said, waving a baggie full of pot.

"Invite him back to your place," I heard Max pipe up after his long silence.

"What about Grandma? What if he steals shit?"

"I'll take care of Grandma," Max replied. "Trust me."

"Wow, I didn't know you lived up at Mayor Andersen's old place," Jayce said in awe as we pulled up in front of the decrepit mansion. "I always thought this place was haunted."

"Oh, it is," I said totally deadpan, but then mumbled "just kidding" when I saw the look of abject horror on Jayce's face.

As Max predicted, Grandmother was asleep and we were able to slip past her to the attic. Fortunately, Jayce had brought his pipe with him, and he spared no time in lighting up the first bowl. I took one hit for three of Jayce's, wanting to keep the upper hand but playing it off as generosity.

Jayce laid back on the big four-poster bed, the top buttons of his gas-station jumpsuit undone to show the dirty undershirt he wore beneath. I thought I detected a stiffening bulge in his pants.

"You know, that's the damndest thing about weed," Jayce said. "Screw the munchies, I just wanna fuck," he said, drawing out the vowel on *fuck*.

Jayce didn't move or say a thing when Max prompted me to unbutton Jayce's uniform the rest of the way down and pull his cock out of his boxer shorts. Maybe Max's gaydar was better than I realized, or maybe Jayce was just one of those straight boys who didn't mind having his cock sucked by another guy if he kept his eyes closed. He lay still and let me go down on him. It had been a long time since I'd sucked another man's cock, not since Johnny. I was forced to admit that Jayce's cock looked pretty good: long, thick, with a hint of foreskin. I was already imagining what it would feel like to get fucked by it.

My brain went blank with pleasure once I tasted him with my tongue, his cock filling my entire mouth and pushing at the gate of my throat. I could feel Max's satisfaction in the background, gently goading me on. My own cock was straining hard in my pants, begging for release. Jayce groaned and grabbed my hair, began fucking my face with a quick rhythm. I knew he was close to coming, and it was as if I could feel the buildup to his orgasm in my own body as well. When he finally went over the edge, I felt a huge flood of energy pouring out of me at the same time that he came in my mouth. Max was entering Jayce at his most vulnerable moment, and it felt like the most intense orgasm of my life. When I finally pulled away, I realized that I'd shot in my pants, and my cock was trapped in a hot, sticky web in my underwear. I panted for a moment, and looked at Jayce, spent on the bed, half-erect cock slick with spit and sperm.

Jayce looked at me with bewildered eyes and I wondered for a moment if Max had failed his mission to enter his body, and if Jayce would pick this moment to beat up the fag who'd had the nerve to get him off.

The dumb look lingered for a moment, before Jayce seemingly regained control of his senses and blinked a few times. Max's trademark smirk curled on Jayce's lips. "So what do you think of me now, Anthony? That wasn't so difficult after all."

"Where happened to Jayce, then? Is he dead?"

"He's not dead . . . just sleeping. It wasn't difficult at all to convince his soul to roll over and make room for the alpha male. Like I said, he didn't have much upstairs to begin with."

Jayce/Max got up and languorously shrugged out of the filthy coveralls so that he stood before me in all of his nude glory, admiring himself in the dusty mirror. If Jayce had been a diamond in the rough when we'd spotted him working at the gas station, he was now a cut gem shining with unbridled glory. I was forced to admit that Max had chosen well. Jayce's body was hard and lean, with a beautiful cock and a handsome face that would clean up nicely. "Come on, let's take a bath," Max said, surveying his new skin. "This body is filthy."

We went into the bathroom on the second floor with the giant claw-foot tub. Max filled the tub with hot water and soap and helped me in. I felt drained and strange after everything that had happened, and a little wary. I felt empty without Max inside of me, and a little sad. Max brushed the hair out of my face and looked at me with Jayce's yellow-green cat's eyes. "You know I love you, right? And I would never do anything to hurt you. . . ."

I closed my eyes and nodded. I felt so tired.

I sat in front of Max in the tub, and he washed my back with a bar of soap, and kissed my neck and shoulders.

"Everything is going to be perfect from now on," Max reassured me. "Leave it to me."

I surrendered to Max. What did I have to lose? It was an escape from the loneliness of my life in Silver City. I had nowhere else to go. Max had a plan. Maybe he could even help me get Johnny back.

Minutes after Jayce's orgasm Max was erect again. I could feel his cock nudging against my ass cheeks, prodding insistently. "Wait, Max," I said. "Use a condom. You don't know where he might have."

"He's clean," Max replied. "I can smell death on people, and he's clean." I decided to believe him because it was easier than making him stop. I didn't want him to stop.

Max began slowly easing his cock inside of me, lubed with soapy water. I winced a little, but somehow he took the pain away and suddenly it felt so good I wanted to faint. Johnny and I had tried fucking like this a few times before but it never felt as good as it did with Max.

"You belong to me," Max said, whispering in my ear and kissing my neck as he filled me to the hilt. "Finally I can take you the way I always wanted to. Give yourself to me."

I whimpered a little. "I love you, Max," I said, forgetting about everything that had happened in the gas station, forgetting my promise that I'd strike out and find Johnny once high school was over. "Don't ever leave me," I sobbed. He began stroking me with his hand as he moved inside of me.

"You're mine. I've waited too long to find you to ever leave you, Anthony. We were meant to be together."

Max somehow managed to time the strokes of his hand and his cock so that we came at the same time, and collapsed together in bliss.

After the bath, Max dried me off, and he began looking through some boxes in the attic until he found what he wanted—old, dusty boxes full of clothes, cut in a retro style. He unfolded a pearl gray silk suit that smelled of mothballs. "Needs dry cleaning, but it's held up remarkably well, regardless." He slipped into the pants, and they fit perfectly. It was as if he had picked Jayce's body because he knew it would look great in his old clothes. Dressed in the suit, Max had transformed Jayce's body from redneck gas-station attendant to elegant movie star.

"He could use a haircut, and some dental work, of course," Max said, primping in the mirror, "But all in all the effect isn't bad. We'll have to get you some better clothes, too. Do you own a suit?"

I had one plain black suit that I only wore when I went to church with Grandma Mabel. "Are we going somewhere?" I asked excitedly as I changed into it, but also feeling a little tired.

"We should leave tonight," Max said authoritatively, "Before anyone suspects anything. We'll take Jayce's truck, stay somewhere for the night, and trade it in for something better in the morning."

"But what about money?" I asked, feeling suddenly panicky and unsure. "When will we come back?"

"Do you really want to stay here?" Max asked with a

twinkle in his eye. "You don't have to come with me if you don't want to."

"You said you'd never leave me," I said defensively.

"Yes, which is why I expect you to accompany me to Los Angeles."

"Los Angeles?" I asked. Suddenly I had images of Max and I wearing color-coordinated designer suits, dining out at expensive restaurants, envied by the other patrons for our love and beauty. Max and me dancing together at a gay club, kissing in front of everybody, nobody to stop us. A beautiful apartment where we would make love in a big white bed, with the scent of jasmine blowing on the warm California breeze. I had never been to California, and suddenly I was overwhelmed by a desire to go. It didn't occur to me that these images might have been planted in my mind by Max himself.

"Are you ready?" he asked me impatiently, once I had finished buttoning my shirt.

"Yes," I replied, without hesitation.

It was only a two-hour drive to Las Vegas from Silver City, but I slept in the cab of Jayce's truck, dreaming thick, clotted dreams about Max as he was in his youth, his terrible beauty, madcap parties, and the drowning. In the dream I was Max's lover Clarence, and I suffered terribly, exiled from town for our homosexual liaisons. I woke up feverish and feeling more tired than when I had laid down to sleep. Max had given the truck to a valet to park on the curb of a plush Las Vegas casino.

It was my first time in Vegas, and the neon lights and clanging racket of the casino seemed unreal in my sleep-deprived state. I felt like a zombie, sleepwalking alongside the confident Max, who didn't appear tired at all. It reminded me of *Fear and Loathing in Las Vegas*, and I almost made a joke about Max being like Hunter Thompson, but I realized that Max had probably missed that tidbit of popular culture during his fifty-year sleep, so I chuckled to myself, too loopy to care about who stared at me.

We entered a glass elevator that looked out over the span of the casino, and Max turned to me and stroked my cheek, pinning me with Jayce's eerie amber eyes. "How are you doing," he uttered as a tender whisper, more of a statement than a question. We were alone in the elevator together, and he leaned forward to kiss me. *It's too late now,* I thought to myself, resigned to my fate. *There's no turning back.*

"But why would you want to?" Max asked with a smirk, as if I'd said it out loud.

Max wanted a drink. We went into a bar that seemed to be made entirely from tinted glass, colored lights, and mirrors, with a panoramic view of the strip, the kind of place that charges ten dollars for a cocktail. The bartender must have surely seen that I was too young to drink, but he didn't ask for an I.D. Max ordered a gin and tonic for himself and a glass of wine for me. The bartender never asked for any money. It was eerie how Max did it. I wouldn't have even noticed if I didn't know we had almost no money between us.

I sipped my wine and stared at my face reflected in the mirror between bottles of liquor. I felt passive and weirdly dead. By contrast, Max was sparkling like champagne, bubbling with liveliness and energy. I looked ghostly, haunted eyes set in a too-young face. Maybe it was the lack of sleep. My hair was still rumpled from sleeping in the car. I felt strangely empty since Max left my body, and needy, as if we now had some symbiotic bond that I needed to survive. Max was talking to another man at the bar, an older, wealthy gay man, struggling to preserve his youth through careful artifice. I couldn't pick out the words they were saying, it was as if a wasp were humming in my ear, and I couldn't be bothered to listen closely.

"How generous," Max said, turning to me suddenly. "Arthur has offered us the use of his private penthouse for the evening. He's quite taken with you."

"With me?" I asked. I thought I looked terrible.

"He likes younger men, don't you, Arthur?" he asked, and Arthur giggled in a creepy way.

I'm not sleeping with him, I thought defensively. *I'm not your bargaining chip, Max.*

Leave it to me, he simply replied in return.

Arthur paid for the next round of drinks, and another, before we left in a cab. He asked me lots of stupid questions: my name, how old I was, where I went to school. Max fed me lies, and I spoke them in a deadpan voice. My name was Anthony Johnson. I was twenty-one years old. I was a junior at the University of Nevada. Max was my ex-boyfriend, but we were still friends. I didn't ask any questions of my own. I felt drunk and passive and allowed myself to be led out of the bar by Max.

We went to Arthur's penthouse in his shiny new BMW. Max drove. We took the elevator up, and Arthur sat on the couch while Max stood before me, took my shoulders in his hands, and kissed me on the lips. When I opened my eyes, I saw that Arthur was asleep on the couch. "That was fast," I said, laughing a little. Max walked over to the sleeping man and touched his eyelids. "He won't be bothering us for a while," he said, turning to face me with a smile.

Max led me into a bedroom with floor-to-ceiling windows, and a huge bed with a black silk coverlet. He laid me down on the bed, and covered my face with kisses.

"How do you feel?" he asked again.

My sleepy torpor had been replaced by a strange giddiness, a light bubbliness. I giggled a little. "Drunk, maybe. I've never felt this drunk before."

"You look even more beautiful by moonlight, Clarence," Max said, kissing my throat.

"Don't call me that," I said, feeling creeped out. But the second I said that, I wished I hadn't.

"All right, Anthony," Max said, unbuttoning my shirt. "If you insist."

Despite my drunken exhaustion, we made love in that big silk bed until the sky began to fill with light, and then I fell asleep in Max's arms, totally nude. I decided I had made the right choice. Nobody could stop us from being together the way they had with Johnny. We were the masters of our own destiny, drifting from town to town unknown, preying on the kindness of strangers.

Once asleep, I dreamed I was Clarence again. In the dreams, there was no division between Clarence and myself, my identity was a composite of his life experience and my own. I saw myself reflected in Max's eyes, and I looked like me, me if I had lived in another era, a blond and freckle-skinned farm boy. I dreamt about the first time I met Max as Clarence. I had been working at my family's roadside fruit stand outside of Silver City, selling peaches and grapes and honey and other things my family grew. It was a hot day in August when Max's roadster pulled up in front of the stand. The mayor's son emerged from the car looking pristine in his tweed knickers and cap, as if he'd spent the day golfing. It was just me that day, minding the stand, wiping dust stirred up from passing cars off the fruit. I was wearing a pair of overalls, my blond hair plastered to my head with sweat, my body hard and brown from picking fruit in the orchard. I had felt nervous when such an important person had come to the shabby little stand. I was worried that I looked like a hayseed Okie to him. But Max put me at ease with his handsome, easy smile and his charming good nature. He overpaid for his peaches and honey and talked me into closing up the stand and going swimming with him. I went along without any protest, knowing I'd have no excuse to give my angry father when I came home.

We went swimming together in the lake, and I had my first kiss there. I wanted to resist, knowing it was a sin, but I let his hands go wherever they wanted to, until he'd brought me to orgasm, and I did the same for him. He dropped me off down the road from the farm with a fistful of cash in hand, and a lie about being offered a high-paying job working on another farm. This was the beginning of the secret life we wove, Max paying me off during our secret interludes, and my family choosing not to ask questions as long as I brought cash home.

When I awoke it was already late afternoon and Max was standing nude before the window with the sun shining on his tan, beautiful body. I moved behind him and wrapped my arms around his waist. He turned to kiss me, and grabbed my head by my hair. I nearly swooned in his embrace. I was quickly growing to like Max's new body.

We showered together and Max moved to Arthur's wardrobe, and selected expensive suits for us to wear.

"You can have this one," he said, pulling out a silvery blue shirt. And I knew without him saying that it was because Clarence had always worn blue, and I found myself wanting to wear the color to please Max.

"I don't know if you should just help yourself to his clothes like that," I said nervously, as Max buttoned the shirt across my chest as if I were a child. "It's one thing to sleep at his place when he offered, but it's another to steal from him."

"He'll never know," Max said, knotting his tie and walking back into the living room, where Arthur appeared to be still asleep on the couch. "We'll put him back in his bed, and when he wakes up he'll remember fucking you, and he'll feel like a big man. It's a win-win situation for everyone."

As we left the penthouse, I glanced guiltily over my shoulder at Arthur's sleeping form. "Are you sure he's not dead?" I asked.

"He'll be fine," Max reassured me, pulling Arthur's car keys out of his pocket.

"You can't take his car!" I said, horrified. "They'll track the license plate."

"We'll take it somewhere and trade it in for something else," Max said blithely.

An hour later, we were on the road to Los Angeles in a speedy black sports car that was barely big enough for the two of us. Jayce's truck and Arthur's Beemer were left abandoned in Vegas. I felt bad about it at first, but Max soothed my guilt by letting me drive our new toy on the highway.

We put the convertible top down, and Max smoked fragrant cigarettes with the wind blowing through our hair. I had only ever driven my parents' and grandmother's cars, nothing as fast and fancy as the sports car. I revved the motor to make Max laugh.

"How do you do it?" I asked, my voice floating on the wind.

"Do what?"

"Make people fall asleep, have false memories, forget to ask for money or identification. Sometimes I wonder how much free will I truly have left."

"I'm not like you, rooted to one body," Max said. "My spirit is still part of the ether. My spirit is borrowing Jayce's body, but Jayce's soul is what's still keeping this body alive. In the ether I can see and touch the thoughts and memories of everyone I encounter, and it's that much easier if they're close to me. It's not difficult to manipulate people's desires to my own advantage. Most people would rather have a feeling that's pleasant than a feeling that's true."

"So you've exploited my own desires to your advantage then?"

"Maybe, but I don't hear you complaining," Max said with a wolfish grin.

"Tell me about Clarence," I said, my curiosity piqued from the dream.

"I thought you didn't want to talk about Clarence," Max replied coquettishly.

"I never said that," I said. "Well, I dreamed about him, that I was him. Was that your fault, too?"

"It's easier to show you what happened than to tell you," Max said. "Ours was the greatest love affair that backwater town has ever known, and it ended in tragedy and ignorance."

We arrived in Los Angeles a few hours later, and had a nice dinner at a jazz club where men in tuxedos danced in twos. I got drunk on champagne and I danced with my cheek against Max's chest. It felt dreamlike dancing on the patio of the club strung with jasmine and white Christmas lights—even though it was December. The winter night in Los Angeles was not cold like it was in Nevada. Max worked his magic chatting up the patrons at the bar, and by the end of the night he had a lead on a house that was being sublet in Hollywood. I didn't ask any questions. We spent the night at a stranger's home yet again, but this time the three of us shared one bed in a more modest apartment.

Our third member was a beautiful blond boy, a struggling actor who moonlighted as a bartender at the club. He could have passed for Jayce's brother, which was no doubt why Max had chosen him. I felt as though I should feel hurt or jealous that Max would share our love with another man, but I didn't. I succumbed to their caresses and slept between the two of them. I didn't dream at all that night.

The next afternoon, after the beautiful boy (whose name was Michael) had left for an audition, we had brunch on the patio of a posh restaurant before meeting the owner of the sublet. The house was a beautiful cottage in a neighborhood where all the streets had the names of birds and butterflies. The house was painted burnt orange and terracotta red, dusky against the blue and purple of the flowers blooming in the little garden. The cool air was filled with the scent of jasmine and tinkling music of windchimes. The place was just big enough for the two of us; a bedroom with a big white bed, a sunny living room that faced the street, and a nice kitchen where I fantasized about making fruit salad and pancakes. It was almost identical to the house that Max had showed me in my mind when he'd asked me to go to Los Angeles with him, and I wondered if he had the power to will it into existence as well. We spent another night at Michael's apartment and moved into the cottage the following day.

And thus, we began our lives together in Los Angeles. Max cut his hair and became unrecognizable as Jayce. The longer he inhabited the body, the more and more he began to look like Max, short of changing his hair and eye color. Something about his mannerisms, the way he looked at me, his devilish smile. Los Angeles was everything Max had promised: exquisite meals we never paid for (Max had a talent for convincing restaurateurs and shop owners that he was an extremely high - profile celebrity and that he should receive his meals and clothes for free), hot tubbing, sex, dancing, art openings.

Max always kept one eye open for fresh talent, and sometimes brought boys home with us. If I complained, he'd go out without me and not come home. I learned not to complain. He had his reasons. He needed fresh energy all the time in order to maintain his powers. It took a lot of control to keep Jayce's soul in subordination while he used the body for his bidding.

"Why can't you just take the energy from me?" I pleaded. "I don't mind, I have nothing better to do here," I begged, bored and possessive.

To punish me, Max did exactly as I requested. One night while making love, he drained my life force until it was so low that I could barely walk for days afterward. I lay in bed ashen as a corpse, unable to feel, unable to move. I began to wonder if Max was really something terrible and unnatural, an energy vampire than feasted on the world around him as if it were a ripe plum. He was more drug than man. He gave his victims the ultimate high while robbing them of their health. I didn't have the energy or desire to escape the situation, even if I knew on a gut level that what we did was wrong. At the depth of my despondency, Max came to my bedside, kissed me awake, made love to me and filled me with a powerful, intense love, poured wave after wave of golden life energy into my body until I felt superhuman and immortal. I knew that he was bloated with the energy of some other beautiful boy, but I didn't care. All that mattered was my faith was restored, my love and devotion stronger than ever.

Weeks passed. The melancholia and loneliness I thought I had escaped when I'd fled Silver City had returned to haunt me again. Even when we were together I felt lonely. I adopted a stray kitten I found in the street, and played with it until it grew sick of me and bit my hand. I began going for long, aimless walks around the neighborhood, sometimes walking all the way to the haunted shell of Hollywood Boulevard. I could've taken the car, but more often than not Max was using it and I felt it was more his possession than mine. I was hesitant to voice my dissatisfaction about my life. No doubt he knew already, and I didn't want to rock the boat. Without Max I was nothing.

The day of my eighteenth birthday came, and Max surprised me with a wealth of paints and art supplies, everything I could have ever desired. I had never painted a picture in my life, but Clarence had, and Max thought that having an outlet for my creative expression would cheer me up. He even talked about arranging a gallery show for me, before I had even touched paint to canvas. That night Max took me out to dinner and a club, and it seemed as everyone we encountered knew my name and wished me happy birthday. Nights like those, I was able to forget all my doubts and bask in the illusion of a perfect life with Max.

I woke earlier than Max the next day, and began experimenting with the paints. Thick jewel-toned smears of color on canvas, eerie swashes of pale, iridescent pigment. It was as if I were vomiting up years of suppressed emotions onto the canvas. The art took form by itself, as if I were merely a puppet that supported the movement of the brush. I finished my first painting in one afternoon and collapsed on the couch exhausted.

Max emerged from the bedroom rumpled with sleep, dressed in nothing but pajama pants with coffee cup in hand, and studied the painting with fascination. "You saw the book?"

I shook my head exhaustedly. "What book?"

Max gave me a strange look and walked over to the bookshelf. He took down a thick book entitled *California Modern*, and flipped through, sipping his coffee. He held the book open and passed it to me, a reproduction of a painting eerily similar to my own. I looked down at the artist's name: *Firestorm*, Clarence Smiley 1952.

"He's inside of you, whether you like it or not," Max said.

"You didn't do this, did you?" I asked. "Make me paint Clarence's painting? I'd like to believe I am capable of doing something on my own for a change. . . ."

Max raised his hands to show his innocence. "I didn't have a damn thing to do with it, I swear."

Chills ran down my spine. So far I'd been semiskeptical about Max's claims that I was Clarence's incarnation, it seemed like a convenient story to me. Now I wasn't so sure.

Max took the book away from me. "The original is hanging at the Getty Museum," he said. "If you like, I'll take you there tomorrow to look at it."

"Don't you have to buy tickets for the Getty months in advance?"

Max shot me a withering glance, and I knew I was stupid to doubt his powers for even a moment.

Although Max had slept all day, he lay beside me when I went to bed that night, and held me until I fell asleep.

For the first time in weeks, I dreamt of being Clarence. This time Max wasn't in the dream, this was after Max's death, long after Clarence had been chased out of town by the spiteful Andersen family, after his own family had turned their backs on him.

The year is 1952, fifteen years after the drowning accident. I am looking in the mirror, blue eyes and light brown hair darkened with age, swept into a pompadour, painting a self-portrait. I look around at my modest apartment with its bare floors, hotplate, and sad single bed. The walls are covered in paintings. I am thirty-two years old. I have a job at the Paramount studios painting sets, and every day I go to work in my painting overalls, toting my thermos of coffee and my tin lunch box. Whatever money is leftover after rent and groceries is spent on paint. I look at the painting in front of me, and I am surprised to see not my face, but an aching blaze of color bursting before my eyes. I run my fingers through the paint and think about Van Gogh eating his paints and going insane.

I'm lying on the bed, staring at the ceiling, wearing a blue shirt and blue jeans like a prisoner, smoking a cigarette, and listening to the radio. Tonight I am too restless to stay in. I'll take my car to a jazz club in Japantown, where I'll hear hot music and smoke reefer and drink red wine backstage. Tonight's the night when I'll meet a man who will become my partner for the next forty years, until I die. I know this somehow, but it's a secret that's dangerous, I must hold it very close to myself and not let on that I know. His name is Charles and he will be responsible for getting me my first art show, a show that will lead to other shows, and someday, big-name recognition.

I woke up feeling strangely defiant. Max was still there, beside me, despondently smoking a cigarette. I glanced at the clock—5:00 A.M. Did you go out tonight?" I asked.

He shook his head no, and took another drag.

"Are you okay? I understand if you need to go out and get what you need. I won't be jealous."

"But I will be," Max mumbled, rolling away from me.

"What are you talking about?" I ask.

"You don't want me anymore. I can tell. I should have never forced you to come with me. I was foolish to think our love could last this time. I'm out of touch."

"Max, no," I said, stroking his back. "You're being paranoid. Nothing's changed."

I wasn't used to being the one who gave comfort, and it made me wonder if my words were sincere or just said to put Max at ease. He should be able to see through me either way, but he didn't seem to care. He stubbed out his cigarette, and rolled toward me, held me so tight I could barely breathe, suffocated by the scent of cigarettes.

We slept through the hours of dawn and rose together, showered, and had breakfast at a cute little café on Santa Monica Boulevard. It was a pleasant drive to the museum in the sports car with the top down, and for a while being with Max felt like everything he'd promised me, and I felt truly happy.

The Metropolitan Museum had been one of my favorite places to visit when I'd lived in New York City, and so I was excited to wander through the many levels of the vast Getty Museum. Max made jokes about fucking on the Louis XIV beds (I had no doubt he could arrange it, but it seemed sacrilegious and wrong to me), and I felt annoyed by his chatter when I was trying to look at the pictures. Max grew bored and retreated to the museum café to smoke cigarettes and drink coffee, and I gratefully continued on my own. I still hadn't found

Clarence's painting, so I approached a docent and asked for directions.

I was startled by how young and beautiful the docent was, and a strange spark of recognition coursed through my body. His name tag said Charlie. He was a tall, lanky man with olive skin, deep brown eyes, and shoulder-length black hair tied back in a ponytail. He looked as if he might be part Asian or Native American.

"Excuse me," I said, struggling to regain my composure, "I'm looking for a painting called *Firestorm* by Clarence Smiley."

"That's one of my favorites," the docent said. "Follow me, it's just around the corner."

The painting was bigger than I expected, much bigger than my own, so that it took up the better part of one wall. The affect of the painting in such grand scale was electrifying—I got goosebumps.

When I returned to my senses, Charlie was still standing there next to me.

"I'm sorry," I said, "I don't know what came over me."

"No need to apologize," he said with a smile.

"I have a special connection with the work of Clarence Smiley," I said. "He was my grandfather, though he died before I ever got to know him." It was a white lie but it would have to do. "I'm a painter, too," I boasted. Who cared if the only thing I'd ever painted was a smaller version of the painting on the wall in front of us. I wanted to impress Charlie, and it seemed to be working.

"I'd love to know more about your family," he said flirtatiously. "Can I give you my card?" he asked.

I cringed, knowing that Max would throw an abusive tantrum when he found the card. I would never be able to sneak out and meet Charlie without Max finding out, and I wasn't willing to risk the security of my home for a meaningless dalliance. If I left Max, I'd have nowhere left to run to.

"I'm sorry," he said apologetically. "I didn't mean to be so forward, it's just that I'm such a fan of your grandfather's work."

"No, it's quite all right," I said cheerfully. "I'd love to talk with you sometime."

I abandoned the scrap of cardstock in the men's room wastebasket, but not without memorizing the phone number first, the digits masqueraded in the swirls of paint of Clarence's picture in my mind's eye where they would be safe from Max.

I found Max thumbing through a book and drinking what appeared to be his third cappuccino. I expected he would be annoyed with me for being gone so long, but he appeared cheerful and indifferent.

"Let's get a hotel room tonight," I proposed. "Just the two of us, a room with a big bathtub. Just like the first time we truly made love together." I still felt a little guilty about flirting with Charlie and I wanted Max to think he was the only man on my mind.

He acquiesced, and we had a dinner of sushi in Beverly Hills before checking into a hotel where the beds looked like white wedding cakes and the floors were carpeted with soft plush carpeting. I seduced him coyly, mixing him a drink from the minibar, and perching on the arm of his chair to slowly unbutton his shirt and kiss him. My mind kept drifting back to Charlie, what it would be like to make love with him, and every time I would catch myself, then quickly think back to the image of myself as young farmboy Clarence to entice Max. If Max caught on, he didn't show it.

I rubbed his shoulders, admiring Jayce's tanned, muscular arms and back that Max had carefully maintained with daily visits to the gym. I felt pale and skinny by comparison, even though we lived in sunny Los Angeles. I barely left the house, I was used to the gray weather of Silver

City, and the sun made my eyes hurt. Max flexed those well-formed muscles for my pleasure, and as if he knew what I was thinking, stood up and pinned me to the chair, daring me to move against his strong grip. He looked more lion than man, a lean golden beast flaunting his power. I couldn't have escaped if I'd wanted to, and I didn't want to. I swooned as he sunk his teeth into my neck, marking me. My breathing quickened with excitement, unable to resist the desire that had initially brought us together. He bent me over the chair and made me submit to his will, and I accepted the force of his thrusts with eager pleasure.

Max slipped out after I had drifted to sleep, as he often did, and I found myself alone in bed when I was awakened by a knock at the door the next morning. I barely bothered to wrap a sheet around my waist before answering the door, figuring it was Max. I nearly dropped the sheet in shock when I opened the door and saw Charlie standing there, holding a bottle of champagne and a bag of croissants from a French bakery.

"Surprised?" he asked with an embarrassed smile.

"I'm sorry, I just wasn't expecting to see you at all."

"I took the liberty of finding out where you were staying," he said. "I got lucky, I guess. I called around asking if there was an Anthony Smiley staying at the hotel, and when they said someone checked into this hotel under the name Clarence Smiley it had to be you."

I was flabbergasted. "Come in," I said. If it were anyone else, it would have been creepy, but I liked Charlie too much to care. If Max came back when Charlie was in the room, I'd tell him that he was a present for Max. I hoped it wouldn't come to that, but I knew Max's weakness for pretty boys.

"Are you staying here by yourself?" Charlie asked, glancing around the room at the damp towels and the dirty glasses.

"I had someone with me last night," I replied tersely, sitting on the bed.

"A girlfriend?"

"A boyfriend," I replied, in a tone that suggested he should know better than that.

"Too bad he couldn't stay for breakfast," Charlie said in a tone that suggested he wasn't sorry at all. "But I guess that means I get to have you all to myself."

He leaned across the bed and kissed me full on the lips. It wasn't that I wasn't attracted to Charlie, I was, very much so. But there was something really weird about this. This wasn't the man I'd met at the museum yesterday. The wheels in my brain turned. If Max could take possession of Jayce's body so easily, it's possible that he could do the same thing with any of his sexual partners. . . . My stomach lurched sickeningly.

"You're more clever than I thought," Max said, smirking in his unmistakable fashion. "I figured it was time for a change before I built up too much of a bad reputation for myself around town. . . . It was either find a new body or move, you know? And you seemed to be pretty happy here."

Clearly Max was deluding himself.

"Max, that's not fair. Charlie didn't deserve this. He's a smart kid with a future, not some redneck burnout like Jayce."

"So you're saying that Jayce got what he deserved?"

"Don't twist my words, Max. It wasn't right with Jayce, either. What did you do with Jayce's body anyway? Is he dead now? Did you suck him dry and leave what remained face down in a ditch somewhere?"

"I left him to sleep it off in an abandoned shack outside of Joshua Tree, where he'll be able to hitch a ride back into town. He thinks he was abducted by aliens. Rather humane of me, I think. I could have saved myself the time and killed him." Max sighed and examined his nails. "Not a bad scheme, you must admit? He'll be the talk of town, no doubt," he said, looking very satisfied with himself.

I sighed. "You're fucking impossible, Max. Sometimes I wonder why I bother with you at all."

"Don't say things you don't mean, Anthony," Max said, suddenly cold. "You're nothing without me."

"Fuck you, Max!" I screamed, throwing the bag of food at Max's head and hitting the wall instead.

"I take it that you're not hungry, then," Max said icily. "Maybe I should leave you here to cool down until you've got a handle on that temper of yours. It's unattractive."

"You can't go on treating people like this, Max," I warned him. "What happens when you get sick of me? Will you abandon me somewhere to die, too? I can't take it anymore. It's not worth it."

"Such fire and passion, Anthony," Max said silkily. "All grown up now, are you? I'd like to see you try and make it on your own. You take me for granted. Some men would kill to be in your position of privilege."

I narrowed my eyes. Something very strange dawned on me. "You know, it seems pretty weird that you've stayed with me as long as you have, when you clearly don't care about anyone but yourself. There's something you haven't told me, isn't there? Maybe you need me more than I need you."

"Well, when you figure it all out, let me know," Max replied breezily. "I'll tell the front desk to give you another night, and when you're ready to apologize you can take a cab home." Max said, tossing a couple twenty-dollar bills on the floor, and leaving as abruptly as he had come. How arrogant of him to think I would apologize when he was the one who had messed everything up. He was far too confident that I'd come crawling back to him. And he had good reason to be: I had no money and no place to stay, I didn't have any friends in L.A., and I didn't have his magical ability to charm the pants off of everyone I met. Max had made sure that I was completely dependent on him.

Alone in the room, I weighed my options. It was either go back to Max or back to my parents. I didn't really like the idea of either, but I knew that if I returned home it would make Max angry, and I liked the idea of pissing him off. I wasn't sure how my parents would react. I was an adult now, they could easily tell me to get lost unless I played by their rules. I would have to play it straight long enough to get a job and make some money, and maybe then I could find Johnny and we could start a life of our own. I decided that I would have to grin and bear it. I wanted to prove to Max that I could make it without him, but money was an issue and I had none. I could always call my parents and beg them to bail me out, but that seemed too humiliating. I needed things to be on my own terms. I couldn't see myself talking an airline into giving me a free ticket the way Max could. I needed money fast, and I knew how to get it.

I knew that Max sometimes cruised West Hollywood for tricks, boys he could take to a hotel to feed on sex and energy for a few hours. They always forgot to ask for money, or maybe they didn't care because he was so good looking he could have been one of them. I wondered how much I could make selling my body for a night. Enough for a ticket home, surely. There was always the risk that I'd run into Max cruising for meat, but it was a risk I was willing to take. I was good looking and young, it couldn't take that long for me to find a john of my own.

I went into the bathroom and stared at myself shirtless in the mirror. Here I was, prepared to whore myself out to strangers for money, and I didn't feel a thing. If anything, the idea gave me a little bit of a sick thrill. Maybe it was a childish way to get back at Max, but for the first time in months I felt truly free, and it was a feeling that was exhilarating.

I found my clothes: a form-fitting T-shirt and blue jeans.

Not glamorous, but it would do the trick. As much as another night's sleep on that soft hotel bed appealed to me, I would need to get an early start if I wanted to outrun Max. I dug into my bag for lip gloss, eyeliner, and hair gel, and spent a few minutes in the bathroom turning myself into a West Hollywood faggot nymph. I had youth on my side, I knew the johns liked young-looking boys. With any luck I'd be able to make enough in one night to not only get a cheap flight back to Las Vegas, to where I could get a bus to Silver City, but maybe even have some money left over.

I had the hotel call a cab for me, and I used my remaining cash to pay for a ride to the stretch of Santa Monica Boulevard where the hustlers cruised for johns. I had nothing but luck to rely on, no pimp, no experience, no money. I primped and posed with the best of them, trying to look as if I were casually loitering in case the cops drove by. Within fifteen minutes a big black car pulled up to the curb, and a ringed hand beckoned for me to get inside.

"Get in the back," he said. I could only see the head of the john from behind, dark hair greased back, a black suit, and sunglasses. Middle-aged, not bad looking, though a little creepy. There was a six-pack of beer on the seat next to me, still cold.

"Have one if you like," the measured voice from the driver's seat instructed me.

I debated for a moment. I wanted to be in control of the situation, but I was so nervous that I decided one little beer wouldn't hurt. I cracked the can and took a sip, which tasted perfectly cool and refreshing. I drained the can in minutes, and started on another.

"Don't overdo it, I want you to be able to perform," the driver snarled.

I nodded ashamedly, and put the beer down in the cup holder in the back of the seat.

The driver was taking a weird route, I didn't recognize

the streets we traveled through. We arrived at a plain-looking concrete unmarked warehouse. I felt scared for a moment, as images of serial killers and abandoned bodies raced through my head.

"It's a sex club," he said, as if to reassure me. The man paid for our cover at the door of the club, grabbed my hand, and led me inside. We walked past a variety of rooms set up with various fantasy scenarios: a hospital, a jail cell, a medieval dungeon. Hardcore porn was being broadcast from TV screens on the walls. Men walked around naked or wearing only towels. Many of them leered at me, but my john tightened his grip on my hand and led me to a plain door with a number on it. He pulled a key out of his pocket and unlocked it, leading me into a room with barely enough room for a bed covered in rubber sheets, lit by a single black-light bulb.

The man grabbed me and started kissing me immediately, which struck me as weird. My stomach turned a little, but my dick was starting to grow hard in spite of itself.

"Wait a minute," I said pulling away. "You still haven't paid me. And I'm going to have to charge extra to do it in here, how do I know there aren't perverts peeping at us through some hole in the wall?" If there was one thing I knew, it was to get my money upfront.

The man pulled out his wallet and passed me a thick wad of bills. "Have it your way," he said, "but for this price I get to do whatever I want to you, and I don't want to hear you complain."

I accepted the bills and counted them. He had given me almost five hundred dollars. I gulped and nodded. I was a little worried about what he might want to do to me, but as long as I got out alive, I didn't care.

"If that's settled," he said, "let's begin."

The man stripped off my clothes and pushed me face down on the bed. He used his knees to spread my legs, and

I heard the crinkle of a rubber package opening, and the squirt of lube. I felt his cockhead at the head of my ass, pushing me open. His cock was the biggest I'd ever felt, and the fact that I was nervous didn't help. I winced, and tried to reach for my own cock, hoping that jerking off would help me relax, but he grabbed both of my hands and pinned them behind my back. I panicked for a moment, and my ass clenched shut again, but he continued to push until his cock was all the way inside me. I had never felt so humiliated and desperate in my life, and for a moment I wished Max would rescue me from my brutal fate of being skewered by a stranger. "If it wasn't for Max, you wouldn't be here," a voice in my head reminded me and rage welled in me anew. The man thrust against me, and I channeled my rage into my burning ass, and thrust against him. It hurt—he was holding my wrists tightly, and his unit was way too big for me to take, but I made the best of it, hoping that if I squirmed more, he'd come quickly and let me go home. Each stroke was agony, and when I thought I couldn't take anymore, he pulled out, even though he hadn't come yet. He peeled off the condom, flipped me over and began to fuck my face, thrusting his cock down my throat, slapping me when I began to choke. Tears began to run down my face.

"Pretty little whore," the man growled. "I know just what you like."

I remembered when Max had used those exact same words with me, but it had never been like this. I felt gutted and dirty as the man abused me to his heart's content, making sure I earned the exorbitant sum he'd paid for the pleasure. When I thought I couldn't take any more, he pulled out of my mouth and shot his load all over my face. Even Max had never brutalized me the way this man did.

He thrust his cock back in his pants and barked, "Get dressed and get out. I'm sick of looking at you."

I scooped up my clothes and scurried out of the tiny room, walking naked down the hallway to a bathroom to get changed. I washed my face with soap until my skin felt raw, wanting to get the slimy feeling of his come off of me.

I kept my hand on that fat wad of cash in my pocket as I hailed a cab to take me to the airport. I cried silently in the backseat all the way there, wondering if I'd made the right decision after all, knowing I could go back to Max's possessive mind games if I really wanted to, but deciding that what was done was done. In a way, it had been easy to exploit my looks to make a quick buck, even if the john had been brutal with me. I understood why the hustlers got addicted to whoring, why they drowned their sorrows in drugs when the day was done. I had been Max's whore in some ways, but he always treated me gently, if possessively, like someone's favored Persian cat. I hardened my face, and decided that if I could endure whoring myself, then I was capable of anything. I was my own man now.

I caught a late flight to Las Vegas, slept in a cheap hotel on the strip, and filled my belly with buffet food before catching the afternoon bus to Silver City. I had stolen the Bible from the bedside of the motel room, and I read it on the bus to kill time and distract myself from the vague sense of dread that haunted my senses. *It would be a waste for Jesus to die for my sins if I didn't have some really good sins for him to die for,* I thought to myself.

It was evening by the time we reached Silver City. It took me nearly an hour to walk from the bus depot to the mansion on the top of the hill. I guess I could have tried to hitch a ride, but it felt good to walk. I had a lot to think about.

When I arrived at Grandmother's house, the sky was pitch black and full of stars, and none of the lights were on inside the house. I turned the doorknob and found it was unlocked.

"Grandma?" I called out nervously. I wasn't looking

forward to facing her after disappearing without any warning a few months previously.

I flicked the light switches but the living room stayed dark. The bulb must've burnt out. I tried the light in the kitchen, but it was dead, too. There must have been a power outage. I fumbled in the kitchen drawer for candles and matches, and carried a big white emergency candle to light the way.

"Grandma?" I asked softly, knocking on the door to her bedroom. There was no response. Maybe she'd gone on a trip with her church group? I turned the doorknob slowly, and was greeted by a cloying, horrible, sickly sweet smell. Grandma was lying in bed, not moving. I knew instantly that she was dead. How long ago had she died? Not more than a week, surely. The members of her church would have called if she hadn't shown up for services. She never missed church. I closed the door as quickly as I had opened it, wanting to get as far away from her body as possible. I would have to call my parents, but the phone line was disconnected, like the electricity had been. She must have forgotten to pay the bills. There was a public phone at the ice-cream parlor in town, but that would be closed by now. I could either drive out to Angleston or wait until morning.

I was exhausted from the long bus ride and walking, so I decided to go upstairs and try to get some sleep. I didn't want to sleep in the attic, it reminded me too much of Max. I found the room that had once belonged to my mother, with its plain, nonthreatening decor, and I laid down in exhaustion, wanting to escape the horror of my life for a few blank hours.

I dreamed about Clarence yet again.

In the dream I am nineteen years old, no longer a boy but barely a man. Max's family has offered me a lot of money to leave town. There are rumors, they say, rumors that could rock the very foundation of the Andersen family. My family is ashamed of me, we eat our dinners in silence. It would be better for everyone if I left, I know this. I have decided I will go to Los Angeles. I do not know what waits for me there, but it's got to be better than this. I'm standing in front of my single bed in the farm house with an open suitcase, packing away my meager belongings. Tomorrow I will catch a bus out of town and never look back.

My family is away, working in the orchards. Max lets himself into our house without knocking, appears in my doorway. I cannot look at him. I am too full of shame. I have been made to feel it is all my fault. Today is Max's nineteenth birthday, his parents are throwing him a lavish birthday party that's the talk of all society. Lots of girls will be there, the ones who are willing to overlook rumors of a homosexual liaison for a chance to be chosen as the bride of the heir to the Andersen fortune. He's been on dates with lots of girls lately, he barely leaves the house without a girl on his arm now. I know it's a sham, but it still hurts. I know that his parents will put the pressure on for him to get married as quickly as possible, put it all behind him. I am not invited to this party, I am an embarrassment to be forgotten.

"Don't leave," he says to me in a small voice. "Stay, and we'll continue in secret. I'll find someplace for you to stay, out of town."

"I thought that's what this was supposed to be—a secret," I reply, bitterly. It was a secret, until Max's sister Mabel spied on us kissing in the yard and ran telling tales to their parents.

"I don't care about those girls, Clarence. They mean nothing to me. You have to understand the difficult position I'm in."

"I understand all too well. You have obligations to your family. It's better if I leave now, Max."

"You're the only one I love. You're the only one I'll ever love, Clarence."

I looked up at him. "Then leave with me. Screw your family, come with me, and be poor but happy. You don't have to live a lie like this."

Max hung his head. "I really wish it were that easy. I have more to lose than you do."

"Oh yeah? Well I got nothing left now, and it's all your fault. Maybe you should take a moment to think about everything I've had to give up for you."

"Come to the party tonight. I don't care what my parents think. You're the only one I care about."

"I can't, Max. You know that."

Max throws his arms around me and pins me to the bed. "I don't think I can live without you," he said.

We make love for the last time in my bed, and Max leaves to get ready for his party. I lay in bed feeling angry and confused for some hours, then decide that it's time to take control of my own life, and confront Max's parents in public. I dress myself in my only good clothes, a suit that Max had given me for my own birthday a few months previously. I have never worn the suit except for the one night that Max and I drove three hours to a Las Vegas speakeasy where men danced with men. I dress myself and walk miles to the Andersen estate. I have lost everything, and I do not care if Max's parents shoot me on sight. It would be a fitting end to the whole debacle. I have to follow my heart now.

I find Max in the gardens behind the house, so drunk that I can literally smell the alcohol coming off his skin. He has a girl with him, but he sends her away, telling her to fetch more drinks. He grabs me and kisses me sloppily. He grabs my hand and leads me back to the party, where socialites are drinking spiked punch by the pool, which is lit up with floating candles. Everyone stares at us. A man I recognize as a younger version of my grandfather approaches me and says "Look here, I thought we told you to never come near our family again."

"Screw your family," I reply coldly. "Your family is a pack of lies." I swing at him with my fist, and soon the party has erupted in chaos and panic. I take the blows I am dealt with pride, knowing I can fight better than all these rich pussies put together. I relish the pain, the blood dripping from my mouth. Somewhere in the chaos, Max has fallen into the pool, or was pushed, nobody knows for sure. His own father, the mayor, dives into the pool to save him, but when he is brought to the surface it's too late—he was so drunk that he'd inhaled water and suffocated almost instantly.

"Max, I'm sorry," I whisper, tears streaming down my battered face. "It shouldn't have ended this way."

"Somebody call the police and arrest this man!" I hear a voice shout, and I am shaken from my sorrow. I waste no time running away, looking like a mess with my black eye and my torn and bloody clothes. "Poor Max," I think to myself. If only he'd had the courage to leave, he would have been alive still. I spend the night sleeping under a bush and hitch a ride out of town the next morning, never looking back.

I awoke the next morning feeling heartbroken and empty, almost as tired as when I had gone to bed. I imagined the burden poor Clarence carried in his heart all his life, having lost his first love at such a young age, and in such a tragic way. I felt my heart soften toward Max. What he'd done wasn't right, but he'd wanted to make up for the love he'd lost and recreate that missing life with Clarence in whatever way he could.

I took a cold shower (thankfully the water was still running), got dressed, and took the car into town to get some breakfast and call my parents. At the very least, they deserved to know that Grandmother was dead. I ate eggs Benedict at the tavern in town, and fed quarters into the pay phone at the back, dialing my parents' number in New York. "The number you have dialed is out of service," a mechanical voice informed me. I clicked the change return and dialed again. Same recording. Things were getting very weird, between Grandmother's death, the disconnected utilities, and not being able to reach my parents. I wondered how much had changed in the few months since I'd left.

And then, something incredible happened on the way out of the restaurant. I saw a head of thick black hair through the window of the ice-cream parlor. From behind, the man looked just like Johnny. It had to be a coincidence. I slipped inside, trying not to look too conspicuous as I sneaked glances at the man who was flipping through a phone book at the front counter. "I'm looking for someone named Anthony Smith," he said in a voice I would have recognized anywhere. My heart leapt for joy. It couldn't be real—could it? I wanted to run into his arms and kiss him, but I worried about the reaction of the other customers in the tiny ice-cream parlor.

"Johnny," I said, and he whirled around, with his beautiful grin on his olive-skinned face.

"Anthony! Oh my god, I can't believe I really found you! What a coincidence, huh?"

"Not really, considering how small this town is. How did you get here?"

"I ran away from the group home and hitchhiked into the city. I worked washing dishes until I made enough money to get a bus ticket. I knew the name of the city where they sent you but nothing else"

Tears formed in my eyes. "You came all this way to see me? I can't believe it."

"Believe it, Anthony. There's no way I could live without you."

"Come on, let's get out of here," I said, glancing nervously at the customers in the store.

I felt too weird about taking Johnny back to the mansion knowing Grandmother's dead body was still there, so I drove the car way out into the woods, where we could talk in private. Johnny had some weed that he'd picked up on the road, so he rolled a joint and we smoked together, and laid together in the backseat, just kissing and holding each other.

"I missed you so much," Johnny said to me with wet eyes. "Nobody is ever going to tear us apart again. We can make a life together now, and no one can stop us."

Johnny told me about the group home where they'd controlled his life every moment of the day, and had tried to brainwash him into being heterosexual. "They even made me go on fake dates with this lesbian. I'd have to get dressed in a suit, and they'd make us watch romantic films in an auditorium. We pretended to be cured so they'd leave us alone, we even got fake-engaged. We wound up escaping the home together when they let us go out for our engagement dinner with our families. I wanted to contact you sooner but I didn't know how."

"Me, too," I replied. "I wrote you letters every day. They're all there in my desk drawer in my grandmother's house."

"Is that where you've been staying all this time?" Johnny asked.

I closed my eyes and took a deep breath. I could tell Johnny the truth—everything about Max, leaving Silver City for Los Angeles, whoring myself for the price of a plane ticket—but how would he respond? The story was hard to swallow, and he wouldn't like learning that I fell in love with another man when he was working so hard for us to be together again. I decided that it was too soon to divulge the whole story, that would come later if necessary. I decided to focus on the present.

"My grandmother died, Johnny," I said, choking up a little for dramatic effect.

"How?" Johnny asked, alarmed. "What's going to happen to you?"

"I don't know," I said. "I came home yesterday and found her dead in her bed. I don't know what to do. I tried calling my parents but their phone's been disconnected. I don't know what to do, Johnny."

"Screw your parents," Johnny said. "I still haven't forgiven them for sending you away like this. But maybe you should call the police about your grandmother?"

"What would the police do other than try to call my parents? It's not like she was murdered. . . . It's just so weird."

"Don't rush into anything," Johnny said. "You have the car, and I still have some money saved up. We can go away somewhere together, but maybe you shouldn't abandon your grandmother's body there . . . it would just be wrong," he murmured, unconsciously crossing himself.

I burst into tears and this time I wasn't sure why. Maybe it was a combination of being reunited with Johnny, the guilt I felt about lying to him, the stress of leaving Max, and the shock of Grandmother dying. If I thought my life was weird before, it had only taken a turn for the worse. On the bright side, I had Johnny back, and we had our future together, still I couldn't help but feel unsettled regardless.

"Shhhh," Johnny said, holding me to him protectively. "I'll protect you." I cried into Johnny's flannel shirt, and lost myself in the feeling of his thick muscular arms wrapped around me.

"We're going to have to stay there tonight," I said with a tearstained face. I know it's creepy but I don't know what else to do, it's too cold to sleep in the car. If we stay up in the attic it will be far enough from her room that the smell won't bother us. It's a big house."

Johnny held my hand as I went up the stairs to the big, dark mansion. "Don't let go," I begged him. "I'm scared."

Once inside, I picked up the candles and matches I'd left in the front hallway and lit candles for both of us. "They turned the power off," I said apologetically. "These candles were the best I could do."

"It's okay," Johnny replied. "I'm not afraid of the dark."

Something shifted in the corridor as we moved toward the staircase. I screamed. The light of the candle shone on my grandmother's wrinkled face. She was standing at the end of the hallway, staring into space as if she could look right through me. Blood trickled out of her nose and mouth.

"Grandma!" I called out and her image faded away, as if I'd scared her off.

Johnny shook me. "Are you okay?" he asked. "Did you see something?"

I shook my head. "I swear I just saw my grandmother standing right over there. It was the most horrible thing, she had blood all over her face."

"You're just exhausted from stress," Johnny said, holding me. "Your grandmother is dead, Anthony, she can't hurt you. You don't believe in ghosts, do you?"

"I'm not so sure anymore," I said, shaking my head.

"Well, I'm not going to let any ghost hurt you."

I shakily led Johnny up the staircase, the candle trembling in my hand. A gust of wind blew down the hallway, a window had blown open. The candles guttered and went out.

"Don't worry," Johnny said. "I can see well enough in the dark. We don't need the candles."

I felt my way up the second flight of stairs to the attic. I would have preferred to sleep on the second floor, but none of the beds there were big enough for two people to sleep in.

After this ordeal, I collapsed on the big brass four-poster bed, feeling as though I would faint if I remained standing any longer.

"Johnny, I'm scared. I don't know what I'm going to do."

"It's all right, Anthony. It's just for one night. We can leave tomorrow and put it all behind us."

Johnny lay on top of me on the bed, kissed my face and stroked my hair. "I just want to make love to you," he murmured. "It's been too long."

I felt his hard muscles through his shirt, his erect dick poking me through his jeans. I breathed the familiar comforting smell of his neck and kissed him until I forgot all about my fear and gave into my desire for him. Part of my brain was worried that he wouldn't be able to satisfy me sexually after what I'd had with Max, but it turned out my worries were for naught.

Johnny undressed me, and used the sash from my dressing gown hanging next to the bed to bind my wrists to the brass bars of the headboard. I was intrigued by his mixture of gentleness and dominance. Johnny had never done anything so kinky with me in the past.

"I don't want to ever let you go again," Johnny said, cupping my face in his hands as he kissed me, the length of our nude bodies pressed together. My entire body felt so sensitive to his touch. My own cock strained against Johnny's belly as he rubbed his thick, uncut dick between my thighs. I knew he was going to penetrate me, make me his own again. He'd always been the one who held the power in our relationship. I wanted him to cleanse all the bad things that had happened to me with his love.

I heard him reaching in his pants for something, but although he applied lube to his cock before entering me, he didn't put on a condom. I wanted to protest for a moment, but then I decided against it. This was the man I planned to spend the rest of my life with, and he would be suspicious if I asked him to use a condom, since he probably still thought he was the only person I'd ever had sex with.

Johnny entered me slowly, and his cock felt huge inside

me. I gasped and moaned as he fucked me with long, smooth strokes.

"You belong to me, and nobody else." Johnny asserted.

"Yes, yes, I do," I replied with a soft sigh, not caring that I'd made the same promise to Max only months before.

Johnny knelt between my legs to fuck me, and stroked my cock with his fist, to ensure I received as much pleasure as he did. I could feel himself timing himself with me, stroke for stroke, so that we came together. He'd learned a lot since we'd last been together, and I wondered jealously for a moment if he'd learned his tricks by sleeping with other men. But I put those worries out of my mind. I had no right to judge him after what I'd done with Max. All that mattered was that he was with me now.

Having spent himself, Johnny knelt before me, my come and his come mixed together on the flat plane of my belly. "Have you been with any other men since me?" he asked, as if he could read minds.

I hesitated for a moment. I didn't know if I had the guts to lie to Johnny outright this way.

"Answer me," he said, slapping my face. His little power play had gone too far for my liking.

"Ow! What's gotten into you, Johnny? Untie me already," I said, squirming against my bonds.

"I know, Anthony, about the dirty thing you did for money in West Hollywood."

Now this was getting way too weird. There was no way Johnny could have known about that—nobody knew about that. The only person who could have figured it out besides me and my trick was Max. My blood went cold. I looked up at Johnny's face. It was Johnny's face, but it wasn't Johnny. In the dark I saw Max's visage, cold and beautiful, looking down at me with contempt.

"No, Max. Not again. This time you've taken it too far."

"You really thought you could escape me, didn't you?

How can I escape you when I am part of you, Anthony? It was your need that brought me back. I'm not going to disappear just because you're sick of me."

"That was you in West Hollywood, too, wasn't it? You were the trick. You wanted to punish me. So what did you do with that body? Not to mention Charlie . . ."

"You're not really in a position to ask questions, are you, Anthony? You've got a lot of pride for someone tied up in an attic with a dead body downstairs. I could make things very unpleasant for you if I wanted to."

"Fuck you, Max. If I created you, I can destroy you, too. Johnny didn't deserve this. None of them did, but especially not Johnny."

I squeezed my eyes shut. I knew that Max was somehow dependent on me for survival. I had called him into existence, there had to be some way I could send him away. If my need and belief had created him, there had to be some way I could destroy that belief and renounce the need. I focused on my happiest memories of time spent with Johnny, memories that filled me with so much warmth and hope that they blocked out all of the desperation I felt. Johnny was here with me now, I knew it. Max might have been feeding on him like a tick heavy with blood, but his spirit was still trapped in his body somewhere, and Max couldn't survive without it. If only I could touch his spirit somehow, strengthen his will and help him push Max out. I sent a tentative feeler with my mind. "Johnny," I whispered, focusing that golden energy toward my captor. "I know you're in there. Be strong."

I felt the warmth grow for a moment, Johnny's energy like a feathery touch on my soul. But it was quickly replaced by a feeling like a blast of cold air, a shooting pain in my head, a sensation of choking in my throat and chest.

"I DON'T LOVE YOU, MAX!" I screamed, gathering what little strength remained in my body.

Max slapped me, and grabbed my face. He reached over and picked something up off the floor. He showed me his gun and pointed it at his temples.

"Say it again," he said. "I dare you. Say it again, and I'll blow him away, and leave you to pick up the pieces. Better yet, I'll leave Johnny alive, and take your body instead. You'll have no choice but to sit back and watch while I control your every move, and Johnny will never know the difference."

That was the moment that I surrendered. I stopped caring what happened, I closed my eyes and went into a state of trance. I hid in the place where I often hid things I wanted to keep from Max—the mental image of Clarence Smiley's painting *Firestorm*. It was the one safe place in my mind that Max could not penetrate without my permission.

I could walk into the painting as if it were a room in my mind, a mad abstract world of red and blue flames, shrieking black trees. When I went into the painting, I became Clarence. The painting was the gateway between my reality and all the dreams I'd had about Clarence and Max. I knew that as long as I stayed there I had as much power as Max did. The firescape began to bulge and warp, and I knew Max was unsuccessfully trying to fight his way in to the last private place in my mind. We were going to settle this on my terms this time. I closed my eyes and I let him in by visualizing him as he once was, standing before me as a nineteen-year-old rich boy.

Max appeared oddly innocent in this incarnation, and overwhelmed by the place. "Where are we?" he asked.

"Clarence's mind," I replied calmly. "Don't you remember this place? It's the gateway you used to enter from the past."

"Clarence," he said softly. "I knew it all along."

"I never denied it," I replied. "But I am not like you. I

wasn't supposed to know about all of this. This knowledge is forbidden to me. It wasn't supposed to happen this way."

"But Clarence, it's a chance for us to do things over again. Can't you see, it's destiny? Finally we can be together, with nothing to stop us."

"That's a nice thought, Max, but it doesn't work that way. You died, but I kept on living. I survived, even when they chased me out of town. I lived, and I painted, and I loved again. I died, and I was reborn, and lived a new life. I wish I could say in good confidence that it's the right thing for us to be together again, but things have changed, Max. It's time for you to move on, to be reborn and live another life as well."

Tears formed in Max's eyes. "I loved you, Clarence. I never forgave myself for what I did. I ruined your life."

"You didn't ruin my life, Max."

Max hung his head. "I never forgave myself for making the wrong choice. It's tortured me all these years."

"But I forgave you long ago, Max, and you have to forgive yourself so that you can be reborn as well. You can't go on living like this. It's not fair to anyone, and it's cruel to Anthony."

"I'm sorry, Clarence. I feel so stupid."

"It's all right, Max." I saw then how young and vulnerable his soul really was, cut down in his prime. I opened my arms and held Max in my arms while he cried. "I love you, Clarence. I never stopped."

"I know, Max. I love you, too." We kissed, and when we pulled apart, I felt him fading from my arms. I felt sadness, but I knew it was the way it was supposed to be. And as Max faded, Clarence did too, the world of the firestorm withdrew and I found myself alone in my mind, calm.

I opened my eyes. Johnny was collapsed on top of me, not dead, but breathing heavily in sleep. I sighed a breath of relief, tears streaming down my face.

"Johnny," I whispered in his ear.

"Hnnn?" He said, still half-asleep. His eyes opened and he jerked awake.

"Oh my god! Anthony! Where—where am I?" He looked at my bound wrists. "Did I do that? I don't remember . . ."

"It's all right, Johnny. You didn't exactly have a choice in the matter. But it would be nice if you untied me now."

"I dunno," Johnny said, with a playful smirk. "You look kinda hot like that. And it's been so long since we've been together . . ." Johnny said, playing with my nipple.

"Johnny, there's some stuff you should know before you decide whether you wanna be with me ever again. Some of it might be kind of hard to believe. Please untie me so I can explain."

Johnny sobered up, and quickly began undoing the knots. "The last I remember, I was in Las Vegas. I took a bus out here from New York to try and find you. A older man at a bar bought me a drink and offered to pay me for sex— I told him no, but I'd already had a few sips of the drink and I guess I blacked out."

"Let me guess, he had slicked back hair and sunglasses."

"Yeah, how did you know?"

"It's a long, weird story, Johnny, and I'd like to tell you all about it, but I think we should get the hell out of town. I never liked this little city, anyway."

A PRINCELY GIFT

CLAIRE THOMPSON

A crane flew over the rice fields, casting a small shadow over the young man bent over his work. Kisho lifted his head, stopping a moment to admire its winged beauty, a lone white bird stark against the relentless blue summer sky. Surely the lovely bird was a sign of good luck? Something was going to happen. Something good. He knew it in his bones.

If only Kisho had wings, he, too, would fly away, far from this little bit of earth from which he barely eked out an existence. The land was poor and too far from the river to yield a lush crop, though Kisho was skilled at coaxing the seed from muddy waters.

Most years there was barely enough rice to support himself and his aging mother. They would barter what they couldn't eat in the village market in exchange for fish and vegetables and perhaps a bolt of cloth for his mother to sew into these rough black pants he wore each day.

Kisho was born the second son of seven to an inauspicious man. One would have thought him lucky, being bestowed with seven sons and no useless daughters, but alas, each one but Kisho had died either at birth or in childhood. Instead of cherishing the one remaining son, his father seemed to find his presence a rebuke—a reminder of his loss. He died before his time, bitter and full of grief.

Kisho had lived at least two decades, though his birth had not been well marked and its exact date was now forgotten. He could have left his mother, forcing her to return to her relatives, who by custom would have been forced to take her back. However, her family was a cruel lot who had mistreated poor Akira before packing her off to marry Kisho's father, a man already once widowed and over twice her age. He had blamed Akira for their weak offspring, finally calling her cursed and refusing to touch her. This suited Akira, for when her husband did touch her, invariably another pregnancy was the result, and she herself could not bear to lose another child.

Kisho loved his mother, and though he longed to travel—to see the famous temples of Kyoto and Nara, Mount Fuji, the canyons of Iwadatami, the imperial palace at Edo with its famous gardens and beautiful plum and cherry blossom trees—he would not abandon her. Instead he toiled, scrabbling for sustenance on a plot of land stripped of its richness long ago.

Kisho was a handsome young man with large, liquid brown eyes and a small, almost feminine mouth. He was slight of build but very strong, having tilled the earth since he could toddle. If women had been given the chance to see him, there is no question they would have found him handsome. The sack of rice on his bowed back and his tattered clothes were all that was noticed when he passed through the markets, bartering for goods.

One day in midsummer the entire village was abuzz with excitement. A pronouncement had been made. The great heir apparent, Prince Yukio, would be passing through the village on his way to the Ryujin hot springs in the Kii Mountains. The springs were famous throughout Japan, known for their restorative properties.

Apparently the prince was ailing, though no physical cause could be determined. His parents, Emperor Shigakazu and his wife Maiko, doted on the young man, who had been designated as the next ruler of Japan, once Shigakazu's spirit passed on to the next world.

The crown prince's happiness was paramount. At age twenty-two, he was the first son and chosen heir to the throne. When the finest doctors could find nothing wrong, and no amount of gifts and diversions seemed to revive him, the suggestion of the hot springs to purge his pain and restore his joy was offered and seized upon.

Accompanied by a small army of guards and servants, the prince set out on horseback for the mountains, only because his parents had wished it, and he wished to honor his parents. He had little hope the waters would restore his happiness, as the source of that happiness had died the year before, when the soul of his lover, Kiyoshi, had flown from its body.

Kiyoshi was a common gardener at the imperial palace. He had created beautiful, detailed gardens, breathtaking in their simple beauty, little haiku of nature. Yukio admired his work and beyond that, found the boy beautiful—with his large dark eyes, small mouth, and slender build. Yukio was drawn to his introspective, subtle nature—evident from his gardens.

One day he had spoken to Kiyoshi, complimenting him on his miniature rock and flower gardens. "You take what is most fine in nature and improve upon it, making it even more beautiful with your little spade and your artist's eye." Kiyoshi had blushed and bowed low, his forehead to the ground, trembling to have been spoken to by the young prince.

Of course it was most inappropriate for Yukio to be fraternizing with a lowly gardener but no one would dare comment upon it. He was discreet, sitting in one corner of a garden on a bench, meditating on its beauty, offering comments and suggestions from time to time as the young man worked. Prince Yukio dismissed his attendants during these quiet afternoon visits to his favorite gardens, and was permitted to do so, as he was safe behind high thick walls.

"Kiyoshi," he said softly one afternoon, several weeks into his daily visits to the gardens. "I want you to come to my chambers tonight. You will enter through a secret passage my trusted servant, Mamoru, will guide you to. You will tell no one of your visit."

Kiyoshi had no choice but to obey, though surely he quaked with terror at the possibility of being discovered in the prince's chambers, invited or not. Yet he appeared at the designated hour, wearing his best kimono and having scrubbed his body and hair with cool, clear water from the garden well.

Yukio had fed the young man from a tray of delicacies, speaking gently with him and putting him at his ease. He sat next to him upon a divan, lightly brushing the young man's thick straight black hair from his face. He was so handsome, and so terrified. Yukio's heart had softened even as his cock had hardened. He knew it was a matter of time before he introduced the young man to the exquisite sweetness of tender love.

He ordered Kiyoshi to come each night, and each night he took him a step further, at first contenting himself with just touching the young man, feeling his firm, supple muscles ripple beneath his soft skin as he whispered his admiration. At first Kiyoshi trembled, eyes downcast or closed as the prince explored his youthful body.

Yukio was kind, his words soothing, his touch gentle. He didn't want to take him by force, though if he had chosen, Kiyoshi would have had no choice but to obey. Yukio's patience paid off as Kiyoshi eventually relaxed, coming to trust the prince. Finally he even ventured to return his affections.

At first they only shared chaste kisses, fingers entwining. Slowly Kiyoshi seemed to open, like a timid flower reaching toward the sun. Yukio was enchanted with Kiyoshi. Forcing himself to go slowly, he introduced the younger man to all the pleasures of masculine love.

Yukio found himself obsessed with Kiyoshi. He set him up with his own apartments not far from Yukio's own at court, bestowing on him enough wealth so he need never work again. They met every night, exploring each other with the passion of young lovers, each insatiable for the other.

Yukio had a duty to his people to create an heir and thus ensure his dynasty. He was to marry that year and his wife had of course been chosen many years prior. Yukio fully intended to perform his matrimonial duties. He already knew and liked his wife-to-be, Aiko, a petite and pleasant woman who had been prepared since birth for her role as his consort and queen.

But as prince and later as emperor, Yukio could do as he liked outside the marriage bed, and his tastes had always run toward the stronger sex, when it came to sensual appetite and pleasure. His discreet affair with the little gardener, while not remarked upon to his face, was surely noted and discussed endlessly throughout the court.

Alas, a prince has enemies, with factions and families always vying for power. He could never prove, but believed in his heart that his uncle Jiro was to blame for the mysterious death of his beloved Kiyoshi. This uncle had never liked Yukio, angry that his brother had ascended the throne when he himself had felt entitled to that position. He was still determined to have his own son adopted by the emperor and placed on the throne instead of Yukio, but as yet his web of intrigue and deceit had not become strong enough.

Yukio, still young and protected, was only dimly aware of the infighting surrounding him and his position. But he knew of his uncle's enmity, which had been clear since he was a small boy. Jiro had never missed a chance to humiliate or embarrass Yukio during examinations or tests of physical prowess, calling him a sissy boy and a fool when no one else could hear. Yukio ignored him, which enraged the uncle still further.

When he had discovered Yukio's homosexual affair with a palace servant, via his vast network of palace spies, he had made his dismay clear to Yukio, threatening to tell the emperor at once.

Yukio had laughed, not caring if he told anyone he chose. Unlike the round-eyed barbarians who sometimes came to their land, the Japanese were civilized. They did not view sex in terms of morality or sin, but rather in terms of pleasure, social position, and social responsibility. Nonetheless, Jiro could make Yukio's life difficult if he implied to the emperor that Yukio was behaving irresponsibly.

"He is my friend, and it is not your affair," Yukio had unwisely said. "Go count your ill-gotten coins and leave me to my business, old man."

The uncle had not told his brother, as the emperor was prone to killing the messenger if the message didn't suit his ears. Oh, if only Yukio had pretended respect for the man he loathed, instead of believing himself and all those in his circle inviolate. If only he had protected his darling Kiyoshi, who still insisted on lovingly attending his gardens, though he needn't have lifted a finger again had he so chosen.

For Kiyoshi was found drowned in his own garden well, his head wedged in an unnatural way that suggested foul play. No one had seen a thing, at least no one who dared come forward. The emperor, blissfully unaware of Yukio's affair, had clucked his dismay that a servant had so stupidly dunked himself in a well, and he had thought no more about it, except to suggest they find a new gardener.

Yukio had been inconsolable; his heart still tethered to

Kiyoshi's departed spirit. Even his uncle had quailed when Yukio turned his eye upon him, his expression promising vengeance someday. Yet in fact Yukio was too full of grief to focus on revenge. Instead he pined, sitting for hours without moving on his favorite garden bench, watching the ghost of Kiyoshi quietly tending his flowers and plants. He forgot to eat and took no interest in affairs of state or his upcoming wedding.

Ironically, Jiro was found murdered in his own bed a few months later, a victim of his own palace intrigue. Yukio felt no vindication at his death, as it did not bring his beloved Kiyoshi back into his arms.

His parents, unaware of the cause of his grief, finally grasped at the idea of the hot springs, and so he set off, mainly to get away from the court and the constant reminder of what he had lost.

He was riding along the outskirts of a small village, his mind empty, the wind blowing through his shiny black hair upon which the sun beat in the heat of summer. Out of the corner of his eye he saw Kiyoshi tending a small field, dressed in rags, his hair long and untamed. Impossible and yet his eyes saw what they saw! It was his lover, sure as life itself.

Was the sun playing tricks upon his eyes? "Whoa," he cried to his entourage. "I wish to stop here. I wish to speak to that man there. Who is he?" His men did not know, as they were all strangers to the village, only passing through with their master.

The captain of the guard pulled alongside the prince. "That is only some lowly slave, some worthless peasant. Why do you inquire after him?"

"I feel I know him. That I've seen him before. But you are right. The sun has addled my brain. Let us stop at this village today. It is too hot to ride farther. The horses are thirsty. Surely there is an inn in town where we can stay, and a stable for our horses."

"As you wish, sir." The captain bowed low and if he wondered at the prince's strange choice of lodging, he certainly made no remark about it.

Yukio longed to ride directly over to the man to see if it was in fact his Kiyoshi, somehow returned to this earth in the guise of a rice farmer. He knew in his mind this could not be so, but his heart was less sure. Yet he didn't want to frighten the man, or draw attention to his actions. He'd learned the hard way he needed to be more discreet in how he conducted his affairs.

The entourage was housed in the village, completely filling the inn and several surrounding houses, with lesser servants and guards finding other lodging as best they might, or sleeping under the stars on the rolling hills surrounding the village.

The entire village was agog. The honor and delight of having the prince's royal entourage pass through had been enormous. To have them stop and stay—it was unprecedented in the history of the small village and immediately brought a new stature and importance to every man living there, or at least so they imagined.

Yukio was fond of occasionally dressing in clothes of the common people, covering his head and moving among them. He was discouraged from this by his advisors and friends, as a prince could easily become the target of his enemies when not flanked by his body guards.

Yukio thus had taken to sneaking out on his own, leaving a lump of clothing and pillows under his covers, with only his most trusted servant aware no flesh and bones lay in the royal bed for the few hours he roamed the city.

Tonight Yukio whispered his intentions to his servant, Mamoru, who bowed and nodded, never questioning his master, whom he loved and obeyed in all things. When the moon had risen high in the sky and the travelers were either sleeping on their tatami mats or getting drunk on rice wine at the village tavern, Yukio, dressed in a simple kimono with a broad sash around his head, slipped unobserved from the inn.

He walked alone under the pale moon, enjoying the rare freedom of no one hovering over him. For the first time since Kiyoshi's death, he felt his spirit rising from where it had fallen, lingering at the garden well, waiting to reunite with a lover who was never to return.

Tonight he felt hope blossoming in his breast, though he knew it was surely absurd. The man he had seen was probably some blockhead peasant, nothing like his delicate gardener. He probably had a wife and six brats at home in his hovel, his thoughts and deeds as coarse as a round-eyed barbarian from across the seas.

Yukio told himself this, trying to tamp down his rising excitement as he moved along the wide dirt road. He came to the rice paddies neatly carved out into tiny fields barely large enough to sustain a single family. Was this the place? It looked familiar. He recognized the little house with its vegetable garden in front.

His heart began to pound as he noticed a small flower garden containing flowers that grew wild in the area, but here were painstakingly cultivated into pleasing patterns and obviously tended with love. Had Kiyoshi's soul somehow found its way to this field? Had this trip been ordained so they could meet again?

The house was dark. This was crazy. Though of course the family would leap up at the knock of a prince, he did not wish to make his true identity known. Yet how to see the man again if he did not?

As Yukio stood puzzling he noticed something move along the side of the house. Quietly he approached and saw it was the very farmer he'd seen that afternoon, now crouching on his haunches, staring up at the moon, lost in thought.

Yukio waited, forgetting to breathe. A shroud of

mourning seemed to fall from his soul as the man looked up. He was the very image of Kiyoshi, his fine features silvered in the light of the moon.

"Kiyoshi-chan?" he said softly, the sound of his own voice obscured by the beating of his heart.

The man looked up. He didn't seem startled by Yukio's presence. It was almost as if he'd been waiting for him. Gracefully he rose from his squatting position and bowed politely. "I'm sorry. You mistake me for someone else, sir. That is not my name, though if you rearrange it a bit it could become so." He smiled at Yukio, his teeth strong and white in his tan face. "I am called Kisho. And who have I the honor of addressing?"

Yukio's heart felt as if someone were squeezing it. He willed himself to be calm. This was not Kiyoshi—of course not. And yet this young man, this Kisho, looked so like him he could have been his twin, though he was older by several years. And his voice, while lower pitched, was pleasing to the ear, with a lyrical lilt and respectful cadence.

How had such a peasant, toiling in the mud of his rice fields have come to speak with such gentle refinement? Kisho stood patiently, waiting for Yukio to identify himself. He would certainly have never seen the prince, and Yukio was dressed now as a commoner. Though Kisho surely knew the royal entourage was lodged in his village for the night, he would never dream he was addressing the prince himself.

Yukio had learned the world was very different when one was not artificially elevated by the status of one's position. People treated one differently, judging one on one's merits, rather than being blinded by the opulence and power of a royal title. It was the primary reason Yukio liked to slip in among the common people when he could. Now he said to Kisho, "I am called Yukio. I am with the entourage passing through your village, and had thought to take a stroll this night to ease my heart."

Kisho replied, "I am honored you pass by my poor bit of land. My mother is sleeping or I would invite you inside my home. If you would be so gracious as to sit with me, I would be pleased to bring you some tea or cool water."

Yukio smiled and bowed. "I would be honored to take tea with you, Kisho." Yukio sat happily against the side of the house near the little neatly tended flower bed while Kisho went into his tiny house to prepare refreshment. Kisho's invitation to a total stranger to stay and visit was not surprising, as a new face was probably rare in his village, and the chance of news from afar was no doubt appealing.

Kisho returned shortly with a small wooden tray containing two clay cups of steaming tea. He sat next to Yukio, his large dark eyes so like Kiyoshi's Yukio fancied he saw the gardener's soul peeking through them.

They sipped their tea for a few moments, each silent. Yukio studied the young man, who gazed calmly back at him. Kisho finally said, "You seem to examine me, as if you were looking for something."

Yukio flushed a little and said, "Forgive my rudeness. It's just that you look like someone—like someone I loved."

"He has gone?"

"He died. Last year."

Kisho nodded soberly. "I know much of death. Of my seven brothers, mother and father, only she and I remain."

"You have no wife?"

"I have nothing to offer a wife." They looked at one another. Yukio set down his mug and moved his hand, reaching out to lightly touch Kisho's leg. Kisho did not flinch or move away.

His thigh was strong. Yukio longed to move his fingers along the coarse cotton to his groin, but his hand remained still. Kisho's hand moved with the delicacy of a swan's dipping head, coming to rest on top of Yukio's.

Kisho's hand was rough and calloused with labor, but its touch was gentle.

Yukio's heart began to pound, and blood raced to his cock, engorging it as they sat together, still as statues. Softly Kisho said, "I saw a crane today. I believe my luck is changing."

Kisho admired beauty, in flowers, in birds, in humans. To him male beauty could be as arresting as female. He had never lain with either sex, except in his dreams. He took his own pleasure with his hand, and hoped someday to find someone to love. But a man such as himself had little prospects, and he'd contented himself with the beauty of nature, finding poetry in the land.

Now he gazed at this beautiful man who had appeared almost as if by magic, suddenly at his door. He was bathed in the silver light of the moon, shimmering like a ghost.

Ever since Kisho had seen the crane that morning he had known something was going to happen. When the thunderous horses had come tramping by and he'd seen the glorious royal procession, he'd been in awe of the strength and power and wondered for a fleeting moment what it would be like to be a prince.

He had thought then that was the luck the crane had portended—to see such a glorious parade pass right by his little plot of land was amazing indeed. But now he knew in his heart his luck lay elsewhere.

He hadn't been able to sleep that night, though he knew the dawn would approach as it always did, and he would rise and tend to his mother and begin his backbreaking day in the fields. He decided, rather than fight sleeplessness, he would sit outside under the calming moon and let his mind drift where it might.

When he had heard someone approach he hadn't been afraid. The day had already been unusual, and it seemed natural for this to continue.

As the stranger had approached Kisho had admired his fine form—the broad shoulders, the smooth high brow, the aristocratic nose, and high cheekbones. The man held himself regally, Kisho thought.

He assumed he must be a part of the prince's royal party, perhaps a guard out for a walk, or a servant sent on an errand. He had been pleased when the man had approached, as he was lonely. When the man had sat down with him, they had stared at one another, and Kisho had found himself falling into the beauty of the other man's eyes. They were a light brown, almost amber, specked with flecks of gold. He'd never seen eyes like that. They held him spellbound. When the man had touched Kisho's thigh, Kisho felt something slide through his blood, moving toward his cock, making it hard.

Without thinking, he'd laid his own hand over Yukio's. It was the softest hand he'd ever touched. This was no laborer, Kisho knew. This was the hand of a poet and a gentleman. Kisho was entranced.

He realized suddenly he must be dreaming. How else to explain this handsome, refined man suddenly appearing at his hut, taking tea with him, gazing at him with such tenderness?

Since it was a dream, he decided to let the dream flow over him, taking him along its currents wherever he was supposed to go. Yukio leaned closer, his hand still beneath Kisho's. It was the most natural thing when their lips touched, lightly pressing. Yukio's hand did move then, sliding up Kisho's leg toward his erect cock.

They remained with lips touching as Yukio's fingers found Kisho's penis, moving over his pants to feel its hard outline. Kisho gasped against Yukio's mouth. No hand but his own had touched him there, not since his mother had washed him as an infant. This dream was so real! So deliciously real.

Yukio's lips parted, his tongue licking over Kisho's lips. He opened his mouth, letting Yukio's tongue find his own. As they kissed, Kisho felt his body begin to tremble. Some part of him seemed to know this man, and his touch filled a great emptiness inside of him.

He reached out, his eyes closed, his tongue dancing with Yukio's as his fingers sought their way into Yukio's fine robes. He drew his hand along Yukio's smooth chest and felt his heart, fragile as a bird's drumming against his fingers. Perhaps the man was as inexperienced as he was. It didn't matter. In dreams one knew what to do.

He continued to move his hands down Yukio's fine, hard body, sliding over his flat belly as Yukio's fingers tightened around his cock, still sheathed in coarse fabric. Kisho longed to feel those fingers on his skin, wrapped around his manhood. Because it was a dream he felt no shyness, only desire, rising like a dragon's fire in his blood.

Gently he disengaged from Yukio, who opened his eyes as Kisho pulled away, his expression filled with longing. Kisho stood and pulled off his shirt and trousers, standing naked, his cock perpendicular to his body.

Yukio licked his lips and knelt up, moving his face close to Kisho's cock. Looking up at him, he took the man's shaft between his lips, sliding his mouth down over the head. Pleasure washed over Kisho as Yukio moved down, taking the length of him into his throat. His lips and tongue created sensations Kisho had never experienced. Now he was certain this was a dream, and he gave himself completely to it.

If he had died at that moment, it would have been enough. But he did not die. Yukio's soft hands moved beneath Kisho's cock, gently caressing his balls as he suckled and kissed his cock. Kisho's hands moved to grip Yukio's head, holding him as his hips began to thrust of their own accord against Yukio's mouth.

He felt his balls tighten and his blood pounding through his veins as Yukio continued his skilled attentions, drawing Kisho's seed into his mouth, making him cry out as he jerked forward, his body spasming with fierce pleasure. Yukio's mouth remained upon him, sucking out the last drops of his seed, his arms wrapped around Kisho's narrow hips to keep him steady.

When every drop of passion had been wrested from him, Yukio sat back, his amber eyes blazing. Kisho stood still a moment, his cock glistening in the light of the moon. He looked down on the handsome man still on his knees, his robes open, his hair disheveled.

Something was wrong with this, even in a dream. The man seemed too regal to be kneeling while Kisho stood. Silently he held out his hand and Yukio took it, rising up to embrace Kisho, who stood taller than he. As his immediate lust had been satisfied, he felt another emotion, a great tenderness, overtake him, for this dream spirit who had just given him the greatest pleasure of his life.

He pressed Yukio's head gently to his shoulder, smoothing the soft black hair with his rough hand. He felt the man's shoulders begin to shake and felt his silent sob as tears stained his bare chest.

Yukio was crying. A cry too deep for sound, rising from the depth of his sorrow. He must be crying for his lost friend, Kisho thought, holding him tightly in his arms. He is grieving for lost love, and I have never known love. Not until tonight.

He held him a while longer, and then, Yukio still silently keening, he lifted the smaller man into his arms and lowered himself against the wall of the house, cradling him in his lap until every tear was spent, and Yukio slept.

Yukio slipped back into his room as dawn rouged the rice paper at the window. Mamoru was pretending to be asleep on the tatami mat at the foot of Yukio's futon as he shucked off his kimono and slid between the soft covers.

Yukio could barely contain his joy. It threatened to lift him from the earth and send him floating away in the heavens. Yet he no longer wished to fly away, no longer yearned for the lost spirit of his little gardener. Though Kiyoshi would always have a place in his heart, Yukio now wanted to remain firmly on the rich earth. His heart soared as he thought of the amazing events of the last hours.

The tears he had cried in the arms of the farmer had washed away the last of his desperate sadness, leaving behind a peace and serenity he had never known in his twenty-two years. Kisho had held him so sweetly, like a mother holding her new babe. What would he have thought if he'd known he was holding a prince? One of the most powerful men in the land?

Would it have mattered? Yukio had been very surprised by Kisho's calm acceptance of the situation. It was almost as if they had been moving together in a dream. A lovely dream scripted beforehand in which they performed an erotic dance choreographed by the gods.

How thick and straight Kisho's shaft had been. It had sprung from his belly, demanding attention, which Yukio happily gave. Surprisingly the farmer's skin had been soft and clean over the iron rod of his cock. Kiyoshi's cock had been much smaller, and he had blushed and wilted when Yukio tried to bestow that particular gift upon him, whereas Kisho had taken his offering almost as his due.

Yukio's cock rose now as he remembered the man, standing naked and proud in the light of the moon, his eyes deep and unfathomable as he stared into Yukio's soul. When he'd swallowed his sweet offering, Yukio had expected Kisho to return the favor. At least he had expected the lovemaking to continue in some way.

His own tears had interfered, catching him by surprise,

unleashed by Kisho's warm, gentle embrace. He realized now that Kiyoshi had always been mightily aware of the vast difference in rank between them. Perhaps he had never even loved Yukio, except as a subject loves his ruler. Perhaps he had only given himself because he had no choice.

Yet with this man Yukio knew the emotions and the desire were genuine. He did not know who Yukio was, and thus he was not influenced by the power of his position. He had stood while Yukio had knelt—he could have lost his head for less at court.

Yukio stroked his cock as he thought of the handsome, enigmatic farmer. He realized up until that moment he had thought of everyone outside his royal family as merely servants, guards, peasants, villagers—but not as people. Even Kiyoshi, while real to him, was still "his" little gardener, there at his beck and call.

He could now reveal himself to Kisho, and force the man to comply with whatever he wished, but how much sweeter, how much more meaningful, to have his love freely accepted. Still he knew it was a matter of time before Kisho learned the truth.

He would keep his entourage here one more day. He was the heir apparent. No one would dare question his decision.

Happily he drifted off to sleep for the few hours remaining before Mamoru awakened him. Though his hand curled around his cock, he was suddenly too tired even to continue, instead transferring his passion to his dreams.

When he awoke after only three hours he felt refreshed. He felt wonderful! Mamoru eyed him suspiciously until Yukio laughed and exclaimed, "Stop staring at me, you old goat! You look as if I've been painted blue or sprouted horns."

Mamoru bowed low but as he stood again his eyes were twinkling. "Your highness, I couldn't figure out what it was, but now I know! You are smiling! If you'll forgive me, sir, I haven't seen a smile grace your countenance since . . ." he trailed off, blushing. He had never mentioned Kiyoshi's death before, though he alone knew this was the source of Yukio's great sadness.

Yukio laughed, further startling the old servant. Gently he laid a hand on his shoulder and said, "I am happy, Mamoru. Kiyoshi's spirit has finally been allowed to depart. I held on to it long enough. It was unfair of me."

Mamoru's smiled lit his wrinkled face. "Shall we continue to the springs, then, my lord, or shall we return to the palace?"

"No, we will go on. I couldn't disappoint the men. They are all looking forward to the famed hot springs. We will go today, and return again to this village on our way back, as I find I am happy here."

Mamoru did not question the cause of Yukio's happiness. He never questioned Yukio's moods and never gossiped about him to other servants. He was utterly loyal and devoted to his charge, with whom he'd been since Yukio was born.

The day was busy, with every person of even the slightest influence in the village vying to see the prince. He had set up an impromptu court in the main room of the inn, meeting with his eager subjects to hear their concerns and receive their praise. He found he rather enjoyed playing at emperor, and he listened earnestly to all the men who bowed and kowtowed before him.

Just before the men were ready to leave, the horses fresh from their night's rest, Yukio found a chance to slip away, dressed again in commoner's robes. He took a horse, leaving it tethered among nearby trees as he approached Kisho's little plot of land.

Kisho was bare-chested and sweating in the hot sun. He had just dunked his head in the trickle of stream that flowed past his property, and his hair dripped water onto his deeply tanned shoulders. As he saw Yukio approaching he smiled and waved.

"Welcome," he said. "My mother is preparing the evening meal. You must honor us with your presence." Yukio guessed they could ill afford to feed a third person, and that his portion, should he accept it, would be at their expense.

"Thank you for your kind offer, Kisho, but I only came to say good-bye." As he said this, Kisho's face, lit a moment before with happiness, seemed to crumble, a spark dying in his eyes as he turned away. Though he didn't like to have been the cause of that sudden sadness, his heart leaped at the thought Kisho did not want him to leave.

He laid a hand on Kisho's thickly muscled forearm and said, "I will return in three or four days. We are off to the hot springs of Ryujin, but we will pass this way again on our return."

The sun returned to Kisho's face and Yukio beamed back at him. He reached into the pocket of his robes and pulled out a small leather pouch. "Please accept this as a small token of my thanks. Last night meant more to me than you'll ever know."

Kisho took the small bag and started to untie the leather string that held it closed. "No," Yukio put his hand over Kisho's. "Wait until I have gone. Share it with your dear mother." He glanced at the sun, already beginning its descent. He knew the captain was eager to begin their trek.

"I will return for you as soon as I can, I promise."

Kisho stared in disbelief at the pile of gold coins on the little table in their one room house. His mother also stared, her bowl of rice forgotten. Neither of them had even seen gold coins so close, much less handled them. Akira picked up a coin in her gnarled hand and whispered, "How did you come by this, Kisho? Are you going to be arrested?"

Kisho smiled at his mother. "I hope not! I didn't steal these coins. They were given to me by a man I met last night. I thought he was a guard in the royal entourage passing through on their way to the mountains. But now I'm not so sure . . ." He trailed off, gazing into the middle distance, his mind roiling. How could a guard or servant afford to give someone a bag of gold? Kisho wasn't sure of its exact worth, but he knew this was more money than he would earn in a year, in ten years. Who was this Yukio, after all?

He thought about last night, his cock nudging in his pants as it, too, remembered. Kisho had never imagined such pleasure was possible at the hands of another. He had never seen a more handsome man than Yukio. And though he had not been aware he was attracted to the same sex, he knew now that he was indeed. At least to this particular man.

He could almost feel those fine, long fingers wrapped around his shaft, that tongue swirling in circles of pure heaven over his cock until he exploded in ecstasy. He had thought it was a dream, and had thus been able to fully accept the beautiful gift without hesitation or fear. He had known it was no dream when the dream lover had begun to cry.

Then he was just a man. A man with a burden Kisho hoped he had helped to ease just a little by holding him until he was spent, and slept. When Yukio had finally awoken and slipped away, Kisho had wondered if he would ever see him again. He hadn't asked, deciding it was better to see what the future held without attempting to sway it.

Seeing him just now, his face glowing with happiness, had warmed Kisho's heart. He had longed to take Yukio in his arms and crush him to his bare chest. But in the bold light of day, with no dreams to hide in, he dared not.

His mother pulled him out of his reverie. "Son! We are

rich! But what can we do with these coins? No one will believe they are ours. Who would believe a man you only just met handed you a fortune? We might as well have been given the moon, for all the good it will do us."

Poor Mother. Her life had been so difficult she had no reason to believe it would ever be different. She couldn't see past the immediate present, as it was all she had. Indeed, Kisho himself had not allowed that dangerous thing called hope to surface very often; he was reconciled to his fate as a poor rice farmer.

He put his hand over hers and said, "Honored Mother, with this gold we can leave this wretched bit of dirt and make a new life for ourselves. There is a whole land out there you've never seen, barely dreamed of. We will travel, you and I. I will build you a home with fresh tatami and a wood-burning stove and a separate kitchen, and we will make a lovely garden for you to sit in the shade and sip cool drinks." His mother smiled and clapped her hands.

"My friend is returning in a few days time. He will be able to advise me on what to do with this amazing gift." It didn't occur to Kisho to refuse the gift. That would have been a grave insult, as Yukio had clearly been intent that he accept it, and seemed quite willing to part with it. Again he wondered, who was this man?

They were both distracted by the rumbling clip-clop of many horses and they rushed to the door to see. The royal procession was approaching, passing them on their way to the mountains. Kisho stepped out to see them better. Somewhere amidst that proud group of men and horses was his lover.

His lover! Dared he be so familiar? They had shared one magical night. He peered out, shading his eyes to see better in the setting sun. Flanked at the front rode the proud figure of the prince, surrounded by a semicircle of the highest-ranking guards. As they passed the little farm, the prince turned toward Kisho and smiled, his amber eyes glittering.

Kisho stared in disbelief, unable to move or fully process what he was seeing until long after the parade had dwindled into the dusty distance.

Kisho borrowed a horse from a villager with whom he was on friendly terms, promising to pay him upon his return the next day. He had told the man he had received word of an inheritance, bequeathed to him by a distant cousin in a village a days' ride away. "When I return, I can pay you for the use of this horse and for your kindness."

The man had agreed, marveling that Kisho was to come into money at last. He liked Kisho, who was always honest in his dealings and properly deferential to his elders.

Kisho rode hard, having left his mother with all but one gold piece, which he held clutched in his hand, afraid to entrust it to his pocket, lest it somehow slip out. As he rode he took out his newfound knowledge and turned it over and over in his mind like a piece of rare parchment, wondering what to make of it.

So Yukio was a prince. The prince! The heir apparent to the royal throne, one day to be ruler of all the land! He recalled now the soft hands—hands of a man who had never labored. He recalled the man's regal bearing, his quiet, assured confidence. The confidence of a man used to being obeyed. But a prince!

A few discreet inquiries finally convinced Kisho that his Yukio was in fact Prince Yukio. He had never heard his actual name, as he was routinely referred to as the prince, or his royal highness, or the heir apparent. His name was rarely used, or if it had been, Kisho had not been aware, living outside the village as he did, with little daily contact except in the marketplace.

Beneath his awe at the discovery was a newly sprouting

fear. Surely a prince would have nothing more to do with him, a peasant rice farmer! Whatever had possessed the strange prince to don common clothes and steal away from his royal entourage? It must have been a fluke, a lark, a way to pass the time. He might not remember his promise to return to Kisho, and why should he? Kisho was nothing, while Yukio was a prince.

He thought now of Yukio's hot mouth locked around his cock as he knelt before Kisho. He blushed a dull red as he rode, though there was no witnesses. The prince had been kneeling before him! The ignominy of it distressed him as he gripped the reins of his horse, hurrying it onward toward his destination.

Yet clearly Yukio had not wanted his identity known. Kisho thought about this for a long time. It made a certain sense, he supposed. What must it be like, to be surrounded, morning, noon and night, by servants and guards, by advisors and fawning courtiers who admired not the man, but his station? It must be a particularly hellish kind of loneliness, Kisho thought, where you are never free to be just yourself.

Perhaps the one the prince had loved before had also been a peasant, someone who didn't know or at least didn't care about the trappings of the man, loving him for his spirit, not his wealth and status. Perhaps Yukio took solace in Kisho's arms, at least for that one night, anonymously held by someone who could offer comfort in some small way.

Kisho contented himself with this, and decided if the prince did return to him, he would try to behave as before, letting his natural impulses guide his actions. This would be his gift to the prince, though it could never compare with a bag of gold.

He rode into the large village and found a money changer who asked no questions of this stranger, happy to give him many silver and copper coins in exchange for the gold coin and a small fee. If that fee was in fact ten times what if should have been, Kisho didn't know and didn't care. The money jingling in his pockets was more money than he had ever had at once in his life.

He used some of it to buy three large bags of fresh fruit, vegetables, fish and flour, as well as a small jar of an expensive ointment that promised to ease joint pain. He still had plenty of money left, and so he bought a small brooch shaped like a songbird for his mother, smiling at the thought of giving it to her, and at the realization she would never again have to wash or mend or cook or clean.

The next few days passed quickly in some ways, as Kisho took his mother into the village and bought her fine robes, new sandals, and several items for the house. She was as thrilled as a small child, spending hours picking through the market, haggling with the stall owners and having the time of her life. At one stall she stood entranced, eyeing the fine white paper, fingering the beautiful little brushes and cakes of black ink. Kisho purchased the items over her voiced protests, though her eyes had shone with desire.

At night, once his mother lay sleeping on the new tatami mat Kisho had bought for her, time slowed, barely moving as Kisho waited for the return of the prince. He tried to put him out of his mind, but it was useless. His heart teetered between certainty his lover would return to him, and certainty that he would not.

Time will tell, as it always does, he reasoned with himself. A craned flapped across his vision, black against the waning moon.

Prince Yukio soaked in the hot waters at Ryujin and pronounced himself cured. He could barely wait to return to Kisho, his every waking thought devoted to that quiet rice farmer who had utterly captivated his heart.

He had seen the recognition in his face as they'd passed by on horseback. He hadn't planned to look at him, wishing to stare straight ahead and thus avoid detection, but he couldn't help but seek one last glance at the man. Their eyes had locked and Kisho had remained frozen in surprise as the prince rode on, leaving the rice paddies far behind.

Was he there still, rooted to the spot? Would he still agree to see the prince? Not that he had a choice, but this did not make Yukio happy. He longed for that sweet intimacy, without the huge mantle of his station weighing them down.

Would it still be so sweet? So easy and so right? He could only hope so. And if not, well, the night had been a gift. It had permitted him to release Kiyoshi's spirit at last, and it had freed him to begin to feel again. For that he had given Kisho the small bag of gold—for him a mere trifle but he knew for Kisho a king's ransom.

He worried over the gift as well. Would Kisho think he had bought his favors? Would he be offended as a result? Yukio finally laughed at himself. He could dissect every act, every thought, every notion, but things would be what they would be, with or without his feverish analysis. He was a prince, worried about a farmer. The notion was absurd on its face, though true nonetheless.

Finally the time crawled and then hurtled toward the moment when Yukio was again ensconced in Kisho's village. His men were free to take a much-deserved rest, as he'd pressed them to make the return journey as quickly as possible.

This time he'd had an entire house procured for his comfort, paying the family that lived there a staggering sum for the use of their home for two days.

Thus he would have complete privacy for his plans, if they came to fruition. Only Mamoru would stay, with guards posted outside the house only. Instead of going to Kisho, he sent Mamoru by horse, in case Kisho wished to refuse. He did not want to command the farmer to come to him. If he was now too in awe of the prince's titles, he would perhaps feel freer to refuse his invitation secondhand.

The prince waited with impatience as his servant was dispatched, but within less than an hour's time, Mamoru returned with a man seated behind him on the large horse. They were little noted as they passed and stopped behind the house where Yukio was staying. Kisho was ushered in by the servant, who discreetly disappeared once Kisho was in Yukio's presence.

Kisho was wearing clean new pants and a white shirt, his long hair tucked neatly behind his ears. It was still the clothing of a peasant, with no fine kimono or sash. Yet he looked handsome, fine, and strong, though his face still suggested the sweetness of a girl. Kisho stood uncertainly for a moment and then bowed low, staying down until Yukio touched his shoulder.

"Please," Yukio said. "If you can help it, let us not stand on ceremony. Let me be the man you met before knowledge of my identity clouded your mind."

"Your majesty."

"No. Yukio. Between us, let us be equals, I beg of you."

Kisho swallowed, his struggle evident on his face. Yukio stood before him, his expression pleading. Slowly Kisho smiled and said, "Yukio. I am so glad to see you. A rock of time has passed since our last meeting."

Yukio's smile was wide, relief evident on his face. He moved into Kisho's arms and they embraced, holding each other as if it had been months, not days, since they'd seen one another. "Can you stay? I have given my men a two-day respite. I augmented their pay so they are all very happy to find what entertainment they may in your village."

"Your gift. It was overly generous."

Yukio put a finger to Kisho's lips. "Please. You've no idea the gift you bestowed upon me that night. You set a tethered spirit free and you set my heart at ease for the first time in a year. What I gave you was nothing, a bag of metal. What you gave me was priceless—a princely gift."

Kisho blushed. "I did nothing. Nothing but respond to your touch, and then hold you. I thought," he dropped his voice to barely a whisper. "I thought you were a dream. At first."

"A good dream?"

Kisho answered by ducking his head slightly so their lips could touch. They kissed tentatively at first, a slight shyness between them. This shyness was soon burned away as their bodies responded to each other's taste and scent. They moved closer, pressing chest to chest, groin to groin.

Yukio felt Kisho's hardness and his own rising response. "I have a bath prepared. The water is hot. Let us bathe together." Kisho followed Yukio into the large bathroom where a tub had been built over a pit set into the ground. Wood could be placed and lit through a side door of the oven and stoked to heat the water. A small fire yet burned, and the water steamed with fragrant oils.

Kisho stared, his eyes wide with amazement. Yukio laughed, wondering what Kisho would think if he saw the royal baths, with their polished wood and marble, much larger than this simple tub. Yukio stripped, dropping his clothes and stepping lightly to the tub. He dipped in his foot—it was hot, but not too hot for comfort. He stepped in, easing his body down on the wooden bench that encircled the inside of the tub.

He watched as Kisho began to strip as well, his fine lean body nearly hairless but for the thatch of hair under each arm and at his groin. His cock was still stiff from their embrace. He seemed at ease with his body and moved with a natural grace.

Kisho touched the water with his foot, pulling it back with a little cry. He had never bathed in anything so luxurious, content in winter with using a towel dipped in boiled water, and in summer swimming in a stream to clean himself. Slowly he climbed in, as Yukio smiled and encouraged him.

"I could get used to this," Kisho laughed, as he settled himself across the tub from Yukio.

Yukio patted the side of the tub. "Come here."

Kisho obeyed, sliding over until their thighs were touching. Yukio slipped down into the water, dunking his head before popping back up. Kisho did the same, shaking his long hair from his face.

Yukio took a cake of soap and began to wash himself. "May I?" Kisho asked. Yukio hesitated, not wanting Kisho to assume the role of a servant. But as he watched Kisho's hooded expression, his lips lightly parted, his eyes glittering, he understood this was no subservient gesture.

He handed the fragrant cake of soap to Kisho, who began to move it slowly over Yukio's skin, creating a lather that he massaged with his other hand. Yukio closed his eyes, letting sensation flow through him.

When those hands at last found his cock, he groaned and shifted forward on the bench. He felt Kisho's hands trembling and opened his eyes. "What is it?"

"Forgive me. I have never touched a man in this manner. This is so new to me."

"Do you like it?"

"I do. Very much. But I'm afraid I don't really know what I'm doing."

"It seems to me you do!" Yukio laughed. "You are making me mad with desire with those strong fingers. Let us finish our bath and retire to the bedroom, shall we?"

Two thick, soft robes had been set out for them, as well as a stack of towels. They dried themselves and put on the robes. "You never answered me, Kisho. Can you stay for these two days? We will have complete privacy."

"I would like nothing more, your maj—Yukio. I must let my mother know. And I must tend to her a little each day."

"Of course."

Yukio moved to the bedroom, feeling as giddy as if he were a virgin, as new and untried as the man following behind him.

Kisho lay on a bed for the first time in his life. Perhaps it was not the bed of a king, but it was certainly thicker and softer than the mat upon which he had slept all his life. His heart was pounding in his throat. He hoped he had stopped trembling. The prince was very kind and had put him at ease—as much at ease as he could be in the situation.

How easy it had been that first night, when Yukio was not a prince, but a golden spirit moving through his dreams. How simple it had been to accept the gift of his skilled touch upon Kisho's body.

His cock rose hungrily at the recollection. Kisho found he was curious what it would be like to taste another man as Yukio had done. Could he possibly deliver the same intense pleasure? Would Yukio permit such a thing?

Too shy to ask, he instead reached over, lightly touching the prince's cock. It responded to his touch, lengthening and rising like a snake under his fingers. Kisho glanced over at him. Yukio was lying on his back, his eyes closed, his hands behind his head. Kisho might have thought he was sleeping if it weren't for that cock, straight as a pole now, pointing toward the ceiling.

Emboldened by the man's implied invitation, Kisho knelt up next to the prince and massaged his penis with both hands. It felt as soft as a rabbit's fur, with a bar of iron hidden beneath.

Kisho's own cock bounced against Yukio's thigh as he leaned over, his heart pounding, his lips parting to taste the hard shaft of the man who would be emperor.

He tried not to focus on Yukio's status, but it was very hard to forget it. He understood Yukio's desire that it not come between them, and he tried to swallow his own fear, thinking only of Yukio's pleasure and his wish to give it to him.

Lightly he teased the head of the cock, as Yukio had done to him. It was spongy and soft, a pleasing texture. He willed his hands to stop trembling as he gripped the base of the shaft and slowly lowered his mouth over it.

Yukio moaned and lightly touched the back of Kisho's neck, the pressure of his fingers a gentle encouragement to continue. Kisho lowered his head, taking the shaft farther into his mouth. As it touched the soft palate at the back of his throat he gagged slightly, pulling away.

"Relax. Open your throat. You are pleasing me greatly." Encouraged, Kisho tried again, slowly taking the full length of Yukio's cock, remembering the prince's mouth on his own shaft and trying to recreate that pleasure for his lover. Letting go of his own fears, he found his hands, lips and tongue moving of their own accord, dancing across the prince's body with a grace that seemed to come from somewhere outside himself. Yukio groaned and his fingers tightened on Kisho's neck.

"Yes. Yes, don't stop," Yukio said, his voice low and urgent. His hips began to writhe, making it somewhat difficult for Kisho to maintain his rhythm. He tried to flow with Yukio's movements, allowing Yukio to guide him with his fingers. He thought of the crane, flying so effortlessly across the sky and tried to summon that grace within himself as Yukio bucked against him.

All at once Yukio stiffened and with a little cry released his seed into Kisho's open mouth. It shot so far it bypassed his tongue, sliding down his throat like a raw oyster before Kisho could even register its presence.

He sat back, swallowing the ejaculate, which did in fact taste faintly of oyster. He couldn't help the grin that spread over his face as he watched Yukio, his features flushed, his eyes closed in what could only be described as ecstasy.

As he watched the young prince, his eyes slowly opened and he smiled up at Kisho. "You cannot tell me you have never done that before. I won't believe you."

Kisho continued to grin, a blush now kissing his cheeks. "I will not tell you, then," he laughed.

He left the prince for a short while, riding home to make sure his mother understood he would be staying in the village. She was sitting outside when he arrived, the fine paper Kisho had bought set out on the ground in front of her. She was dipping her brush into a little bowl of water and then running it across the cake of ink. Kisho looked at her work and was stunned. With just a few strokes she had created the scene in front of them—the rolling hills, the cultivated fields, and in the sky, a single crane drifting past the clouds.

She smiled and nodded when he explained he would need to stay in the village for two days to take care of business. She hadn't questioned what business, her world now on its head since, for the first time in her life, things seemed to be going her way. Her belly was full and not only of rice, but of fish and fresh fruit. The ointment had actually helped ease her joints, and she had her brushes and ink.

Kisho smiled as he realized she probably wouldn't even notice if he was there or not. He saw a neat row of paintings drying in the sun, held down at the corners with little pebbles. She must have been painting for hours. It was gratifying to see her smile—something he'd rarely seen her do over the years.

Kissing her good-bye, he mounted Yukio's steed and rode back, eager to return to his lover, wondering what the night held in store for them.

Two nights.

That was all Yukio had asked. Kisho sighed. Of course a busy prince couldn't possibly stay longer. He would return to his palace at Edo, and Kisho—what would Kisho do? With his little bag of gold, he had no intention of remaining a rice farmer. He had dreams of studying at a university. Of learning to read and to write, of studying the works of the great thinkers and the science of the stars.

Would this be enough to make his life complete? Would he miss his prince? Long for him? Would Yukio think of him as he went about his royal duties and held his fancy balls and presided over festivals and great affairs of state?

Kisho sighed. He realized that for Yukio this was merely a stopover, a break from his "real life" where he could indulge in a little secret play, far from the prying eyes of his court. Of course he would never want anyone to know he had allowed a lowly rice farmer into his bed! He, who was used to consorting with the highest strata of society, would never want to be seen with a peasant like Kisho, however sweetly he held him when they were alone in the dark.

Stop, Kisho told himself. It was ungracious to expect any more. He had been honored beyond anything he could have ever dreamed of just a few days before. Even if it would always be their secret, Prince Yukio had kissed him. He had wrought such pleasure with his mouth and hands. And he had allowed Kisho to try, in his own effectual and novice way, to return that pleasure.

Kisho tied the horse to its post and hurried back into the house, eager to the see the young prince, happy again to accept what he would offer, and prepared to expect no more than that.

Time was suspended. It had lost its meaning. Under strict orders, no one disturbed the prince. He was taking complete rest as the final part of his restorative cure. Only Mamoru came and went, bringing fresh towels and sheets, and leaving delicious perfectly prepared meals of the freshest fish, vegetables, fragrant rice, tea, sweet honey cakes, plum wine, and saki.

Kisho had been true to his promise, leaving Yukio only

to check on his mother from time to time, returning within the hour to fall back into the arms of his lover.

To his delight, Yukio would forget for hours at a time that he was a prince. Kisho told him stories about his life as a rice farmer. Yukio had never given a thought to the backbreaking work entailed to grow rice when one didn't have rich soil or an ox to plow the fields. He was amazed at the self-sufficiency of the farmer. A whole new world seemed to open before him, one he wondered if he would have the courage to face. When he responded with many questions and much interest Kisho had laughed. "I had no idea I lived such an interesting life until you showed it to me through your eyes!"

Yukio shared his stories as well, of palace intrigues and gossip, and of his training and preparation to one day assume the mantle of ruler. Kisho listened wide-eyed, laughing with glee at Yukio's inventive ways of handling the too-serious role into which he was thrust, and holding him close as Yukio shared the joys and loss of his little gardener. Kisho marveled that this important man would want to spend even a moment with such as he.

"Do you ever wish you had not been born a prince?"

Yukio pondered this question. Always those around him had envied him his position, even plotting and planning to take his rightful due from him. No one had ever asked him such a question. "I suppose," he said finally, "I could no more wish that than a mouse could wish it had been born a horse. I am what I am. This is my destiny."

Kisho nodded. This was a proper response. He himself was less content as a rice farmer, but perhaps that was because it was not his destiny. His luck had changed. He no longer knew what he was or where he belonged. He would wait patiently for this to be revealed.

Amidst the feasting, hot baths, naps, and long talks, of course they made love. For the first day and night they confined themselves exclusively to kisses and embraces, touching and enjoying each other's bodies. Each took the other's cock lovingly into his mouth, bringing the receiver to orgasm before lying back for the same hot kisses.

Yet Yukio longed for more. He found himself falling in love with the quiet, grave farmer. He wanted to consummate that love as only two men can. The knowledge they had only one day left made him press more quickly than he might otherwise have.

The second morning, after breakfast and another hot soak, Yukio said, "Today you will experience something new. It might frighten you, but when executed with care and love, it can be an experience more intense and lovely than any we've yet shared."

Kisho nodded, intrigued and not a little nervous. He was not quite as innocent as Yukio imagined. He had seen the picture books in the village, detailing quite alarming sexual positions between a man and a woman, and between two men. He understood the mechanics of sexual intercourse with a woman, and the reason for it.

He was vague about sexual intercourse between two men, and though it alarmed him somewhat, he was also intrigued. Beyond his fear lay a trust in Yukio that had been forged their first night together, and had only strengthened the more time they spent in each other's arms.

After a long nap, Yukio awoke Kisho by taking his cock into his mouth, pulling it to erection. "This day you lose your virginity," he announced. Kisho couldn't help the sudden intake of breath at this statement.

The thought of Yukio's thick cock penetrating his nether entrance was frightening. Would he be sufficiently clean? How would it push past the tight ring of muscle? Would it cause him to bleed? Would it be pleasurable, as Yukio had promised, or painful? Would he be expected to do the same act in kind?

Yukio, watching his lover, laughed softly. "Your fears are written on your face, my friend. You must trust me. Your body will know what to do." Yukio opened his hand, revealing a small jar. He opened the lid and showed Kisho its contents.

"This is a lubricant. It will make the passage easier, and also is said to be an aphrodisiac for both parties, not that we would need that!" He caressed Kisho's cheek, smiling. Kisho smiled back, nervous still, but less so.

Yukio instructed him to get on his hands and knees. Kisho obeyed, hoping his limbs did not give away his nerves by trembling. Yukio knelt behind him on the low bed, positioning himself so his cock was poised at Kisho's ass. Dipping his finger into the small pot, he smeared a generous amount over his own cock and dabbed a bit at Kisho's tight opening, which made him jerk a little.

"Close your eyes," Yukio commanded. "Empty your mind. Be at peace. Imagine something that soothes you."

Dutifully Kisho tried to picture the lone white crane he had seen the first day he had met Yukio, gracefully gliding by his field. His heart began to pound as Yukio's cock head lightly touched his anus. Yukio placed his hands on Kisho's hips, holding him steady as he slowly pressed forward.

Kisho jerked suddenly, startled by the pain. Everything they had done together to this point had been pleasurable. He clenched his body instinctively as Yukio tried to push past the virgin entrance. Again the head penetrated and again Kisho jerked, this time grunting.

"This is not for me," he said urgently, trying to throw Yukio off him.

He was the stronger of the two by far, and easily dislodged Yukio, tossing him over onto his side. Yukio's face darkened. A prince was surely not used to such rejection, no matter its form. To be sexually rebuffed was an even greater insult.

Kisho turned to look at him, chagrin and humiliation

burning on his face. He felt disquiet, even fear. Though Yukio had insisted that when alone they were just two friends, equal in love, at this moment it did not seem so. Yukio's voice was tight with suppressed anger. "You refuse me?"

Kisho slipped from the bed, dropping to his knees on the floor. Bowing so his forehead touched the tatami, he said, "Please, sir. My apologies. This is new for me. I confess, I am afraid."

Yukio sat still for a moment. Kisho did not move, awaiting the prince's decree. Yukio touched his head, stroking his hair. His voice was gentle. "Forgive me, Kisho-chan. In my lust for you I forgot myself. Please," he touched the kneeling man's shoulder, "do not kneel before me. If you are willing, we will try again. I will do a better job of preparing you, if you will give me another chance. I will not force you. What we have is too special to destroy. Please."

Kisho rose, settling back naked on the bed. Yukio knelt next to him. He stroked Kisho's smooth, hard chest, his fingers lightly massaging the strong muscles as they trailed down his belly. Long supple fingers found his cock, teasing it back to erection as he cupped the pouch beneath.

Kisho's eyes closed. He let his mind wander, empty as a blue summer sky, giving himself over to the lovely sensations being wrought by the prince's skillful hand. When Kisho's cock was stiff and erect, pointing to the heavens, Yukio whispered, "Kneel again on your hands and knees. I will be gentler."

Kisho obeyed, nervous but eager to please his lover and to find more courage within himself. Yukio again knelt behind him. Again he felt Yukio's finger at his anus, this time slipping the slender digit in, moving slowly and carefully. It didn't hurt at all, and actually felt rather good. He relaxed further as Yukio reached around his body with his other hand, sliding his hand up Kisho's hard shaft as he continued to finger his opening.

Kisho was aware when the finger was withdrawn, replaced by the spongy head of his lover's cock, but this time he didn't clench. Yukio's hand felt so wonderful moving up and down his cock in light, sensual movements, and Kisho focused on this.

When Kisho felt near to orgasm, his body bucking a little toward Yukio's hand, Yukio again focused on the little puckered entrance with his cock. Gently but firmly he held Kisho's hips as he guided himself into Kisho's virgin ass. Kisho felt the cock, thick and hard as it pressed past the entrance, sliding inexorably into him.

He tensed for a moment, and as he did, he felt the pain of his muscles spasming around the thick member. Yukio whispered, "Relax, my friend. Empty your mind. Be at peace. You are pleasing me. You are my beautiful lover. Give yourself to me."

Kisho sighed and was at last able to let go, his body opening to Yukio, who now slid the length of his cock fully into Kisho's ass. Yukio moaned with pleasure as he began to rock slowly back and forth, withdrawing and then penetrating his lover, each thrust easier for Kisho to handle than the last, as his body fully adjusted to the invasion.

Kisho wasn't sure how he felt at this point. It no longer hurt, but he wouldn't have said it was precisely pleasurable. He would have preferred Yukio's mouth on his cock, or his strong fingers dancing over Kisho's body, exciting each nerve ending until he was on fire with lust.

Yet he found himself getting more aroused as Yukio shivered and moaned against him. Kisho was pleased to be the source of such pleasure—to be the vehicle that provided his lover with such satisfaction. When Yukio again reached around to fondle Kisho's cock, his moans mingled with Yukio's, and he forgot to analyze the situation, finally letting his body take the lead.

They moved together in a slow motion lovers' dance,

Yukio riding him with greater frenzy as he approached his climax. Kisho felt Yukio's heart pounding against his back as Yukio suddenly grabbed him hard, thrusting with such force Kisho fell forward on the bed, Yukio's cock still buried inside of him. Yukio continued to thrust, oblivious to Kisho's discomfort, lost in his own heated pleasure. He jerked several times, crying out, his sweat wetting Kisho's back as his semen spurted deep inside Kisho's body.

Yukio stilled against him, his heart still drumming, his breathing loud and ragged in Kisho's ear. Kisho lay still, not sure what to do, his own cock mashed uncomfortably beneath his body, but still erect.

At length Yukio slowly pulled his cock from Kisho's passage. He reached for a soft towel and wiped both himself and his lover. "You were splendid. I have never experienced such pleasure." He pulled the covers lovingly over Kisho, patting his still semi-erect cock with a grin. "I will have Mamoru draw us another bath."

Yukio smiled gently, touching Kisho's cheek, which was stained by a single tear. He himself had learned when still a child to hide all emotion. The royal court was no place to show one's feelings. Yet inside he felt sorrow welling like a tsunami.

"Take heart, Kisho. We will meet again, I promise you. You must take this." He thrust another leather pouch filled with more gold coins than the first into Kisho's hand. "And, as a further token of my love, take this as well." He pulled a gold ring with a single red stone in its center from his finger and pressed it, too, into Kisho's hand.

Kisho bowed, accepting the gifts graciously. Reaching into his kimono, he withdrew a small bird—a crane— made entirely of paper, cunningly folded so its wings moved when the tail was pulled. Yukio's heart filled at this simple gift. All his life expensive and lavish gifts of every description had been heaped upon him, and because of the sheer amount and worth, most had meant little.

"I will cherish this," he said sincerely, his voice cracking a moment before he recovered himself.

They were standing at the sliding shoshi door of the borrowed house. It was dusk on the second day, and Yukio's company was going to set out in the cool of evening to begin their return journey to Edo. "Take this scroll," Yukio said, handing Kisho a piece of parchment, folded in the traditional ceremonial style. "This contains my seal, and will gain you admittance to the royal palace when you arrive in Edo. You will come to me, will you not, Kisho-chan?"

"Nothing could keep me from you, Yukio-san. If you will have me." They embraced. Yukio was returning to his wedding celebrations, preparations for which had been in progress for the past two months. There would be a month of joyous celebration and festivities, during which Yukio would be expected to actively participate. He would also be expected to consummate the marriage and hopefully get his new bride with child.

He gently told Kisho it would be better to wait to visit until the court was again settled down to its everyday routine. When Kisho arrived, Yukio would introduce him as a friend made while at the hot springs, a traveling lord who had wished to view the imperial palace while in Edo. "You must dress the part," he warned him, grinning. "No more peasant's garb or even this common kimono. You will make a brilliant lord, Kisho, one I will be honored to present to my family."

Kisho smiled and blushed, "I will always be who I am— the second son of a failed rice farmer, but thank you just the same for your confidence."

"That may be what you once were. I believe your destiny has changed its course, my friend."

• • •

So they had parted, Kisho slipping away on foot, returning to his mother, whom he had visited several times a day over the course of the two-day hiatus spent in his lover's arms. As he walked he thought about the amazing time they had spent together.

Yukio had penetrated him several more times, each time less fearful, more pleasurable than the last. Kisho had not felt ready to return such attentions. Yukio had not pressed him, telling him they would have time when they met again to continue in their explorations.

When they met again . . . would the prince, soon to be married, soon to return to his duties and the pageantry of his office, really want to see Kisho again? His passions were fiery and heartfelt while the two of them were alone in this little village, with the prince out of his element and away from his ken. Could he honestly wish to see Kisho again? Even to remember him?

Kisho touched the gold ring on his finger. He knew he would never remove it, not as long as he lived, but for the prince perhaps it was merely a casual gesture, offered on a whim as a token of passing affection.

He put his hand in the deep pocket of his kimono, feeling the bag of gold. Now they were wealthier still, he and his dear mother. He would find the finest doctors to help with her joints, and the pain she sometimes felt in her heart. She had told him it was only grief, when from time to time she clutched her sides, rocking and moaning, her face white with pain. Kisho had suspected this was more than grief, but until now they'd had no money for doctors or remedies.

He hurried home, eager to see his mother and to see what else she had painted with her ink and brushes. When he arrived she was lying down, though it was only barely dark, the sun still streaking the sky in purples and oranges as it slipped down below the horizon.

"Mother, I am back. Why do you sleep so early?"

His mother turned to him, for a moment her face blank. Then she smiled. "Kisho-chan. You have come back to me. Are you here to stay? Is your business done?" Her voice was weak.

Kisho felt a disquiet slip into his heart. Trying to dispel it he answered, "Yes, Mother. When you are ready, we will pack our things and leave this place. I will buy a horse in the village. We will ride to the sea and hire a boat to take us all along the coast, stopping at each port to see the sights. At last we will come to Edo, and to the imperial palace. We will see things we have never dreamed of, Mother. And I will buy you a lovely house in Edo, with your own gardens and servants. Would you like that, Mother?"

She nodded, approximating a smile, but her face contorted suddenly with pain. Alarmed, Kisho touched her forehead. "Mother! Are you all right?" Her skin was hot to the touch and felt dry as a funeral drum. Hurrying outside, Kisho grabbed a bucket and filled it with cool water from the stream. He returned, dipping a rag into the water and smoothing it over his mother's heated brow.

Surely this could not be! If only he hadn't left her alone! Because of his own lusts and appetites, because of his absorption with his newfound lover, he'd left his mother to fall ill!

He loosened her robe, dabbing the wet rag over her frail, thin body. How had she grown so old, so fragile? Tenderly he bathed her skin as she drifted in and out of consciousness, her eyes opening wide each time another spasm wracked her.

He sponged her body and held her head as she sipped some cool water. The fever broke several hours into his ministrations, bathing the old woman in sweat. She opened her eyes, smiling at her son. "Kisho-chan. You are tired. I feel much better." She touched his arm. "You must sleep. You have work in the fields."

He didn't remind her he no longer needed to till the soil, plant the seed, coax it from the ground, and reap what he could. Never again would he bend his back for hours on end, toiling to grow just enough to sustain them.

Instead he nodded and smiled, relief flooding him that the worst seemed to be over, and his mother would soon be well enough to travel. She closed her eyes, a little smile on her face. It seemed she had aged twenty years on that night.

The last remaining son, exhausted, unrolled his mat next to hers and fell into dreams.

Kisho held the brush, staring at its tip of fine horsehair, stained black from the ink. He'd known the moment the sun had returned that she was dead. The small house had felt empty, her shell lying on the mat, her spirit having fled sometime in the night.

Silent tears rolled down his cheeks as he stared at the gray face. "Mother. Mama-san, why did you leave me? Why now, when I could at last give you the things you deserve? The things you never had?"

He stared at the pile of papers she had covered in delicate strokes of black. There were birds, the rice fields, the distant mountains, even faces. Baby faces—his own and others he did not recognize—the faces of the children she had lost?

He stared again at the brush. Standing slowly he moved outside, taking with him paper and the cake of black ink. He sat down in the dirt, a bowl of water at his side. He dipped the little brush in the water and drew it back and forth over the cake of ink. Lifting the brush to a clean white page, he began to paint.

Kisho stood in front of the imperial palace astride his fine steed. He had purchased the horse he'd once borrowed from the villager, giving him silver, as well as his small house and field as a generous payment. That horse had taken him, alone, to begin the journey he had planned to take with his mother.

Dressed in mourning white, he had given her a proper ceremony, and had taken her ashes to be strewn into the sea she would never see. His heart was at once heavy with the loss of her, but light with excitement at the life before him.

In the month left to him, while Yukio was busy with his wedding ceremonies, Kisho traveled. He saw mountains, canyons, temples, beautiful gardens, bustling cities filled with more people than he had known populated the earth.

All along the way he painted, carrying a portable easel he'd built for himself, always supplied with fine paper, a cake of ink, and his growing collection of delicate paintbrushes. He kept his work in a heavy rice paper portfolio, painting everything he saw along the way—the mountain and sea landscapes, a lone fisherman, a school of goldfish in a shimmering pond, butterflies moving over flowers in a garden.

He found to his delight he had a talent for this art, much like his mother's. What had begun as a way to honor her had become his own passion. Perhaps her spirit had found a way to remain tethered to this earthly plane by slipping itself into his fingers, allowing him to create what she had not had the chance to do.

Now he sat on his tall black horse, recently purchased in the huge city of Edo, with its wide elegant streets, its fine houses and estates, its endless markets and press of people, all who seemed very busy and intent on getting to their destinations.

Because he rode the impressive steed, and was dressed in fine robes of silk and beautifully patterned and richly colored cottons, people made way for him. He still wore his hair long, but it was pulled back in a shiny braid that fell down his back. His angular features had filled out some, now that he could afford to eat more than rice and fish slivers. A fine sword hung at his side, completing the impression he wished to create, mindful of Yukio's advice that he "look the part."

As he waited patiently at the huge iron gates, a guard moved toward him, asking him his business at the imperial palace. "I have come to see the Crown Prince Yukio." He handed down the parchment he'd been carrying throughout his journey. What if the guard barely glanced at it, and told him to be gone? Kisho sat quietly, his face impassive, his heart pounding.

Slowly the guard unfolded the paper. Carefully he scrutinized it, noting the prince's seal. With a low bow he handed it back to Kisho, his tone respectful. "Please follow me, my lord. I will take you to the inner guards, who will escort you into the compound."

Kisho's heart soared. He had done it! The lowly rice farmer had fooled the royal guard. He was to see his Yukio again, after a month of holding him only in his dreams.

Another guard met the first, who spoke quietly to him. This guard bowed low as well. He indicated that Kisho should dismount. With the help of another guard, they took down his saddle baggage, which contained his clothing, a few trinkets he'd picked up in his travels and, of course, his portfolio of ink and brush paintings. With Kisho's permission, his horse was led away to the palace stables where he was sure it would be well taken care of.

Kisho stood uncertainly, trying to appear calm and as if he had a clue what was expected of him. Yukio hadn't told him much beyond that he was to arrive after a month's time and make his presence known. After perhaps ten minutes, another person approached. It was not Yukio, as he had hoped, but a palace servant.

"Lord Kisho," he said formally as they bowed to one another, "I will escort you to your chambers. The prince has been expecting you, and has asked me to convey that he will visit you as soon as his duties allow."

Kisho forgot to appear haughty and impassive as a huge grin broke out on his face. Yukio had been expecting him! He was taken to a small house on the grounds set quite a distance away from the main palace. The guards brought in his things and placed them in the outer room, which contained a low dining table set off by embroidered silk cushions on the polished wooden floor.

They bowed and left him, just as another servant brought him hot green tea, rice wine and many red lacquered bowls filled with a variety of cold noodle dishes and steaming, fragrant shrimp dumplings. The servant didn't say a word, only smiling and bowing as he set down the food and drink.

Kisho didn't have the courage to question him. He would wait, and rest, and try to take in the amazing fact that he was on the grounds of the imperial palace, and his prince was somewhere close by.

Exploring the tiny but lovely little house, he went into the bedroom. It was simply but richly decorated, with a fine teak bureau inlaid with brass and mother-of-pearl, a raised bed with an elaborately carved headboard, and two beautiful wooden and silk screens depicting mountains scenes painted in brilliant colors.

A sliding door led to a smaller room, in the center of which was a large tub already filled with water. It was much like the one in the village house they had shared together those two glorious days and nights. Kisho smiled, sure Yukio had chosen this little house just for him, both for its privacy and for this tub.

Kisho took off his outer formal sash and robes, and placed his heavy sword carefully on the bureau. He returned to the bathroom, moving toward the tub. It was built on a raised platform, a covered space beneath filled with kindling and wood, ready to be lit.

As the delicious smells of the food wafted throughout the small house, Kisho realized he had not eaten since early that morning. The servant had only set out one plate, so he presumed he was to eat alone. He would rather have broken his fast with Yukio, but knew he must be patient. He was waiting for a prince!

Settling himself on a soft cushion, he washed his hands and face with the hot wet towel the servant had thoughtfully left for him. Picking up the beautiful black lacquered chopsticks, he admired the delicate mother-of-pearl designs along their sides. How different from the crude wooden sticks he had fashioned for his mother and himself, as they ate from clay bowls on the dirt floor of their little hut. Wouldn't she have been awed and amazed with this lavish display, all of it prepared just for Kisho!

He ate slowly, thinking Yukio still might be along at any moment to see him, and would join him. Perhaps forty minutes passed and still Yukio did not appear. Kisho tipped the last of the saki into the tiny enamel cup and drank it.

He realized he was exhausted, the excitement of the day at last overwhelming him. The sun was only just setting outside. He didn't dare leave the little house, having been told to wait there for the prince. And anyway, where would he go?

He walked back into the bedroom, taking off his clothes and lying down on the soft covers of the sumptuous bed. He felt like a prince as he lay there, marveling anew at his situation. Soon the good food and the strong wine overcame his anticipation, and Kisho drifted into sleep.

When he awoke the room was softly lit by an oil-burning lamp on the table near his bed. Someone must have entered while he was sleeping. It took him several moments to recall just where he was. Where was Yukio? He could sense the hour was late and that he had slept long.

Almost as if on cue, there was a soft knock at the outer door. After a moment Yukio himself slipped into Kisho's bedroom.

Kisho came fully awake as Yukio ran to him and threw himself into his arms. Kisho hugged him tightly in return.

"Kisho! You came back to me! How I have missed you!"

Relief and joy flooded through Kisho. Yukio had finally come to him, and was glad to see him. He had not forgotten him! "My apologies for coming to you at such a late hour. My duties went long tonight. I had to host a banquet and I didn't think it would ever end. I knew of your arrival just after you came, but a prince must first honor his obligations, as I'm sure you appreciate."

"I am only delighted to see you again, my prince. I would wait a thousand years for the privilege."

Yukio laughed, clearly pleased with this response. "Now, my little rice farmer, let me see you! Stand up so I can admire that strong manly body of yours."

Kisho obeyed, standing tall in only his underclothing. "Take off those things," Yukio said softly, though the command in his voice was clear.

Blushing a little in the soft light of the lamp, Kisho stripped, his cock coming to attention as Yukio lustfully eyed him. Yukio quickly took off his own robes, his lean body bare beneath them. With a small groan of appreciation, Yukio knelt before Kisho, wrapping his arms around his hips as he took the length of Kisho's cock into his throat.

Kisho touched the top of the prince's head, sighing low with pleasure as Yukio sucked and caressed him. Quickly, all too quickly, Kisho felt his pleasure rise and overflow as he ejaculated into the prince's hungry mouth. Yukio swallowed and continued to suck, coaxing out the last pearly drops.

He sat back on his haunches grinning widely up at Kisho, who knelt and took the prince in his arms. "Forgive me," he said. "Your lips and tongue are too skilled for my poor body to resist for very long."

"Don't apologize," Yukio said, laughing. "That is what I

wanted to do. See how my body is pleased with you?" He pointed at his own cock, erect and bobbing toward his lover. Slowly he stood as Kisho stayed kneeling, opening his mouth and closing his eyes as Yukio slid his shaft past Kisho's lips.

Lovingly he suckled and kissed Yukio's cock, reveling in his sweet, pungent taste as he gripped the standing man's hips to hold him steady. Soon, almost as quickly as Kisho had erupted, Yukio spurted his royal seed into Kisho's willing mouth. Kisho remained on his knees, his arms around his lover's body, his own cock rising with the quick recovery of youth.

They climbed onto the bed and lay wrapped in a tangle of arms and legs, kissing, fondling each other's bodies and talking until the sky turned light gray and pink as a seashell.

"The sun will rise soon, my love," Yukio whispered. "I will return to my chambers to sleep awhile. My day is less busy tomorrow. Your breakfast will be brought to you. You are free to roam this part of the compound. I have informed my staff and my parents of your arrival. They think you are an important lord I met in my travels. I hope you will take pleasure in the small garden outside your little house. It's only partially cultivated, as I thought perhaps you might enjoy working there. I recall your carefully tended wildflowers."

Kisho was overwhelmed at this thoughtful gesture. A house and a garden implied permanence. What were Yukio's intentions in that regard? Kisho did not ask. He only kissed his lover and said, "I will await your return when time permits, my prince."

The next day Kisho slept late, awaking refreshed. A breakfast of fruit and tea had been set out for him. He ate sparingly and just as he was finishing, there was a soft knock at his outer door.

"Enter," he said, little wings of hope soaring though he knew it couldn't possibly be Yukio so early. It was not Yukio, but a servant, the same one who had brought his food before.

"I am called Taku. I will be your personal servant for your stay here, honored sir. Prince Yukio has asked me to prepare your bath. It takes a while to heat. Perhaps I could show you the garden, sir, and your method of alerting me to your needs." Kisho nodded, following the young man outside. It was a lovely day, the waning summer's heat no longer so relentless.

"The prince does not wish me to reside with you, but instead, when you need my services, please place this red lantern on this hook, here." He held up a little red tin lantern. A candle was placed inside so it could be used at night as well. They walked around to the side of the house, where Kisho saw the gardens Yukio had referred to. Some plants were in place, and others were still in wooden crates, waiting to be planted. Kisho smiled, as he found tending flowers to be a peaceful, healing activity. In his old life, it had been his only joy.

Kisho passed the day agreeably enough, though his mind was ever on Yukio's return. The sun was low in the sky when Yukio appeared. Taku came soon after, bringing them a sumptuous meal brought on a rolling cart.

"I have cleared my calendar for this evening. We will have a full night uninterrupted. No one is to disturb us and you can be sure no one will." His quiet authority reminded Kisho he was used to having his orders obeyed to the letter.

After they ate, Yukio said, "Now, it is time you learned something new."

They sat together soaking in the fragrant water of the tub, the embers below it keeping the water hot. The full moon was already beginning its descent. Yukio felt a great happiness as he sat with his lover, all his cares for the moment forgotten.

He treated his wife with the honor her position required. He had done his duty by her, though it was too soon yet to say if she was with child. Indeed, he enjoyed sex with women and would continue to visit her bed. But it did not compel him as sex with another man did. The little gardener had not been the first man with whom Yukio had made love, though until Kisho he had been the only one to touch his heart.

Kisho not only touched his heart, but consumed his passions and encircled his soul. He found himself almost frightened by the intensity of feeling when he was with the quiet, handsome man. There was an inner serenity to the rice farmer that fascinated Yukio. He didn't seem overly in awe of the prince, which was in itself refreshing, as Yukio had spent his life being fawned over and indulged because of his status.

He had been stunned when Kisho had showed him his ink paintings. Yukio had always been surrounded by the finest art from both Japan and abroad. He had a good eye for quality and at first refused to believe Kisho had done the work himself, thinking he was making a joke.

Kisho had blushed and pressed his lips together, as he did when he was feeling self-conscious and overly praised. He showed Yukio his ink cakes and his brushes. Shyly, he took out several paintings that were likenesses of the prince himself, painted with a loving hand from Kisho's memory.

"It made me feel less alone to have your likeness near me," he confessed sweetly, to Yukio's delight.

"These paintings are no mere dabbling, Kisho. This is fine work, very fine. Fine enough to hang in the imperial palace! And it works well for us, as my father has a mania for portraiture. You will have a secure and legitimate spot in the palace for as long as you care to remain. I am certain once the emperor sees your work, you will have your hands full painting the likeness of all two hundred and twenty-seven relatives that reside in the compound!"

Yukio was well pleased. He had been wondering how he would justify Kisho's presence for much longer than a month's visit. He did not intend to lose Kisho, but he was mindful of the discretion necessary when housing lovers. This would make things much simpler.

As they lay quietly together he thought back over the wild night. Kisho was no mere plaything. Where Kiyoshi had been passive, even submissive, Kisho had a fire that, once stoked, was not easily put out.

Yukio had learned that well this night. Now lying in Kisho's arms, he thought back over the evening. He had been curious to see how Kisho would react to *kinbaku*—the erotic art of Japanese rope binding. Yukio had been introduced to it by a woman, much older and very skilled. She had bound Yukio and sexually teased him in devious ways that still made his cock rise to think upon. More importantly, she had taught him some of the techniques for binding. Special knots were used, their aesthetic appeal as important as their ability to bind. The beauty of the presentation was as important, if not more so, as the effective restraint of the subject.

He had tried to introduce Kiyoshi, but the younger man had been too frightened. He had submitted, of course, as he did to everything the prince asked of him, but his heart, and certainly his cock, were not engaged.

Kisho's eyes had widened as Yukio removed several lengths of brightly dyed rope from his silk kinbaku bag. "Sometimes," he said softly, "the eroticism of an experience is heightened by restraint. And sometimes, it is the restraint itself that is erotic."

He had watched Kisho carefully, gauging his reaction. "There is a beauty to the stillness of the bound subject.

And for you, if you let it, this bondage can take you to an inner stillness, a place where pleasure is heightened to an unimaginable degree."

To his delight, Kisho's cock had swelled and lengthened as Yukio added, "When I bind you, naked and beautiful in your helplessness, you will be at my mercy. Whatever I choose to do to you, you will be powerless to resist."

"I would never resist you," Kisho had whispered.

How beautiful he had looked, his strong thighs encircled with red rope that forced him to stay in a kneeling position on the floor. He was kneeling on his haunches, back straight, on a padded mat Yukio had produced for the purpose, his legs spread wide to display his cock and balls. His bound arms behind his back forced his chest out proudly.

"Stillness is the key. Do not struggle. Let me take you where you need to go. I will listen to your body. You connect with the inner peace and meditate on the submissive beauty of your surrender."

Kisho had been a natural, relaxing completely as Yukio bound him until he was completely immobile, even winding soft rope over his eyes to blind him and between his lips to silence him.

At last he had focused on the bound man's cock, selecting a narrower rope that he entwined around and between Kisho's balls, forcing his erect cock to jut out even farther.

Once his lover was completely immobilized, Yukio had admired his own handiwork, stepping back to gaze on his lover. Kisho looked like an exotic flower, the stamen at his center erect with lust, dripping with his sweet nectar.

Though Yukio was tempted to taste the offered prize at once, he wanted to heighten the experience for Kisho. Taking a silk scarf, he drew it over Kisho's shoulders and chest, making him shudder. Teasingly he moved the silk over Kisho's cock and drew it under his balls.

Moving behind him, he pulled the scarf through the

bound man's legs, drawing it up between the cheeks, which were splayed and spread by his position. Returning to his front, Yukio finally knelt and took the hard cock into his mouth, savoring its taste, licking along the silky smooth flesh as Kisho moaned against his rope gag.

Yukio began a slow erotic torture with his tongue and lips, teasing Kisho just to the edge of release and then withdrawing, letting Kisho's body tell him just when another stroke, another lick, would push him over the edge.

Yukio's own cock was eager for attention and he had had a devious idea. Stepping behind Kisho, he gently pushed him forward, forcing Kisho to tip so his forehead was touching the mat as he balanced on his knees, his ankles still bound to his thighs. Kisho was completely out of control now, his balance reliant on his staying perfectly still.

His hands trembling with lust, Yukio took the little pot of lubricant he had brought with him, smearing a generous amount of it on the head of his cock. He pressed a small amount into Kisho's helpless opening. Kisho shivered a little in his bonds.

Because of his position, his legs spread and bound, his ass offered up with splayed cheeks, he had been very easy to penetrate. Kisho was unable to clench his muscles in fear or anticipation, tied open as he was, powerless to resist Yukio's invading thrust.

He had grunted against the soft rope in his mouth. Yukio reached around, massaging Kisho's cock as he filled him from behind, always careful to keep him on the edge, never letting him slip over. Kisho's cock was rock hard, his chest rising and falling, his neck red and straining as he held his awkward position, sometimes assisted by Yukio's strong hands on his hips.

As Yukio neared his own orgasm he had grabbed Kisho's bound arms like reins, pulling on them as he rode his stallion lover to a searing release. He fell against Kisho, knocking him from his precarious position. They rolled together on the mat, Yukio's cock still buried in Kisho.

They lay still until Yukio's heart stopped drumming enough for him to disengage himself from his bound lover. He removed Kisho's rope blindfold and gag first, kneeling next to him, their faces almost touching. Kisho focused on him, his eyes glittering darkly.

For a moment it had frightened Yukio. Had he pushed his lover too far? "Untie me. Now." Kisho's voice carried a command, the usual deferential tone absent. Yukio had raised his eyebrows. He could have had Kisho executed for his tone of voice alone, but he didn't want to have him killed. Oh no. He found himself thrilling to this new dark side of his lover.

He knew he himself was to blame, or congratulate. Through the erotic bondage, and through the denial of Kisho's sexual release, Yukio had helped Kisho move to a higher plane of sensation and erotic experience. He knew Kisho was now past the peaceful, almost meditative state kinbaku can create, having been fueled by Yukio's sexual teasing and anal penetration into a state of fierce arousal.

When he had finally relented, untying and unwinding the ropes and freeing Kisho's limbs, he had expected Kisho to want to make love, but he had not expected what had happened next.

Kisho had stood, tall and strong, his slim body and narrow waist seeming too small suddenly for his huge erection. His eyes were wild, not the eyes of the serene rice farmer, but those of a raging, lustful man, determined to have his way.

Without a word, Kisho had lifted the smaller man, dropping him on his belly onto the bed. Yukio pushed himself up on one elbow, looking back at his wild lover. Kisho's hair was loose, falling into his face. His red lips were parted, the white teeth glistening below.

Yukio had watched as Kisho took the little pot of lubricant

and smeared it over his erect cock. Gone was the shy but eager lover, replaced by a raging bull determined to take his own pleasure. Yukio found himself thrilling to this dominance, his own cock already erect though he'd only just spent himself deep in Kisho's ass.

Crouching behind Yukio, Kisho lifted him up by the hips, forcing him to his hands and knees. No one had ever dared treat him like this. Though they might respond passionately to his advances, no one had ever dared take him without permission, without the leave of the prince.

Breathing hard, Kisho reached around, grabbing Yukio's cock, which was now as hard as his own. Apparently satisfied, he dropped it and focused his attention on Yukio's firm buttocks. Spreading the cheeks, he touched the head of his cock to Yukio's nether entrance.

But unlike Yukio, who had been very careful and slow with his virgin lover, Kisho pressed hard. He was not rough, but nor did he stop or pull back, nor take time to see how Yukio was handling the penetration. Inexorably he had pressed past Yukio's tight entrance, wresting a moan from his lover as his shaft slid into that dark tunnel.

After only a moment, Kisho began to move, thrusting his pelvis, his balls slapping against Yukio's thighs as he took his pleasure. After the initial slight pain of penetration, Yukio had become faint with excitement, delirious with lust. His beautiful boy had become a man!

Kisho used him hard but not for very long, as his own apparent passions drew him to a quick release. Yukio, his hand stroking his cock as his lover pummeled him from behind, came as Kisho did, spurting his sticky offering onto the silk sheets beneath them.

They had collapsed together, sweating, hearts pounding, their labored breath mingling. They had lain as they had fallen for some time, the sweat cooling their bodies, time easing the fierce rush of blood in their veins.

Now they sat in the heated water, lingering and soaking as the warmth and fragrant oils restored them. While they soaked, the old, more familiar spirit returned to Kisho's body.

"Yukio-san," he said softly. "I don't know what happened. Something overcame me. If I have offended, I offer my most humble apologies."

Yukio laughed. "Kisho-chan, you have made me happier than I ever dreamed! I have taken my pleasure, even great pleasure, in the arms of others, and I believe I have also given pleasure in return. But never has someone taken that pleasure from me. I had feared, perhaps because of my status as prince, no one would ever have the courage to dare treat me as an equal.

"And though you have treated me with love and respect, never making me feel you were merely a subject obeying my wishes, until tonight I hadn't thought it possible to give of myself with such abandon."

Kisho listened, nodding as he took in the words and considered their import. After some time he said, "I consider myself a peaceful man. I strive for serenity in all my actions, as this was the only way in the past to survive the life I had been given. It was the only way to maintain my spirit in a balance that made sense for me.

"But now my world has been turned on its head. I have traveled throughout the land, seeing things I never imagined and others I could only imagine. I have no more rice field to plow. Instead here I sit with a prince in this beautiful house you tell me is mine for as long as I care to stay in it, my pockets filled with gold and silver.

"I have a future here, you tell me, with my inks and my brushes, doing something that feeds my spirit instead of simply my body. The spirit of my honored mother lives in the work I create.

"My body, once used only for toil, has become a vessel of pleasure and happiness. I never knew a body could experience such sensations, while at the same time feeding the soul.

"I have no family—I am alone in the world. Yet for the first time I feel truly cherished. All of this has come from you. But beyond all these marvelous things, tonight you have taken me to a place within myself I didn't know existed.

"To be bound as you had me, unable to move while you touched and aroused me to such a fever pitch—it was indescribable."

"Try. Try to describe it."

Kisho paused, thoughtful as always as he sought the words. "Because I was bound, silenced and blind, I couldn't respond to you. I couldn't jerk forward as your hand or mouth withdrew. I couldn't take you in my arms. I couldn't return your sweet hot kisses. The arousal was great, almost more than I could bear. I found my mind responding as my body could not. My spirit began to travel into the deep recesses of my sensual being, releasing pleasure of a more profound sort than I'd experienced up until now." He paused for a long time and Yukio, also a patient man, waited. "No. Those aren't the right words. I am sorry. I cannot explain."

Yukio smiled. "I think you expressed it very well. That is very nearly how the kinbaku masters describe the experience. But afterward, Kisho, you seemed to change before my eyes!"

Kisho blushed, looking away. "A demon entered my blood. You had heated me so thoroughly, pushing all gentle and delicate feeling from my head. I was inflamed with the need to take you, to claim you, to use your body as you had used mine." He kept his head turned away, his lips compressed, his eyes cast down.

Gently Yukio reached out, forcing Kisho to look at him. "Be at peace. I liked that raging demon! I hope we can get him to return!" He laughed and dipped his hand below the water, moving his fingers along Kisho's thigh, stopping only when his hand found Kisho's manhood.

They dried one another's bodies, sipped some plum wine, and slept. For the first time since his mother had died, her spirit did not visit Kisho in his dreams. Held in Yukio's arms, he dreamt the dream of lovers.

Kisho watched, smiling, as the little princesses and princes ran laughing and rolling together in the grass like sleek little kittens. He was no longer called Kisho, except by the prince, but was addressed respectfully as "my lord" or "Lord Kisho, Imperial Artist in Residence."

Yukio had been right—the emperor had taken a fancy to his work, commissioning him to paint not only faces, but landscapes and scenery, and even the entire wall of the imperial dining room. The honor had been large, and Kisho had often worried he was not up to the task. When this happened, he would close his eyes and will the spirit of his mother to return to him. She would always comply, soothing his heart and calming his fingers so he could continue to create, following the visions she offered.

He was given paints of many colors and taught to use them by the finest masters. His days passed happily painting, tending his gardens, and visiting with the other artists, artisans, and craftsmen who worked in the palace, filling it with beautiful creations and tending to the ancient treasures already housed there.

But it was the nights he lived for. Yukio could not slip away to see him every night, but he did come often, at least several times a week. If his wife, Aiko, minded, she never made mention, not that she would have dared. Kisho hoped that she did not mind. Most if not all, noblemen took concubines as a matter of course. Kisho knew Yukio was good to Aiko, showering her with gifts, and, most important, allowing her to raise their children herself, despite his mother's urging to have them removed to the heart of the palace where she and the emperor resided, to be raised by tutors and servants as was often the custom.

Kisho had become friendly with Aiko, though his natural reserve kept him at something of a distance. Only with Yukio did Kisho feel completely at home. This was enough for him. He had no desire to marry, and his life was full.

The days slipped into weeks, months, and finally years. The four children laughing and playing on the rolling lawns were soon expecting a new baby brother or sister. They all called Kisho "uncle" and he loved them as if they were his own.

Kisho sat quietly under a pagoda by a large pond, alternately watching the children play and staring out at the peaceful water. It was a clear spring day and Mount Fuji loomed majestically in the distance, some sixty miles away. Kisho had been there, and to many other places throughout Japan over his ten years at the imperial palace. He had never left the island, but knew, when the time was right, he would do that, too.

Right now the emperor was gravely ill, and Yukio had not been by to see Kisho as often as either of them would wish. Kisho missed him, but understood that affairs of state and affairs of the imperial family must take precedence. It was the proper order of things. He would wait, and when the time was right, Yukio would again slip into his little house, sliding between the silk sheets and taking his pleasure.

Kisho never forgot that first heady night when Yukio had introduced him to erotic bondage. Kisho had developed a passion for it, learning from Yukio many of the intricate and beautiful patterns one could create with the ropes. The student had surpassed the master when Kisho had secretly found a kinbaku master, learning from him many complicated but sensual knot-tying techniques. He learned about the symbolic importance of each bondage knot, as well as a technique for binding using no knots at all.

Yukio became his willing subject, almost at once stilling

and entering a kind of submissive trance when Kisho bound him with the twisted and braided ropes now kept in Kisho's home, and augmented with his own collection. Yukio had tried to explain how the experience altered him. They both struggled for the words and Kisho had decided the language wasn't sufficient to capture the beauty. No matter—they shared it and together understood it.

He thought perhaps Yukio had come closest when he had said, "When I am held in your bonds, I feel as if the ropes surrounding my body are an extension of your hands. I have learned of the ultimate freedom to be found within the restraint."

Kisho also thought the experience had an added level of profundity for the prince, weighed down as he was with his titles, his duties, and his status. When he was naked and bound, at the mercy of his lover. Kisho was no longer his subject, nor his servant, nor even his friend. The ropes freed them both, diminishing and eventually removing any barriers between the two, forming a bond of dependence that strengthened both rather than weakening either.

Kisho's thoughts were disrupted as Yukio suddenly appeared, his face weary from tending his dying father. Yet, as always, his eyes lit up with pleasure as he greeted his friend and lover. Kisho smiled back, his heart warmed.

Yukio sat beside him, sighing deeply as he looked across the shimmering pond. He turned toward his children, still laughing and playing, unaware death loomed close, or that their father was about to become the most powerful man in the land.

The men's robes flowed over each others, allowing their hidden fingers to touch. Kisho closed his hand over Yukio's, giving it a gentle squeeze. "Things will be as they are meant to be," he said softly, by way of comfort.

Two white cranes flew overhead, their bodies casting a soft shadow over the still waters.

BEAUTY
CATHERINE LUNDOFF

If I said I met my vampire prince at a ball at the king's palace, would you believe me? Of course, it is easier by far to believe it now. But then it seemed an impossibility. The king was my father and the queen, my mother, or so I thought. I was merely the fourth son and sixth child of the king and queen's eight children, with no hope of the throne. When have you heard a story about the fourth prince before? I flatter myself that this may be the first.

At least my status meant that the courtiers and servants did not trouble themselves to hide their thoughts from me. I learned much of what happened in my father's kingdom from them, most important, that none of my father's subjects had any reason to love him. I also heard the whispers before Prince Raven arrived. "Did you hear? One of Princess Aruna's suitors, he's a real vampire! From beyond the mountains of the Western Wall, I heard." And so it went until I might have pitied the fellow were I not so intent on pitying myself.

Still, something about him intrigued me and I imagined what he might be like before he arrived. I wondered, along with the court, why one of the vampire princes would aim so low as one of my sisters. Not merely because I loathed each and every one of them, mind, but because the vampire kingdom beyond the mountains was rumored to be full of beautiful women and men alike.

It was also said that the vampires were rich beyond the dreams of mortal men, and deathless in the bargain. They seldom intruded on the lands of men since their infatuated victims often gave themselves up by choice. Why bother with a living bride, especially one like Aruna who was neither beautiful nor kind? True, there were other tales that said that the vampires' powers were fading and that they could no longer hold their lands as they once had. But I had no way to judge the truth of any of these rumors and gave them small consideration.

On the night that the vampire prince arrived, I sat sulking in my usual corner of my father's banquet hall with Kriun the jester. Kriun, like me, was short and blond, slender and elfin in the court of dark giants that ruled over the peasants who looked like us. That was one reason I liked him so much, the other being that, as the butt of all the jokes that weren't directed at me, he was my companion in suffering.

Not that he saw it as such. "Fine fish, tonight, lad. Eat up! We may not eat so well again tomorrow." He belched contentedly as the last of the fish he had purloined from the kitchens vanished into his gullet, then scowled at the door. The scowl made the scar on his cheek twist into something fierce and harsh for a moment before his face lapsed into his usual foolish smile.

I turned to see what he was looking at and saw that the vampires had arrived. The word does no justice to the way they appeared, their eyes old and full of secrets, their faces perfect in their weird splendor. They came in, silent as cats but for the clink of their armor, trailing in the wake of their prince.

To see a score of them in company, shining in my

father's court like small suns, was a magnificent sight. And yet there was something about them that sent shivers down my spine, as if they might turn and begin to hunt amongst us without warning. There was a bit of the monster about them still, despite their wisdom and beauty.

Then it was that I caught my first glimpse of my sister's suitor. He was tall and slim like the others but somehow gave the impression of a speed and strength that would be hard to match in battle. His face was pale, white and beautiful, and his hair flowed long and black in a queue down his back. But it was his eyes that made me believe that he was the creature of the rumors. Their silver-gray gaze swept the court with a cold, hungry look like a hawk newly unhooded.

He caught my own stare in their grasp from across the room and I gasped, struggling like a fish on a line. There was something in his gaze that felt as though a single black-gloved hand held my soul and saw all that I thought and felt. I blushed and tried to look away, afraid of having been caught gawking. The strange prince smiled a thin smile with no hint of fang and slowly, oh so slowly released me from his eyes. When I was able to breathe again, Kriun was giving me a strange look. "Don't look at him directly again, lad. He can command your soul if he's all they say he is. The King would kill you with his own sword if he saw even a hint of that come about. Let Aruna lie down with the living corpse and have whatever good there is of it."

He spoke true. The king, my father, had wished me left to the mercy of the wolves when I was a child a thousand times. I could not have said why he hated me so, other than I was the only one of his children to resemble my slim, golden mother. Perhaps it was more than he could bear to see her in my face. Whatever the cause, any infraction, real or imagined, could spark his rage and give him the reason he craved to be free of his least-loved offspring.

I glanced at the scar on Kriun's face, a relic of a time

when he stepped between the king and the object of his wrath, my ten-year-old self. It took no effort to nod my agreement. What was he to me, this vampire prince from beyond the Western Wall who desired the hand of my most hated sister? I turned away.

Once the pleasantries were complete and the prince had been presented to Aruna and the important folk of the court, the evening began in truth. My father had not stinted the flood of gold necessary to bring about the most magnificent feast I had ever seen or heard of. If all manner of delicacies and gallons of sheep's blood alone were enough to sway the heart of the prince, then Aruna was as good as wed.

Idly, I wondered if the blood had truly come from sheep or if my father was bleeding the unfortunates in the dungeons. I spared a small thought for their agonies, poor souls. The cold distance of my father's face as he sat on his throne brought me no more comfort than usual. In fact, the vampires looked almost kindly in comparison. I shuddered and turned to the small plate of food that Kriun had seized from the main table.

The banquet went on around us, turning from food to entertainment and from thence to dancing. I would have sat on in my corner at peace were it not for my sister Eria. When the dancing began, nothing would please her more than that her ugly brother would stand up to dance with her, painting her as a beauty in comparison.

Eria simpered and pretended to smile down at me, her eyes cold as the prince's, withholding all her usual taunts behind closed lips. Yet her face spoke volumes and it was as if she spoke aloud, so her silence was no boon. By the time we finally danced in a pairing with Aruna and her prince, I would have given anything to be forgotten.

He glanced at me again, eyes burning through me with a mocking stare. Aruna whispered something to him and he looked deliberately away, contempt written all over his features. At that moment, I hated him more than my entire family, were such a thing possible. Had I any skill with a sword, I might have challenged him at once but since I had none, I finished the dance with what dignity I could muster. Then I turned on my heel without a word to Eria and left the hall to begin the long, weary climb to my half-ruined tower room. I was done with feasting.

I seized a flagon of my father's finest wine as I left and I sipped it as I walked, remembering the prince's eyes. He had looked at me as though I were nothing, as though I could never be worthy of his notice. The realization made my flesh start and burn as though I had been struck and my heart raced with anger. I stormed along the passage, paying little attention to my surroundings.

That was why I didn't see Aruna's vampire when he appeared in the corridor before me so suddenly that we collided and I dropped the flagon. He looked down his nose at me. "Are you always so rude, dwarf prince of the Northern Kingdom? You leave your sister unpartnered and unescorted, you smash your unwanted self into your father's guests—these things do not bode well if we are to be one clan."

He towered above me, as did all at the court except Kriun, and blocked my passage so that I could not ignore him. "Move aside, sir. My sister may barter her body and soul to you but you will never be a brother to me as long as I draw breath." I was shaking with fury now, glaring at him as if I could force my way past.

With a speed that made me gasp, he spun me back against the stone wall and braced his hands against the rock at either of my shoulders so I could not flee. His face was inches from mine as he hissed, "You are quick to assume that your sister is good enough for one whose lineage stretches back to the Elder Kings, foolish brat. I see that the blood of your kingdom's Old Ones runs true in your veins, yet even they are children compared to the years of my people."

What Old Ones did he mean? I had heard the tales of the ones who lived here before my great-grandfather conquered the kingdom but all of those folk had been destroyed or enslaved. There was nothing left of them but the tiny, blond peasants and they had naught to do with me. I nearly shrugged as I dismissed my thoughts. Who knew how the vampires entertained themselves? Perhaps he simply lied.

His eyes burned into me as if he read my doubts. I was wrenched back from my thoughts to find myself still held captive by a being I despised. I found the words to say as much. "What do you want with her, then? Our lineage is as good as yours, creature of the night. My sister can marry any one of a dozen lords."

"You were simpleminded farmers when my people took the Western lands. Your sister is worth nothing more or less than the alliance she brings and the lands that will be linked to mine. As her husband, I will occupy the throne of this sty and this kingdom will be mine, or have you forgotten that?"

The blood burned in my veins. "Sty? I wonder that you bother to soil your hands with us then, great Prince! Or are the tales true? Do your powers fade with time and your lands slip from your fingers?" I did not expect an answer and he did not grant me one.

"As for you . . ." he bared his fangs as he hissed, "Do you think I could not command you to love me if I wanted to? You would beg for the honor of my notice then."

I could see his fangs when he spoke and I knew that some of what I heard was true. He might control me or even kill me in an instant and I was powerless before him. I looked deep into his eyes, forgetting Kriun's warning and took a long breath. He smelled of wild magic and something else, something I could not name but it pierced me so that I found my anger again. "Oh, all-powerful Prince! Now I see the error of my ways and prepare myself to adore you in any way you see fit! How weak do you think I am, monster? Save your powers to bend men to your will for my father and my sister, and let me pass."

His eyes darkened at my sarcasm and for a moment my knees trembled. I could feel the cordlike strength of the muscles in his arms on either side of mine and I knew I could not defeat him in battle. So we remained for an eternity until he dropped his arm and turned from me with a curl of his lip. He stalked away before I could demand to know what he was doing in that corridor so far from the guest quarters.

I opened my mouth to call after him, to demand an accounting of his actions but no words came. Instead I, too, turned and continued toward my tower, trying to ignore the shaking of my hands and knees. I reached my room without further incident and bolted the door behind me before I collapsed on my hard bed. There I lay, wrapped in my threadbare blankets and tried to forget what I had seen.

But even after I fell into an uneasy sleep, his face haunted my dreams. When at last I fell from the bed to land on the cobbled floor, it was because in the final dream, he ripped my tunic from me to sink his sharp fangs into my neck. His flesh was cold as ice against mine and my body craved his, even as he stole my life away. It was my yell of denial that helped force me awake to see the dawn outside.

I groaned and passed my fingers through my shoulder-length hair with a shudder. What had that creature done to me? Even now, my flesh was still hard from my dream and it made me sick to see it. Was I so reduced that I wanted a monster to take me and consume me like a pheasant at my father's banquet? And the monster was not even one of the beautiful vampire women from the tales. I retched and dove for the icy harshness of the washbasin, determined to wash all such thoughts from my head.

When I went to the kitchens to break my fast, I avoided the corridors near the guest quarters. Maybe the legends which said that the prince and his people must spend the daylight hours asleep were not true. I wanted to see no more of my monstrous brother-to-be than I was forced to.

But despite my precautions, it was clear when I reached my destination that I could do nothing to avoid hearing about him. All the talk was of the prince and his retinue, his wealth, his thirst for blood. True, he had drunk sheep's blood last night and seemed pleased enough with it then, but what would happen once the lovely princess was in his bed? And on it went until I fled to avoid hearing more.

I chose the library as my hiding place for the day, knowing that I would not be discovered there. I curled up in one of the decaying chairs with a dusty leather book that none of my brothers or sisters would dream of reading. But eventually, the dry history was too much even for me and I fell asleep.

I do not know how long it was that I drifted in slumber but there was a fire on the hearth when I awoke. I smiled to see it, warm for the first time all day. Then I stretched my stiffened limbs, swearing softly at the small pains. It was then that I realized that there was a cloak spread over me and that I was no longer alone in the library.

The prince sat watching me, an unread book open in his own lap. I started and the book I held fell unheeded to the floor with a loud thump. "What are you doing here? You startled me." My words sounded unnecessary, hovering in the air amid the cloud of dust from the books.

"Afraid to wake and find the monster feeding from your

open veins, princeling? I'll trouble you for my cloak if you're done with it."

I scrambled to my feet, holding the cloak out to him as if its touch stung me. He took it with a wry and twisted smile that did not reach his eyes. Somehow it gave me my courage back. "You visit a room you'll never see Aruna in when she comes to your castle." I smirked in the knowledge of my own superiority.

The prince rose so fast I leapt backward only to be stopped by his hand under my chin. He tilted my face upward so I had to meet his eyes and they swallowed me. It almost felt as if his lips brushed mine but I knew that could not be. Instead I heard the sting of his words. "You bore me with your assumptions, princeling. Mayhap I come here only to feed my people and not to wed at all. Do your nightmares not tell you as much?" I found my voice with an effort. "It's a long way from the Western Wall to my father's court. Were there no peasants or barbarian ladies you might have tasted along the way with greater ease? Or is the throne of this 'sty' temptation enough?" I hated him more in that moment than I had ever hated anyone before and my hands trembled with the strength of my anger.

. "Perhaps it might be. If I wed Aruna," his lips twisted, "I shall live here in this delightful castle with her equally delightful family. I might even come to their chambers on moonlit nights to sample all they had to give me. What do you say to that?"

"Let me go. They say you do not take unwilling victims. My sister is willing to give herself to you. She should be enough." My anger cooled just enough for me to feel afraid and I hated myself for it.

"What do you know about it, princeling beast?" I flinched. How kind of Aruna to share the family's nick-name for me with this thing. He ran his thumb over my lower lip, tugging it downward and leaning in close to whisper in my ear. "I think I will always call you that. It suits you."

"Am I to call you 'beauty' then?" I snorted as I jerked away. "Begone, monster!" I fumbled at my neck for the old silver cross that my grandmother had given me and yanked it free of my clothes. The vampire prince looked at me and laughed. It was a hearty laugh, one that showed his fangs and made me shudder. Then he turned and left the library, still laughing.

I shivered and shuddered at the heat coursing through my veins and the anger that filled me from head to toe. And yet . . . I could feel such sensations within me that I could scarcely bear to contemplate. My lip burned where his finger had touched it and my ear echoed with the sound of his whisper. Some part of me longed to encounter him again. My senses reeled with confusion.

Clearly he was a monster and nothing more, and yet he laid his cloak on me while I slept. He had a servant start a fire or had started it himself so that I would be warm. In a life unaccustomed to kindness, he had shown me a little and it was more than I could bear. I flung myself into the chair by the fire and gave vent to my anger in silent weeping until my hunger sent me to the banquet hall for dinner.

There I sat in my distant corner and ate my usual fare of the king's leavings. I watched the prince and tried to hate him more than my father who sat at his side. But I could not find it in me since I had hated my father far longer. A voice pulled me from my thoughts. "The prince sends this with his warmest regards." Cheeks flaming, I glanced up at one of the prince's servitors. He set the tray he carried down on the bench next to me and vanished as silently as he appeared.

For a moment, I thought about throwing it to the dogs. But there was Kriun watching me askance and a plate of food finer than I had ever eaten set before me. I ate, sharing it with my father's jester, fearing that my father or Aruna had noticed this strange act of kindness and would make me pay for it later. Or that the prince himself sought only to fatten me up for his own future meal. Still I ate, savoring the sweetness of the roast bird and tried to ignore all that it might mean.

My father called Kriun to entertain his guests but I could not bear to stay and watch my friend play the fool. Too often I had helped to ease his bruises when the king or one of the courtiers did not find him amusing enough. My intervention would only mean more punishment later for both of us so instead I slipped quietly from the hall.

This time, it was Aruna and not her prince, who found me in the corridors. She slipped up behind me, wrapping a meaty arm around my throat and squeezing until I flailed the air with my arms, trying to get free. "I've seen the way he looks at you, beast, and I won't stand for it. He's mine and I won't have any of his misplaced sympathy for our mother's mistake interfering. You are to stay away from him or I will have you brought to the dungeons and tormented until you beg for death."

"Father would never permit it," I gasped, barely able to get the words out.

Aruna laughed, a harsh cruel sound that echoed off the stone walls. "Father would help heat the irons. You're none of his get, fool. Surely you've realized that by now. You live only because our mother protected you. Now that she's gone, it's just a matter of time."

I flailed harder, breaking her hold as the sound of approaching servants came up the corridor behind us. She watched me scamper away, her look burning its way through the back of my tunic. So the king was not truly my father? This was almost too much to hope for, despite my terror. I ran up the stairs to my tower, barring the door and barricading it with the old bureau. My sister was quite capable of carrying out her threats, as I knew of old.

I spent a sleepless night turning what she said over in my mind. True, she might have lied, but her words had the ring of truth. When the sun rose the next day, I had decided on a plan. It would take me several days to steal all that I needed, but once I succeeded in that, I would leave the castle of my father and go out into the world. It could be no harsher than my family and there would be no monsters to haunt my sleep or baffle me with periodic kindnesses.

The decision brought me some peace as the day passed in a blur. I darted from hiding place to hiding place, taking an apple here, a pack or a waterskin there. Ever since I'd been able to walk, I had explored every hidden cubby, every secret passage in the castle until I could vanish for hours, completely undiscovered. It was in one of these that I hid what I found, confident that no one would find it there. When I thought I had purloined all that would not be missed in a single day, I went openly to the kitchen and begged some bread and cheese. This I took once more to the library, though trepidation filled me at what I might find there.

I would say that I didn't think of the beautiful, monstrous prince during the long hours of hiding and stealing but there would be no truth in it. I imagined his thumb on my lip, his teeth in my neck, until it seemed as if he might emerge from any one of a thousand hidden corners. I berated myself soundly for this sickness of mind that seemed to hold me whenever I thought of him, but to no avail.

Still, I was relieved not to find him in the library. True, that meant no fire and no warm cloak, but the cold was a small price to pay to be at peace for a time. To my surprise, there was enough wood in the hearth to make a fire myself, so I indulged myself in this small luxury and sat watching the flames and warming my half-frozen feet. Idly, I found that the flames reminded me of his eyes and I wrinkled my nose in disgust at the quality of my own dreams.

At the time, I thought that this was how he was able to appear so noiselessly at my side, but then I was not so used to his powers. "Little beast. We meet again." His voice was dry, richly amused, and I started a little from my chair, heart pounding.

"My sister has threatened my life if I speak to you again, my lord." I was afraid of Aruna, but I said it mainly to ruin her chances. I would be gone long before their betrothal was announced, surely. And he should know that he had found his match for brutality. I looked up at him, noticing the open neck of his shirt and the lean muscles it exposed, and I tried to look away.

He knelt before me with a soft crackling of wool and leather and black silk so his eyes were level with mine. They went on forever and I was not surprised to feel his gloved hand on my chin. "Are you afraid of your sister, beautiful little beast?" I nodded, unable to take refuge in a brave lie. Part of me wondered about his new name for me; no one had ever thought me "beautiful" before. I wondered then if he spoke to all his meals this way and I shuddered.

"Then I'll speak and you keep silent," he murmured. I tried to tug free of his hand, his eyes, but found myself immobile, frozen. He fastened his mouth on mine, leaving me to howl my protests into the muffling softness of his tongue.

I flailed, trying to free myself from the awful pressure of his mouth, but he held me in a grip like iron, pulling me close to his cold flesh. I made the futile gesture of shoving at his breast, gasping for air as his mouth relentlessly claimed mine. I could feel the edge of his fangs against my tongue and wailed in pure terror. He broke off his terrible kiss then, and reaching his hand up into my hair, bent my face backward so that my neck was exposed.

"Let me go, monster!" I found my voice in a single burst of sound.

"I could take you now and make you one of us. I can tell that you are not completely unwilling." He murmured the words against the skin of my neck, sending shivers all over my flesh. I could feel his fangs rest against me like a dagger's edge and I writhed to get away but he held me fast. He opened the neck of my tunic to bare more of my shoulder and he showered me with obscene, burning kisses, agonizingly slow.

Then his hand found its way down between my legs, cupping what it found there. To my shame, I hardened at his touch and he laughed at my flesh's betrayal of my spirit. He lowered his face, still holding me in place and kissed his way down to where it strained at my leggings. He kissed me through my clothes and I moaned, a small tortured sound. I burned with sickened desire, feeling it engulf me like a wave even as I fought it with all my strength. He murmured, "Such a beautiful boy should be immortal. Don't you agree?"

Sheer terror took me then, and I kicked at him in a fury. He laughed and raised his face to my neck. His fingers continued to stroke me, cupping and caressing until it was almost more than I could bear. "Stop it! I'll kill you if you make me one of you! I swear I will!" I screamed the words as he bit me gently at the base of my neck. My body was betraying me to his touch but I would not let my weakness deny me vengeance. This I swore to myself.

"You seem to be enjoying my touch." His fingers lingered until my breath quickened in pace with my heart.

"No! Let me go!" I wailed even though my body begged for things I could not bear to imagine.

"So fierce a princeling should be taken willingly." He smiled down at me, fangs barely visible at the corners of his lips and gave me a final kiss, more gentle than the first.

He released my face and removed his hand from between my legs, leaving me to spit and swear at him from the safety of the chair. "But I am accustomed to getting what I desire, little beast. I do not think that you will be an exception. Remember that."

"My name is Allain, not 'beast,' you foul creature. I'm not a boy, either! I came of age this year." I spat the words as I managed to fling myself from the chair and leap behind it, giving myself the illusion of security.

"In that case, you may call me Raven, little beast. And I will call you whatever I please."

The arrogance of this . . . thing left me as breathless as his ruthless kiss had earlier. I stared after him as he left the room in a swirl of black cloak, fuming but unable to find the suitable words to hurl at his departing back. I made due by wiping my mouth furiously as though that would clear his kiss from my lips. How dare he make me feel this way? My entire body still shivered and shuddered at the memory of his touch.

Finally I could bear it no longer and doused the fire. I was ravenous and I needed to eat more than bread and cheese or I might faint the next time I had to elude my sister or her suitor. I would also require all my strength to flee before the next banquet three nights hence. That was when the prince would make his official proposal to her and I could not bear to sit and watch that particular farce.

That determination filled me as I darted into the kitchen and tried to beg some tidbits from the cook. There it was that Kriun found me. From the dark frown creasing his normally cheerful face, I knew something was amiss and my heart sank even before he spoke. "Hello, lad. It seems that your sister's suitor has a desire to see her entire family at dinner. The king bids me make sure that you're ready and present." He looked as though the words burned his lips in passing.

I met his eyes and knew that he would pay the price if I

failed to appear as ordered, so I gave him a cheerful smile. "Well then, let's make me look like as much of a prince as we can before the ordeal begins." He smiled back at me, gratitude and some other fleeting emotion crossing his face in rapid succession.

We climbed up to my tower in silence, holding back all questions until we were far from prying ears. But a startling sight met my eyes when I flung open the door. Stretched across my pallet was a tunic and cloak made, seemingly, of silver and moonlight, with leggings and boots to match. I reached out cautiously to touch the fine silk and embroidery, almost as if I were afraid that it would vanish once caressed. This must be Raven's doing, since I could imagine it coming from no other. I would be fortunate if my sister did not poison me at dinner.

"That prince of Aruna's takes too great an interest in you, boy. Nothing good can come of this," Kriun grumbled.

"That's why I've decided to leave, old friend. I need only to steal enough gold and warm clothes to sustain me until I can get further south. I've already got food and waterskins and the other supplies that I need hidden away." I yanked off my threadbare tunic and stripped out of the rest of my old and nearly outgrown garments. Kriun looked away, as if he could not bear to watch.

I felt a moment of shame that I had not thought of the effect of my news on my only friend. But the words could not be unsaid, so I went to the wash basin and cleaned my face and what I could of the rest of me. When I was done, Kriun was staring out the window at the mountains outside. "There's something I must tell you, Your Highness." He paused and I froze at his tone. He gestured and I sat, sinking slowly down onto my bedding. He never used my title unless he was very serious. Hoping he would not attempt to dissuade me, I waited for him to continue.

"You know that I served your mother; the past is

common knowledge in the kitchens and servant's halls." I nodded. There were even whispers that he had been her lover but I had never given them any weight. Now I wondered. He continued, his eyes still fixed on the mountains outside, an audible knife-edge of hatred in his voice now. "She was the last of her line, the last of the rulers of the Old Blood who were not wiped out by the present king and his ancestors. I remained at her side as her counselor as long as she sat as queen."

"So the king is not my father? Aruna said as much." I trailed off at the look in his eyes.

"That monster! The creature who sits on the throne of this land is as much a thing of evil as the one who seeks Aruna's hand. He stole the throne from you and rules your people with the sword. Remember that, my prince. Your mother had a lover of the Old Blood, one of the last surviving scions of the merchant houses who stayed faithful. He was your father. This is why the king hates you so. He cannot kill you openly because he acknowledged you as his to stop tongues from wagging."

"Where is my real father?" I felt the relief of placing down a great burden. Aruna and others were not my true brothers and sisters. I could not keep a smile from my lips.

"He's long dead by your father's hand, lad. And now you have come of age and have no protection. We must flee to the wild lands of the border. There we might be able to raise an army of your people and retake your throne." He held up his hand to stop my questions. "I must go with you. I swore to your mother that I would always protect you."

I watched his face for a span of breaths, imagining a life far from the castle, which was all I knew. My mother died when I was but nine winters old, and my memories of her were fading, despite my best efforts. She had been kind and beautiful, teaching me to read in the old library and training me in the ways of the land. Now Kriun and the blood in my veins were all I had to remember her by. I went to embrace him, wrapping my arms tight around his shoulders. "Thank you, Kriun."

When he turned, there were tears in his eyes but all he said was, "Come lad, let us get you ready for tonight. Do not trouble yourself to steal any gold since I have enough coin put aside for us both. I also have some of your brothers' clothes that should fit. We can leave tomorrow night." I grinned my agreement at him as he helped me put on the magnificent clothes.

Once he was done and I was dressed, I caught a glimpse of myself in the bit of broken mirror that served me for a glass and paused in shock. I knew myself to be plain and drab. I had been told as much since I was a child. Now I barely recognized the figure I saw. A prince, in truth rather than name alone, stared back at me and the sight filled me with foreboding. Aruna would recognize the source of the change and either she or my father would make me pay dearly for it.

But, alas, we would be missed tonight so I could not flee before the banquet. I squared my shoulders and slipped my eating knife into the sheath that hung from the magnificent silver-embroidered belt. Perhaps the prince would pay no attention to me and all would be well. My heart ached a bit at the thought and I swore silently at myself for my strange weakness. But Kriun had begun the long climb down the tower stairs so I forced myself to follow at his heels.

We arrived in the hall just as the king and my half brothers and sisters entered. I was able to sit several seats down the table from Aruna and the empty chair next to her, something that I hoped would keep me from notice. The others favored me with nods and predatory glares, but nothing more. But that changed subtly when the prince arrived with his retinue.

Raven's gaze took in my family with a lazy contempt

that sent a thrill through me. In it was all the loathing I feared ever to let them see, and I very nearly liked him for it. But I remembered the library and thought instead of throwing my eating knife at him. They made me feel ugly and unlovable. He had made feel unclean and ashamed. I could not be away from them all soon enough, and it was all I could do to remain at the table.

At that instant he caught my eyes in his own, and his thin lips curled in a smile both wanton and cruel. I gasped for breath, my heart racing and cheeks flaming as he tilted his goblet toward me before he turned to Aruna and the king. Now my half sisters and brothers watched me side-long and a frown darkened the king's brow until I trembled in my chair. I forced myself to eat and drink as though nothing was amiss but it seemed an eternity before it was done and the servants began to clear the table.

All rose and I was able to slip from the hall unnoticed in the confusion, or so I thought. Kriun was nowhere to be seen so I followed the corridor that led to his room in hopes of finding him. Aruna's retainers must have followed me from the hall because it was there they found me and seized my arms, stopping my mouth with a gag so I could not cry out. A sharp blow to the head ended my attempts to break free and I sank into a cold darkness.

When I awoke, I was chained facing a dank stone wall, my arms and legs outstretched and fastened so I could not move them. From the corner of my eye, I could turn enough to see that I was in one of the lower dungeons and that all the men present were my sister's creatures. I knew then that I would be shown no mercy and I gave myself up for lost.

That feeling only worsened when Aruna herself entered carrying a long carter's whip in her hands. She would think nothing of beating me to death or nearly so. I tugged frantically at the chains when I realized what was about to happen but could not free myself. She laughed to see it and I ceased rather than give her amusement. "I told you what I would do to you, beast. And I am a woman who keeps her word." She snapped the whip through the air and I bit my lips to hold back a whimper.

The first blow stung a little but since they had not removed my tunic, I was able to bear it. I found my thoughts turning to Raven and marveled that I should be punished for attracting the attentions of a prince whom I hated. Still, a part of me rejoiced that I had taken something from Aruna, even if she killed me for it.

The fourth blow made me moan and the eighth to shriek as my sister's whip began to cut through the fine cloth to my skin. Now I stopped thinking, stopped imagining the vampire's face as I had seen him in the library when he caressed my flesh. Once my tunic hung in shreds and each blow landed on my bare flesh, I ceased to count or to attempt to hold back my cries. Thus it was that I failed to hear the door creak open.

"My, what an interesting entertainment. I had no idea that you enjoyed the sight of blood so much, my dear." Raven's voice was bored, slightly cruel with twisted amusement. Over the sound of my labored breathing, I could hear the hiss of my sister's displeasure. He continued, "Perhaps we can add to your enjoyment once my hand is joined to yours. For the moment, however, your brother amuses me and I intend to take him with me. I assume you're done?"

Something dark and menacing crept beneath his tone, like a snake coiling and the retainer who had brought me the food now appeared at my side with a key. In moments, I was released from my bonds, crumpling to the floor as my legs failed to support me. The vampires carried me from the dungeon and their prince followed behind them still chatting with my sister as if naught was amiss. I hung half-swooning from their arms and wondered a little at what my fate was to be. I saw him kiss her hand as the darkness took me and I surrendered to the pain.

When I awoke, I found myself in the prince's chambers. I was lying naked and face down on a huge soft bed. My wounds had been treated and they pained me far less than they had earlier. For that I was grateful. But then Raven chose to lie down at my side and drowned that feeling in a flood of pure terror. He had removed his cloak and tunic and the white flesh of his breast gleamed in the firelight. I forced myself to turn and sit up despite the agony of the motion. A tear I could not hold back leaked from my eye.

He reached out his hand and ran a white finger down my cheek following the track of the single tear. "It seems that I am to blame at least in part for your punishment, princeling. Your sister is quite vicious in her defense of what she feels to be her own." He was much closer now, leaning so close that I could feel the coldness of his bare flesh. Somehow, I could not move away, despite my terror.

He stroked my breast, caressing me lightly until his hand reached the leg I had pulled up to shield myself. "Let me atone for my sins, little beast, little Allain. I can make you forget the agonies of the whip if you will but surrender to me for a time."

I shuddered and tried to turn away but he held my face and kissed me, a long deep kiss that left me breathless. I tried to summon the strength to defy him but somehow it had all fled under the whip's caress. I wondered if his desire had been heightened by the sight of blood pouring from my back as my clothes were flogged from me. I tried to ask him as much, though I had no longing to hear the answer.

Somehow he understood what I was trying to say, despite my inability to form the words. "Your blood was every bit as sweet as I imagined. I took only what you had already lost, princeling. It is my nature to drink even if I do not often kill to take it." He pressed himself against me, stirring my reluctant desires until I reached out my hand and touched his face.

Then he leaned me back against the pillows with a care and tenderness that brought fresh tears to my eyes and I wept as he kissed me again and again. His lips and hands were everywhere on my naked flesh and I hardened against him, longing filling me until I could remember nothing but wanting him.

Then, to my horror, he lowered his face between my legs and took my hardened flesh into his mouth. I screamed then with the last of the strength that I had to resist him, "No! Let me go!" I flailed my legs a little but he rolled over so that he lay on top of them. His mouth did not falter, wet and warm somehow, in spite of the coldness of his flesh. His tongue caressed me and I could feel the edge of his fangs touch my skin.

He watched me as he moved his mouth up and down on me, his hands doing things to me that made me scream and to beg him to stop. But to my shame, I found that in my secret heart I wanted him to continue, to taste my flesh with abandon, and that he did.

Soon it was more than I could stand and my body shook in ecstasy as I spilled my seed into his mouth. He licked it from my body, his eyes never leaving mine. There was an expression in them that I had never seen before and it made me blush to see it, even when I could not give it a name. He rose from between my legs and unfastened his leggings so that I could see the hardness of his own flesh and I gasped at its size and length.

I drew back fearfully as he stretched himself over my legs with his head on the pillow next to mine. He guided my hand to the swordlike hardness between his legs and forced my fingers around it. Then he twined his own fingers with my own and moved my hand on his flesh. His face twisted in a grimace of pleasure and he kissed me once more as he spilled his own seed on my bare flesh.

It burned strangely against my skin, sending a shudder through me that was enough to bring me to my senses. "You monster! I would never have let you touch me if . . ." If I wasn't wounded. If I didn't long for you so. I bit the thoughts back before they could become words. But he smiled down at me as if he could read them unsaid.

I gathered all my remaining strength and rolled from the bed with a painful wrench of my flayed skin. I found the rags that my silver clothes had become and pulled them on as if they would still cover me. The prince watched me from the bed, his lips twisted in a wry smile. "You know, I like them better that way." I looked down. My tunic and leggings hung in rags from me, exposing more of my flesh than they covered and I blushed despite myself. "There's a small cloak in the wardrobe if you insist on leaving."

He got up, body gleaming white and beautiful in the firelight. I watched him approach as the mouse watches the snake, knowing it is doomed yet unable to flee. "I never thought to find so beautiful a boy in one of the barbarian mortal lands. Come with me to my kingdom, princeling beast. Leave this clan that is no clan and join me." He circled me, running caressing fingers over my bare skin then pulling me close so he could kiss my neck and bare shoulder. Then he sent his hand once more between my legs.

"Nooo!" I wailed, determined not to succumb to him again. He would kill me; this I knew in the depths of my very heart. He would make me a vampire catamite, forever young and forever enslaved. And Aruna would hunt me down and stake my sleeping body during the day. I knew what she was capable of.

I exerted all my powers of resistance and to my surprise, I was able to break free of his grasp and run to the door. I flung it open to flee into the darkened corridor beyond. Once there, the madness of the night overtook me and I ran until I went to ground like a hare in one of the secret corridors. Both sister and prince knew where I slept so there was nothing to keep either or both from my tower room. I was safer in hiding for the moment. Despite the coldness of the stone around me, I fell into an uneasy sleep filled with unclean dreams.

Perhaps it was one of them that awoke me some time later. I could hear noises in the main corridor beyond the wall, the swishing drag of something being hauled across the stone floor. I wondered what it was that would be dragged instead of carried. Surely, I thought drowsily, moving whatever it was that way would simply rub holes in it and let the contents drain out.

Then I heard Aruna's voice and tried to curl even deeper into the darkness of my hiding place. At first I could not make out the words but then she drew closer to the wall and I heard her say, "This will bring the creature out of hiding. Then he is mine." And she laughed coldly, sending echoes through the hollow stone that made me cover my ears.

Did she mean Raven? Why would he be hiding? And what could they be doing that would bring him into my half sister's unkind hands? Of course, it was no concern of mine if she sought to harm her own suitor. So I told myself and so I tried to believe. But as hard as I tried to tell myself that his fate was nothing to me, I could not drive his face from my mind.

Finally I could stand it no more and I rose to follow the passage I occupied as far as I could before it ended in an exit in a hidden alcove. I slid out as soundlessly as a mouse, my skills honed by years of practice, and found myself in the corridor behind my sister's men. An ancient stone statue hid me for the moment but I was very cautious as I peered around it to see what they were doing.

I could see little at first but as they passed under one of the few torches well down the corridor from my hiding place, I could see that they dragged a limp body behind them. I wondered who the unfortunate was, since all who

went to the dungeons in my father's house were unfortunate or soon would be. I could not see his face but a
strange and morbid curiosity took hold of me. I needed to
know who this was. I crept along the wall behind them,
avoiding the circles of torchlight as much as possible. Then
they paused beneath a torch well ahead of me and tossed
the limp body onto the shoulder of the biggest guard. Its
hood fell off and I saw the flash of golden hair. Kriun.

I managed to strangle the cry that leapt to my lips. My
heart raced and it was only with difficulty that I imposed
order on my thoughts. If they saw me, I would join him
and they would simply kill us both. I had to see where they
were taking him first. Then I could devise a plan to rescue
him. My heart was in my throat as I trailed after my sister
and her men, hoping they would do no more than chain
him up in the dungeons.

Yet something in my sister's voice made me fear that was
a vain hope. Trembling with fear for my only friend and
myself, I followed them down and down into the depths
of the castle, into the darkest levels of the dungeons. Eventually they stopped and I managed to hide myself in a
recess as they carried Kriun inside. I slunk closer, my back
always to the wall, my feet sliding over the stone as if I
walked on air. As if our very lives depended on it.

Finally I got as close as I dared to the open door, just near
enough to make out some of what they were saying. I heard
Aruna laugh before she spoke and the sound sent chills down
my spine, "Your life will be short but less merry than you
might have dreamed, fool. You should have left the kingdom
after the queen died instead of troubling yourself about the
boy. What does it matter to you who sits on the throne?"

Kriun's voice was faint but stern. "The prince is of the
Old Blood. He bears the right to rule the kingdom, not
your family of usurpers." I pressed myself against the wall,
imagining myself as king, the dungeons emptied and the

peasants free, those demons I thought my family in exile. The vision filled me with indescribable gladness. Not that it mattered, since I had no army to take back what was mine. Better to flee, perhaps to build an army in hiding, perhaps only to live in a less hostile world.

But not without Kriun. His words were followed by the sound of a ringing blow, of flesh meeting flesh. How long they beat him I could not say because I fled. Not from fear, you understand, but because I realized that I could not aid him by myself. There were too many of them and they might kill him while I lingered, trying to find a way to trick them away from his side. That realization lent wings to my feet and I scrambled up the stairs toward the upper levels with every bit of speed I could find in my trembling limbs.

When I reached the corridor with the guest quarters, I slowed, appalled by the only option before me. I had no other friends in the castle. The king and his children would turn their hands against me and though some of the servants were kind, I could not trust them to aid me in this. There was only one who had the might to help me rescue Kriun. But the price would be all I had.

I froze before the door to Raven's chamber, trying to find my courage. I remembered how Kriun had stood between myself and the enraged king. I remembered how he had soothed my back after beatings, had listened to the futile wailing of my young heart at the cruelty of my family. How he had stolen food and clothes for me and done all that my true father could have done. Then I knocked on the wooden door, praying that it was still dark outside and that the vampires were yet awake.

At first, I heard no sound within and I rested my head against the wooden planks of the door and knew despair. Then at last I heard the bolts being pulled with a great shrieking of iron on wood. The door was opened by the same servant who had brought me food from the king's table. He raised an astonished eyebrow to find me there, but stood aside to let me enter the same chamber I had fled hours before.

Raven was buckling on his sword when I entered and several of his people appeared to be donning armor. All paused to stare at me in what seemed to be astonishment. "Ah. It appears that our rescue efforts were a bit premature." Raven smiled at me and I made myself smile back. He tossed me a piece of parchment with a scrawled message on it. Prince Allain is in the princess's hands. Please, please as you have been kind to him, come and save him now. It was signed with Kriun's name.

I flung it to the floor in disgust. "It's a trap! Kriun never wrote this! She must have thought you would come to rescue me. It's Kriun who she's imprisoned. I fear that she may kill him." The words came out in a rush while the vampires looked on impassively. "Please, Your Highness, I beg your aid as one prince to another. Help me rescue my liege man."

No one even blinked. Finally, Raven broke the silence. "Who is this Kriun to you?"

"He was my mother's counselor. You have seen him at the banquet." I stopped, aware for the first time that I was begging a group of vampire knights to save the king's jester. I hunted for the words to persuade them.

"The jester with the scar? The one who bears the look of the Old Blood of this misbegotten land?" Raven sat on the edge of the bed, one eyebrow raised in cynical astonishment.

"He is my friend, my liege man. The only one who called me 'prince.'" I thought of mentioning love but such an emotion would be too alien to these creatures. Loyalty, I thought they might comprehend. "I am prepared to . . ." I stumbled over the words until I could force them out, "to give you whatever you desire in return for your assistance." I drew in a deep breath, preparing myself for the sacrifice that I intended to make.

Raven frowned, then waved his hand at his people. "Wait for me in Lord Nekaron's room until I call. Prepare the others." His people filed out, taking the servant with them and leaving us alone. I closed my eyes and waited. "Now, Prince, perhaps you might tell me what it is that you think I want."

I moved as close to him as I could bear, close enough to reach out and touch his face. Then I leaned in and kissed him, my lips tentative and nervous against his cold ones. I pressed my body against his but still he did not reach for me. For a long moment I thought I would fall weeping to the floor at his feet. Then I realized what I must do.

I pulled his dagger from his belt and stepped back. With an effort that made me tremble, I rolled my sleeve up to expose my arm. Then I ran the knife's edge in a line from my hand to my elbow so that the red blood gushed to the surface. The pain was almost more than I could bear but I made myself remember Kriun and I did not faint. "Take me." It was the only command I had ever issued and it rolled from my lips with an assurance that I did not feel.

Raven watched the blood run down my arm and I could see the monster rise in his eyes. He was fighting it, looking away. I brought the dagger up to cut off the rags of my tunic, exposing my flesh. I cut off the remains of my leggings, too, and stood before him naked. His nostrils flared, breathing in the scent of my blood, but he still resisted it for what seemed an eternity.

Then he met my eyes, his face going cold and fierce like a wolf's. My heart raced as I saw him become the thing I feared. I was shivering so much I thought I would swoon but I forced myself to hold the dagger up before me like a shield. "Will you honor our bargain, Prince? My blood, my body, for Kriun's life?"

He tilted his head sidelong to study me from those cold eyes and for an instant, he was the Raven from the library. He nodded and I knew that this was the only reassurance I would receive. I could only hope that I would be alive to see Kriun safe. It was my last thought before he moved, his hands a blur as he seized my arm and brought it to his lips. This time he sank his teeth into me without hesitation and drank, pulling me closer as I swayed on my feet. I watched him draw the life from my veins for a breath or two before I fainted.

When I awoke, I was face down on the bed and he crouched naked above me, his cold legs capturing and pinning mine. He rested his fangs on my neck for a moment as he worked his fingers inside me. I could feel the hardness of his flesh above me and I writhed, fearing what was to come and trying to escape.

"Too late for that now, little princeling. You offered me all that I desire and I want my payment now before you change your mind." His voice changed with his looks, and it rolled from his lips with the growling cadence of a wolf. I was but a deer before him and I had to bite my lip to keep from wailing in terror and begging for my life. *Kriun*, I thought, trying to drown myself in memory as my body began to surrender to him. Despite my yielding, some instinct made me writhe against him, hoping to break his hold.

Instead the movement only seemed to inflame him. He reached under me to where my own prick hardened and I moaned a soft, "No!" He laughed, an unnatural sound with the echo of a howl behind it. Then he plunged himself inside me, sinking his teeth into my neck at the same time. I screamed as the first wave of pain shook me, then gasped for breath as he drank from me as if from the king's largest flagon.

The sensation was a terrifying one yet it filled me with some unknown emotion. I knew then what it was to be at the mercy of a monster who wanted all that I had to take, whether I willed it or not. My desire to fight him faded as I thought at first merely to endure his attentions. It was replaced by a lassitude so dreamy that I feared I might swoon again.

He was cold inside me, his spear freezing me even as he thrust ever deeper. It burned inside me until I thought he would pierce me through. Gradually, as my blood fled from my veins, I opened to welcome him despite my terrors. His hand was fierce and demanding on my prick, forcing me to give him all that he desired. I spilled my seed on the bed, surrendering as he took me completely, spending himself inside me with a growl that terrified me. I slipped a little further from my waking dream then, and he released me and forbore to drink further from my veins.

I could feel his lips trail icy kisses up my bare back as he pulled himself from me. I wondered that one so close a kin to the wolf could be so brutal, yet so tender. The thought was too complex for me in my present state and I soon abandoned it in favor of contemplating Kriun's fate. I have never known such an effort to form words before. "Please. I gave you what you wanted. Kriun. You must help." I collapsed into the pillow, unable to summon my legs beneath me to rise from the bed.

"You did indeed, little beast." He caressed me, sending chills over my bare skin. Then he turned my face to kiss me once more and I could taste my blood on his lips. "Where is the jester being held?" I remembered the corridor that I had followed and murmured some incoherent instructions. He held my eyes with his own, seeming to read my thoughts. Then he nodded and rose from the bed. A single clap of his hands and his servant appeared, silent as a cat.

It seemed only moments before a blanket was flung over me and Raven was appareled for battle, long sword at his side. His knights emerged to join him and the sight was as the coming of a terrible dawn. For the first time, I wondered what I had done, calling such beings as these to slake their thirst on my fellow humans. But it was the only way.

My head dropped to the pillow and I surrendered to oblivion before they left the chamber.

It was some time later when I awoke with the hand of the prince's servant on my shoulder. We were no longer in the chamber that had brought me pleasure and pain in such equal parings. Instead, I recognized one of the disused passages where I was accustomed to travel, far from the watchful eyes of the court. I wondered that Raven's servants would know of such a place but spoke another thought first. "Kriun?"

The servant pressed a finger to his lips and gestured at the other servants around us. Only Raven and his knights were missing and we were in hiding. The descent of despair was so sudden and so black it took my breath away. Raven had failed. His life, Kriun's life, all of our lives were forfeit. I blinked tears away, trying to prepare to hear the worst. "Is he dead?" I whispered the words, realizing that I could be speaking either of my friend or Raven, unsure which loss would bring me greater pain.

"We don't know, Highness. Our prince bid us hide here in case he failed, but it is daylight outside now and he is not returned. We fear that he is dead or captive." The servant met my eyes in the flickering light of the torch and I read a despair nearly as great as my own. In that moment, I realized that he was a mortal like myself. I marveled that he would choose to serve the vampire lords, at least until I remembered the cold perfection of Raven's flesh against my own. Then I knew how close I was to the Western Wall and what lay beyond.

I looked up along the stone walls, noting that the pale light of dawn was trickling through the arrow slits on the wall behind me. I closed my eyes to shut out my fears, to shut out the doom that might have befallen my one true friend. One thing I knew beyond all doubt: if I lay here doing nothing, then all hope was lost. I did not know what I could do to save them, if indeed they could be saved, but a way must be found. Else I was unworthy of Kriun's love and unworthy of the throne of my fathers.

I forced myself to my knees, relieved to see that I was clothed once more. I rolled up the overlong sleeves of the tunic and winced at the sight of my arm, ravaged by Raven's teeth. I forced my trembling knees to hold me as I stood and the prince's man rose with me to hold me steady. We stood swaying together a moment as I thought of what to do next. I knew well the secret passages of the castle. Perhaps there might be more beyond the ones that I knew. Perhaps even some that entered the deepest of the dungeons.

The determination to begin, to know the fate of my friend and the prince, propelled me forward as I muttered my thoughts in a rambling surge of words to the servant. Then I realized that I had not even asked his name, he who had saved my life by hiding me. "What is your name?"

"Raoul, Your Highness."

"You will accompany me, yes? Good man. Are there any others here who might be of assistance?" I gestured at the other servants and Raoul beckoned to two of them. No plan came from my fevered brain at first so I simply began to walk. My strange escort moved behind me as I walked held upright by his strong arm.

Soon, I knew where we were and I began to lead us down broken stairs and through deserted corridors. Betimes, we stepped warily across the open corridors to reach more of the secret ways. And all the while my blood beat with the rhythm of fear warring with hope.

I would say that I thought of Kriun and I did, hoping and praying that he was yet alive and unharmed. But it was the vampire prince's face which rose before me and lent wings to my feet, despite all I could do to banish it. I hoped that my fears would lend me strength to do whatever I must at our journey's end.

Lower and lower we descended through stone-lined

passages dank with cold. Now I had to stop more frequently to find holes to look out of, doorways into the known passages to see where we were. Once we hid when some of the king's troops walked past, one of them wiping blood from his hands. I shuddered, praying that it did not belong to one whom I loved. It seemed an eternity before we found our way down to the level where I thought Kriun was held.

I opened the door from the hidden corridor cautiously, unsure of what I would find on the other side. My heart raced to see nothing but an empty corridor before me, lit only by the sputtering of a single torch. I stepped into it, staggering a little as I was still faint. Raoul steadied me. "From here, I am lost," I whispered to my companions. "We need to find out where your master is being held captive." I gestured in either direction.

One of the servants shrugged and slipped down the corridor to see what he could see. After a moment, the other went the opposite direction while Raoul leaned my swaying form against a wall. An eternity passed before the man who had taken the right-hand path appeared and waved from the far end of the corridor. I walked toward him, my hand against the rough stone for support while Raoul went to fetch the other servant.

For some reason, the fellow seemed further and further away with each step of the winding corridor, almost as if he moved away from me deliberately. I followed him around several turns and past some other passages, still vainly trying to catch up with him. Finally I opened my mouth to call to him to wait, only to find that there was no need as I turned the corner.

He lay on the stone of the corridor at my sister's feet. The king stood at her side, wiping his dripping sword on the body's clothes. Behind them stood ten men at arms. Aruna gave me a smile that might have been birthed from deepest winter. "Hello, 'brother.' " She reached out, catching my arm in an iron grip. "You see the wounds, Father? He has given himself to the vampires. No doubt the fool told him that he was the rightful ruler of the land before he died or some such other nonsense. The beast thought to make an alliance with his grotesque little body. How pathetic."

News of Kriun's death shot through me like an arrow and I bit my lip hard to hold back a sob. The king glowered down at me from under fearsome black brows. "I have spared you until now, traitor's get, for your mother's sake. Now it seems my mercy was misguided. Your true father, my jester, is dead at my hand." Here he seemed to spit the words, his cold eyes alight with hatred. I gaped at him in astonishment. Kriun, my true father? Why had he not told me this?

The king smiled grimly at my surprise. "He did not tell you then. He did not speak of the Old Blood or that you might rule in my place, were I as weak as he? How droll. As if a race of weaklings like you could drive us from this land." Aruna laughed but he waved her to silence. "I give you to the princess, who you have wronged. She shall determine your punishment." He turned away with a look of contempt.

I was in truth doomed; I could see it Aruna's eyes. Still I found the strength to be defiant. "At least my body was sufficient to gain an alliance, my 'sister.' Can you say the same?" I growled the words, somehow twisting free of her grip. For an instant I thought to run but the armsmen circled around behind me and I knew that I could not succeed.

Aruna's slap knocked me to the ground a moment later and left my head ringing too much to think further on the subject. Then I was seized by the arms and dragged down the corridor. I cursed the king and his daughter with every drop of the Old Blood in me, hoping it was strong enough to do them some harm.

The king growled some order at the guards and Aruna

laughed, the sound trailing fingers of ice down my spine. I had failed and now she would succeed in killing all of us. Or at least in marrying Raven if he still lived. The realization that this was a cut near as unbearable as all the rest made me groan, made the hot helpless tears threaten to spill down my cheeks. I could not bear to see her win, could not bear to see him kiss her. I would die before I would see that happen.

Soon it became clear that my wish would be granted. The guards dragged me into a cold stone chamber and chained me to the wall by my neck. A second set of manacles were fastened on my wrists and I was left alone for a few moments to mourn the loss of the only being who had loved me since my mother's death. It seemed only moments but my eyes were raw with weeping when Aruna entered, five of the guards at her heels.

I backed away from them as far as the chains would permit, my eyes anxiously searching the gloom for the whip she had used on me before. "No whip this time, Allain. Now I'll make the punishment fit the crime and there will be no rescue. Your monstrous lover sleeps until sunset and by then you will be dead. But not before you know what it means to try to take what is rightfully mine." Her eyes were feral in the dim light now and I shuddered, making the chains rattle with it.

She stepped away and waved her men forward and I knew fear greater than any I had known before. They encircled me, each one bigger and uglier than the last. One of them grasped the flesh between his legs and said something in a lower-class speech that I did not understand, though it made the others laugh. But the gesture, that I understood, and I bit back a wail of pure terror before it could escape my lips.

Then two of them reached down with knives in their hands while the others seized my arms and legs. I struggled and flailed but to no avail and the shining blades descended to cut the clothing from my trembling limbs. Once I was naked, they held me up suspended before the largest guard. Lenash, Aruna's lieutenant. I remembered his tortures of old and I very nearly begged for mercy. He smiled and one of his huge hands went to untie his trousers, exposing a fleshly spear of such a length and breadth as could split me in two.

I stared at Aruna in horror. "Your body will not seem so desirable to my prince when they are done, beast. And I shall enjoy your screams as they all take their turns with you. Now beg for mercy until Lenash plugs your mouth for you." She leaned against the wall, anticipation lighting her features.

I was forced to kneel before him. The others had unfastened their own trousers and watched me from eyes turned savage with lust and rage. I wept then but I would not beg. I was a prince of the Old Blood and my enemies might break me but they would not humble me. So I promised myself. Lenash's huge fingers closed on my nose, trying to force my mouth open. I fought as best as I could, determined to suffocate before I drew breath.

The room had begun to whirl around me when a mighty slap jarred the side of my head. My gasp of pain was enough and he crammed his filthy length inside my mouth. His pawlike hands held the back of my head while I choked and gagged, trying to push him away. He thrust his way inside me, nearly breaking my jaw and forcing my mouth wider. His movement jerked him against my teeth and tongue while I tried to bite him. The effort only amused him and earned me another cuff on the head.

Then all at once, the torture of my mouth was over and he withdrew to run his fingers down his spear. "Nice and wet now for what comes next." He grinned at his companions and I was seized and bent at the waist. My arms were held and they kicked my legs apart. I wailed a little then, dreading what was to come. Lenash stood behind me, pressing his spear against my flesh, pawing at me in his efforts to force his way inside me.

I tried to squirm away, tried to think of Raven and how different that had been but it was no use. Another guard seized my head and shoved himself inside my mouth as Lenash at last found what he was looking for. He pushed up against me, beginning to wrench me open, to pierce me through until it killed me as I knew it would.

The sound of voices from outside could be nothing, must mean nothing. There was none to save me or even to avenge my death. Raven would marry Aruna and forget me. The vision pierced me with a pain of the heart, greater still than that of my body. I screamed as well as I could with the guard's spear in my mouth. He yanked my head forward so that his length choked me and I could scream no more, could make no other sounds than the low animal-like moans that fell from my lips and that I could not suppress.

Only Aruna's scream was louder. Lenash released me with a bellow and the other guard pulled himself from my battered mouth. I fell to the cobbles, too weak for a moment to lift my head and see what had forced them to stop. All around me the guards grabbed for their swords and I was kicked once or twice in the melee. I curled up in a ball as swords clashed over my head. Lenash's head dropped to the floor nearby and I smiled to see it, no matter who wielded the other sword.

Suddenly, Raoul was by my side and I was pulled away from the fight to the safety of the opposite wall. Raven and several of the vampire knights still faced the last two guards but the latter were no match for them. My vampire prince turned as they fell, fangs bared and face awesome and fearsomely white with rage. I quailed and rejoiced at once, but realized that his eyes were not fixed on me.

It was then that I saw Aruna being held near the door by one of his knights. Her face was nearly as white as the prince's, even down to her lips. She struggled against her captor's grip, but it was to no avail. For a moment, her gaze fell on me and I thought that she might beg me for mercy. But she read the answer on my face though I could not speak and looked away. Instead, she threw herself on her knees before Raven as best she could. "Mercy, my lord! All I did, I did for love of you!"

Raven stood before her, his blade dripping with the blood of the fallen guards and said nothing for a moment that seemed an eternity. Raoul dropped a cloak over me then and I wrapped it around me and sat up slowly to see what the prince would do. Aruna tried to bare her throat but the knight would not release her arms. Across the room, Raven's knights fed on the fallen; the sight seemed to stir her greatly. She cried out, "Take me, highness! Make me one of you and I will serve you for the rest of my unending days."

I saw Raven's face change, become wolflike as he sniffed the air, laden now with the scent of blood. He looked first at me and I huddled deeper in the cloak, as if it was enough to conceal me. Then he turned back to Aruna. Time seemed to stand still and I wondered if he fought the monster he held within. If so, it was not for long. I watched in horror as he pounced on her like a cat with a mouse and sank his teeth into her throat with a growl. Aruna gave one short scream and her back arched. She pushed against him with hands growing weaker as he drained her.

When she stopped moving, Raven looked up and met my eyes. I shuddered and looked away; there was no prince there now, only a monster. The blood of one who I had thought my kin ran down the alabaster flesh of his chin, red as rubies. His fangs dripped with it and I found I could not bear to look at him again. In that moment, he was more like the king and his children than like the prince I had known. True, I had hated Aruna but now her fate seemed almost too cruel.

Then Raoul lifted me, carrying me from the chamber of the horrors I had witnessed. I was weak, far too weak to walk unassisted and soon I found that my eyes closed on their own and I rested my head on his breast. Darkness took me soon thereafter and I knew no more for a time.

When I awoke next, I was dressed and we were in the palace stables. Raven's horse was saddled and his people already mounted. Raoul picked me up and handed me to the prince as if I was a feather to be passed among them. The memory of his fangs carmine with blood came back to me at a moment and I flinched away with a cry. His cold arms wrapped themselves tight around me and he tilted my face up so he could see my eyes. "Are you so afraid of me now, little beast?" His cold fingers stroked my cheek and he searched my eyes for an answer.

Was I too afraid to go with him? True, my fear wailed within me that he would feed on me as he had with Aruna. That my broken corpse would be flung from his bed to be taken away by the servants. But if I stayed, the king would kill me. It was then that I remembered Kriun and what he had told me. "I must stay in my lands if I am to become the king. Yes, I am afraid of you but I am more afraid of what will become of my people if I abandon them." As I spoke the words, I knew them to be true. A weak king I might be but better by far than one who ruled awash in blood.

Raven spoke at last, interrupting my thoughts. "We must go into hiding then, at least for a time." With that, he set spurs to his horse and we loped swiftly from the stables, vampire knights and servants at our heels.

For the first time, I realized what he had sacrificed to save me. Both knights and servants were fewer in number and they crept away at his heels, who had ridden into the court in triumph. They were fugitives for my sake unless they returned to their own land. What right had I to ask this? I resolved to send Raven away when next we stopped. For now, there could be nothing but flight and pursuit, for I knew the king would seek to avenge his daughter.

Night had fallen and the moon shone brightly down on us, lighting the stone road before us. I saw the guards at the gate felled before they could raise the alarm, saw the torches and beacons lit on the walls behind us. For the first time, I cursed myself for not knowing the lands outside the castle. I could not guide us to sanctuary. Instead I clung to the monster who had saved me while the motion of his horse's galloping hooves jarred me until I was sore. Exhaustion forced me to ignore the questions that boiled in my brain, begging to be asked.

So passed much of the first night. We stopped to walk and rest the horses once we were in the mountains and away from the road. I saw then that we were bound for the mountains of the Western Wall and I thought for a moment that I might flee, hide myself away before we journeyed to the land I feared above my own.

The moon came out from behind the clouds then and a single beam lit Raven's face. It was pale and wise and beautiful as he spoke to his knights and they decided on the route. My heart twisted inside me as I watched him, sending a pain so sharp through me that I gasped for breath.

Then behind him, I saw distant torches on the trail. "They have found us," I whispered, pointing. Raven snarled, a trapped animal staring from his eyes and I flinched away in horror. He leapt up into his saddle, catching me by the arm as he rode past. His arms were iron bands holding me prisoner as he guided horses and men higher and higher into the mountain passes. I knew I could do nothing to save myself then. In my secret heart, I wondered if I wanted to.

Our flight went on forever, or so it seemed. We hid in caves by day and I watched Raven sleep when I could not.

He lay so still that it wrung my heart to see him, fearing him dead each day until he rose at dusk.

Once Raoul managed to steal fresh horses. Once the king's soldiers were so close that I could hear them breathe but they so outnumbered the knights that we hid, flattening ourselves against the rocks and behind bushes. Raven told me nothing until the third evening after we left the castle though I knew he could see the questions in my face.

Finally, I could bear it no longer. "Where are you taking me? And how were you able to save me? All the stories say that you cannot walk when the sun is in the sky." I did not ask why he had saved me; I was not sure that I could bear to hear the answer.

"Don't believe everything you hear from the bards, little beast." He smiled at me to take the sting from his tone and I almost forgot what I knew of him. Almost. "I have trained myself and my men to walk before sunset if there is need enough. There is a price to be paid for it, so soon we must eat and feed." His gaze lingered on me like an icy caress and I felt the hot blood rise to my cheeks.

"And where are we going? I have never been so far from the castle before." I detested the whine in my voice. I sounded not like a future king, but rather like a child and a foolish one at that. I spared a thought for Kriun, my father, and resolved to act more as I had seen him behave when not obliged to clown for the court.

"Do you grieve for him, little one? I am sorry that I failed you. He was dead when we reached his cell." Raven's face showed nothing but the disappointment of a noble lord who had failed in his purpose, but there was pain in his voice. I wondered how I could ever begin to understand this creature, so kind yet so cruel and brutal.

"He was my true father, my mother's secret lover from one of the families of the Old Blood. I did not know this until it was too late."

"Ah. Then my grief on his behalf is the greater." Raven turned away, jaw working a little and my heart burned inside me.

Despite my terrors, despite anything proper that I should have felt, I reached out to him, turning his cheek so he faced me. Then I pressed my lips to his, slowly and cautiously. He tasted like metal, like the tang of blood. He pulled me to him, half-straddling his legs as his tongue sought mine. For the moment, I forgot the rest of our company, I forgot the danger of pursuit all to lie safe in his arms for a moment.

Then I remembered my shame and the face of the one who I thought my sister. I remembered the eyes of the wolf watching me from Raven's face and I pulled away, trembling in every limb. His grip on me only tightened and he pulled me closer, his lips caressing my neck until I was torn between desire and revulsion.

It was the sentry giving warning who saved me from debasing myself further. Raven put me aside and went to him, leaving me gasping for air and my flesh burning wherever he had touched me. I could not look at any of the others. Raven vanished for a time, followed by some of his knights and there followed the screaming whinnies of terrified horses, then silence. A thin trickle of blood ran down his chin when next they stepped back into the firelight and my flesh turned cold.

Then we fled again, riding all night toward the Western Wall. Always, I rode before Raven on his saddle, and felt sometimes his lips at my ear or caressing my hair. I wondered if my blood called out to him the way my flesh did. Part of me wondered what it would be like to be immortal. I rejected it firmly, yet it appeared again and again. To be beautiful and wise, for somehow I believed that his deadly kiss would remake me, and to be at his side forever. A vision came to me of what it would be like to be in his bed forever as well, sending a rush of heat and horror through me. These were my dreams despite all I could do to think purer thoughts.

So we rode, each wrapped in our own thoughts and fears until the mountains of the Western Wall loomed above us. Once on the other side, we would leave my lands behind and, I feared, all chance of reclaiming them. Never had I desired the throne so much as when I knew that it was mine, yet I could not attain it. My head spun with plans, each stranger and more complicated than the last, each discarded as impractical in turn.

I nearly missed it when Raven turned from the road we followed and sent his horse in a weary gallop up to a tower, overgrown with vines. Looking about showed me the remains of an old castle, with enough of the wall still standing to make it defensible. "Here we shall find sanctuary until you gain your throne," Raven whispered in my ear, sending chills through me.

I looked around at my new domain and knew not whether to laugh or cry. Still, I must begin somewhere. With that thought, I dropped from the saddle to the ground. I helped the servants and the knights as best I could to clear the tower's floor and stairs and to build a fire. Raven hunted, bringing several hares for us to cook and eat once he and his people had drained their blood. We covered the windows and the door and prepared for the coming of day and sleep. Thus we ended our first night in our new home.

But I am forgetting to speak of what passed when Raven laid out his bedroll for us to share. I will not say that I approached it with the same terror that I had before. The press of his body against mine as we rode had accustomed me to the cold feel of his flesh. But this was not the same as being naked before him once more. Almost I found it in myself to flee rather than let him remove my clothes.

"Allain." His voice was tender and he said nothing more

than my name, yet he had not spoken it before now. I came to him then, no more master of my feet than I was of my kingdom. He undressed me with gentle if cold hands, his lips finding the scars from the bites he had inflicted as well as the marks of older beatings on my body. Each of these he kissed slowly and carefully until I buried my fingers in his hair and pressed myself close against him.

This time when his hands slid between my legs to caress me into hardness, I did not stop him or cry out in protest. My memory of the wolf inside him had faded a bit but not so much that I did not realize that the prince I longed for and the demon were one and the same.

Still, I did not offer him my life's blood this time, only my body. That he took gently, turning me so that I kneeled before him and slipping his fingers inside me until I groaned and rocked against the blankets seeking release. Then he crouched behind me, thrusting carefully into me to make a path for himself. I opened as best I could but the exquisite agony made me cry out.

He reached between my legs, his hand steady and sure on my hardened flesh. He coaxed and rubbed, all the while thrusting his way further inside me than I thought possible, pulling more pleasure and pain from my weak form than I thought any mortal could withstand. When he spilled his seed inside me, his groan shook its way through me until I spilled mine on the waiting bedroll.

My legs could no longer hold me then and we fell to the ground in a tangle of limbs. I twined my arms around his neck, all power of speech lost as we kissed once more, our bodies hot and cold flowing together until we were as nearly one as was possible between mortal and immortal. He held me close and buried his face in my neck, making me flinch away.

He stroked my cheek in the darkness. "Little beast, I will not take your blood unless you give it to me."

But Aruna's dead face hung before my closed lids and I could not stop shivering. The birds outside began to twitter and I felt him sink into a deathlike sleep. I crawled free of his arm and found my scattered clothing. I was too tired to sleep so instead I began climbing the tower stairs in hopes of seeing where we were.

The steps were rotting but I was able to traverse them by the early dawn light, following their spiral curve upward to the top. They emptied finally into a room whose windows looked out on the mountains of the Western Wall and my vampire prince's lands on the one side and my own on the other. I went first to look at the mountains and tried to imagine life there. I realized then that Raven had never told me why he left, only mocked me when I thought he was my enemy.

With that thought, I turned to look out on my own land and wished with all my heart that Kriun was by my side to see it in all its beauty. I could see a tiny village some distance north and figures in the fields. I looked back toward the castle, the only home I had ever known but it was too far away to still be visible. I thought about the Old Blood in my veins and the bloodstained swords of my family's conquest. I wondered what I could do to undo the wrongs that had been done until I fell asleep facing the windows.

Raoul woke me when the day's shadows had grown long and I knew that Raven would be awake soon. The thought filled me with longing, desire, terror all somehow mixed in a way I had never imagined. I followed Raoul down the stairs and shared the servant's meal of stewed rabbit. We heard the sentry cry out, and Raoul and one of the other servants slipped out to see what it was. Curiosity overcame me and I followed them, staying well back in case of danger.

But it was not so far back that the old peasant woman on the path did not see me. She gaped and pointed at me before sinking to her knees. Raoul, who had moved to intercept her if she had any evil intent, spoke in wondering tones, "She recognizes your golden hair and bows to you as the rightful prince."

I went to her side and raised her then, realizing that her hair had once been as yellow as mine and that she was bit shorter than me: one of my people then, the people of the Old Blood. Inspired, I remembered my true father's words then and gave the second command that I had ever issued. "Tell your neighbors that the true king is returned and that those who would serve him should gather here by sunset three days hence." She kissed my hand, a wondering look in her faded blue eyes, then vanished into the brush.

"Was that wise, Highness? Your father will be able to find you, too." Raoul frowned at me in the fading light.

"My army must come from somewhere, Raoul. Do not fear for your prince. I will send him back before I will let further harm come to him." I rested my hand on his shoulder for a moment and watched the reluctant dawn of trust in his eyes.

"Send me back where exactly, princeling? I'm the third heir to our throne, sent forth to marry and build alliances, perhaps to make more like myself. Do you think my queen wants me back?" Night had fallen and Raven stood behind us, listening to all I said.

Raoul vanished silently and I trembled a little to see him go. If I provoked my prince into a rage, would he serve me as he had my sister? For I still could not think of her otherwise, having thought of her that way for so long. He continued, his voice a low, steady growl. "And since when do you have the skills to command an army, even one composed of untrained peasants?"

"I meant no insult. Only that I could not bear—"

"To perish, as you surely would without your consort's aid? I thought as much." His lips curled in a mocking smile and something else, an expression that went through me like an arrow and deprived me of speech. "Or did Kriun not mention that particular tradition among the ancient rulers of your land? Several centuries past, I believe, one of my ancestors sat on the throne next to one of your own. We'd have to find you a queen to bear your heirs, of course."

Now I knew he mocked me and I grimaced back at him. Surely I could not mean so much to him. He could not want to be a mere consort when he might rule as king himself merely for the price of marrying a mortal princess. I concealed my hurt as best I could. "Teach me to use a sword, demon prince. There is much I need to learn."

He smiled then bowed slightly. Moments later, I stood before him holding the lightest sword any of the company possessed. Some hours of practice passed, first through a series of movements like a dance, then in combat with a figure of bundled wood.

It lasted until I could stand no more and wove in my stride as if overcome with drink. "Enough, little beast. Rest now and we will do more again tomorrow." Raven swept me up into his arms and took me into the tower.

He laid me carefully on the bedroll and removed my clothes but tonight he did no more than kiss me before he vanished. I wondered where he went but was too tired to think about it for long. I slept until the sun was high in the sky. This time, there were several baskets of food by the path and a trio of peasant lads standing before the tower when I emerged. I broke my fast with them awhile before the others woke. Thus I learned some of how the peasants lived under the blades of my family's conquerors.

More joined us that night, including one of the border lords with his small retinue. He had been driven into exile by the king and sought to take back his lands and his standing. His sword was mine if I would return what had been his. He watched critically as Raven took me through the exercises and arms training, shouting the occasional suggestion as I learned to swing the sword. When I could do no more, he produced two staffs tipped in metal from the pack on his horse and tossed one to Raven.

Wordlessly, they faced each other as all of us gathered to watch. Raven dropped into a fighting stance and the lord made the first attack. A moment later the staffs whirled, their metal tips gleaming in the firelight as they clashed, then fell away from each other. The border lord was gasping moments later but my prince showed no sign of weariness.

It could not last and finally Raven felled him with one deft swing. The lord bowed his head unsmiling but took his hand to be helped up. He gave Raven a nod of approval then he sent one of his men away and sat down to break bread with us.

More farmers trickled in as the night wore on, no few with mighty spears and bows. The borderlands were per-ilous ones. At dawn the lord's man returned, bringing word of more of the border rulers coming down from their mountain castles. For once, I might be grateful for the wages of cruelty. My army grew apace until by the third night, it numbered near a hundred men and boys.

"Now what?" Raven asked me as we looked down from the tower. "It is not enough to fight the king's armies yet, even if all the rest of the land rose up to join us."

"Ah, but that would be enough. We must show them we are here first. Only a few men are needed to take a castle by surprise, provided always that their commander knows the secret ways." I felt strangely confident, as if my father's spirit guided my steps and my words. Somehow, I knew this was what he intended.

Raven smiled tenderly at me, no trace of mockery on his face. "It will be an honor to celebrate with you if we suc-ceed, to die at your side if we fail." He vanished before I could respond, leaving me to welcome a small group of wild boys and a few girls who rode up the path in a thunder of hooves.

Training and provisioning my new army took a few days, as did telling Raven and one of his knights all I knew of the ways into the castle. Finally we decided on a three-pronged attack, each entering by a different way. Most of the king's commanders dwelt in the castle under his eyes, since he did not trust them. Once the commanders and the king himself were gone, the army would collapse, or so I hoped.

Finally, all was ready and we left under cover of darkness, our army as hidden as it could be. We followed some shepherds through hidden paths in the mountains, avoiding the roads where the king's men patrolled. We rested by day, sleeping in caves and hovels and Raven lay beside me all the while I wondered when he would leave. Would it be after we defeated my father? Or after the coronation? Or simply when it appeared that all hope was lost and the king would win? I found no clues in anything he said to me.

On the final day of our journey, we slept in the caves above the castle. Or I should say the others slept. At first, I tossed and turned, trying to fire my courage with dreams of avenging my father, of taking back the throne that should have been mine. A lifetime of fear was not so easily overcome, however, so I tried instead to think of what I could say to persuade Raven to stay with me. I lay and watched his sleeping face until at last, I could not keep my eyes open any longer and fell into a restless doze.

That night, we gathered ourselves to enter the castle by the secret passages I had known so well. I feared to make a map lest it be discovered and the passages closed to us. Without them, all hope was lost. Instead, I allowed Raven to use his powers to see the passages in my mind, then to pass it on to those of his knights who he trusted most.

I have spoken much of his touch upon my body but how shall I speak of his touch upon my mind? He had told me that he had few such powers in comparison to the older vampires so I did not fear that he might read all my thoughts and hidden desires. Instead, I thought fiercely about the routes we must take to enter the castle and gain the king's apartments. He held my face and looked into my eyes until I thought that my legs would give way beneath me.

I hoped that he would press his lips to my own and tell me all the things that I longed to hear, but the border lords were watching. I resigned myself to pain and agony, what I feared might happen if my mind was not my own. Yet when it finally came, his touch was feather-light and cautious, as with one who takes only what he has been given and I loved him for it. That understanding shook me to my core and I was barely able to hold back the words. There would be time later, or so I hoped.

Once he gave the routes to his knights, we were ready. He and I were to command one group, his knights the other two. We hoped in this way to overwhelm the guards and commanders and allow one of us to reach the king. This decided, we began our journey into the castle, moving as quietly as could be done with a hundred men. Raoul we left in charge of our sanctuary and the other servants. He had orders to take them all and flee over the Western Wall if we were defeated. I trembled, thinking of what would be done to us if we failed.

Despite my terrors, we were able to enter the castle and gain the secret passages undiscovered. In the end, it was our decision to separate into three groups that saved us. The king's men found the first group. I'm told that they died valiantly, knights and farmers alike. But the alarm spread through the castle, alerting the guards and they were waiting for us in a force that greatly outnumbered our own when we broke through to the king's chamber.

I had steeled myself for blood and for battle but I had not thought to shield myself for the burning look of contempt and hatred on the face of him I had thought my father. Despite all I could do to command myself, I shrank away, expecting a blow. He laughed, a sound without mirth but strong enough to give me the courage I lacked. I stood before my men then, my sword in my hands, Raven at my side.

He said nothing and I knew that I must speak, must act first. Otherwise the men would never follow me as their king. "Put down your swords and you may follow the king into exile." My voice was steady and I met each man's eyes as if I were a stranger to fear and terror. The king drew his sword in answer and ordered them forward.

"For Kriun!" I yelled and Raven echoed me. I tried to remember all that Raven had tried to teach me and I met the first man's sword with a clash that shook my arms. An arrow from one of the border girls took down a guard and then battle was joined.

Raven was before me in an instant, his sword a blur of light as he dueled against one of the king's commanders. Soon the floor ran slick with blood, both theirs and our own and it became hard to keep our footing. Still, I acquitted myself well, slaying two of the guards and wounding several others. But we were losing and for every one we slew, two more took their places.

It was then, when all hope seemed lost, that our second group arrived. They were greatly reduced in number from battling their way here, but still there were enough knights and determined peasants to turn the tide a little our way. That was when the king slew the last of those who stood between us and faced me, hatred burning in his eyes.

I would not let him see that I feared him, but I sought Raven without realizing that I did so. That was nearly my undoing. The king swung his blade. It was nearly as long as my body and had it not caught the ceiling in its descent I would have had no time to leap away. Raven had seen this and I could see him assume his demon form, face fixed in a monstrous rage with fangs out of a nightmare. Men fell before him like wheat but he was too far away to save me.

I danced away from the king's mighty blade once again before I struck back. I chanted Kriun's name silently to myself to give me the courage to cross my sword with his. I remembered an attack that the border lord had shown me and I slipped beneath his longer blade to strike at his leg. I drew blood and I gave him a wolf cub's smile as I danced away from another weighty blow. We circled as well as we could and he slashed at me suddenly, wounding my shoulder.

Gripping my sword in both hands, I shot forward, sending my blade through his already wounded leg. The king bellowed with pain and gave me a blow that sent me flying backward to land at his feet. The sword fell from my limp fingers and the king stood swaying above me, raising his blade to end my efforts. I could do nothing but wait and I prepared myself for death.

Then, with a howl of inhuman rage, Raven was between us. His blade caught the king's, knocking it aside before his own sword swept across his opponent's neck. The man who I had thought my father looked almost surprised as his body fell to the floor.

I lay looking up at my preserver, my vampire prince, and he looked back at me with his wolf's eyes. Blood ran from his fangs and for a moment, I almost turned away. Then I forced myself to my feet and pulled his face down to mine. I kissed him then, my very heart in my mouth and I whispered, "I love you." But I shuddered as I said it.

His features grew less distorted but his expression was guarded. Several of the commanders surrendered but a few fought on. Raven pushed me gently away and went to finish the battle while I crumpled to my knees next to the king's body. There was nothing more I could do and the pain from my wounded arm soon made the room darken around me.

I lay in my mother's old room, my wounds bandaged when I awoke. Raven did not lie beside me and my heart caught in my throat. Soon the king's own physician came to me and with him a group of those who had served him. I called for those who had followed me and those few of the border lords and peasants who could stand came to wait on me. I made the first lord to join me one of my chief advisors and told him the rewards I wanted to give my men.

Then I asked where the vampire knights were. "Asleep, Majesty. You slept past the dawn." He answered me, a look of slight amusement on his features. I nodded, ignoring the tears that threatened to well up in my eyes. Raven had left no word and though he might walk past the dawn, he had not done it for me. I forced myself to rise and dress and began to go about the business of being a king, though my heart was heavy within me.

Raven slept for several days and I did not see him, busy as I was in planning my coronation, exiling my half siblings and other kingly tasks. I missed the feel of his body when I went to my lonely bed at night and I wept until my pillow swam with tears. But I would be a king in fact soon, and I could not bring myself to beg him to come to me. Or to love me in return when he did not.

Instead, I pledged my troth to the daughter of one of the border lords who had ridden with us. It was her arrow that had brought down the first of the guards. Thus I cemented the loyalty of the bordermen to me and made my first alliance. But I did not choose a consort because the one who held the first place in my heart had not come to me.

Even after he woke, he came only to the court and not to my chamber, and though my heart broke within me, I did not ask. At last, my heart was numb and I could weep no more. I was crowned king and I rewarded all of my men, including the vampires, with all that was in my power to offer. Raven sat in council at my right hand but still did not come to my chamber.

The emptiness inside me consumed me, but I wed my

betrothed and took her to my bed, hoping to sire an heir quickly. When she quickened with child, it was she at last that intervened. I could not have said why she did it but I shall always love her for it. It was she who sent word to Raven and ordered him to come to me in my private chamber.

I turned from the window, starting a little to find him there with a slightly mocking look on his beautiful face. He bowed. "Her Majesty sent me hither to await your commands." I dismissed the waiting servants and petitioners with a gesture, already practiced. "And how do you enjoy being a king, little beast? I see the queen is already quick with your child. I congratulate you." He bowed, a fleeting look of pain crossing his look.

"Why haven't you come to me, Raven? I thought . . . I thought after what I said that . . ."

"Do you think I don't realize that you are afraid of the vampire in me? That you turn away from what I am? I have tasted you only when you hoped to save your father. I thought you would come to my side after the battle, but each night I woke alone." His eyes were the hawk's look that I had seen before but now I could face it without fear. I knew what I must do.

I said nothing but only drew the dagger I wore at my side. With a single motion, I bared my shoulder and held it to the skin near my neck. He met my gaze a moment before he crossed the floor to my side, knocking the blade away. His features distorted, the wolf gleaming from his eyes. Our garments fell away like leaves from a winter's tree and I wrapped my arms around his neck as he sank his fangs into my flesh.

He fed on me, his hands rough on my body as they forced me into readiness for him. I wailed my need, my desire so long suppressed into the flesh of his neck, and he wrapped my legs around his body, holding me up. I bit back a scream as he pierced me, my limbs convulsing as he fed from me and took all that I had to give him. I spilled my seed against him and he laughed to feel me writhe in surrender, making my body beg for what my lips could not, would not.

He pulled away from my throat to look down at me, my blood coating his fangs and his lips. He was a demon in truth and I loved him more than my land, more than my crown. "Little beast," he growled and thrust against me, cold inside me until I thought I could feel nothing more ever again.

"Beauty," I whispered against the coldness of his lips.

"I love you," he growled in return and joined himself to me as only the best of consorts can do.

THE WINGED LEOPARD IN A FOREIGN LAND

STEVIE BURNS

Ichiro sat in the tub, soaking away his worries and doubts about the important trip to New Mexico ahead of him, the business trip he did not want to take. His boss had suggested it was a great opportunity, a chance to prove himself as a lab technician worthy of leading his own science team. That would mean a promotion, and Ichiro needed the money. Not that he had a desire for many things or required an apartment of his own, but his aged mother was very sick, and because it was only the two of them now, it was up to Ichiro to see that her needs were provided.

He knew that even now as he rested his head on the back of the tub, letting the scalding hot water soak into his very bones, his mother was in the kitchen bending over the burner to make more tea. Her hands would be shaking, all her joints swollen and her slim leg muscles barely able to shuffle across the floor to the cupboard for a fresh cup. Every move was painful to her, and for Ichiro, watching her every move was painful because there was nothing he could do about it. He could not afford the specialist care she required.

Ichiro moved a leg slightly and the steaming heat rising from the water swayed, the heat of the water feeling like a shift of hot pain that would be replaced by numbness. His fingers were wrinkled from the soak, but still Ichiro did not want to get out of the tub to rinse. Not yet. It was as if getting out of the tub would mean the trip to New Mexico would come all the sooner. Ichiro shook his head, and eased his body out of the water. He sat on the shower chair and rinsed himself off, slowly and thoroughly, to match his mood.

Then he looked back at the hot water. If he sat in it long enough, would the water accept the essence of him? He wanted to be like a tea, to ooze out his angst and frustration, to dissolve the hardness he had created around himself as a false protection, just let it rinse away and be replaced with a warming sense of—what? Hope? Ichiro wished for a softer, distilled version of who he was, to let it become him fully.

He sank back into the tub, his flushed body, cooled by the air, shuddered with little bumps of protest as he relentlessly pressed himself down, and then eased back into the steaming water. The bumps were replaced with smoothness and then with glossy shine. He lifted a knee above the waterline and watched the water teardrop down back into the pool. His breath awakened the fine hairs on his leg and their erection was taut and pleasing. He watched the wet hairs, watched his light brown knee, the steaming water softly swirling around his leg. He thought about the water enveloping his cock, the hairs lightly waving back and forth around the sensitive skin there like seaweed in the ocean. Ichiro thought about the last time he had sex, and his dick began to swell and twitch. The sensation was torturous and he sank back deeper in the water to let the torture deepen with him. His mind wandered to the touch of a hardened nipple beneath his fingertips, to the way the bud mouth that kissed him and wrapped around his cock spread open and wide to let him in.

His stomach was tense, his stem throbbing in a beautiful

pain. He touched his cock lightly, sensitive to the water swish-swish and swish around him, the scorching hotness heightened by movement. It was too much. He had to get out of the water.

Ichiro splashed steaming hot water all over the floor and tub-side, and rinsed the stinging heat away with the showerhead that lay ready for him by the tub, soaped and rinsed again, towelled dry and slipped on his bathrobe.

The living room was quiet and dimly lit. Tatami mats lightly crinkled beneath his footfall, massaging his softened soles.

Ichiro padded along the woven mat floor and by the kitchen he slipped on his kitchen shoes. The hardwood floor was relatively new but was already scuffed, scratched and discolored from use. Ichiro was an admirable cook and took care to keep his workspace clean. His mother once commented that if he had never learned to use a Bunsen burner, he never would have learned to prepare a decent soup.

She now sat at the *kotatsu*, their old heated table that Ichiro used to associate with wintertime. She sat, preparing an arrangement of Ikebana flowers she had sewn out of old silk scraps. She claimed the heat of the kotatsu enhanced the color of the fabric, but Ichiro knew it was because her hands were always too cold. The kotatsu was always in use now, even in the summer.

"O-iki." It was all she said, but it was in that sweet-natured dimpled-cheek manner that she had about her, delivered with a look that pierced into the heart with her unwavering lavender eyes.

It was enough. Ichiro nodded. She wanted him to go; she was asking him to go. It was a request as much as a grant of her blessing. She was letting him know that she would be fine in his absence.

"The neighbors and I have made plans to have big parties while you're gone," she said with a warm twinkle in her eyes. "We're going to have a grand time with you out of the country."

"Oh really? And who is coming then?"

"My boyfriend, of course." She placed an indignant hand on her hip when Ichiro's eyebrows shot up. "I'm quite a catch, you know."

Ichiro laughed. "Yes, I know that because you tell me so often." His smile faded, and his mother noticed the change.

"Don't worry, 'Ro-chan. I can still do certain things and the neighbors have decided to take turns coming over to keep me company. You should go. It will be an adventure!"

Ichiro boarded his plane thinking about those words. It will be an adventure? He didn't think so.

Ichiro sat upright in the plane and waited for the other passengers to board. He felt tense and nervous and couldn't calm his nerves. He mentally berated himself for it. There was no reason to fear the plane crashing down somewhere over the ocean. Not really.

The engines hummed and thrummed, but just as the plane was about to eddy from the terminal, the pilot received a message from the control tower. He was to stop the plane immediately to allow an enplanement passenger.

"Some big-shot investor, no doubt," sniffed the pilot, and waited impatiently as the air hostess behind him exited the cockpit to escort the late boarder to an available seat.

"Ladies and gentlemen, we are pausing shortly to allow a late boarder," announced the speakers. It was the pilot's voice trying to not sound annoyed. "Once he has been seated, we will be taking off. Please remain in your seats." There was a slight pause, and the speakers added, "This will not cause a delay in our flight plan, this will only take a few minutes. Please. Be. Patient."

The other passengers looked about curiously as a tall blond man in a dark trench coat entered the plane as if walking onto a stage. He nonchalantly brushed aside the air hostess waiting for him, removed his trench coat as if it were a cape, and with great authority claimed the aisle seat next to Ichiro as if he owned it and had merely allowed the airline to borrow it so long as he had no use for it. But today, the blond man had a use for that seat. The woman raised an eyebrow at the sheer cheek of the man but, saying nothing, turned to close the door hatch and return to the cockpit.

The man draped his trench coat over his seat as if he wouldn't deign to sit on just any surface and, crossing his legs, smiled briefly at Ichiro and then turned his attention away to look out the window on the other side of the plane. Ichiro was glad. He didn't really want to talk with anyone. He gulped with nervous anticipation as the plane moved away from the building, pulled into the runway, and started to accelerate. He gulped again but this time his mouth was so dry it made his throat burn. He held on, and hoped, and tried to keep his breathing steady.

"Ladies and gentleman, we have now reached a flight level of 25,500 feet. Our air hostesses will be with you momentarily with drink carts." There was a slight pause. "Enjoy your flight."

"Perhaps we should introduce ourselves," began the blond man. "This will be a long flight, so we might as well be comfortable." The man grinned toothily, his thick moustache looking as though all color had been drained from it and then small specks of orange flung back into it. "My name is Howard. Howard Mansion. But everybody calls me HM."

"My name is Hashiki Ichiro," replied Ichiro.

"Nice to meet you, Hashiki. You fly often?"

"No."

The man wiped his hand over his blond hair, which had been combed neatly back and away from his eyes. "On vacation then?"

"No."

The man's thick, heavy brows shot up in surprise. "No? Why are you on this plane, then?" His brows were colorless, and made his eyes appear strangely swollen.

Ichiro didn't want to talk with this man, Howard Mansion. "Business."

"You don't look like a businessman," said the man. "And you said yourself that you don't fly much. What kind of business trip is this supposed to be?" His moustache twitched over his lip like a poisonous caterpillar, the tiny thin hairs introducing every word uttered with quiet secrets and stinging pseudorevelations.

"It isn't supposed to be a kind of business trip, it is a business trip. And the nature of my business is none of yours." This was, Ichiro knew, going to be a very long flight.

"Hey, Hashiki. Didn't mean any offense. I was just curious." The caterpillar cleared his throat. "I'm going on a little trip for enjoyment, myself. Pleasure. Going to make sure I have oodles of fun, if you get my drift." He bumped Ichiro's elbow with a sly grin.

Yes, he got the drift. The air hostess's cart was a welcome distraction.

"What would you like to drink today?" she asked. Thick dark hair hung down over her shoulders, framing delicate pale skin.

"How about you, then, sweetie?" The caterpillar squirmed excitely. "I could order two tall drinks of something like you."

The air hostess smiled thinly. "Pepsi all right?"

"No, no. Poor substitution for the real thing," he cooed, softly patting her thigh as if to help straighten her skirt. "Let's have champagne." Turning to Ichiro, he added, "What do you think? It'll be on me, my treat." Before Ichiro could answer, Howard put up two fingers, "Two bottles, please."

"We have a law-enforced limit, sir. I can offer each of you a glass." Ichiro, for one, was amazed at the woman's calm and composure. Clearly, she had dealt with this kind of treatment before.

"Well, we wouldn't want you breaking any laws, now. Would we?" His smirk assumed too much. "You legal, honey?" His hand reached up her thigh a little higher. Without a word, she took his hand and removed it from her body. But he didn't let go her hand and tugged lightly, just enough to throw her off balance.

To catch herself from falling, the woman rested her elbow on Howard's shoulder. Her jacket puckered to reveal more cleavage and the man made no pretense at not trying to take advantage of her position. He glowered hungrily at her chest, and if she had not been able to pull herself up in time, would have done more.

Ichiro couldn't take any more of this. "Leave her alone," he said. His voice was hard and other passengers turned to look at what was happening.

The caterpillar moved, and Howard Mansion stood then, a hand brushing lightly over the woman's breasts. "Excuse my manners, miss. I didn't mean any offense." Then he leaned over and whispered something into her ear. She closed her eyes, and when they reopened she was smiling, happy.

She turned, bending over, pressing her ass playfully against Mansion's crotch.

"Here are your bottles, Mr. Mansion." The airhostess pulled two bottles of champagne from her tray and handed them to Mr. Mansion with a gracious smile. He placed one on his chair, and broke open the seal of the other, slowly screwing it open. Then the airhostess took three glasses and held them up for him to fill. The caterpillar smiled, and allowed the champagne to spill over her hands as he filled the glasses.

"Oh my, look what I've done," he said. He took a glass and handed it to Ichiro. Then he took the other two glasses from her grasp and began to lick and suck the liquid from the woman's hands. Ichiro looked into her face. She was in ecstasy, breathing heavily, her face and chest flushed with excitement.

Howard Mansion took a glass and slowly tipped it down her top, letting the golden sparkled liquid slowly slide down her chest and fill her bra. Her eyes closed and her head fell back.

"Oh no. I'm so clumsy," he whispered. "Let's go in the back and get that cleaned up." And the two left together, Howard's hand casually cupping her buttocks and guiding her movements.

Ichiro was stunned. What had just happened? Another air hostess appeared and pushed the drink tray forward to the next row of passengers. Ichiro glanced around him. Fellow passengers were reading, or content to talk among themselves as they drank, or gazed out the window to look at the clear blue sky.

Mr. Mansion didn't return to his seat for some time. And no one seemed to notice that the crew was shorthanded.

Ichiro sipped his champagne grudgingly. He hadn't wanted it at all, but was so thirsty that his throat hurt and his body felt shrivelled and dry. He had tried to ask one of the other hostesses for a drink. He waved his hands, stood and called out, but they just ignored him. Frustrated, he figured the one young woman with Mr. Mansion in the back must have been specifically assigned to his section. He drank champagne.

He had plenty to drink. Mansion had left both bottles behind. When Ichiro had opened the second bottle, the caterpillar returned to his seat, chuckling.

"Now see? That's just the beginning. Pure pleasure, my friend." He grabbed his crotch and adjusted himself with a groan. "Oh, and she was sweet. Yummy." He noticed that Ichiro had not said anything. "Why the silent treatment? Don't you like pussy?"

Ichiro took another drink.

"Oh," Howard Mansion giggled. "I see you've drained a bottle without me already . . . was I with her that long? How nice. But then, maybe you just drink fast." He patted Ichiro's leg lightly, almost playfully. "Maybe you need a little release, you know? Looks like maybe it's been a while."

Ichiro got up. "Excuse me, Mr. Mansion—"

"HM, call me HM."

"HM. I need to . . ."

"Ah. Say no more, Hashi. Say no more." He stood up and let Ichiro into the isle, and as HM sat down again he whispered, "Nice package."

Ichiro felt his face flush and fumbled his way into the men's bathroom. He was drunk, very drunk. He relieved himself, threw water on his face and arms, and went back to his seat to find that Howard Mansion was sitting there, in Ichiro's window seat.

"Want to sit on my lap?" Then he burst out in laughter. "Just kidding with you. I figured you might prefer the aisle. Do you?"

To his surprise, Ichiro heard himself say, "Yes." He sat down in the aisle seat, feeling strangely exposed.

HM leaned over, conspiratorially. "To be honest with you, that little bit of pussy wasn't quite what I had in mind. You know?" He put his hand on Ichiro's knee, stroking it like his own pet, rubbing it lightly, playfully. "Let me ask you something. What do you want in the world, more than anything else?" His hand stopped, and the weight of his fingertips felt like lead weights on Ichiro's leg, "More money?" The brows that looked like lumps on his eyes lifted for emphasis, "That's what most people say."

Ichiro felt the alcohol and the bubbles and the vision of pale delicate skin swimming in his mind, trickling down the back of his neck like lava. Ichiro couldn't remember ever feeling this drunk before, more than numb, much worse. He thought his eyes were open, but he wasn't sure. He saw something then, colors and nonshapes, but he didn't know what anything was, everything became so blurry. He could feel a pleasant warmth fall over him, something that felt so good. Then the world went away, blacked out.

He could feel his cock harden, filling with blood. Ichiro moved his leg to a more comfortable position before opening his eyes. The pang of pleasure was filling him, as it often did when he awoke, but this was different. He moaned. He was still drunk. Ichiro glanced down through a thick haze with much concentration and saw that the zipper on his pants was open, his dick out. A hand stroked him but it wasn't his. Whose hand was that? Ichiro struggled to concentrate, fought hard to see the arm that was attached to the hand, and fought to see the face above the arm. It was that strange man with a caterpillar moustache. What was his name? The caterpillar twitched. The caterpillar had unzipped Ichiro's pants for him, and placed his hand down over his cock. Lightly stroking it, playfully, just as he had done to his knee before. His knee. That's right, he had stroked his knee earlier.

Ichiro opened his mouth but he didn't know what he was about to say. He released a sigh, sensations of pleasure trembling up and down his body. He saw feathers, black and gray. Where did those come from? It was a vulture. How did a vulture get in the plane? It was perched on the shoulder of the man, what was his name?

Ichiro was going to ask how the vulture got there, and exhaled a sigh of ecstasy instead. His head lolled back onto his seat as he struggled to place the word *how* on his lips. The air in the plane was thick with stale air shared by too many strangers, the coarse blue fabric upholstery covering the seats all around him became claustrophobic, closing in on him, pressing against his arms, pushing his shoulders down, then covering his eyes. Blackout.

"Sir, wake up! Wake up!"

Shaken, Ichiro sat upright, eyes wide. The emergency lights of the cabin were on, overhead lights off, and a strange red glow emanated from all the exits. What was happening?

"Sir, I need you to put on your seatbelt. Are all your possessions stowed away?" The air hostess with delicate pale skin bent over him now, a look of barely controlled fear shown across her face.

He glanced around. He was alone; there was nothing there. "Yes, there's nothing here," said Ichiro, fastening his buckle. There was no turbulence. Everything was quiet. What was the problem?

Before Ichiro could ask, the woman was off and checking other passengers.

In the cockpit, the two pilots were trying to stay calm. "Why aren't the controls responding? Mayday, mayday, we are headed on a direct collision course with an unidentified plane. We are unable to contact her pilot. Our controls are jammed and we are unable to adjust our trajectory."

"Descend to an altitude of eighteen thousand feet."

"We can't! Our controls are jammed. Can you contact the pilot of the other plane?"

"The other plane is not responding."

"Please advise! We are headed for a direct collision. Situation critical. What are you boys doing down there? You've known our controls have been jammed for half an hour!"

"Calm down, pilot."

"You calm down. This is a mayday!" He flipped a switch that controlled his headset. "If no solution, I will cut engines."

"What are you talking about?" The air hostess was frightened. She didn't want to die. "If you cut engines you won't be able to get them back on again. We'll fall out of the sky so hard we'll all be dead before impact."

"It may be our only chance to at least drop our altitude enough and in time to avoid a collision if the other plane doesn't change course." He stared out the window. "Then at least they will survive this." Flipping the switch once more, he repeated, "Mayday, mayday!"

Ichiro looked out his window but couldn't see anything. He looked out the window across the isle, and saw what looked like a vulture, flying. There was something in its beak. Ichiro blinked and the bird was gone, out of view. Had he really seen that? Ichiro didn't know what was real any more, his head was pounding so hard he thought it might split. He could hardly think at all.

Then the lights came back on, the red glow dissipated into amber, and the speakers clicked on with a crackle.

"Ladies and gentleman, our status has returned to normal." Ichiro felt his chest relax. "You can land knowing that you survived an NMAC, near midair collision, today. Our situation was critical, hence the emergency lights, but we are in the clear now. We would appreciate your staying in your seats with your seatbelts fastened, however, as safety protocol requires that we make an emergency landing at the nearest airport large enough to house this plane." There was a slight pause. "Thank you."

In the cockpit, the pilot was unhappy, even though he was alive. "I don't know what happened, damn it. The controls just suddenly kicked back on." He wiped the sweat off his brow with the back of his sleeve. "Once we land, I want this hunk of metal checked, top to bottom. Then I'm going to have a good stiff drink."

"I'm just glad we're landing and not crashing," sighed the copilot. "Even if it is in Brazil."

Ichiro's plane made an unscheduled emergency stop at the International Airport in São Paulo, Brazil, which as it happens was where it was flying above when the controls started functioning again. Protocol demanded that the plane land immediately, and it was just pure luck that they happened to be above one of the largest cities in the world. Their systems were jammed long enough to bring them off course, but no one could fully explain how the plane had managed to get so entirely off course. The GPS must have conked out, providing wrong coordinates for their location from the very beginning of the flight.

The passengers stayed aboard for two hours as the plane's control systems were checked, top to bottom. The crew of six fully licensed mechanics could find nothing wrong. Safety protocol required that they find something wrong. Until such time, the plane would be permanently grounded.

Now the passengers deboarded and stood in line to receive alternative seats on other already scheduled flights. By the time Ichiro reached the counter, there was nothing available until the following day. He would stay overnight in Brazil, with dinner and sleeping accommodations provided for him by the airline. Once in his hotel room, he called work to explain what had happened and that he would be a day late reaching New Mexico and would they please explain to whomever planned to pick him up? Great, thank you.

Ichiro entered the shower to relax his muscles and unwind, wondering if anything he had seen or experienced during the flight was real. He couldn't remember when he started getting drunk but he could well have hallucinated everything. He wasn't even sure if there had been a man

sitting next to him at all. No physiology could have with-
stood such a quantity of alcohol at that altitude. Some part
of Ichiro knew he was lucky to be alive. Some part of him
knew he should in fact be dead or collapsed in a brain
coma. But the part of him that was conscious, and thinking
about what to eat that night, was doing a fair job of
ignoring all of that.

He dressed for a dinner down in the hotel lobby. People,
sexy Brazilian people, would be a nice distraction from
thinking about death, death and a vulture.

Ichiro entered the hotel restaurant and found a small
table to sit at. What he did not realize and could not have
expected is that the moment he crossed the threshold, a
handsome young waiter took note of him and asked the
waitress assigned to Ichiro's table if he could work it.

"Why, what for?" asked the waitress.

"Why do you think?" Ronaldo winked at her. "He's just
so cute. You can have two of my tables, okay?"

"All right. But don't take my tips this time, okay?"

"Yeah, sure." Ronaldo rubbed his hands together with
glee. This was going to be fun. He pushed his pants further
down his hips to accentuate the line of his strong torso and
walked to Ichiro's table.

"Good evening, sir." Ronaldo handed Ichiro a menu with
a gleaming smile filled with perfectly straight, white teeth,
accentuated by his bronzy skin. "Can I get you something to
drink while you consider what you'd like to eat tonight?"

Ichiro gulped hard. He was shaken by the intensity of
the waiter's charm. He could smell warm cologne emanating from the warm, trimly muscled body standing so
very near his left arm. "Vodka straight."

Ronaldo smiled wide. "Certainly, sir. I'll bring that to
you momentarily." As he turned and walked away, he
knew Ichiro would be watching him go, so he made the
best of it and let his ass wiggle and pump a little with every

step. Ronaldo prided himself on having a shapely, round ass. It was pure fuck waiting to happen.

Ronadlo poured a good stiff drink for his customer and when he brought the cooled glass and saw the look on Ichiro's face, he knew the guy was hooked. He smiled, "Have you decided what you would like?"

"Steak." Ichiro could hardly speak. He let out a slow breath. Exhale. Relax.

"And how would you like that?" Ronaldo looked at him now with meaning, "Well done?"

"Oh, yes, please."

"Fine. I'll just take care of that for you, if you'll meet me down that hall over there." Ronaldo pointed. Then he bent down and said quietly, "Just meet me in the storage room. The two of us can take some real pleasure in a nice, thick piece of meat tonight, and have it very well done. What do you think?"

Ichiro smiled and nodded. He could hardly believe his luck.

Ichiro sat on the hotel bed, thinking back to what had happened. It was incredible, unthinkable. When he had reached the storage room, Ronaldo was already naked and half erect. He had an incredible body.

"Tell me, sir, what would you like this evening?" Those had been the first words out of his mouth.

"Suck my dick," Ichiro had said. Where did that come from? He had never done something like this before, never said something like that before. It felt so good, so empowering. It was a new sensation for Ichiro.

"I can't do that with your pants on, Sir."

"Unzip my pants," ordered Ichiro, "with your teeth."

Ronaldo grinned. He knelt down in front of his customer and unfastened the top button of his pants, then grabbed the tab of the zipper between his teeth and pulled the slider down with the pulling motion of his head. The chain size was large and thick, and it made a low tick-tick and tick as the two halves opened, and Ronaldo let his face brush smooth against Ichiro's cock.

Ichiro closed his eyes and let his head fall back against the wall behind him.

Even now, several hours later and just thinking about that moment, Ichiro found himself doing the same thing, closing his eyes and putting his head back, letting the desire soak into him. He brought up his legs and hugged them to his chest. It had been such a sexy experience with Ronaldo, two close, warm bodies in a poorly lit storage room of a four-star hotel restaurant.

And Ichiro remembered, letting the images come streaming back into his mind.

Ronaldo took Ichiro's boxers in his two strong hands and ripped them open. Rip! All with one strong pull, and the fabric fell to his sides, hung open and shredded, revealing the thick dark hairs that made an appealing shape, a teardrop that started at Ichiro's navel and stretched downward, cupping his erection.

Sitting on the bed now, alone and in silence, Ichiro grinned. He had taken the boxers with him, stuffed them into his pants pocket afterward. They were discarded now, on a small pile of clothes that required laundering.

Ronaldo brought his right hand under Ichiro's cock and brought it to his mouth. Then he let that hand slide back to Ichiro's tightened balls.

It had been so delightfully tortuous.

Ronaldo toyed and squeezed the tender skin between his fingers, all the while lightly sucking and nibbling the cock head. He waited, teasing Ichiro until his cock was good and hard. Then he brought his middle finger back and up, and in the same moment brought his mouth over the full length of Ichiro's erection.

Ichiro groaned with the memory. His erection was coming back again, but this time he fought it.

Ichiro saw Ronaldo's heavy erection and wanted it. The pulsing energy of it was an ache he had to experience. Ichiro pumped lightly into the waiter's face, slowly pulled back just a little, and back. Slow.

There was a knocking at the door and the two men jumped. They were as quiet as could be, waited and hoped that whoever it was had moved on already.

"Can you hear anything?" whispered Ichiro.

Ronaldo shook his head.

From the outside of the storage room door called a voice, "Hello? Is someone in there having fun without me?"

It was a familiar voice to Ichiro, though he could hardly believe his ears. Ronaldo jumped up from his kneeling position and opened the door wide.

"HM! How fabulous to see you again!"

Ichiro shook his head at the memory, HM had just appeared, right at that door. Ichiro sat on his bed, hugging his knees, still unable to grasp the situation. How? He didn't know if he was in a dream or a nightmare.

HM. He stood there, eyeing Ichiro's nakedness and lightly fondling Ronaldo's penis as they spoke.

"You've missed me, haven't you, Ronnie." It wasn't a question.

"Hmm, yes. HM, oh yes."

"I think our friend is feeling left out. Why don't you suck him off while I make introductions?"

Ronaldo obeyed and resumed sucking Ichiro's cock. Ichiro's pleasure was so intense he thought he might split in two. He came almost immediately, but Ronaldo kept licking and fondling him so that he got hard again. As Ronaldo continued pleasuring Ichiro, HM introduced two women and a man, all scantily clad and looking as though they were ready to join him and Ronaldo in that cramped storage room.

"Hi there," said the other man. Ichiro had already forgotten his name. He couldn't remember any of their names. The women looked like twins.

"And these are the Nana sisters," said HM. They were twins. "They're twins, I can assure you. I checked the birth certificates myself to make sure." With that, he laughed out loud in a bark. The caterpillar approved.

The door closed.

Ichiro closed his eyes, banging his head against the wall behind him. Why hadn't he just pulled up his pants and walked out of the room? He could have. Maybe he just hadn't want to, maybe he wanted to stay. But the vision of the caterpillar moustache bothered him. It frightened him.

Before Ichiro knew what was happening, he was stripped completely naked, finger-fucking the twins. One twin saddled over his right hand, the other twin on his left, and both women were sliding up and down his arms, pumping and squeezing their breasts over him as if his arms were giant dicks. They twisted their torsos over his hands, taking in his fists, grinding over them, writhing in ecstasy, both of them pulling and twisting their tits.

Then Ichiro felt the other man, the one who'd said, "Hi there," move behind him. Ronaldo sucked Ichiro's dick and played with his balls, happy to be on his knees. Then there was the pressure, the push of a well-lubricated dick pressing against his backdoor. Ichiro exhaled, relaxed. He wanted more. The twins took turns kissing Ichiro, then each other, pressing their nipples against his face, dripping wet all over his arms. He wiggled his fingers, feeling against the fine velvety walls, and then he was penetrated. "Hi there."

Ichiro groaned, remembering the incredible sensations he had felt. He looked at his toes, bent them, scrunching up the fabric of the bedclothes in them, then letting go again. It was something tangible. When he had been in the storage room, there was something unreal about it, and as it progressed, it became less manageable . . . the more heightened his physical sensations, the less tangible it all became.

"Hi there," was an incredible rush, and Ichiro came. He came again. He came. The twins wriggled and pumped over him, their soft round breasts stroking his arms and torso. Ronaldo stayed on his knees, sucking, handling. Ichiro came again. His body was taut and every muscle flexed, every muscle alive, intensely. He couldn't see. For just a moment, like a flash, he could not see anything, just white, the color white. But he was fine.

The two twins both stuck their tongues in Ichiro's mouth, and they both groaned, exhaling their sweet breath into him. He came again, and when he did, the world went white again. Then he could see black feathers.

"Hi there" started bucking so hard that it made Ichiro's pelvis buck, bang-bang and bang into Ronaldo's mouth went Ichiro's cock. Bang. Ichiro realized his feet were not even touching the ground. Bang-bang. He was lifted up, suspended. Bang. His feet were not touching the floor. Whiteout.

Then he could see a vulture, and he recognized it. It sat on HM's shoulder.

Whiteout.

The vulture perched calmly now on Ronaldo's head, and it held something in its mouth, something that wiggled.

Whiteout.

The vulture was all Ichiro could see; there was nothing else. Nothing else except the white caterpillar with orange spots wiggling happily in the vulture's beak. It was happy. It wanted to be put into Ichiro's mouth. He heard a scream. It might have been him.

Whiteout.

That's all that Ichiro could remember. When he had opened his eyes again, he was naked, sleeping on top of his bedcovers. He felt strangely exposed.

Ichiro sat, hugged his knees and rested his head there,

wondering if the caterpillar now wiggled somewhere inside of him.

The flight from São Paulo to New Mexico would be another twenty-two hours long, with a two-hour layover in Frankfurt, Germany. Like most people with a layover in Frankfurt, Ichiro went to the food court. But he didn't eat. He wasn't hungry. He meandered behind the indoor play-ground, past the vat filled with soft plastic balls and loud children, and then he saw the view that the bright colors and bright children had been hiding. Vast windows reached up three stories high, reaching from one side of the court to the other. He walked to the windows, and looked out over the landing, watching planes like the one he had flown in, as they rolled by to the right, to the left. One came in a rush, landing gracefully and then quickly disappearing out of the window frame.

He wanted to put his hand on the glass, to see if maybe the surface that witnessed so many people come and go would feel different than his windows at home, which only saw him and his mother come and go. Something caught at his leg, and pulled three times. Ichiro looked down to see a young boy not more than five years old staring up at him.

"You better not touch the glass," he said. Then he pointed a thumb over his shoulder, "My mother will notice." The boy looked out the window, and with great seriousness said, "It won't feel like home, you know. It will feel like glass, but you will not recognize it. You don't belong here." The child then pulled a bright red plastic ball out of his pocket. "I was going to take this home, but I think you should have it." He held it up for Ichiro, waiting.

Ichiro took the ball, recognizing it as one of the many plastic balls from the playground just behind them. He mused how strange it was that the child's mother would have issue with people touching the windows, leaving greasy fingerprints behind for someone else to clean, but wouldn't think anything of stealing. Ichiro quickly glanced around behind him. "Where is your mother?"

The boy didn't answer. Ichiro looked back to the boy, but he saw only a young couple making out just a little farther away. The boy was gone. Ichiro stared blankly at the teenagers, experimenting with their tongues as they kissed, the young man's hands slung lazily in the back pockets of his girlfriend's jeans.

The little boy was gone.

Ichiro boarded his third plane still holding the red plastic ball in his hand. If anyone looked at him strangely because of the peculiar way he solemnly held this small plastic red ball in front of his body as if he carried the staff of a king, Ichiro paid no notice. He sat down in his seat, and only then did he briefly stand up to place the ball into his pants pocket.

"Excuse me, you're in my seat," said a man.

Ichiro checked his ticket and realized that indeed, he was sitting in the wrong place. He made his apologies and got up once more, edging to the isle without seeming too terribly clumsy.

"Ouch! My foot," complained a second man.

"Sorry, excuse me please," was all Ichiro could say as he stumbled out of the cramped row and into the isle. Smoothing out his clothes he said, "Sorry . . . sorry." He looked at his ticket again and found his proper seat. His eyes had been playing tricks on him. He must be tired. He was in seat 21, not 12.

So tired, Ichiro used his coat as a blanket and fell asleep before the plane took off into the air. When he awoke some time later, his pants were moist with the warmth of his cum. It felt so nice, and he felt so relaxed.

He turned in his seat to get up and use the bathroom.

His chest cramped when he realized that a certain man was sitting next to him. He was there. Ichiro was awake and sober and the neighboring seat to his 21 was 22, Howard Mansion. He seemed a little different, but Ichiro couldn't think what it was.

"I see we're headed in the same direction," said HM. The smile was yellow and smelled peculiar, like something rotten and spoiled.

"Excuse me," said Ichiro. He stood abruptly and made his way down the aisle toward the lavatory in a brisk walk, just in time to throw up. The quiet rage and frustration, the embarrassment, it overflowed and gushed and splashed down into the toilet as he grasped for any surface that was stable enough to hold him up. He cleaned up the mess. Then he got out of his clothes and cleaned his face, his mouth, his body. He could sense the stench of spoiled milk rinse off of him.

Ichiro dressed again, and sat down on the toilet. He didn't want to face number 22. He checked his watch only to realize he had no idea what time it ought to be at that point in the sky. How much longer would this flight last? Ichiro shook his head with disgust. He was being foolish and weak. He would go back and confront Mr. Mansion.

But the man was not at his seat anymore. He must be using the lavatory. He would be back. And when he did, Ichiro would be ready. He sat, arms folded across his chest, and waited. But the man never came. The plane landed, eddied to a stop at the gate, and Ichiro deboarded, wondering and looking for the man so many people knew as HM.

"Greetings! Welcome to America, Mr. Hashiki Ichiro. I'm Andrew Bonny." The tall brown man smiled with a broad and professional grin. Ichiro was not sure if this was someone he would ever trust, but Mr. Bonny grabbed his hand in a firm clench and shook his arm until it hurt. "How was your flight?" Before Ichiro could answer, his escort released his hand and asked, "Shall we get your luggage?"

"Yes, thank you."

The two men walked down sun-filled marble floors that had been well polished so that people would slip. The air was arid and thin, and Ichiro could feel his lungs working harder. He coughed on a pocket of dry air and said, "You work at the labs?"

Mr. Bonny barked a laugh. "No, no. I'm not a scientist. I work in PR, promotions, and sales. I work for a small firm called U-Nexus. We are subcontracted by the laboratory to handle certain aspects of this deal." Bonny smiled.

Ichiro knew that a deal had not already been made— not unless it was signed during his flight. The whole point of his coming to see the labs was to evaluate whether the product the labs wanted to develop showed any promise of working, to see, in fact, if their proposed experiments were worth financing . . . or not. "The contracts have not been signed, Mr. Bonny."

"No, of course not. But I'm sure they will be." He smiled, "You'll see. I know."

Ichiro saw that Mr. Bonny carried self-assurance with every stride, and wore strength like a tailor-made suit. It hung well over his trim and muscular body.

Bonny noticed Ichiro noticing his body and grinned warmly. It was an invitation. "Are you very tired, Mr. Hashiki?"

"Not too tired. Why?"

"I could take you to your hotel later this evening, and help you loosen up a bit. You know, unwind from the long flight." He stopped walking and looked down at Ichiro. In a soft voice he added, "Besides, I could use a good fuck."

"Seducing me will not cement the deal, Mr. Bonny." Ichiro slipped on the shiny surface of the floor, but caught himself from falling.

Three boys, none older than thirteen, glided past, one knocking into Bonny's elbow with a hurried and unconcerned, "Sorry." The boys kept going, giggling and skidding along the shiny marble, each one trying to slide along the floor farther than his friends.

"No, no. Of course not." Bonny smiled in a way that betrayed his meaning, exaggerating his words and moving his arms too much. He hoped a seduction would make this business deal a foregone conclusion and didn't mind Ichiro having seen through the charade. In fact, he hoped it would help to be openly dishonest. Sexual corruption in the form of bribery was his hobby and he was very good at it. His every seduction brought him more wealth. Bonny's experience showed him over and again that seducing men was far easier than seducing women. Not that seducing women was hard, not at all.

Bonny grinned again, glad that he lived in a time when most decision making was left to men in this business. His dick was half-hard just thinking about the new car he could buy if everything worked to his plans. Bonny imagined his naked ass sitting on soft leather seats with built-in air-conditioning, imagined cool air seeping through the air pockets in the seat, drifting along his skin, and then he decided he would want someone sucking him off while he drove to his next business deal. The daydream was working and his dick was uncomfortably poking against his slacks. A none-too-subtle shift showed off the promised length that would reveal itself to Ichiro should he feel up to a proficient fuck.

"Now look what you've done, just walking next to me. You are so incredibly hot." Bonny was such a tease, but a tease with promise. He stood closely to Ichiro, knowing that his quarry was at that moment imagining a thick brown cock getting harder under his pants—and it was. To emphasize the point, Bonny flexed just the right muscles so that his dick kicked against the waistline of his pants.

Bonny smiled to himself when he saw the glossy hunger unveiled in Ichiro's eyes. *Oh yeah,* he thought.

Ichiro wanted. Brown and thick, long and warm. A dislocating flight, a stiffened, stale sadness had crept into his heart and then he looked at the hardened form there, waiting to be released, waiting for the release, and that it was his for the taking. The take, and then release. Ichiro felt small waves of a distant throb growing from deep in his stomach, reaching down and spreading, filling him.

A woman slipped on the marble a couple of meters behind them and yelped in pain. The two men turned, the spell of pulsing sexuality disappearing. Ichiro reached the woman first.

"Are you all right?" Bonny asked from a small distance, not waiting for an answer as he casually walked toward the fallen woman. "Perhaps we can help you with your bags?"

"Let me help you up," offered Ichiro.

The woman smiled and, looking up to Ichiro, thanked him. He wondered how old she might be. She didn't appear particularly elderly but her hair was almost entirely silver, more so than his mother's hair. Crystal blue eyes twinkled warmly as Ichiro picked up her purse and small bag, and handed them to her.

"Are you staying here long, dear?"

"Just a week, on business," said Ichiro.

"Well, should you ever feel like you need to get away from the business you're here for, perhaps you can come visit me. I'll show you something . . . something I think you'll find of great interest."

Bonny hated the old bat for interfering. She was ruining everything, and if he didn't know better, she was actually flirting with Ichiro, too. Shit. He had to do something.

"Well, that's really nice of you, but we have to get going," he said. It was a dismissal.

But Ichiro didn't want to go. "I wouldn't want to be of any trouble to you," he said. He knew he had never seen this woman before, but there was something that felt strangely familiar about her.

"Don't be silly, child. It's something I want to do." She pulled a slip of paper out of her purse, something she didn't need anymore. It was stained and had been crumpled up. She smoothed out the paper enough to write on it, and gave it to Ichiro. "That's my number. Just come by, anytime is fine with me." Her eyes twinkled again, "Thanking the young and able is something older women tend to do more as the years pass. I'm sure your mother is very proud of you." With that she gently patted his hand, the hand that still held the dirty scrap of paper she had given him.

Ichiro placed it into his breast pocket, watching the woman walk around the corner and out of view. It wasn't until he was sitting in Bonny's car that he realized he didn't know the woman's name. He pulled the paper out of his pocket and looked at it. Just a phone number. He turned it over. It was a ragged, ripped corner that had been torn off of some ad or pamphlet. He couldn't quite make sense of anything on that side. In any case, she hadn't written her name there, either. No introductions. The woman didn't even know his name. Ichiro had heard that Americans were like this, very casual. But to invite someone to your house and not even exchange names—it was absurd. He shoved the scrap into his pocket again and decided he would throw it away later.

Brown, flat buildings and a brown, flat land passed by the car window. Everything about the land felt wide and exposed, but the bare blue sky above felt close enough to touch. It was pressing down on Ichiro. He wanted to go home.

"Since you're a day late, I'm afraid you won't have the luxury of settling in at your hotel tonight," said Bonny without apology. "All the business meetings have been arranged and we couldn't have everyone drop what they were doing just because you were coming a day late. As a result, I need to drive you to your first meeting now, and then we can drop by your hotel later." He glanced at Ichiro and asked, "Is that all right with you?" He didn't wait for an answer. "Too bad your plane schedule was altered like that. Otherwise, we could have had some fun on your first night here." He smacked his lips and said, "Well, that's life, I guess."

Ichiro was almost glad of the meetings and wondered how he might get out of having Bonny drive him to his hotel later. He would think of something.

The men were on the road for some time, driving smoothly over the asphalt, travelling the wide straight roads that seemed so near the Sandia Mountains Ichiro imagined the craggily rocks were near enough and rough enough to scrape against his soul. Spiked boulders hung precariously on the side of the mountain as if they didn't particularly want to be there, held in place by spiked weeds and cacti. The stones were needled in place, in danger of rolling down and smashing onto the foothills into tiny bits of dust, becoming a pebbly nothing on a vast desert floor.

Large, lumbering, rambling tumbleweeds nearly as big as the car Ichiro sat in rolled along the road at the speed of the wind, perhaps 15 miles per hour. Drivers swerved around the weeds and continued on. Such a weed, thorny, made of wooden splinters and exaggerated rounded spikes would never be damaged by a car, was never in danger of being flattened by wheels. But it may well puncture the tires and flatten the car, and scratch up the paint job just fine. Ichiro wanted to go home, and sighed. He stared out the window, trying to ignore the tumbleweeds, his welcoming committee.

The flat, low buildings that spread out across the land became sparse, and then vanished, being replaced by commuters.

"Where are we going?" Ichiro asked, feeling a sense of panic well up within him.

"Los Alamos, of course. Where do you think?" Bonny shot Ichiro a puzzled smile. "That's what you came here for, isn't it? To visit the Los Alamos National Laboratory, discuss the experiments with the other lab technicians?" Bonny didn't wait for an answer. "Just lay back and relax . . . take a nap. I'll get you there on time." He flashed a brilliant white grin and added, "Trust me."

Trusting Bonny was the last thing Ichiro would do, but he did lay his head back, and he did doze off.

He dreamt of a cowboy, a tall man with chaps and no pants, and very well hung.

"Howdy," said the cowboy, tipping his hat. It was a brown cowboy hat, like the ones Ichiro had seen cowboys wearing in so many movies. His jaw was unshaven and his chin cleft, a strong jaw. The cowboy took a step toward Ichiro and the chink of spurs sounded in his ears. The wind howled.

"Ichiro? Ichiro, wake up. We're here." Bonny rattled the car keys near Ichiro's ears again, *chink-chink* and *chink*. "C'mon, wake up."

Ichiro groaned, his stomach grumbled, and he opened his car door to let in a surprisingly chill air, delivered with the force of a powerful desert wind. He closed the door again. He sighed, fleetingly allowed himself to hope that there would be food platters at this meeting, and barred up his strength to face the wind. Bonny lead Ichiro to what looked like an army barrack that was positioned slightly angled and in front of a cluster of other metal-bodied barracks.

Once inside, the smells of coffee and doughnuts permeated the air, the sound of a phone ringing in one of the offices toward the back and a man answering it, and several people stomping across an elevated surface that was not permanently fastened to the ground, a deep and hollow echo accommodated each step taken.

Stomp-stomp and stomp, "Hello, you must be Ichiro Hashiki, or should I say Hashiki Ichiro?" boomed a tall and slender, gray-haired man. He held his hand out for a hearty shake.

"My first name is Ichiro, and my last name is Hashiki. In Japan we place the surname before the first."

"Ah, yes. Well, isn't that interesting. I'm Jonathan Johnston, and as you probably know, the director here. Welcome to America," he said with a sweeping gesture of his arm, as if the barrack and the people within it were a microcosm and well representative of the nation as a whole. Grinning, he asked, "How do you like it so far?" For a moment Ichiro felt as though the barrack had gone silent, all breaths held as they waited for the verdict of a Japanese man. The scientists who founded these laboratories had developed the bombs that had been dropped on Japan in 1945. Now he was sent to evaluate a product that these same labs hoped to develop. It was Ichiro who would determine whether or not these experiments would receive funding. It was a peculiar position of power, one that Ichiro didn't particularly enjoy or desire.

"It's nice," Ichiro lied. He wanted to go home.

The room exhaled, almost as a tangible relaxing of metal sheet.

"But I'm very hungry," added Ichiro with a weak smile. The room laughed nervously. The kind of hunger caused by travel was well understood.

"What? Didn't Mr. Bonny feed you before your drive here?" Johnston shot Bonny a look of disdain, as if this wasn't the first time he had escorted a guest to official business on an empty stomach. "No matter. This meeting is catered. Please help yourself, Mr. Hashiki. After such a long flight, you must be famished."

Ichiro ate carrots, celery, a roast beef sandwich with lettuce, potato salad, drank copious amounts of tar black coffee, and stuffed himself with three sugar-glazed doughnuts. No one commented, but everyone noticed. It didn't matter.

The meeting was cursory and general. The laboratory's plan was to reduce the quantity of radioactive waste. Theories about rocketing it to the sun had been rejected years earlier, as any technical failure of the rocket in transit would be catastrophic. But the lab felt that the basic idea of incinerating the material was a good idea and wanted funds to develop a super-oven, a special oven that could heat to temperatures equal to that of the sun, a controllable hydrogen bomb, sustained within a fabricated gravity field. Ichiro was skeptical. This was not the first time such a concept had been toyed with, and previous attempts had failed miserably.

After several lab technicians had finished their individual presentations, and Ichiro had been subjected to a slide show of graphs and tables projecting how successful the experiments would be at solving waste storage problems worldwide, Ichiro was escorted to Mr. Bonny's car for a drive back into Albuquerque.

"I'd rather not just now," said Ichiro. "I'm actually very interested in seeing more of the sights, the places of interest right here," he said, indicating the immediate surroundings. He would have said anything to stay away from Bonny.

"Oh, well, if it's sightseeing you're interested in, I can show you the local places of interest," cooed Bonny, his meaning sexual rather than cultural.

"What did you have in mind, Mr. Hashiki?" Mr. Johnston looked expectant.

"Cowboys and Indians," said Ichiro. "I'm in the Wild West, I'd like to see cowboys and Indians."

Mr. Johnston boomed a laugh.

"Ha! Of course you would. I should have thought of that." He smiled, "We locals sometimes forget the allure of

our surroundings, and take them for granted." Turning to
Bonny he then instructed, "Why don't you take Mr.
Hashiki to a wrangler range? There are a few in this area,
not too far away."

"Or I could show him the neighboring Indian reservation, how would that be?" Bonny smiled in a way that suggested a certain shared understanding, but Ichiro couldn't
have guessed what it was. Something unspoken had just
been communicated, and Ichiro suspected it might have
been a threat.

"There's a very good steak restaurant down the road,"
said Mr. Johnston, pulling a thick wallet from his back
pocket. "Here's some money. Why don't you eat there
tonight?"

Bonny took the money. "Do you mean the steakhouse?
This won't be enough." Johnston have him another bill.
Ichiro couldn't quite see the denomination in the dim light
of the setting sun, but it was sufficient in meeting Bonny's
expectations. "That's better, thanks, Mr. Johnston." Bonny
gleamed a white broad smile, fit for Hollywood glint.

"Fine, fine. Have a relaxing evening, and we'll meet
again tomorrow." Turning to Ichiro, the man remarked, "I
hope you take the opportunity to enjoy the city so long as
you're here, Mr. Hashiki. It isn't Tokyo, but it's the place I
like to call home."

In the car, Bonny said, "I have something you should
see. We'll eat at a great Mexican food restaurant I know,
and then I'll take you to the Indian reservation. The only
real cowboys left in this area are the Indians. Native Americans. Some people prefer to say Native Americans. Stupid.
Anyone born in this country is a native American." Bonny
jabbed his own shoulder with a hard thumb, "I am a
native, damn it." They drove in silence.

The dinner of fajitas and baked beans with melted
cheddar, some spiced red rice, and a salad they no longer

had space in their stomachs to eat was also one of tall, iced and salted margaritas, mariachi music, and crude sexual jokes. There were a few cowboys in the place, wearing plaid shirts and jeans with large silver belt buckles studded with turquoise. Some wore boots, some sneakers. They all talked very loud, thought Ichiro.

He wasn't used to eating such heavy food, but it was delicious and very satisfying.

Then they left for the Indian reservation.

"Have you ever experienced an hallucinogenic drug?"

Ichiro wondered why Bonny would ask him such a question, and answered, "Yes, but many years ago, when I was a student."

"Good," he grinned. "It's more fun if you already have had a little experience with some sort of psychotropic drug."

What was more fun? "Where are you taking me, Mr. Bonny?"

"I told you, the reservation. I've known the chief for a long time, and told him that I wanted to bring you with me tonight." He paused, glancing briefly at Ichiro. "I'm quarter Comanche Indian on my mother's side."

Bonny pulled the car around and off the paved, lit road. They travelled on a dirt road now, a vast open space with no lights but for the starry sky that hung so low above their heads. The rumbling sound of crunching, sandy gravel rattled the car along the way, creating a sound like distant thunder rolling in over the desert mesa.

The car came to a stop very near what appeared to be a series of campfires. Ichiro got out of the car, feeling as though he might be able to touch the stars they were so big in the New Mexico sky. The air was crisp and cool, and a light wind cut through his clothes, carrying the scratchy, glasslike desert sand with it. He felt like a cowboy tonight, his skin marked by dusty winds and the cold evening brushing over the tightness of exposure to a sun that hung low in the sky, a dry and windy day. Ichiro had been driving around the desert most of the day, and during the few hours he was indoors it was in a metal barrack, a giant heat conductor. He thought his skin felt like dried leather, toughened, cooked.

"Good evening, Bonny." A voice that sounded ancient and tired drifted on the campfire embers carried by the desert wind. "You brought him?"

"Yes," said Bonny.

Who was there? Ichiro wondered.

As Bonny and Ichiro walked toward the voice, Ichiro could see that they were walking now around a tepee, and on the other side of it was a fire, and sitting before the fire, was an old Indian.

"You do not know why you are here," said the Indian. "Sit down, and I will show you the things in yourself that you cannot see."

Ichiro sat near the Indian and waited.

"I am Chief Rising Sun, and if you are ready to see who you really are, then we will go inside the tepee together." Then he asked, "Do you know what peyote is?"

Ichiro shook his head.

"It is a psychotropic drug derived from the peyote cactus, outlawed in the land outside this reservation. But here, it is sacred, a holy means of communicating with the spirit world, and with God. We have different rituals and different ways of administering peyote. Tonight, if you believe you are ready, you may join us in the peyote sauna."

Ichiro wasn't sure that he was ready, and asked, "What do you do in the peyote sauna?"

Chief Rising Sun looked to Bonny and made a motion with his hand that suggested he should explain to his friend.

Bonny said, "We enter the sauna; the peyote is set to fired coals in the middle of the room. Some of the elders also eat small amounts of peyote, or smoke it, and as you sweat out your sins, you allow the peyote to open your soul to the heavens. It is a cleansing ritual, and one that will help you to understand things you would otherwise never know and never understand."

Ichiro nodded, surprised to see this side of Bonny, a sincere aspect of the man that up until now he had not revealed.

Bonny and Ichiro followed the example set by the old chief. Outside of the large sauna tepee, they stripped out of all their clothes. They poured water over their naked bodies and entered the tepee, one by one.

The tepee was dark save for the fire in the middle, and the air was thick, heavy, and sweet. Ichiro could taste it on his tongue, and it swelled a little, numbed. Naked men and women sat on benches circling in two rows around the fire, sweating quietly.

Ichiro sat down next to Bonny, on a bench toward the back of the tepee. Bonny smiled reassuringly.

A gourd-shaped pot was passed to Bonny, and he stuck his hand in it. Some kind of golden, shiny, thick substance that looked like liquid amber clung to his fingers. He began to smear the viscous stuff over his skin and handed the pot to Ichiro. Then, with both hands, Bonny continued to spread it over his entire body, standing up briefly, so that every bit of his naked self glistened by the dim firelight.

"What is it?" Ichiro asked. "Peyote?"

Bonny smiled, and brought his middle finger up to Ichiro's mouth. Honey. It was honey. Bonny read the question in Ichiro's eyes and answered, "With the heat of the sauna, it softens and cleanses the skin. You won't feel sticky, trust me."

Ichiro took a big gob of honey in his hand and passed the gourd to the next person. Standing up, he then smeared it over his entire body, just as Bonny had.

"You missed a spot," whispered Bonny, and glided a hand up and over Ichiro's ass. The touch was caramel-colored stickiness, and then the stickiness yielded, melted, vanished into skin and heat and sweat. Ichiro dripped and glistened gold and fire.

Chief Rising Sun stood and poured sweet-smelling water over the coals, then a rag was flung around and around through the air, circulating the heat like a propeller. When the sting of the heat wave hit Ichiro full in the chest, he realized that the liquid thrown over the coals had been a form of peyote, perhaps a peyote tea.

"That's the peyote," explained Bonny. "Keep your head down and over your knees until the heat subsides again." Ichiro did as he was told. "Otherwise, you'll pass out."

Ichiro blinked. Everything was so vibration-ish and colorfully something-or-other. A wave of heat pressed against his face, tightening his pores and then opening them again, breaking the sweat, forcing it out, flushing and fleshing out, draining and releasing. Ichiro blinked. He was tea. He could drink himself in, and be distilled. Colors of gold and bronze glistened softly in the firelight. A rag whirled through the air and made a pretty rainbow.

And then he was there, standing before him with chaps, boots with spurs, and no pants. A broad bare chest and the most enormous cock Ichiro had ever imagined walked toward him, and asked him to spread honey over his shaft. Ichiro found the gourd filled with honey and poured it over the cowboy's cock, and spread the honey up and down the length of it, using both hands because it was necessary. The cowboy was shiny and golden, a glint of calm satisfaction flinted from under his broad-rimmed cowboy hat, sparks, sparkling golden. The fire was renewed. Bonny was shiny and golden, too. Ichiro thought maybe he was confused and that Bonny was the cowboy. He looked down at Bonny's dick and realized, no, it was different. A nice cock, though. Bonny smiled with big white teeth, admiring Ichiro's body, admiring Ichiro's erection. His dick was getting bigger, harder. Ichiro sat down on Bonny's lap and took his honey-dipped stick in with one swift movement. The warmth spread over him, the honey soaked into them, and the towel made another pretty rainbow.

Ichiro and Bonny stepped out of the tepee around 3:00 A.M., and dressed under the stars.

"I feel so great!" exclaimed Ichiro, and Bonny laughed. Then behind Bonny's head Ichiro saw a symbol painted onto a nearby tepee, a shape that seemed somehow important to him, a circle with a swirling cross running through it. He saw in his mind the face of that silver-haired woman who slipped and fell at the airport. Checking his pockets, he found the scrap of paper she had given him, the one on which she had written her phone number. Turning it over, he realized that the scrap had that very symbol printed on it, part of a larger picture that had been torn away.

He pointed to the tepee. "Do you know what that symbol means?"

"Sure, it's the sign of the four ages: infancy, youth, middle age, and old age, sometimes a fortune-teller's icon, sort of. It's a tribal thing."

"Can we go in there?"

Bonny considered, "Maybe. I'll ask the chief." With that, Bonny removed his clothes again and reentered the sauna. The two men came out together.

"You want to see the soothsayer?" The chief didn't wait for an answer. "Hold on, I'll see if she is awake."

He called out from the tepee and a woman's voice permitted his entrance. He disappeared and shortly thereafter reappeared. "She said you can come in," he waved.

Bonny and Ichiro went in together, and she was there. It was the woman, and she seemed to have been waiting for them. "Sit down, please." She looked into Bonny's eyes, and said, "It's nice to see you again, Bonny." Then she turned to Ichiro and said, "I'm glad you finally made it, 'Ro-chan."

'Ro-chan? Ichiro was stunned into silence. That was the nickname by which only his mother called him. And he wondered, *Who is this woman?*

The two men sat together side by side with great anticipation.

"Yeah, I heard about you, and I know what you're doing here." He spat. Ichiro never thought, never once in his whole life, that he would meet a laboratory technician who chewed tobacco. But this one did.

"But I'm here to tell you something you need to know, something I can't do anything about, but maybe you can." The man paused for a moment, looked at his feet. "Somebody ought to."

Ichiro was inspecting the radioactive waste storage facilities, maintained by the laboratory and funded by the government. This was part of the working itinerary that Mr. Johnston had arranged for Ichiro, meant to show exactly how waste was currently handled as a stark contrast to the alternative solution that the labs wanted to provide, given time and the money to develop that solution. They very much wanted Ichiro to tell his boss that their plans were worth the time and money to develop. But when Ichiro reached the storage facility, he was met with a very disgruntled technician by the name of Smithers. The tour of the radioactive waste facility was scant and rushed, and the two men now stood on a makeshift metal porch outside of Smithers's office barrack.

The storage facility stood behind them, a strange building that looked like a shiny, white, plastic tent the size of a warehouse, and before them, was a cruel and untamed nature. An open sky, an open land.

Mr. Smithers and Ichiro looked out on the horizon, the vast dry desert land expansive before them. "You see that, out there?" He pointed at the horizon. Ichiro looked out in that direction but could see nothing, nothing at all, just dirt, cacti, and some scraggily heatstroked bushes. Ichiro shook his head. He saw nothing.

"No, right there. There, see that?" He was getting impatient.

"No, I don't see anything. What am I not seeing, Mr. Smithers?"

"Junk. Radioactive waste. It's out there, just out in the open. And I know how it got there." He paused to look hard into Ichiro's eyes. "We did it. The labs, a bunch of guys got the idea to just start dumping some of their stuff out there, save their own departments a good amount of money doing it, too. Johnston don't give a shit, it was probably his idea in the first place." He spat. "Know what else?" He squinted his eyes, making himself look meaner. "That's the reservation, that is. It don't even belong to us, it belongs to them." He spat again. "That's right above the underground water supply, too." He grinned, unhappily, as if the world had conspired to prove to him that men were evil. "You go over there, you won't even believe the mess you'll see. But when you go, be just sure to wear a white suit, gloves, everything. That whole place out there is radiated to shit." He spat, and turned back toward his doorway to indicate that the conversation was over. Then he stopped with his hand on the doorknob, and looked over his shoulder.

"You do what you do, but if anyone asks, I don't know nothing about you, why you're here, nothing." He turned fully, pointing angrily at Ichiro. "You got that? You tell anyone I said anything to you about this, and I'll make sure you spend the rest of your days in living hell." He spat once more for effect, then added, "Believe me, that's something I know about."

Ichiro packed what he needed, borrowing some items from one of the laboratory barracks, got in Bonny's car, and drove out in the general direction Mr. Smithers had pointed. Toward the horizon, somewhere to the right of where the storage facility stood. The government had given the tribe's people land, and then built a radioactive waste storage facility right on the border of it. When Ichiro stepped down off of Smithers's porch, he was already standing on the reservation.

Ichiro drove along the dirt road, and then he saw what Smithers had warned him of. He would not be getting out of the car for a closer look, even with his protective lab gear.

The junk that had been dumped here was clearly toxic. Radiation cannot be registered by any human senses, but Ichiro's radiographic instrument showed unquestionably that the area was highly radiated. The small lightbulb indicator flashed emphatically at a fevered rate.

This was against the law. The waste should be contained in fifty-five-gallon T-208 drums and packed in halite before being stored in a facility where it can be monitored by a technician and tracked by computer. It is an extraordinarily expensive endeavor to properly store radioactive waste but to do otherwise? Simply unthinkable. Ichiro was looking at the unthinkable now.

Discarded office furniture that had been chemically burned by experiments gone awry lay splintered amongst the trash as if it had been tossed off the back of a truck. Perhaps sixty leaking T-208 containers, cracked and rusted, some of them tipped open with the tops popped off and the liquids already drained into the sandy dirt, emanated a toxic smell that caught at Ichiro's nostrils even with all the windows rolled up. There was no question at all as to who was responsible for this. It could only have come from one source.

Ichiro noticed the grade of the road beginning to slope upward and hoped that by situating himself high enough he might get a clear look of the entire area that was being used as an illegal dumpsite.

After driving for twenty minutes, Ichiro parked and stepped outside the car. It was expansive, the dump, perhaps spanning an area twice as large as the laboratory's legal storage facilities. Ichiro went back to the car trunk for his camera. There was an obstruction and the shock of seeing it made Ichiro's legs collapse under him. He fell hard on the desert earth and looked up in shock.

"Hi there, Hashi. Did you miss me?" HM stood before Ichiro now, wearing a gray suit and black trench coat. "I think you have something that belongs to me."

Ichiro didn't know what the man could have meant. "I don't have anything of yours, I took nothing from you. Except the champagne."

HM grinned. "Yes, the champagne. That you can keep. But there was one thing that I gave you, just something on loan, really. And I want it back." Again, the yellow smile. "Haven't you felt as if maybe, something was eating at you? Isn't there something bothering you, itching to get out?" The gaps between his teeth were black and vacuous, as if there was no end to the back of his mouth. His mouth. That's when Ichiro realized what was different about HM, why it was he looked changed. His moustache, the caterpillar moustache, he had shaved it off.

"Ah, I see the truth is starting to dawn," smiled HM. "I miss the little tickle over my lip, if you get my drift." He raised his arms and revealed long feathers. He flapped them twice and as his feet lifted off the ground, they became talons. The combed-back hair seemed to mold itself onto his head, shifting and melding until a lumpy hairless head was revealed. The vulture.

Before Ichiro could move, before he could think what to do, the vulture was upon him, stabbing, pecking and tearing away at him with his thick, heavy sharp beak, scratching viciously with his thick talons, easily ripping through fabric and skin. Ichiro screamed, rolling onto his back in agony, trying to fight sharp ripping and stabbing tools, distracted and confused by the flapping, bobbing movement of uneven feathers. He wished the ground could shift underneath his body, let him just sink away, and disappear right into the earth. He heard another sound, a man's yell. He looked up and behind him, and saw legs running. Two legs. A man with chaps was running to help him. He wore boots. *Whap!* A cowboy boot kicked the vulture. *Whop!* Ichiro heard more than saw another boot connect, kick the beast.

The vulture screeched hideously, "Kyaa!"

Ichiro glimpsed the flash of a broad knife shining in the sun. There was silence, the wind. Ichiro squinted into the desert sun, trying to lift his head. His chest hurt, and he knew he was bleeding. The face of a man blocked out the sun's intensity.

The man asked, "Are you all right?" Ichiro knew the face. It was the face in his daydream, the face that came to him in a haze of peyote. It was the cowboy. Ichiro closed his eyes, and allowed himself to be unconscious.

He was sitting on a tatami mat facing north in a beautiful tearoom with softly lit shoji screens, and the cowboy was his guest, sitting on another tatami mat, and facing south. They would represent the yin and yang, and share the ritual Japanese tea, and then . . .

Ichiro opened his eyes to the robust smell of cherry pipe tobacco and the crackle of a modest campfire. He could hardly register what he saw sitting before him, his head was so battered and his eyes so resistant to focus. It was the cowboy, smoking a pipe. He sat on his saddle wearing his chaps over a pair of worn jeans, and big boots. A white T-shirt stretched over his muscled chest in a warm and inviting hug.

Ichiro sat up, and the immense pain in his chest was debilitating. He stiffened with a groan, tried to relax his muscles again, and used his hands to push himself up into a seated position. He folded his legs in and assessed his situation. It was just he and the cowboy, a horse, a fire, and his wounds had been cleaned, treated, and then bandaged.

"What did you use to clean the wounds?"

"Peyote." The cowboy puffed his pipe.

"Oh, uh. Peyote is also medicinal then?" The cowboy closed his eyes, and it was answer enough. "Thank you for—everything," muttered Ichiro.

The cowboy nodded, and it was understood that no further acknowledgement would be necessary. Honor was what a man like the cowboy simply had. He didn't require thanks for being who he was. He sat and squinted into the fire.

"How did you— I mean, how did you come to be right there, right when I needed you? Were you following me? Who are you?"

The cowboy puffed on his pipe, and stopped to consider the man sitting opposite the fire from him. "Does it matter?"

Ichiro was silenced, stilled, and a little stunned at this question. He wasn't sure what mattered, but he did know that he wanted to know something more about the man who saved his life. So he answered, "You saved my life."

The cowboy grinned, and replied, "What else would I have done? Let the damn bird shred your chest open?" He shook his head in a silent chuckle. "That's no way to treat a fellow." He puffed on his pipe, and added, "Smoke?"

Ichiro shook his head. The peyote sauna still affected him a little. He saw colors in the objects around him that could not possibly be real. The fire was lavender, orange, and green. The cowboy's hat seemed to glow red. Then he realized he had inhaled a great deal of peyote, enough to stay in his system for several days, and his wounds had been additionally treated with peyote. Could I overdose from peyote? "I took a peyote sauna last night. Should I worry? With my wounds, I mean . . ."

The cowboy looked at Ichiro straight in the eye. "Did you enjoy it?"

Ichiro considered, and nodded his head.

"Then you don't need to worry."

Ichiro touched the bandages on his chest, and picked at it, tentatively.

"Don't mess with it," ordered the cowboy. He started to tap the spent tobacco out of his pipe and into the fire. "You hungry?"

Ichiro shook his head.

"Well, you're going to eat anyway." He grabbed for a skillet that was sitting atop the log. There was a fork resting on the lip; obviously the cowboy had used it earlier. "Take it," he said, offering it to his patient.

Ichiro took the skillet and fork, and asked, "What is it?" Some kind of brown food that Ichiro could not identify was cooked and mushy looking. It smelled good, though.

"Food." And with that, the cowboy slid down the log so that he sat on the ground, pulled his cowboy hat down over his eyes, and leaned back against the log. " 'Night," he said.

In the stillness, Ichiro sat under the stars with a skillet of brown food and the sounds of crickets as a serenade. "Good night," replied Ichiro. He looked at the cowboy and down at his skillet of food, then at the cowboy again. He didn't even know his name. "What is your name?"

"Jim." He pushed his hat up his forehead enough to peek out from under the rim, and said, "You're the winged leopard from Japan, I know." He closed his eyes again, and fell asleep under his hat.

The next morning at early dawn, Ichiro woke stiff and cold. The campfire had been stoked and refueled by Jim the cowboy, fresh wood already burning and crackling under the pressure of fire. Ichiro rolled onto his side and saw Jim, naked save for his chaps. He was shaving with a single blade, his cock gently swaying as it hung, thick between his legs.

"'Morning," said Jim. "Coffee's on the fire. Help yourself."

The *scratchy-scratch scratch* sound of a man shaving thick dark hair off of his neck lightly echoed across the desert floor. Once the word *coffee* registered in Ichiro's ears, he could smell it through the crisp morning air. It smelled like warmth, and Ichiro poured himself a cup of the hot black stuff. This early morning, he would drink it and be glad for it. It was not a morning for tea.

Jim's dick was alluring, frightening in its sheer length and breadth even while limp, a tempting challenge. Ichiro felt rough, he felt like maybe this morning he could handle a ride like that. He wouldn't mind trying. Jim the cowboy was a man, a true man's man. Being taken by him would be an experience to remember and treasure.

"That looks very inviting," said Ichiro.

The cowboy finished his shaving and wiped the residue cream off with a small towel. He turned to face Ichiro, his dick shifting heavily with his movements.

"How do you manage to sit on your horse with that?"

"I don't see why you'd be asking, unless you wanted to find out for yourself." Jim looked at Ichiro with meaning. "You wanting to find out if you can straddle this?" Ichiro could see that Jim's cock was growing, getting harder, and rising. He could not keep his eyes off of it.

"Yes, yes I do."

Jim walked around the campfire and to Ichiro, standing before him. "You know what to do," he said.

Ichiro took the cock in both hands and started to stroke it up and down, pressing it between a firm and steady grip. Both hands. He needed both hands. He bent forward in a movement that hurt the wounds on his chest, and kissed, licked. Even half hard, Jim was too much to put into Ichiro's mouth. It was almost too much, when he rolled onto his back and lifted his legs up and over Jim's strong shoulders, to take him in.

Bonny was crouched down on the hard desert floor, dusty and dirty, ruining his suit. "I could ring that old bat's neck," he muttered to himself. He could hardly believe he was involved in this fiasco at all, and here he was with his stomach to the ground, in hiding.

A white, extra-long stretch limo appeared from the distance, glittering under the sun's intensity. Waves of reflected heat emanated in wiggling images from the limo's metallic body, as if an invisible cape flapped behind it, distorting the desert in its wake.

This was the moment Bonny had been waiting for, his calling.

The limo pulled up to the barrack and stopped. Mr. Johnston got out, and a trio of people got out with him. There was one man Bonny didn't recognize, and two gorgeous blonde who could only have been twins. Bonny pulled his binoculars out and focused on the man. He knew, from the detailed description he got from Ichiro and the old bat, the second man could only be HM. It had to be him.

Mr. Johnston paused for the two blondes and waited for them to catch up with him, each one flanking his sides. He stuck his hands up their miniskirts as they embraced him, lifting their skirts slightly to reveal tight and shapely buttocks. Bonny smirked. He knew who the real seducer was in this situation. Johnston would think that he was the one in charge—until it was too late.

Once Johnston, HM, and the twins were inside and the door closed, Bonny pushed himself up and rushed to the side of the limo, crouching down beside it so he would remain hidden. He pulled the small bit of plastic and metal and wires from his pocket, fastened it to the underbelly of the limo, and scampered back to his hiding place.

Jim was kicking dust over the campfire to extinguish it, looking at Ichiro with a particular intensity. "You ready for this?"

Ichiro smiled, a little sad, "As ready as I can be." He looked out to the horizon, the clear blue sky spanning ahead endlessly. Then he added, almost to himself, "I think you've done all you can to prepare me," and he turned to Jim and winked.

Jim laughed out loud and slapped his knee. "Let's do this," he said and grabbed his saddle. Holding it in both hands, he watched Ichiro and asked, "Need help?"

Ichiro withdrew the red ball he had been carrying with him since his brief stay in Germany. It seemed to all appearances like any other simple bit of plastic. But the old soothsayer had shown him, or rather, helped him to see that it was much more than that.

Ichiro stood naked now, and placed the ball against his forehead. It began to glow, and Ichiro was able to let go of it, and it stayed there, hovering above the slope of his nose. Ichiro closed his eyes, and envisioned in his mind what had happened in Brazil. Images of large breasts, a thickness filling him up from behind, the innocent-looking Ronaldo kneeling before him, with Ichiro's dick in his mouth. The caterpillar. Then there was the vulture, so near him Ichiro could hardly breathe, the foul stench of rotting and spoiled milk filling his nostrils, a sweet stench. Just remembering it all, that horrible image filling and overwhelming his view, made Ichiro shiver. He heard a chinking sound, the sound of Jim's spurs.

"Stay back," ordered Ichiro. He would do this part alone.

Jim kept his distance, but put the saddle down so that

his hands would be free should Ichiro need his help after all.

A black, wiggling, squirming sensation niggling at Ichiro's neck made all the hairs there stand on end. It tickled and hurt, and it had to come out. As if speaking through a thick fog, Ichiro said, "Give me your knife."

Jim pulled a large hunting knife from his left boot and placed it in Ichiro's hand. He squinted against the brightly glowing red emanating from Ichiro's head; its brightness ever increasing.

Ichiro's neck was swelling, a thing inside it was swelling with anger, turning and spinning, coiling itself in some kind of webbed, sticky cocoon. Ichiro fisted the knife so that he could cut the back of his own neck open if he had to. There was a vivid crackling sound in Ichiro's neck, as if a gooey ripping inhabited it. Ichiro's eyes popped open wide at a fluttering sensation, part of something that felt like a wing. Ichiro screamed in agony, and dropped the knife.

In a flash, Jim was at his side, picking up the knife and pulling Ichiro around so he could see his neck, and he saw the blackness there. Both wings were out of their cocoon now, he could see them flapping through the skin. It was perched on Ichiro's spine. The red glow was fierce now, emanating redness so bright that it made the desert look pink.

Jim used the point of his knife and made a small puncture wound right where he could just locate the butterfly's body. There was no blood, just blackness. It oozed out but instead of dripping down it dripped up, and each droplet of black took part in forming the blackness flitting in air, a hovering butterfly, deathly beautiful as of an evil spirit that feeds off of the living so that it can strengthen itself in perverse form. It flapped its wings, *hih-hih* and *hih* was the sound of a wing hitting the air and it infuriated the cowboy. He drew up his knife and plunged it into the butterfly, but it made no impact, it made no difference. The knife passed through the blackness, and the evil thing flitted away over the hill, heading toward the laboratory.

"Are you all right?" Jim asked, both worried and amazed that his friend was not bleeding from his neck.

Panting, Ichiro nodded. "We've got to track it," he said. The red glow still pulsed in front of his eyes, and he kept them shut. "It's going to find someone else it can inhabit, someone . . . more . . . corruptible." Ichiro struggled to get his words out as the light began to overwhelm him, spreading across and over and down and around and through his entire body.

It felt hot and thick, like raw honey warmed by fire, smoky ringlets of warmth floated over 'Ro-chan, making all the little hairs on his naked body stand on end. And they began to grow, and thicken, and he could hear the creaking crackle of splintering bones. They were his bones, but it felt good, like a long-awaited stretch. He flexed his thick, broad claws into the dusty earth beneath his leathery paws, opened his maw in a wide stretching yawn, and roared with delight. He felt so alive! His tail swished happily behind him and the wings that sprouted from his back rose and fell a few times to test their strength. They lifted his feline body from the ground, and 'Ro-chan couldn't wait to fly! He pulled himself higher into the sky, whiskers at the corners of his toothy mouth twitching gleefully, and a bright pink tongue playfully licked over the thick and sensitive hairs. He grunted, confused that something was holding his tail and pulling.

"Hey, come down! I've got to saddle you!" It was the cowboy.

Oh yeah, thought 'Ro-chan. He let his wings fold in and he pounced heavily to the ground with a great *thud!*

Jim placed the saddle over 'Ro-chan's large leopard back, just in front of his massive wings, and mounted. He wore nothing but chaps, boots with spurs, and his holsters held two guns shining silvery white. His heavy cock hung to the left and his bronzed upper body flexed in anticipation. The cowboy adjusted his hat to be sure it wouldn't fly off his head and lightly kicked into 'Ro-chan's ribs. "Giddy-up!"

'Ro-chan flapped his wings and in two great bounds they took to flight, higher and higher up into the warm desert air. The wind bolstered them up, and 'Ro-chan glided with ease in great swooping movements. He roared happily and licked his chops. This was fun! Jim grabbed his cowboy hat and clenched his legs tight around the leopard's body as 'Ro-chan playfully reared up and clawed at the sky with a great roar.

"Woohoo! Yee-Hah! Heeyah, yah, yah!" Jim hooted and howled, urging the beast on, pushing and pressing and helping 'Ro-chan to free himself, to stretch his wings, to roar! The cowboy and the winged leopard from Japan flew high in the open skies, their muscles flexed and taut, their voices thick with resonance.

'Ro-chan's growling voice rumbled in his vast chest when he asked, "How did you know? From the beginning, you knew who I really was. Even when I did not."

The cowboy smiled a quiet smile. "Does it really matter?"

'Ro-chan remembered this question, and it had the same effect. So he answered, "You freed me."

"Did you enjoy it?" Jim prodded.

'Ro-chan didn't need to consider, and nodded his enormous, furry head. His big leopard ears perked up and his tail whipped at the air.

"Then you don't need to worry," replied the cowboy, and lightly spurred him on.

Kaboom! A loud explosion came from the laboratories.

"It's happened," said Jim. "That's our cue." The partners swooped down in a rush, the speed of air pressing against their bodies in hard resistance. When they reached the labs, the limo was in charred, smoky pieces, HM was screaming up into the sky, holding a gun to Bonny's head, and Mr. Johnston had collapsed, unconscious. He was naked and sprawled out on the ground next to his obliterated limousine, and the twins were holding each other tightly in a 69, pleasuring each other to multiple climaxes.

"Our plan has gone awry," observed Jim. "They've got Bonny." He drew his guns and aimed for Johnston. "Let Bonny go, Mansion!" Jim bellowed. "Let Bonny go, or I'll obliterate your little butterfly."

HM giggled, and replied, "You won't kill something you can't see, you fool. You'd just end up killing your Mr. Johnston."

To that, the cowboy smirked threateningly, and said, "Hardly matters. I'd just be doing the locals a great favor. And your butterfly will perish without him. You chose the host, Mansion, there's no going back at this point and you know it!"

HM opened his mouth to shout a retort, but instead let out a sudden shock of air. "Oof!" Bonny had elbowed him as hard as he could, and ran, heading for 'Ro-chan as fast as he could. HM lifted his arm, aimed the gun at Bonny's back, and fired.

Bonny collapsed, dead before he hit the ground.

A deafening roar filled the air and rebounded, echoing against the desert valley and reverberating off the thin wisps of cloud, and thundering against the sheet-metal barracks. 'Ro-chan extended his claws and dove as Jim fired with both guns right into HM's chest. HM fired into the sky, missing all but one shot, which hit Jim in the thigh, piercing his chaps. Howard Mansion buckled under his legs and fell to his knees, but there was no blood oozing from the multiple holes in his chest. His chamber was empty.

'Ro-chan hovered above HM, flapped his wings and reared back so that a single claw from his hind leg could entrap a bit of HM's hair. He lifted, and pulling his hulking leopard body up into the air, pulled on a strand of HM's head, and the higher into the sky he went, the more of HM would unravel, and spin out, and stretch up into the sky like a single strand of thick thread, a presence that was not a presence, something without substance, a thing that, once locked onto by the thinnest and most insignificant strand, could unravel in an instant. There was no blood, no bones, no flesh that could be hurt. Just a thin whine, like the sound of a spinning top skidding along a table, and the thin facade of HM unraveled completely, disappearing until he was nothing but a bit of yarn.

The twins pulled apart, as if in a daze, and realized with a shock that they were topless, and that there were men scattered about on the ground and that there was also, right in front of their eyes, what looked to be the remains of an explosion. Looking up, they then saw the vision of a winged leopard riding a half-naked cowboy with the biggest cock either one of them had ever seen. The sheer thought of riding a man who was hung like a horse was too much and they fainted straight away.

Mr. Johnston was sick, and his body was turning blue. His eyes popped open, and he howled. To 'Ro-chan's amazement it was a howl of anger rather than pain. The black and blue man jumped to his feet and ran toward the winged leopard as if to tackle an enemy. He jumped up into the air and grabbed onto the yarn, the stuff that had been HM. He yowled and howled, screeching like a vulture. His back started to poke out and move strangely, and suspended in the air, the beginnings of sheer black wings poked out of his body. Blood was draining down the man's legs, falling with a loud hiss as it hit the ground.

The cowboy knew what to do. He put his spurs into 'Ro-chan and they headed toward the reservation. Approaching the area where Johnston had allowed his employees to illegally dump, he began to hiss viciously and pulled harder on the strand of HM he clung to so desperately. 'Ro-chan flew higher up into the sky, higher and still higher, the altitude almost blinding, the air so difficult to breathe. They were now at a flight level of 25,500 feet.

It was not difficult to let go, just let it all fall. The string, the butterfly thing that had tried to inhabit and inhibit the 'Ro-chan from emerging and actualizing, those who would damage and pollute and seduce for their own gain, all fell, stumbling and hurdling at an increasing velocity. It was like the sound of a top spinning across a table.

And then it was over.

When the twins inevitably woke several hours later, it would be in the hospital, and for the rest of their lives neither would remember anything that had happened to them in those few days. The only imprint or evidence that either one of them shared an existence with Howard Mansion would be the bizarre and inexplicable urge to begin every sentence with "Hmm," and since they had frequently made that noise before the incident, the incessant habit went largely unnoticed.

'Ro-chan did sign his authorization on the new experiments the labs wanted to develop, and he also made sure to contact the EPA about the illegal dumping on reservation land so that the government would be forced to clean up their mess.

The funeral for Bonny was a sad event, attended by several hundred former lovers who grieved his passing for the rest of their days. Bonny had been right: his deal did go through.

'Ro-chan's trip had originally been scheduled for two full weeks and he had only been in New Mexico for a few days. He had some time. 'Ro-chan purred deeply as Jim the big cowboy absently stroked and scratched the spot behind his fuzzy ears. His tail swished happily, a simple, unrestrained reflex.

He could wait a little while longer before he went back home.

LEGACY OF BOY

MARILYN JAYE LEWIS

In the Lower Kingdom, there was existence and there was death. Aging had no meaning for the inhabitants of the Lower Kingdom. Time crept so slowly across its lush centuries that it appeared as if nothing changed there. And so it felt to everyone that Boy had been their trusted king since time began.

Boy propped himself against his pile of satin pillows, unwilling this morning to leave his royal bed. His mood was contrary as usual, but now he felt strangely resentful of his duties. His balcony doors had been thrown wide the night before and his bedchamber had filled with an ethereal night music, a music of wanderlust. It had swelled up to his windows from down along the river somewhere. Its unearthly strains had haunted him. They had seeped into his dreams and muddied his sleep. He hadn't rested well. Then before he knew it, the morning air had stirred him and he found himself awake once again.

A hint of sun filtered down through the towering pine trees that covered the Lower Kingdom, pines that had grown so enormous, century upon century, that only the bare minimum of light ever made it to Boy's bedchamber. It was a sun not bright enough to scatter the morning mist that forever hung lazily over the River Sargine.

"Your Highness!" A voice called from the great hallway outside Boy's royal bedchamber.

He didn't reply. He was reluctant to leave the plush comfort of his bed even to unbolt the door. He remained propped against his pillows, his tousled black hair hanging loose about his slender shoulders. He was in a funk this morning and he didn't know why.

"Your Highness?" It was the voice again, more insistent now and accompanied by loud knocking. Boy scowled and got out of bed. The stone floor was cold beneath his royal bare feet.

"What is it?" he demanded irritably, unbolting his door and throwing it open. He stood bare-chested before the startled servant, his muscular yet quite hairless upper body was a provocative sight. The king never appeared less than fully dressed in front of anyone, least of all a servant. After all, he was the king.

The servant rushed to explain himself. "I apologize for disturbing you, Your Highness, but there's been a message from the Upper Kingdom—from the king himself."

"From Shooter?"

"Yes, Your Majesty. From Shooter."

The servant handed Boy the tightly scrolled message. Boy grabbed it impatiently, feeling alarmed but trying to mask his agitation. "Thank you," he said abruptly. "You can go. I'll ring if I need you."

Boy slammed the door and practically ripped open the scroll as he headed back to the protective security of his still-warm bed.

It was an unsteady script on the parchment, but it was Shooter's handwriting without doubt.

"Boy, my sacred one," it began.

*The terrible fate that we'd feared might befall
one of us one day in some make believe, far-off*

future, has now befallen me. Hecton's hordes have succeeded in overrunning my kingdom. I am certain it won't be long before Hecton himself breaks through my defenses and overruns my very palace with his horrible Warrior Beasts.

Long ago, when you and I were innocents, naive princes, ignorant of the true unbridled ferocity that stormed across the borders beyond our kingdoms, we made a pact regarding Hecton. Perhaps we did make it in innocence, but I hope with all my heart that you are prepared to honor it. If Hecton himself, or one of his wretched warriors, comes near enough to infect me with the awful curse of the Beasts, you alone have courage enough to rescue me—to release me from the curse and somehow reclaim my kingdom and keep our people united.

I fear there is not time enough for me to ever receive your reply. Hecton's warriors are at the very gates. I am counting on my heart to counsel me in its wisdom, even as my destiny assails me. I blindly await your help and your mercy. If and when you do reach me, Boy, do not be fooled by appearances. You must release me, as we swore on our honor we would do for each other so long ago.

I close now in love and fellowship. May we meet again in full knowing on the other side of the wild river. Yours eternally,
Sparkle Shooter

Sparkle Shooter was king of the land of the never-rising sun, far north in the Upper Kingdom where all was ice and snow and darkness, where the people were all of a color: azure blue eyes and their hair as shockingly white as their translucent skin. On the fastest steed, it would still take Boy at least the rising of one full moon to reach him. If what Shooter feared proved to be true then it would surely be too late to save him.

You must release me, Shooter had written, as we swore on our honor we would do for each other so long ago. . . .

But death was the only release from Hecton's curse. Boy knew this. They both did. What Shooter asked of him was impossible. "I can't kill you," Boy spat aloud, tossing aside the scroll in outrage. "It's unthinkable." And yet . . . had an oath not been sworn?

"But we were only princes then," he argued with himself. "How could we know the gravity of what we were proposing? I can't kill the one I love—I won't."

And yet . . .

Boy wrenched himself from the comfort of his bed. Still clad in only his silken leggings, he stepped out on to his balcony, looking for all the world like a king serenely surveying the grandness of his kingdom on a beautiful misty morning. It was an impression that could not have been further from the truth. Inside him, Boy's rage was roiling. When would Hecton be done away with, once and forever? When would the dreaded curse of the Warrior Beasts cease to be a threat to all the kingdoms? Boy was not ready to take his men into battle with Hecton and yet there was no other choice. Already it appeared to be too late—the mere thought of it was nauseating to Boy: the vile flesh, the monstrous, heaving bodies of the Beasts roaming at will in the sacred Upper Kingdom, violating the smaller, weaker people there, violating their very king, raping him and passing on the repugnant curse.

Shooter as a Warrior Beast! It was beyond imagining, the torment he would go through. But that was indeed the fate awaiting poor Shooter. First, the ravaging, then the grotesque physical transformation into a Beast, then utter subservience to Hecton. The only way Beasts ever regained free will was through the final transformation of death.

But if our fates were reversed, Boy thought, and I were unlucky enough to be the one whose kingdom was invaded by Hecton's hordes. If it were I succumbing to the violence and the curse, facing a life of subservience to the likes of Hecton, would I not rather a fate of death?

The answer went without saying. What king would want to lose his omnipotence, his very identity to Hecton and become an inhuman killing machine? It was why the two had sworn the oath in the first place, to choose annihilation over ignoble living.

"We must keep our kingdoms pure, our people free," a young Sparkle had proposed in earnest so very long ago, and Boy had been quick to agree with this fair-skinned prince from the far north country. Sparkle had gone on in rapture, "We must vow to unite our kingdoms, come what may, in our mission to keep Hecton's hordes in retreat. To do whatever be required of us to keep our people, and our souls, free."

Sparkle's intensity had left the young Boy breathless. "Death, even?" he whispered.

"Yes, even death."

The two idealistic princes had lain together in the eiderdown, naked legs entwined and hearts enthralled. In their noble innocence, they had fallen in love. This was back in the days of the old castle, the one last occupied by Boy's grandfather so many centuries ago. Yet the memory still burned in Boy's heart, bright and hot as the fire that had cast its dancing shadows on them from the old stone hearth that night.

Boy felt disgusted with himself as he remembered those long-ago days of chivalry and early lust. How naive he'd been. Boy had not known how to execute a kiss, let alone a royal order, back then. How clumsily he had stumbled over his heart, his secret yearnings for Shooter. He'd been inarticulate and inexperienced. But how that had changed. In time, love had guided them both into knowing what was needed to be known, how to satiate their erotic longings for each other.

Boy went weak in the knees remembering it, how their love had indeed grown; had risen up and made itself undeniable. Until they could not help but consummate their lust. Until Shooter was the only soul in all the kingdoms that Boy gave his heart to unflinchingly and with abandon. Until Boy's skill as a lover had taken on a new, controlled intensity and he could gaze steadily into Shooter's eyes while they made love. His own rapture overtaking him as his thick shaft sank deep into Shooter, who opened to accept Boy with trust and ecstasy. Shooter's thighs spread wide, his legs thrown over Boy's arms as the two conjoined in sweat, in their hard-earned pleasure . . .

"And I'm to kill this man now?" Boy cried out to the universe, his voice trailing away from him and tangling ghostlike somewhere up there in the needles of the towering pines. "How on earth—how? How can I kill my own heart? Who can answer me?"

There was the faintest of echoes, and then silence was the earth's reply.

Boy was brave and, if need be, he could be a ferocious king. He did not fear war, nor dying in battle. What he did fear was dying and leaving his kingdom adrift. He'd been lazy in begetting an heir and now he knew that it was likely too late. The odds were high that he would not return from this war.

In his royal chambers, he chose to dress for battle unassisted. He wanted the time alone. He did not yet know it, but he was grieving. He was too caught up in the preparations for war to show much justice to his heart, or to how broken it was. He refused to entertain thoughts of Shooter's succumbing to Hecton's impurity or to any of the indignities he might be suffering at the hands of the Warrior Beasts. Instead, Boy focused on the elaborate ritual of dressing for battle. It was good discipline—keeping his thoughts trained on minute details and clear from anything too emotionally charged.

So focused was he that he barely registered his own reflection in the enormous mirror before him. The flowing black hair, the black eyes that stared back at him, his lean yet exquisitely muscular frame—he saw none of these attributes. He saw himself first in a layer of silk, then a layer of leather. Lastly, he laced his boots. The iron and brass plates of his armor would not be attached until he was down in the courtyard, ready to mount Sebula, his trusted black steed. Only then would he be presented with his father's legendary sword, the sword that, hundreds of years ago, had infamously slaughtered countless Warrior Beasts.

In the courtyard, Boy kept his conversation fixed and to the point. Were the men ready, the supplies loaded? Silently, though, Boy surveyed his palace loyalists who were staying behind. There were none among them that Boy felt truly confident could rule his kingdom in good stead should he be killed in battle.

I must not be killed, then, Boy advised himself. *That's all there is to it.*

Then he mounted Sebula and leaned close to his aide-de-camp. He said, "Blitzkrin, remind me when the war is over and we've returned, I need to go into the land beyond the River Sargine and find a suitable female to give me an heir."

Blitzkrin nodded, eyeing his king strangely over this oddly timed request. "I will, my lord," he assured him.

Boy gave Blitzkrin a faint smile, knowing full well that the thought of his mating with a female—no matter how regal or high-placed she might be—would be a strange notion to any of his men. In the Lower Kingdom, females were rarely seen by men of the palace, even though there were thousands of them living beyond the River Sargine. What the king's men couldn't guess, however, was that the idea of mating with a woman seemed strangest of all to the king himself.

Boy's spurs gently urged Sebula out of the courtyard and through the palace gates. What little sunlight there was streamed down through the trees, illuminating a regiment of brave and capable men. Some on horseback, experienced at waging war. Some merely foot soldiers, green and untried. But all were ready, even though it would be weeks before they were far enough north to engage in any serious battles. A minor skirmish with a roaming Warrior Beast would be the worst in store for them for several days. But once the Lower Kingdom was behind them, the farther north they moved into the realm of ice and snow, the danger would increase exponentially.

In that gray middle ground between the Upper and Lower Kingdoms where the sun rarely shined, ran three treacherous rivers, the rivers of Lust, Forgetfulness, and Sleep. Crossing any one of them was a harrowing test of physical endurance and spiritual strength. Combined, they posed a formidable triple barrier, making it unlikely that mere common people could ever complete the arduous journey between the Upper and Lower Kingdoms. Though animals could cross the rivers at will. They were not at all affected by the spells cast by these daunting rivers. It was why the cursed Warrior Beasts, who were no longer human, were often encountered roaming wild between the kingdoms' borders.

The first challenge that Boy and his troops would face was a relatively minor one, crossing the River of Lust. It was still a few days away. It was a deceptively calm-looking river, yet so potent were its arousing waters that virgin females from kingdoms far and wide bathed in it when they were needed to conceive a child. Indeed, if it weren't for the River of Lust, it was unlikely the two sexes would ever mate at all. They had lived separate from each other for so many centuries that no natural physical attraction remained between the females and males of the human species. Yet once every century or so, the population of a given community dwindled and young females were called upon to make the great sacrifice of conceiving and giving birth to children. They were taken to the River of Lust, whose waters were so bewitching that once the virgins were immersed in it, their distaste for the male gender all but evaporated. Unsuspecting men in their villages were assailed from all sides then, and great orgies ensued, lasting several days, until the men were as aroused as the women, until every ready male was thoroughly depleted of his seed. Until conception was underway, and the effect of the lusty waters was over.

Out ahead of the regiment, Boy rode Sebula, holding a steady pace as the black steed's sturdy hooves ably made their way through the dense forest. As they journeyed, the king kept an eye always on the farthest trees, scanning them for any encroaching Warrior Beasts. Yet in his mind, he stewed over this unpleasant notion, this mating of the female with the male—it was his only hope of begetting a true heir to his throne, a male from his own bloodline. Boy had been born no less than a king, descended from kings in a hereditary line that reached as far back as the beginning of time. It was only right to continue that legendary line with a bona fide blood heir to ascend the throne.

As his father and grandfather were before him, Boy was biologically equipped to produce nothing but a male heir. Yet it still required a woman, and an unordinary woman at that, to conceive a king.

As unusual as she might prove to be, Boy thought, the whole idea is still disgusting.

He strained to keep his thoughts on Shooter instead.

Poor Shooter. He, too, had neglected to beget an heir and now his entire kingdom was likely overrun by the enemy, with no one closer than a month's journey away who could even attempt to salvage the situation.

Shooter, Boy thought longingly. What has become of you?

As boys, they had braved those treacherous rivers countless times to be together, to roam the forests unaccompanied by palace chaperones, to unearth their own princely adventures.

The third river, the River of Sleep, was the worst of the three rivers, as its waters caused one to be laden with unbearable fatigue. If a person didn't make it quickly to the opposite shore of that roaring river, he would be overcome with sleep and drown. For strapping young princes, however, it was the most short-lived of the effects of the three rivers. With just a little endurance on their part, it was surmounted and shaken off. And the second river, the River of Forgetfulness was more like a lark. As long as the boys held fast to each other while crossing that bewildering river, the plague of forgetfulness was often more uproariously funny to them than dangerous.

But it won't be so funny, Boy thought now, to cross that river with a regiment of soldiers. Keeping my troops from wandering aimlessly away in forgetfulness will be imperative. Yet if I myself can no longer remember why we must cross that river . . .

The prospects for success seemed grim. In truth, the entire mission seemed doomed to failure. But such was love; it strove onward in spite of all odds.

Love . . . Boy's heart ached. It was creeping up on him now, around the edges of his soul—the truth about his love. His one great love. Sparkle Shooter was more than likely cursed now, lost to him and to all time, with the dim hope of death at the hands of Boy being Shooter's only salvation.

It was that first river in fact, the River of Lust, that had forged their love for each other so long ago. They'd plunged into it together on a morning in late spring and were not seen again at the palace for the rising and setting of seven suns. When the palace envoy had finally located the princes, they were both sprawled naked and exhausted on the mossy banks of the river—no older, but they were wiser princes indeed.

This was while Boy's grandfather had still been king, was still ruling the Lower Kingdom from the old castle. When the truant young royals were at last returned, Boy's grandfather was stern. It was suddenly undeniably clear why these two princes were always striving to skip their studies and carouse together. They were in heat—for each other. It was not a good distraction to succumb to; learning to rule a kingdom was serious business. Down came his merciless decree: Sparkle Shooter was to be returned to his own kingdom for good. The boys were too young to be this inseparable. They each had kingdoms to learn how to maintain.

Sad as it was, a decree from the king was final.

Ah, but not insurmountable! Boy smiled to himself now, the tall trees casting his stunning face in light and then shadow as he and Sebula led the troops ever farther northward through the rocky hills and towering pines. Not even a royal decree, it turned out, had been powerful enough to keep Boy apart from his beloved Shooter.

That night they set up camp in a clearing. Boy's elaborate tent was erected first, then meals were served to everyone. Outside Boy's tent, a foot soldier tended to Sebula as darkness fell on the Lower Kingdom.

Boy paced inside his tent distractedly. Blitzkrin was quartered with his king and he lay dozing on his own pillows. "Your Highness," he suggested, half-awake now, "you might want to walk among the troops or survey the stars. You seem much too preoccupied for sleep yet."

Boy smiled compassionately at his exhausted aide-de-camp. "Perhaps you're right," he agreed. "I am only keeping you awake."

Boy stepped outside the royal tent and was happy to discover the foot soldier, nearly finished tending to Sebula. "You, there," he said. "How did the day seem to you?"

The foot soldier, startled, turned and stared at him.

"I said, how did the day seem? You foot soldiers bring up the rear. You see things others of us might not see from up on our horses."

The foot soldier nodded his head uneasily.

"What does that mean?" Boy asked impatiently.

The foot soldier shrugged. He was young, with dark eyes and black hair, like Boy's. But this soldier's hair was cropped unusually short. The lack of hair served to highlight the delicate features of his beautiful face. The soldier's beauty was not wasted on Boy.

"Why don't you answer me?" Boy demanded. "Can't you speak?"

The soldier shook his head no in earnest.

Boy was stunned. He expected a young man of such beauty to be flawless somehow. "You're mute?" he asked. "You're actually mute?"

The soldier nodded his head in relief. They had communicated.

"Well, I guess it would do me no good to ask how someone such as yourself winds up in the royal army. Why don't we just stick to yes or no questions?"

The soldier smiled uncomfortably.

"Were you raised in the palace?" Boy asked.

The soldier shook his head no.

"That would explain why your presence among my soldiers is news to me. You were raised in one of the male villages beyond the River Sargine then?"

The soldier nodded his head yes.

Boy studied him in silence for a moment. The soldier was quite a fair specimen of manhood. Boy could not recall ever having seen a young man with fairer features than this strange mute. The young man was done tending to Sebula now and clearly longing to be dismissed for the night. But Boy had other ideas. He said, "Tell me, where are you quartered?"

The soldier pointed vaguely toward a mass of tents.

Boy stepped closer to the young man, reached out and gently took hold of the mute's chin. The skin was quite soft. "Not tonight," Boy informed him. "Tonight you sleep here in my tent."

The soldier pulled back in horror.

"You're going to disobey your king? You, a mere foot soldier who has not yet seen battle? A mere peasant from beyond the River Sargine? I am offering you the comfort of my luxurious pillows instead of the cold ground in your tent."

The soldier stared hard at his king, unmoved.

Boy clarified. "I'm not giving you a choice, soldier. Come." He took the soldier by his muscular arm and pulled him into the royal tent.

"A virgin," Boy announced to a snoozing Blitzkrin, who quickly woke.

"The mute!" Blitzkrin scoffed sleepily. "Where did you find him?"

"You knew we had a mute among our troops?"

"Of course I knew. He comes from beyond the river. It doesn't surprise me that he's a virgin."

"Well, I don't know it for a fact, but see how he trembles?"

Blitzkrin gave the foot soldier a cursory glance, then turned over in his pillows and went back to sleep.

Boy let go of the soldier's arm and went over to his own makeshift bed. The soldier did not follow him. He stood planted in the spot where Boy had left him.

"You know that if you disobey your king, you are

stripped of your soldier's uniform and treated as a common prisoner, don't you? You're aware of this, aren't you?"

The mute did not respond yes or no. He simply stood and stared.

"If it's fear that's worrying you, you needn't be afraid of me. I don't need much to feel satisfied. And besides, it's fun. You can't go through life being afraid of sex, can you?"

The soldier slowly shook his head no.

"So what will it be? Will you come over to my bed, or do we strip you of your uniform and treat you as a prisoner? It gets very cold in the Upper Kingdom, you know. Your uniform might come in handy. It is nothing but ice and snow there."

The soldier seemed to weigh his options and then, in defeat, he went over to Boy's bed and knelt down beside it.

"You don't want to get up here among the pillows?"

The soldier shook his head and then reached in the opening of Boy's leggings, deftly retrieving his royal cock.

It was Boy's turn to be startled now. The soldier's hot mouth quickly encompassed Boy's stiffening member. "You're no virgin at all," Boy whispered in ecstasy. "What a strange mute you are." The soldier's mouth worked up and down Boy's thick erection. It was happening very rapidly. The mute's mouth was soft and wet and so warm, and it thoroughly worked every inch of Boy's swelling cock. This mouth was experienced. "You know," Boy declared between quick breaths. "When we reach the River of Lust, I'm going to take my time with you. Don't even try to stay out of my field of vision. I will find you in the chaos of that river bank and fuck you."

Boy could not believe how quickly he was reaching orgasm. Something in him knew this soldier was purposely working quickly, that he wanted to flee to the safety of his own tent, far from his lascivious king.

Boy spasmed uncontrollably, the fire of his orgasm

searing through his loins. He grabbed the soldier's head and emptied his royal seed into the soldier's mouth. Before Boy had even taken time to gain his composure, he released the soldier and told him, "Go. You're free to sleep where you like. But I'll be calling on you again. I can assure you of that. You're an intriguing one—you please me."

The mute rose abruptly and, in haste, fled the king's tent.

It was two nights later, at a different camp, the night before Boy and his army would reach the River of Lust, when Boy was lurched awake from sleep by a sound he had never heard before. A piercing shriek like an animal might make, some unknown animal in the throes of extreme pain.

Boy looked over at Blitzkrin's bed and found it empty.

The shrieking continued. What was happening? Boy leapt from his bed and tore out of the royal tent. In the bright moon light, he saw his soldiers gathered in what could be only called a mob. He heard Blitzkrin's shouts as the aide-de-camp tried to regain order. Meanwhile the piercing shrieks filled the moonlit night with a horrible cacophony of anguish.

Boy ran to his men, hollering, "What goes on here? Step aside."

As the men realized their king was among them, they fell into their roles as soldiers without delay, halting their pack mentality.

Boy shouted out, "Blitzkrin, what's going on here?"

"I'm not sure, Your Highness," he called back anxiously. "I was trying to find that out myself."

Boy pushed through the men and at the center of the ugly brood lay the mute, flat on his back on the ground, naked. A soldier on top of him, ravaging him. Boy was outraged. "You there, soldier! Since when do we rape each other in this army? Are you already succumbing to the filthy behavior of Hecton's hordes?"

Blitzkrin pushed in through the crowd next to the king

and immediately grabbed the soldier from atop the mute and hurled him aside. Then Boy and Blitzkrin both recoiled in shock at the site of it—the mute's naked body. "A woman," Boy sputtered. "But how? In my army? Blitzkrin, how could this happen?"

Blitzkrin had never seen a naked female before. He stared at her stupidly. He was now as speechless as the mute.

Boy stared in turn at his aide-de-camp. "Blitzkrin! Speak up. Explain this!"

Finding his voice, he admitted weakly, "I honestly can't say, Sire."

This, of course, changed everything. Females who willingly left the security of their villages to roam the Lower Kingdom alone, forfeited the right to protection. And this was even worse! Masquerading as a soldier in the king's royal army. Privately, though, Boy blanched. This mute had even fooled a king into pleasuring himself in his—her—mouth. Still, something in Boy could not in good conscience leave her to her fate. "Give her to me," he said. "No one is to harm this one. She will be my prisoner."

Back in his tent, Boy dressed the cowering mute in a pair of his own silk leggings and a silk sleeping gown. There were no other clothes to give her. He tied her hands together and then chained one of her ankles to a sturdy tent pole. "Here," he said, stuffing one of his own pillows under her head.

Then he returned to his bed and stewed. He wasn't quite sure what one did with a female prisoner. He didn't think a thing like this had ever happened before.

"What were you thinking?" he asked her. "Why would you want to leave the safety of your village, where all your needs were provided for? And to become a soldier, of all things? To put yourself in harm's way?"

Of course the king received no answer from the mute. But he kept his lantern lit for the rest of the night. He barely slept. When he wasn't sleeping, he was staring at her.

At daybreak, all around the camp the air was thick with both excitement and apprehension. By midday they would reach the River of Lust. The excitement was mainly among the inexperienced foot soldiers, those who had never seen the river before, let alone attempted to cross it. To them, it was a promise of sexual excess, of unbridled orgies and satiation—all in the name of doing one's duty and serving one's king.

To the wiser soldiers, though, a feeling of apprehension was more appropriate. The River of Lust was at the farthest edge of the Lower Kingdom. It meant that the first real possibility of encountering Warrior Beasts was at hand. To succumb to the arousing passions brought on by the river put the soldiers at an extreme disadvantage should any of Hecton's hordes actually be in the vicinity. When at war, crossing the River of Lust required vigilance and a near-superhuman sexual restraint. It was not a time for surrendering to one's baser instincts.

The journey from the camp to the riverbank took several arduous hours. As always, Boy rode out ahead of the others, keeping careful watch on the distance. Only this time, he had a female prisoner in tow—a mute, no less. She walked and sometimes stumbled along beside him, tied to his saddle by a length of rope. What was he going to do about her, he wondered. I should send her back. I should just untie her and send her home. But it went against protocol to simply release a prisoner, a prisoner who'd been impersonating a soldier in the king's army, no less, and he was already interfering with the divine order of things by protecting her. She herself had gone against divine orders by leaving her village in the first place. By rescuing her from her fate, wasn't he, in effect, setting a very bad example? Soon women from all the villages would be roaming the Lower Kingdom at will. How could he possibly hope to protect them from Hecton's hordes, then?

Still, Boy knew for certain that keeping her with him like

this was only delaying her doom. The Upper Kingdom was overrun with Warrior Beasts. They were in the habit of eating females alive. He couldn't be expected to wage this upcoming war against Hecton, then ferret out Shooter and somehow find it in himself to slaughter him in cold blood, and all the while keep his eye on this perplexing female. I should just untie her and send her home, he told himself again.

But on they rode. When they reached the banks of the river he had new problems. If he didn't release her now he would have to cross the waters with her and then, with passions so aroused among the troops, who could tell what might happen? He looked down at her and said, "You are a true thorn in my side, miss."

She glared up at him, black eyes blazing. He had no way of knowing what she was thinking, but he knew that she understood him.

Now that she was no longer masquerading as a man, Boy could see that she was quite an interesting specimen for a mere female. There was a strangeness to her that practically crackled with life and he had to admit it, there was something erotic in that mute but fiery strangeness. It still perplexed him that he'd had an orgasm that had involved this mysterious creature. He'd had his manhood in her mouth—a woman's mouth. He couldn't allow himself to consider it too deeply. The whole notion of it disturbed him.

At the riverbank, Boy dismounted Sebula. An aid assisted him in removing the iron and brass plates of his armor, then stowed it carefully among his effects. Boy personally untied the prisoner from Sebula's saddle but he did not go as far as to untie her hands. The river was not overly deep but it was deep enough that he would have to ferry her across the river in his arms.

All around him chaos had suddenly erupted. Many of the soldiers had already taken the plunge into the arousing waters and most of the younger men were not even trying to keep their lust under control. They were tumbling over each other in the river, in a hurry to make it to dry ground, to drag themselves up onto the riverbank and get the groping and fornicating underway. Boy left it to Blitzkrin and the other officers to keep the chaos in some kind of order, to make sure the horses and supplies made it safely across the river. His own attention was focused on his prisoner, on keeping her head above water as he swam her to the opposite shore.

Her body felt foreign to him, pressed against him at is was. It wasn't long before he felt the effects of the river, too. But it made him think of Shooter; of the many times they'd traversed the river together in secret defiance of his grandfather's decree. The sensuous waters bathing over them as their tongues mashed together in passionate kisses. Then their bodies ignited with forceful desire and they grappled each other in blind lust. The body Boy longed for was Shooter's; the body he held instead was shocking to him. True, it was muscular but it curved where there shouldn't be curves. It felt supple where it should feel hard as bones. He thought now that his mother's body must have been just like this woman's was. Boy had never known his mother. Women did not stay long in the palace. They gave birth to their royal offspring and were then returned to the security of their villages.

When Boy reached the opposite side of the river, he practically threw the mute woman up onto the riverbank. Then, as quickly as he could, he hauled her off with him into the woods. There, he would wait it out until the mood of his lascivious troops subsided into a more manageable and coherent state.

Boy's breathing was labored and heavy. He saw that the woman's breathing was uneven, as well. *What could she be feeling,* he wondered. *Surely, she, too, was as affected by the lusty waters as any of them. After all, it was how the women of the Lower Kingdom were enticed to conceive. . . .*

Just then, something in the distance caught Boy's eye. Beyond the tangle of men cavorting in erotic abandon, past the more disciplined officers trying to corral the horses. A sudden movement in the trees—was it merely caused by the wind? He stared keenly across the clearing to the woods opposite his hiding place. Instinctively, he held tightly to the woman's arm lest she move and give them away.

There it was again. There was no mistaking it now. It was some kind of movement, but was it an animal or the enemy, stalking them by the riverbank?

Boy held his breath and then heard it, that sickening sound. The heaving breath of a Warrior Beast. Without stopping to look behind him, Boy yanked the woman by her arm and headed for his troops, shouting, "The Beasts! To arms, men! To arms!"

If the situation weren't so dire, it might seem comical, all these copulating soldiers suddenly scurrying for their uniforms. But it was dire. They were practically surrounded. Clearly, the situation in the Upper Kingdom was worse than Boy could have imagined. Never had so many Warrior Beasts strayed this far south. Had he ventured out with his troops even a day later, the Beasts might have made it across the River of Lust into the Lower Kingdom. Then what havoc might they have wrought on his unsuspecting people?

A foul smell preceded the Beasts on the wind. In mere moments, they made themselves known. There was a thundering sound of cloven hooves as the Beasts began their assault. Like most of his men, Boy was clad only in soaking wet underclothes and was without the protection of his armor. With the first sharp instrument he laid eyes on, Boy sliced through the ropes that bound the mute woman's hands together. Thinking that she would surely flee in the direction of home, Boy was surprised to see the woman take up arms and join in the defense against the oncoming hordes.

In some ways, it felt like an ethereal dance. The soldiers clothed only in soaking silk that at first clung to them, then seemed gossamer-like as the fabric dried on the horrible, stirred-up breeze of war. There was not much sound of clanging metal, there were few swords to clash, so taken by surprise were they all. There was a scrambling for any weapons they could find, there was madness as the more seasoned soldiers attempted to find their horses.

Boy found Sebula and mounted him in haste. His father's sword was stashed securely in Sebula's saddle. He made for the center of the horde and began slashing methodically at every Beast in his path. Blood ran fast and furiously. And every Beast that was slaughtered fell to the ground not as a Beast, but as the man he'd been in life. It was a gruesome sight to Boy. He feared that each Beast he slaughtered might fall to the ground in the body of his beloved Shooter.

I am blessing these men, he thought strangely. *I am returning them to their birthright. I am releasing them from their curse. They are men again because of me.*

Would he feel this same heady feeling when his father's legendary sword sliced through Shooter? It was merely a question of time when Boy would know for sure.

In the aftermath, it was difficult to tell who had won the first battle. Dead bodies were piled everywhere and all of them were the bodies of men. At first glance, it was difficult to tell who among them had served in Boy's royal army and who had been enslaved to Hecton.

As was the custom, the soldiers set fire to the dead. They did not differentiate between which men had served Boy and which had served Hecton. Their spirits would all go as equals across the wild river to meet again in the Sacred Fields. And for each man in his own time, the grand pageant of living would eventually start all over again.

• • •

When the fires had been set and the weary soldiers moved on, it became clear just how much damage had been done to Boy's troops. It was a laborious task to determine which soldiers had simply died in battle, and which had been captured and ravaged and turned into more Warrior Beasts to serve Hecton. Either outcome had the same result: Boy's troops were severely depleted by the ambush.

Blitzkrin remained, as did several of the seasoned officers. Far too many of the inexperienced foot soldiers had either parished or been taken captive. Against all odds, the mute woman had survived. Of her own volition, she sought out the company of Boy.

He felt relieved to see her. He wanted to tell her that she was a fine soldier, but it was nonsensical—putting the words *woman* and *fine soldier* in the same sentence.

Under the stars, under the soothing canopy of the tall pines, Boy lay on the ground outside of the royal tent. In his bed that night, the mute slept soundly. All around the encampment, guards were on point.

Alone in the darkness, Boy grieved. At last, he was facing the full truth of it. Sparkle Shooter could not have survived. The Warrior Beasts had made it too far south. Being a king, Shooter would have been ravaged, without question, and ravaged thoroughly. He was now roaming the Upper Kingdom, or perhaps ruling in the palace, as a Warrior Beast in service to Hecton. For all intents and purposes, the Shooter that Boy had known and so deeply loved was gone.

Boy's heart gave way under the finality of it and he wept quietly. Not only for his own loss, but for how Shooter had probably suffered at the end. The indignity of it. The foul stench of the Beasts and the assault, the rape that, without doubt, had defiled him and passed on the incurable curse. If it weren't for Boy's duty to his people back home and to whoever was left in the Upper Kingdom, Boy would surrender to complete and utter dispair. The images of Shooter's demise filled his imagination like a black and ugly rain. And what was worse yet was that Boy must still make it to the Upper Kingdom, track down Shooter, and slice him from sternum to pelvis with his father's weighty sword.

To have been first to die would have been a blessing. Boy understood that now.

In the twinkling twilight, a twilight mesmerizing with its keenness as can only happen in dreams, Shooter appeared to Boy in the flush of manhood. Boy's heart erupted in gladness at the sight of Shooter, uncursed, standing before him. Arms open to welcome Boy close to his still-beating, still-human heart.

Not understanding that he was dreaming, Boy exclaimed, "Shooter! You are not lost! In fact, you look better than ever."

Shooter's brilliant white hair shimmered in the twilight. His azure blue eyes twinkled as brilliantly as if they, too, were twin stars. He was in the prime of good health. Still, he knew the truth, he knew he was lost. "To everyone on the earth, I am no more. But here, beyond the wild river, I exist again."

Boy looked around himself in disbelief. "What do you mean, beyond the wild river? I am not lost. How can I be here with you if we are beyond the wild river and I am not dead?"

"You visit me in dreams, Boy. It is perfectly allowable for us to meet in dreams."

"But I don't feel like I'm dreaming."

"And yet you are. In fact, you have visited me here every night since I was lost to Hecton. It is only just now that your heart has accepted that loss and so you are aware of being here with me. In fact, when you awaken and for every night after this, you will have perfect recall that we now meet in dreams. Boy, it is the only way that I can lead you to the Beast I've become and help you release me from the curse."

To Boy, it seemed unthinkable, it seemed utterly fantastical. And yet what else could explain this feeling? This feeling that he was not dreaming, but was in fact wide awake in an unknown but oddly familiar landscape and that Shooter was vitally himself again and even thriving?

That's it, I'm dreaming, he told himself. *I'm here with Shooter and I'm dreaming.*

"And you will remember it," Shooter added.

"I'll remember it," Boy repeated aloud.

He fell into Shooter's arms and held him. It couldn't be a dream. It felt too real. Shooter's arms were really around him and Shooter's heart was beating close to his own heart. They kissed. At first, tentatively. Then, with all the passion they had ever known as lovers. Miraculously, they were suddenly each without clothes as they tumbled together to the ground and made love on the banks of the wild river. It was lovemaking that felt as real to Boy as anything ever could. The velvety wetness of Shooter's mouth lowering around Boy's aching shaft made him swell with a palpable excitement unknown before in any dream. In turn, Shooter's thick member filling Boy's mouth, as it searched for the soft place at the back of Boy's throat, felt exquisitely solid. He moaned on that fleshy intrusion as it filled his mouth, making him pump his own shaft into Shooter's mouth with increasing vigor. It was no phantom mouth that sucked him. No phantom tongue caressing the sensitive head of his cock. It was real.

Wasn't it?

And weren't those crystal blue eyes real? Those eyes that looked up at Boy with such longing and sweet ecstasy when he pushed his cock into Shooter's hole; a hole that opened around Boy's probing tool and accepted it with unabashed desire?

It was real. It was all real. The sweat, the groaning, the acute pleasure that built to unbearable intensity. And then the peak sensation, the burst into orgasmic delight, the surge of hot semen shooting out of him—it was no wet dream. It happened. It delighted and depleted him. And it happened for Shooter, as well. The world beyond the wild river was real.

They lay together on the riverbank, breathing unevenly and slowly coming back to normal. Or to what could only be called normal in this dreamlike place.

"Is this what we do every night?" Boy asked.

Shooter smiled sweetly. "This is what we do, as if we had never parted from each other."

"How is it possible?"

"Look there," Shooter explained, pointing to the far distance. "Those are the Sacred Fields. I haven't entered them yet. I've stayed here on the riverbank, close to the realm that used to be home for both of us, but is now only home to you. Once I enter those fields, though, I cannot come back here to this river until I live the cycle of life all over again."

Boy studied the fields in the distance. They looked like any fields he might see in the Lower Kingdom. Ordinary fields, yet to hear Shooter tell it, they were extraordinary fields indeed.

"Don't ever go into those fields," Boy begged him quietly. "I'm not ready to live without you, Shooter. I'm not ready."

When dawn came, Boy was startled to find himself alone under the pines on the cold ground outside the royal tent. It was quite early, but many of the soldiers were already stirring and busying themselves about the camp. There was a moment of blankness, a fragment of empty unconsciousness in Boy's brain until a flash of a dream sparked in him and then the night before with Shooter on the banks of the wild river came back to Boy's memory full blown.

His heart ached as he realized what it meant. That Shooter was indeed under Hecton's curse and lost forever more to the land of the living. That, even while surrounded by moving, breathing people, Boy was now utterly alone on earth.

Or so it felt. He went through the motions of commanding his troops, of consulting with his officers, but it seemed meaningless. Perhaps this was a sign that he was no longer fit to be king. The war in front of him threatened the very existence of his people but all that mattered to Boy was finding the Beast that now inhabited Shooter's rightful place on earth and destroying it. Beyond that, he had no ready interest in what he might do with the rest of his life or in how he should best serve his kingdom. A future without Shooter seemed lackluster indeed.

Boy mounted Sebula and this time, he had the mute woman ride along with him. Her slender arms held tight to Boy's waist as they rode. More than ever he was undecided about her. She confounded him. She was a fine foot soldier, yet she was a woman. She'd had her chance, free and clear, to flee back to her village in the Lower Kingdom but she seemed to not so much as consider it. What would he do with her? Select a soldier from his dwindling troops to escort her back to the palace against her will? He could ill afford to part with any of his soldiers now and, besides, what would he have them do with her at the palace? Have her locked up as a prisoner? It wasn't suitable to imprison women. Yet if she were simply returned to her village unpunished, it would serve as the worst possible example to everyone else.

For now, they rode onward, north to the River of Forgetfulness.

"Forgetfulness," Boy mused quietly. "I wouldn't mind

forgetting about everything right now. Except my dreams," he added. "I wouldn't want to forget those."

The woman's arms hugged Boy more tightly. She was listening to him, responding. What did she know about Boy's dreams? Or was this simply her way of communicating?

Boy kept his eyes trained on the distance. He was on a constant lookout for Warrior Beasts. "I'm going to confide in you," he said as they rode, knowing she could never repeat his confession to another living soul. "The Upper Kingdom is gone. The king has fallen under Hecton's curse. The entire Upper Kingdom is overrun with Hecton's hordes and there is likely very little we can do to change that. We are on a doomed mission. We're outnumbered. The best we can hope for is to make it to the Upper Kingdom alive, find the Beast who has now become their leader and at least put him out of his misery. A safe passage back home is in question now, too."

The mute gave him another quick hug, an indication that she understood him.

Why am doing this, Boy wondered. *Why am I putting all the troops in jeopardy? They aren't responsible for rescuing Shooter, I am. They're responsible for defending the Lower Kingdom from Hecton's invasion. I should command them to retreat. To return home and regroup. To map out a fresh attack while I carry out my mission alone.*

Night had nearly fallen when they reached the banks of the second river. It would be better if they crossed the river in daylight but camping by the riverbank overnight would leave them too exposed. Boy consulted with Blitzkrin. Not just about when it would be most prudent to cross the river but if they shouldn't in fact retreat, rethink the attack altogether.

"Your Highness, we can't let you go on alone. You would be done for, surely."

"Perhaps, but perhaps not. On my own, I might be

better able to elude the hordes. I don't intend to fail in my mission but I don't want to lose my entire kingdom in the process. If for any reason I do fail, at least I would know that the Lower Kingdom was still protected, was still able to defend itself and fight on."

Blitzkrin gave the matter some serious consideration. If they did decide to retreat, they should do so immediately, in order to conserve strength as well as supplies. But he honestly felt his king's desire to forge on alone was fool-hardy. "How could you survive, my lord, when it would be you against so many thousands?"

"I might. After all, I can travel swiftly while they are still just lumbering Beasts."

It was decided then. What more was there to say? An advance into certain doom for so many men was senseless. An advance of one on a singleminded mission posed less of a threat to an entire kingdom if it proved fruitless—even if that one was their king.

The entire army, Boy included, retreated to a more secluded area to rest for the night. Once again, Boy forfeited his bed to the mute and slept outside his tent, under a canopy of tall pines. He was going to have to get used to it, sleeping on the ground, since a tent of any kind on the treacherous journey he had ahead of him would be out of the question. He would have to travel very light in order to keep himself well hidden.

He looked forward to sleep, hoping it would once again reunite him with Shooter on those banks beyond the wild river. But for the longest time, sleep eluded him.

The camp was well protected on all sides yet every sound in the night alerted him, jolting him from the precipice of sleep. Until at last, he slipped quietly, effortlessly, to the other side.

Once again, it was not really night there but more of an enchanting twilight. Sparkle Shooter waited for him on the riverbank, his white hair shimmering. His royal blue robes billowing in the ethereal breeze.

"My sacred one," he said. "I've been waiting for you."

Boy felt weak in the knees with both lust for his lover and relief that he hadn't fooled himself about what had happened the night before. He went to Shooter's arms and held him.

"So you've made the decision for your army to retreat? To go on alone?"

"Yes," Boy replied quietly. "How did you know?"

"I can see you from here, whether or not you're sleeping. I can't interfere, but I can see you, hear you, even stand inside your bones and feel you."

"But why can't I see you unless I'm sleeping? It doesn't seem fair. It's too much torture to be apart from you like this, knowing that you're no longer in your palace, you're no longer on the earth as I know it. If you're close enough to see me and feel me, or even enter into my very essence, then why can't I do the same with you?"

"But you could, Boy. You could. You only have to believe that a world exists beyond your senses. Feel it for certain with your whole heart. Eventually, you will develop that second vision, the one needed to see through the false facade of accepted dimensions. I am always here for you, believe it. I'm here—at least until I enter the Sacred Fields."

Boy knew so little about the properties of time. After all, the passing of it was negligible, at best, in all the kingdoms. "Is it possible for you to wait for me here on the riverbank until my time has come, too? Can we enter the Sacred Fields together?"

Shooter looked directly into Boy's eyes. His gaze intensified. "I will wait if you ask me to. It's not usually done, but I don't care. I'll wait for you."

Boy kissed Shooter then and it felt as exhilaratingly real as it had felt the night before. Why even bother to go back, Boy wondered, when everything he wanted was right here? Except that very real people were counting on him back home.

Shooter ran his fingers through Boy's silky black hair. "You must go back. I won't be completely free in this world if I'm still cursed in the last."

"You're reading my mind," Boy said. "How is it you can do it?"

"We're communicating, that's all it is. It's nothing more mysterious than that."

But truthfully, what could be more mysterious than this ebb and flow of meaning between them, with or without a spoken language? They lay down together once more on the riverbank, their clothing gone, their bodies entwined. Their hearts beating, each with an increasing rhythm as their twin arousals coursed through their bloodstream and blossomed in thick, aching erections for both of them. Gifts of their desire, each for the other as well as for himself.

Boy's lean, muscular body served him well in this unreal never-world. His strong arms supported his weight as he balanced over his naked lover, the weight of Shooter's legs once again draped over Boy's shoulders. They kissed ravenously as Boy entered him, this time with the brute force of his arousal. As always, Shooter accepted the intrusion by pushing back on Boy's cock, by relaxing and opening for it and returning the force of his passion even in submission to it.

Entwined as they were, pleasuring each other without restraint, they were like some rapturous swell of music. The rhythm of give and take fueled them on. For Boy, it was the height of ecstasy. Not only in his blood-swollen cock, but also in his lips as he devoured his lover's kisses and on the surface of his very skin; every square inch of his being was peaking, driving deeper toward that orgasmic release of ecstasy.

If I don't need the earth to feel such exquisite sensations, then what is the earth for, he wondered.

And then he heard the distinct silvery sound of it, of a voice that was not a voice, filling his head with sweetness. *I don't know the answer, Boy. I have thought about it, too, but I don't know, either.*

It was the true pure sound of his lover. The essence of Shooter that existed beyond his physical voice. Boy wondered if his own true essence sounded as sweet to Shooter.

It does, came that silvery reply. Your sound flows over my soul like the warm timbre of a curious music. The sound of your essence reverberating inside me is almost better than making love. Almost.

The sound of Boy's own blood pounding in his ears, nearly drowned out this ethereal voice. His orgasm was flooding his sensitive body like a crackling electric wave. It felt even better than it had felt the night before. He pounded hard into Shooter's hole. He was merciless in his pursuit of orgasm. He didn't know how he would ever find enough meaning in life now to keep him back on earth. This feeling was too precious to him, too seductive, to leave behind for long.

In the afterglow, the two kings shared a sense of bittersweet peace between them. They would be parting again soon. "I am going to fulfill my promise to you, Shooter," Boy said. "But I'm going to get my affairs in order."

For a change, Shooter was at a loss for a reply. He wasn't sure what Boy intended.

"I am going to seek out the Beast that cursed you and destroy it. And I am going to see to it that my kingdom is provided for. Beyond that? Well . . ."

It was then Boy awoke in the old world. The land was still steeped in the dark of night. The stars had shifted in the sky but it was nowhere near morning. He was startled to discover that the mute was lying beside him on the cold ground.

"What is the point in both of us suffering this discomfort?" he asked her. "Why aren't you inside the tent, asleep on the royal pillows?"

She looked at him, but of course she didn't reply.

"I'm leaving you in the morning, you know," he went on. "You're going back to your village in the Lower Kingdom and I'm continuing on alone. I'll cross the River of Forgetfulness tomorrow and with any luck, I'll forget about you and all the perplexing questions you've brought to my disquiet mind."

She shook her head no.

"Yes," Boy insisted. "You're going back with the others, back to your village, and you're going to stay put from now on."

She shook her head more emphatically.

"It's true," he conceded quietly. "You're an extraordinary woman. But I'm going on alone."

An extraordinary woman. The phrase resonated in his soul. It took an extraordinary woman to give birth to a king. . . .

He turned to face the woman. In an instant, he was on top of her, his weight pinning her down to the cold ground. "I am not likely to survive my mission," he explained to her in quiet earnestness. "I'm choosing you," he said, his fingers fumbling to tug down her silken leggings. Curiously, she didn't struggle. Rather, she seemed to be assisting him. "You must bear me a son in my absence. You must live in the palace until he is born, until you are certain he will survive."

The mute indicated that she understood him, the seriousness of it.

Boy found himself brimming with the heat of an unfamiliar erotic fever. His cock was already thick and swollen when he felt her small fingers guiding him into her opening. She was tight and wet in there. It was unlike anything he had felt before. The strangeness of it provoked a disturbing desire in him to satiate himself. His body pressed down close to hers as he increased his feverish rhythm and took his pleasure in her. Over and over, his cock drove into her.

So this is the shameful secret that kings have shared throughout the ages, Boy realized. How delicious this strange and slippery fruit does feel.

His orgasm shot through him in fiery bursts then. The intensity of his release caused him to cry out several times. He was unconcerned with whether or not anyone could hear him in his ecstasy, or hear the strange guttural sounds of the mute as her body accepted the full force of his thrusting cock. All that mattered to Boy was that he get this unusual woman with child immediately. By dawn, his life's path would shift irrevocably. His destiny would be nipping at his very heels.

Dawn crept up along the eastern horizon. A golden layer of light rose at the very edge of the dark blue sky and promised a day of clear, cool weather.

Boy took the mute inside his tent and presented her to Blitzkrin, who was already awake and assembling his things for the journey home. "I need you to take extra care with this woman now," Boy informed his aide-de-camp. "She is no longer to be considered a prisoner."

Blitzkrin studied his king with unwavering attention.

"She is carrying my child—the future king of the Lower Kingdom. Perhaps even the future king of the Upper Kingdom as well, one day. If the fates are kind and see fit to help the kingdoms truly become one."

Blitzkrin felt alarmed now. "Your highness, surely you are not anticipating defeat in your mission? Yesterday you seemed more inclined to think you would succeed somehow. I will abide by your orders to look after the woman and see to it that she arrives safely at the palace. But I will await your return there not long after us—with keen anticipation."

"Thank you, Blitzkrin. Your loyalty has always been

steadfast. Above and beyond the call of duty. Knowing that you will be in charge of things until my son has come of age, I can face whatever my destiny throws at me with a renewed sense of purpose and a quieter conscience. I'll leave you to announce my decision to the troops. It's best if I'm on my way before the sky is too light. As for Sebula, I am giving him to the woman now. See to it that she and Sebula are given safe passage all the way home."

"I will, Your Highness. You can depend on it."

What supplies Boy could carry were strapped to his back. He gave a quick farewell to the mute, knowing that he left a small piece of his heart with her. He was so very grateful now that she even existed. Then he was off through the woods on foot, heading toward the River of Forgetfulness. It eased his mind knowing that Shooter traveled with him in spirit. It comforted him to know that in some other realm, he was not alone. And he felt complete now, knowing that his son would one day ascend to his throne, that all would be as well as it could be if he did not return home from his journey.

To keep to a path heading true north, Boy would need to leave the wooded areas and cross the river at a point that would leave him out in the open. He hated to waste precious time, but he felt it would be prudent to wait until as near to sundown as possible before making his journey through the treacherous waters. It seemed like hour after endless hour passed as he waited at the edge of the woods, just in site of the river. As always, he kept a cautious eye on the distance, but in his head, he kept company with Shooter. He was determined to achieve that second vision of which Shooter had spoken. The vision that would enable Boy to see past the false facade of accepted dimensions and enter the very essence of Shooter where they could communicate without a spoken language.

For the longest time, it seemed a futile endeavor. Boy felt

as if he were merely babbling to himself. Still, believing that Shooter did in fact hear him was better than feeling utterly alone.

At dusk, Boy carefully ventured out in the open and down to the riverbank. In full armor, supplies on his back, he waded into the River of Forgetfulness, his father's legendary sword in a sheath at his waist. But he was waist-deep in the water in no time, the sword straining against the steady current of the river. And soon the water was rising above his head. He began swimming then but without concern—as if he were suddenly taking a leisurely evening exercise. With all his clothes on—his armor, even, and his father's sword. Why would he do this, he wondered. He was rapidly losing track of everything, of why he even needed to get to the opposite shore.

Boy flipped over on to his back and floated lazily down-river, staring up blankly at the first evening star as it pierced through the darkening sky. He was unaware that his pack of supplies was emptying into the river. The temperature of the water was warmer than the evening air and Boy was in no hurry to leave behind the delicious feeling of warm water flowing over and around him. In his peripheral vision, Boy was aware of the many tall pine trees that extended in all directions. For as far as the eye could see, in fact. He dimly recalled that there was a reason to be suspicious of all those trees. But what was the reason, exactly? It completely escaped him.

Another star pierced the evening sky, followed by another and yet another. It was captivating, the beauty of it all. The water lapping rhythmically against his ears lulled him even deeper into a state of forgetfulness. Soon it seemed that the rhythm in his ears carried with it a silvery melodic tune. It was hypnotic. It almost sounded as if the tune were calling his name. *Boy*, it singsonged in his inner ear. Occasionally adding what sounded like *my sacred one*.

Boy, my sacred one. It was bittersweet—how it reminded him of Shooter. Yes, he remembered Shooter. Boy had a crystal clear image of him in his mind's eye.

Shooter, Boy wondered. *Where was Shooter?* For some reason, he knew that Shooter was no longer in his palace in the Upper Kingdom, even though Boy hadn't been to the Upper Kingdom in what felt like ages.

Whatever an age was . . . a measurement of that thing called time, whatever that was . . .

Boy!

Now it sounded more like an urgent shout and it startled Boy from his lazy reverie. He looked around. There was nothing but darkness. Where was he? He was in some river. Why? How? He quickly made his way to the riverbank and dragged himself from the water. The air was cold and he was soaking wet. Why had he gone into the river with all his clothes on? And why was he alone? Where was Blitzkrin? Where were the others? He looked down at himself and saw that he was wearing his full armor, his father's sword. His supplies were gone . . .

Instinctively, he headed for the safety of the woods. He would find warmth first and, with luck, solve this puzzle later.

From the banks of a very different river in a very different world, Shooter called out to Boy yet again but Boy still didn't answer. Shooter was trying with all his spiritual might to keep in close contact with him throughout the unfolding ordeal. He'd almost lost him in the River of Forgetfulness. The mental effort it had taken to shake Boy from the spell of that powerful river had exhausted Shooter, would it be equally as depleting to keep Boy conscious in the River of Sleep? Shooter sat down on the riverbank and stared up at the ethereal twilight. Like his old home in the Upper Kingdom, the sun never fully shown in this land, nor

did darkness ever really come. All that was missing here was
the endless ice and snow. It was a strange in-between existence. It was losing its sense of enchantment for him. The
lure of the Sacred Fields called out to him daily, but Shooter
was determined to hold on for Boy's sake.

Boy hid himself in a copse of trees at the edge of the
clearing and he settled as best he could into the under-
growth—for warmth as well as protection. He shivered violently and longed for at least the comfort of his royal tent,
if not his royal bed in the palace. A little food.

"The palace . . ." he muttered aloud. There was something about the palace that struck an unusual chord with
him. It reminded him of his mother, whoever she'd been.
There was an aura she'd left embedded in his memory, a
succinct feeling of love, but there was no memory of a face
to go along with the feeling.

"The mute!" Boy caught himself from shouting it too
loudly. "She's carrying the future king," he reminded himself. It was her memory that burst through the flood gates
and the full awareness of his present circumstances came
pouring back to his consciousness.

That damned river, he realized, hyperaware of his surroundings now. *That's what did this to me. I crossed the River
of Forgetfulness.*

His memory came back to him none too soon for on the
breeze came that foul stench of Warrior Beasts. They were too
close. It would be dangerous to sleep now. Boy was determined to keep his vigil in the safety of the copse. It meant
missing a night communing with Shooter, but tonight he
wouldn't sleep, no matter how inviting it seemed.

Several times throughout the night, the stomp of cloven
hooves skirted the tall grass of Boy's hiding place. He
longed to whip out his father's sword and, exploiting the
full power of surprise, fell them in their tracks. But he knew

he would be quickly outnumbered. He lay impossibly still instead, waiting for dawn.

In the final hour before sunrise, Boy thought he felt the presence of Shooter in his frozen bones. He wondered if it might not be true after all, strange as the idea of having Shooter in his bones seemed. It gave him comfort to think he was not alone.

When the sun was up, Boy dragged himself from the safety of the copse and moved on. His clothes were still damp and he trembled relentlessly from the chill. He tried to stay as close to the edge of the woods as possible, to keep himself hidden but also to soak up whatever sunlight he could without overly exposing his presence. The farther north he moved, however, the less the sun shone at all. Boy resigned himself to the constant chill, focusing what energy he had on the mission that lay before him.

He traveled two more nights and one more day before reaching the River of Sleep. By then, the cold had penetrated so deep into Boy's bones that the mere thought of wading into the rushing water pained him. He was starved for food. With what little presence of mind he had left, he surveyed the edges of the woods on all sides before stumbling into the mighty river. In mere moments, he was on that distant shore, the one beyond the wild river. He was flat on his back on the riverbank and Shooter was shaking him violently.

"Wake up, Boy! You have to wake up! It is not your time to be here."

Boy's eyes were slits, he could barely focus. "Shooter?" he said haltingly.

"Yes, Boy it's me. You can't stay here. Not yet. Go back, do you hear me, Boy? Go back. Once you cross this final river you will nearly be at the palace. You must look for a Beast that goes by the name Gunnar. Can you hear me, Boy?" Shooter shook him again. "You must find the Beast they call Gunnar. You must kill him, Boy."

"Gunnar," Boy repeated feebly. "I must find Gunnar. I must kill the one they call Gunnar."

Shooter felt a measure of relief. Boy was somehow absorbing what he was trying to tell him. "Boy, remember. The Beasts are wickedly clever. If Gunnar sees you first, he will manifest to you in my likeness. Don't be fooled by appearances, remember? Boy," he shouted. "Do you remember?"

"I remember," Boy assured him with what little strength he had left. "They are wicked and clever. He will appear to me in your likeness if I don't spy him first."

With every ounce of determination Boy could muster, he woke himself in the old world, only to find himself battling the freezing current of the River of Sleep. He tried with all his might to swim to the northern shore. "Gunnar," he repeated over and over. "Find the Beast they call Gunnar." The words gave him the strength he needed to swim across the current and reach the riverbank.

Digging his frozen fingers into the hard mud, he heaved himself up out of the rushing waters. He was positively frigid, through and through. He sputtered and coughed when he at last lay prostrate on dry land. He knew he had to be as quiet as possible, to not attract the attention of the Beasts that surely abounded in great numbers in all the surrounding woods. But Boy could barely breathe, he choked violently. His chest was impossibly heavy, his lungs clogged with fluid. And he was still overwhelmed with the need to sleep.

Gunnar. The word repeated like a single reverberation across the frozen tundra of his brain. It was Shooter calling out to him from the other world, Boy was certain of it. Shooter was living for both of them now, supplying whatever energy he could from the spiritual plain. It was likely all that kept Boy from sliding into unconsciousness. It pushed Boy to his unsteady feet.

He stumbled on, moving deeper into the land of ice and snow. He felt for his father's sword. Somehow it was still sheathed at his side. It was all he now possessed. Boy hoped it would be all he would need to accomplish his mission. He headed for the safety of the snow-frosted trees and continued on.

It was long past dark when Boy reached the walls of what was once Shooter's palace.

The western wall. The silvery voice in his head guided him. *Go to the western wall. There is a breach there. It's how the Beasts found me in the first place.*

Boy trudged through the deepening snow, making his way west, sticking close to the icy walls surrounding the palace, walls that seemed to reach halfway to heaven they had been built so impossibly high. And yet, in the final tally, they had been useless in saving Shooter from Hecton's hordes. They'd squeezed in through a crack in the western wall.

The snow was blowing furiously when Boy found himself at last at the breach in the wall. He carefully pushed himself through. The warmth of the palace compound enveloped him immediately, rushed over him like a blessing. But the foul stench of the Beasts washed over him, as well. It nearly overpowered him, in fact, the air was so thick with their stink.

They must be everywhere, Boy realized in alarm. *I've never smelled anything so foul.*

At least the terrible smell outweighed his terrible hunger. He no longer thought of finding food. His only thoughts were of exiting the palace as quickly as he could. He needed to complete his mission. He needed to—

"Halt!" A dark growl of a voice boomed from behind him. "You there! Halt!"

Boy didn't stop to look in the direction from which the voice came. He felt a renewed burst of energy fill his being. His legs carried him effortlessly in the opposite direction. He ran until he found an entryway into the actual palace.

He was certain that the news of his presence had already spread to a multitude of Warrior Beasts, but it was the Beast called Gunnar that mattered most. If Boy could somehow, someway, catch Gunnar unaware, the killing would be over in a heartbeat, his mission on earth accomplished.

But it was unlikely to unfold that way.

Boy knew the palace by heart. In what seemed like another lifetime ago, Boy had roamed these halls with Shooter. He had slept many nights in this palace, dined here, made love here. Talked long into the night with Shooter by the warmth of a blazing fire.

Long ago days. A life long gone. The palace was filled with the filth of Hecton's hordes now. For all Boy knew, Hecton himself was sequestered here.

Boldly, Boy bolted up the grand stairway that led to the royal bedchamber. He was spotted by guards immediately, causing a renewed outbreak of pandemonium in his wake. But it didn't stop him. For now, his fleet body easily outran the lumbering Beasts. Who knew how long his energy would last. Who knew when his congested lungs would do him in or his hunger would once again overtake him. He would play that hand when it was dealt him. Right now, he was on a singleminded mission. He was headed for the royal bedchamber.

He turned the corner and there it was at the end of the hall, heavily guarded. It was a sure sign that Gunnar was indeed in there. In the nick of time, Boy slipped unnoticed into the bedchamber that had once belonged to Shooter's manservant. The pursuing Beasts were soon barreling down the hallway outside the closed door.

Boy's pulse was racing out of control. The urge to cough was quickly overtaking him. He felt like he would suffocate. He didn't want to make a sound but he couldn't help it, he was once again choking on the fluids that filled his lungs. He was soon incapacitated from all the coughing.

Then the door that led to a private hallway connecting the servant's bedchamber to the king's pushed slowly open. This private hallway was why Boy had chosen this room. He had hoped to assail Gunnar through this passageway but now it was too late. Boy had been discovered.

A wretched Beast stood in the open doorway and stared at Boy.

That's him, a silvery voice sounded urgently in Boy's inner ear. *That's the one they call Gunnar. That's the Beast who carries my curse in the old world.*

Boy was on full alert. He tried as best he could to regain control over his breathing, but he felt as if he would collapse.

Hang on, Boy. Don't let him overpower you. Don't fall victim to my fate. You can't. If you do, then who will save our kingdoms?

Boy felt a surge of renewed energy fill him from his bowels upward. "I know who you are," he shouted at the Beast. "You are the one they call Gunnar, the one who has taken Shooter from me!" He drew his sword from its sheath an approached him.

The Beast let out a low, grumbling growl. And then something utterly fantastic happened right before Boy's eyes. The Beast transformed. Gunnar took on the appearance of Shooter, and Boy's heart began to give way at the sight of him, of his lover, standing before him in his palace once more.

"Shooter," Boy said weakly.

It's not me, the voice in his head urged him. *It is only the empty shell of me, Boy. I'm no longer on that plane.*

"Shooter?" he said again. It was bewildering.

"Boy," the vision said. "My sacred one. You've come to rescue me. I had all but given up hope."

The vision approached Boy, unconcerned with the sword that remained poised to impale him. "What has happened to you, Boy? Don't you recognize your lover? Why this sudden need to defend yourself against me?"

The apparition shimmered and glowed. There was no longer the foul stench in the air. To Boy, it seemed convincingly real. His lover was here in the palace, safe in the Upper Kingdom. The other world, the place Boy had imagined to be beyond the wild river—those were only dreams. No harm had come to Shooter after all.

Or had it? The silvery voice persisted in his head. With increasing urgency, the voice begged Boy to remember the curse of the Beasts, that they could transform, at least in outward appearance, and take on the body of its host. Yet it didn't change the curse. It was only an apparition meant to trap him.

Boy, with sword drawn, held his ground though his heart was breaking. "Shooter," he said, his voice trembling. "I've come to release you from the curse. As I swore on my honor I would do so many years ago."

"But what curse?" the vision scoffed, inching closer to the blade. "What do you babble about, Boy? I'm not cursed. You can see as much with your own eyes, can't you?"

"I've come to release you," Boy repeated, his weariness overwhelming him, tears coming to his eyes. "I swore an oath to release you from Hecton's curse, to reclaim your kindom and keep our people and our souls free."

"You're too precious. What fancies you do go on about. You're worn out from your journey, that's all. Look at you, you aren't even well. Come," it beseeched Boy. "Come lie with me in the royal bedchamber as in the old days. I will nurse you back to health. I will restore your vitality. Then you will realize what nonsense this is you now speak."

Memories of pleasures past exchanged between them in the royal bedchamber flooded Boy with erotic desire. Nothing would please him more than to find renewed vitality in Shooter's bedchamber, to pass even a single moment in the arms of his lover. Boy felt weak in the knees with lust. The apparition inched ever closer to him and it seemed as if all that Boy hungered for could be his in a heartbeat.

Instead, he waited until the vision took a single step closer . . . then, with all his might, Boy ran his father's legendary sword through the Beast from sternum to pelvis. And he wept when, at his feet, fell the body of Sparkle Shooter. Dead by Boy's own hand.

Sobbing, Boy fled the servant's bedchamber. Running in the opposite direction of the royal bedchamber, he was not immediately pursued. But within moments, the guards were once again at his heels. The anguish of his bloody deed, combined with hunger and fatigue, made him feel too weak, too lightheaded. All he wanted was to stop running, to catch his breath. But on he ran; down the back staircase he stumbled. Still his lithe body was better equipped for descending stairways than the monstrous bodies of the Warrior Beasts. It bought Boy much needed time and soon he was well out ahead of them.

He went back the way he'd come in. He would need to slip through that breach in the western wall in order to leave the palace grounds with even a modicum of safety.

The thought of facing the endless ice and snow again unnerved him. It unleashed another fit of coughing that felt now as if Boy would cough his very lungs out. But he pushed on, until he'd slipped safely from the palace itself and was back on the palace grounds.

Slowly, hindered by incessant coughing, he staggered through the dark courtyard until he came to it, that breach in the wall. He squeezed himself into the crack. He felt like he would suffocate from lack of breath. And halfway through the breach, it came to him, a crystal clear vision: he would not survive this journey. He would never reach the Lower Kingdom, never see his own palace again. But he consoled himself. His son would be born soon enough. He would grow up to be a powerful king and reunite the Upper and Lower Kingdoms. Boy and Sparkle Shooter will not have died in vain. Boy's son would be a brave fighter, a clever warrior; it was now written in the stars. Boy could see it plain as day. His son would rise up to be blessed among men. Even now, the tiny fetus squirmed restlessly in the womb of its extraordinary mother, eager to get on with the business of living . . .

On the riverbank, Shooter waited in the twilight. The curse had been lifted in the old world. He was free now to enter the Sacred Fields whenever he wished. And how it called to him! He was exhausted with this in-between existence. Still, he would wait for Boy as he'd promised. He knew what the outcome would be. Shooter felt Boy's suffering as Boy struggled to breathe in the old world, to find the tiniest bit of space in his lungs to draw air, but it was useless. Boy was passing. His time, too, had come.

When it happened at last, Shooter watched in awe as Boy emerged from the wild river. Always entrancing in life, in death Boy seemed even more enigmatic; his father's trusted sword still sheathed at his side.

The peaceful twilight beckoned them both. The journey to the Sacred Fields awaited. Beyond that, only Destiny could say what new adventures lay before the eternal lovers, the legendary kings.

CONTRIBUTORS

Stevie "Chazda" Burns, instigator a.k.a. guilty party of *Yen Relish Quarterly*, started publishing erotica for women in *The Voracity Beat* e-zine (2003–2006). Currently available titles that showcase Burns's writing and/or artwork include: *Sex and Many Chiropractor Bills, Picture Held in My Hand Not Framed, The Right Words,* and *Sex and Guitars.* Visit Burns's e-portfolio at Chazda.com for the nitty-gritty and updates on her latest writing, publishing, or art project.

Bianca James spent four years in Japan studying Bishonen in their natural habitat, which makes her uniquely qualified to write yaoi from an American perspective. In her free time she publishes dirty stories (most recently in *Best American Erotica 2006*), plays capoeira, and performs as a drag king. She recently appeared on the Tyra Banks show as a "gay man trapped in a woman's body." Add her MySpace profile: www.myspace.com/scandalpants.

Marilyn Jaye Lewis is the award-winning author of *Neptune & Surf.* Her short stories and novellas have been published worldwide and translated into French, Italian, and Japanese. Her popular erotic romance novels include *When Hearts Collide, In the Secret Hours,* and *When the Night Stood Still.* She is the founder of the Erotic Authors Association. Upcoming novels include *Freak Parade, A Killing on Mercy Road,* and *Twilight of the Immortal.*

Catherine Lundoff is a professional computer geek and transplanted Brooklynite who lives in Minneapolis with her fabulous partner. Her short stories have appeared in such anthologies as *Stirring Up a Storm, Naughty Spanking Stories from A to Z, Hot Women's Erotica, Blood Surrender, Ultimate Lesbian Erotica 2006, The Mammoth Book of Best New Erotica 4,* and *Best Lesbian Erotica 2006.* Torquere Press released a collection of her lesbian erotica, *Night's Kiss,* in 2005, and she has a bimonthly writing column called "Nuts and Bolts" at the Erotica Readers and Writer's Association (www.erotica-readers.com). Her personal Web site lives at www.home.earthlink.net/~clundof.

Claire Thompson has written erotic fiction since 1995. Much of her work focuses on the romance of erotic submission, as well as the darker exploration of BDSM. Claire has published numerous novels and short stories, both in print and e-book format. Says a reviewer for eCataRomance, "Claire Thompson draws a compelling, graphic picture of a loving dominant/submissive relationship. Erotic and confronting, yet tender and intimate." Claire's Web site address is www.clairethompson.net, where you will find all of Claire's novels, new releases and upcoming releases, as well as more detailed information about the author.

Nix Winter lives in Seattle, by the ocean and the bookshops. Author of many stories, she's been involved in writing and illustrating yaoi stories for lots of years. She is also an award-winning cover artist and wants to draw manga. (www.darkfedora.com)